THE
ROAD
TO
MURDER

—

CAMILLA
TRINCHIERI

Published by

Soho Press, Inc.

227 W 17th Street

New York, NY 10011

Library of Congress Cataloging-in-Publication Data

Names: Trinchieri, Camilla, author.
Title: The road to murder / Camilla Trinchieri.
Description: New York, NY : Soho Crime, 2024 | Series: A Tuscan mystery; 4
Identifiers: LCCN 2023018592

ISBN 978-1-64129-556-7
eISBN 978-1-64129-557-4

Subjects: LCGFT: Detective and mystery fiction. | Novels.
Classification: LCC PS3553.R435 R63 2024 | DDC 813/.54—dc23/
eng/20230605
LC record available at https://lccn.loc.gov/2023018592

Interior design by Janine Agro, Soho Press, Inc.

Printed in the United States of America

10 9 8 7 6 5 4 3 2 1

In memory of Wendy Pesky,
who spread grace and beauty wherever she went

———

THE
ROAD
TO
MURDER

ONE

*Gravigna, a small town in the Chianti Hills of Tuscany
A Monday in May, 5:05 A.M.*

Nico's cold feet searched under the bedcovers for Nelli's warm ones, found them and dropped back into his dream. In the adjacent room a cell phone started to ring, heard only by OneWag, curled up on the sofa. The dog raised his head seeking the source of the persistent sound. The thing on the table. He allowed himself a low growl of protest. He'd been chasing rabbits. The ringing continued. OneWag jumped down, padded over to the bedroom door and pushed it open with a vigorous thrust of his snout.

The louder ringing finally woke Nelli. She lifted herself up on one elbow and nudged Nico's back. "Wake up, your phone is ringing."

Nico hugged his pillow. "Mmmm, no. Yours."

"Wrong. Mine's right here by the bedside table." She glanced at the clock radio and started shaking Nico's shoulder. "Get up, Nico. It's five in the morning. It must be important."

Nico mumbled, "It's some joker having fun."

"You're impossible." Nelli started to climb over him to get to the phone.

Nico pushed her back. "I'll go. I'll go." He gave her a quick kiss on the nose and grunted out of bed. Yesterday's mind-blowing meal was still sitting heavily in his stomach, and he took his time reaching the phone.

Seeing Nico, OneWag wagged his tail in greeting but was ignored. Miffed, he jumped back on the sofa and gave Nico his back. The ringing stopped just as Nico picked the phone off the table. He rubbed his eyes to read. *Missed call.* Great. Back to sleep. As he turned back, the ringing resumed. Perillo's name gave Nico a jolt. He swiped. "What's wrong?"

"I need your help."

"Are you okay?"

"Just fine. For the past twenty minutes I've been standing with a dead woman at my feet and an alive English one who doesn't speak Italian."

"Do you want me to talk to her?"

"Please."

In strongly accented English, Perillo said, "Signora Barron, my friend speak English." Then Nico heard a strong female voice declare, "Thank God for small mercies," followed by the sound of soft footsteps and Perillo's phone changing hands.

"Sir, what has happened to my friend is an abomination. I will not say any more until we can speak in person."

After the phone shifted hands again, Perillo asked, "What did she say?"

"She wants me to come over. Where are you?"

"A few kilometers south of Vignamaggio. Just past a very sharp curve you'll see an uphill road flanked by cypress trees. The villa is on top of the hill. Villa Salviati."

"Give me time to get dressed and I'll be there." Nico clicked off.

"Who was that?" Nelli called out. She was out of bed, tying her wool bathrobe around her waist.

"Perillo." Nico walked to the bedroom and started dressing.

"What happened?"

Nico told her while he buttoned up a plaid collared shirt. Nelli handed him his gray corduroy slacks. "Who died?"

"I didn't ask."

"How sad." Nelli's forehead creased. "A heart attack?"

Nico didn't think the carabinieri would get called for a suspected heart attack but said nothing. There was no point in alarming Nelli. He reached for the dark blue sweater she had given him for Christmas. "I don't know."

Nelli crossed herself as she walked to the stove. OneWag jumped off the sofa and ran to greet her. She picked up the dog and kissed his head. "I'll put the moka on."

Nico ran the electric shaver over his cheeks and chin. For some reason, he felt he needed to make a good impression. The English lady had sounded very refined. He combed his still-full head of graying hair and brushed his teeth.

The moka was gurgling when he came into the living room/kitchen. "I don't have time."

"Two more minutes," Nelli said, not wanting to see him go.

"I can't, Nelli. Perillo needs help. Drink a double for me. Ciao, bella." He meant to kiss her lips, but she moved her head and he ended up kissing OneWag. Nico took a moment to study her face. Her expression was soft, still full of sleep. "Are you upset I'm going?"

Nelli smiled. "The reason upsets me. Don't worry. Rocco will keep me company."

Nico kissed her lightly on the lips. She kissed him back. "Let me know."

"I will."

After Nico left, Nelli poured herself a double espresso, added some milk and took her cup back to bed. OneWag stretched himself out against her leg while she sent a little prayer to whoever was listening in the sky. *Please let it be nothing more violent than a heart attack.* These past five months with Nico not playing homicide detective for Perillo had been good. He was cheerful and loving, the sadness he seemed to carry almost gone.

Nelli leaned back on her pillow. And yet she had noticed a restlessness in him. Nico had told her he had not enjoyed his detective work in New York, but it was obvious he liked working with Perillo and Daniele. Here he was needed in a way that maybe he had not been in New York. He had more experience with murder than Perillo. It was clear he loved being helpful. It was how he had entrenched himself in his Italian life. He helped at Sotto Il Fico, coming up with new recipes for Tilde, but during the winter months, with Gravigna empty of tourists, the restaurant had only opened for weekend dinners. She had enjoyed more of his company, his love, the attention he gave her.

Nelli shrugged and finished her coffee. If it was murder, he would have less time for her. Maybe that would be good for both of them. She had a job she loved at the Querciabella vineyard, and she'd have more time for painting.

WITH THE DARK OF night bleaching out of the sky, Nico easily spotted the long, climbing row of cypresses. At the very top of the hill a wide, handsome two-story building in pale yellow stone overlooked an expanse of straggling trees. *A fancy place*, Nico thought as he turned off the paved road and noticed the bronze plaque embossed with the names SALVIATI-LAMBERTI on one side of the tall cast-iron gate. Probably built back in the Renaissance. A place rich in history. Money too. Nico shifted gears and prayed his old Fiat 500 would make the climb.

Daniele Donato, Perillo's right-hand man, met Nico at the double-doored entrance. "Buongiorno, Nico."

"Ciao, Daniele. Are Vince and Dino here too?"

"Yes, checking all the rooms. I'll show you the way. It's a big place." Daniele held out a pair of shoe covers and gloves.

"Thanks," Nico said, slipping them on.

"I'm sorry the maresciallo had to wake you up," Dani said.

"We'll all catch up on sleep tonight."

They walked through one sumptuous room after another, past tall windows adorned with brocaded curtains, walls with gilt-framed paintings and drawings. Daniele's covered boots and Nico's covered sneakers made different sounds as they strode across gleaming marble and soft carpets.

Perillo appeared from a side doorway just as Nico and Daniele entered a room lined floor to ceiling with books. "There you are." He walked down the wide Persian carpet toward them and clasped Nico's hand. "Thank you for coming." Perillo turned to Daniele. "What news from the forensics team?"

"No one answered. I left a message."

Perillo spread out his arms in surrender to the inevitable wait.

"It's murder then?" Nico asked.

"Indeed. Strangled with a piece of curtain cord."

"Who is it?"

"I suspect the owner of this place, but the Englishwoman wouldn't even give me her name."

"Probably too upset. No one else here?"

Perillo shook his head. "We got the call at four-fifteen. All the woman said was 'Villa Salviati, morto, morto.' She hung up before Dino could ask anything."

"Do we know who the owner is?" Nico asked.

"I looked it up on the way," Daniele said. He was Perillo's computer whiz. Scouring the net was his favorite hobby. "It's listed under Eleonora Salviati Lamberti, a widow. The house hasn't been ransacked, but we'll have to wait to find out if anything was stolen."

"My knees are collapsing," Perillo said. "Dani, please, find the kitchen in this mausoleum and see if you can get us some coffee."

Daniele did a military turnaround and hurried back the way he had come.

"The woman has finally accepted a glass of brandy," Perillo said. "That's the only way I was able to convince her to leave the victim and wait in another room."

"Let me see the body first."

"This way."

Nico followed Perillo through a double door at the far end of the library.

The room was cold and in semidarkness. A predawn light from two windows on one side barely reached beyond the curtains.

"She turned the light off when we walked out," Perillo said.

Nico used his handkerchief to click the light switch, and a chandelier sparkled to life. In the center of the far wall was an ornate marble fireplace stacked with unlit logs. From there Nico's eyes traveled over two worn velvet sofas and a few armchairs before landing on the grand piano in the far end of the room. Something dark was covering a section of the piano keys. Nico walked closer. The victim was slumped over the piano, her head resting on one arm, her face turned away toward the wall. The hand of her other arm rested on the keys. She looked as though she had fallen asleep while playing. Her feet were bare, her slippers tossed behind the piano seat.

As Nico got closer to the body he saw two cut ends of a gold cord protruding from under the woman's thick black hair and running down the back of a yellow bathrobe.

"No one sits quietly while being strangled," Perillo said. "She's been posed."

"The killer has left a message."

"Not one I understand."

"We'll have to figure it out. Maybe the Englishwoman can help us. Where is she?"

"In a room she chose." Perillo walked back out into the library and opened a door between two stacks of books. "Signora, my American friend," he announced, and stepped aside to let Nico enter.

The only light in the room came from a small porcelain lamp on a side table. Its soft light revealed a light-blue wool lap on which rested a pair of thin, bare hands.

"Good morning," Nico said, and introduced himself.

"Hardly, Mr. Doyle. Under different circumstances I would say it's a pleasure to meet you, but today it is not. I am Laetitia Barron."

Nico took a step closer. "I'm sorry to disturb you at such a sad time, but we need your help to understand what has happened here."

"It's self-evident what has happened. Last night Nora and I said good night a few minutes before or after ten o'clock and while I slept someone strangled her."

Nico thought he heard a tremor of anger. "Finding her must have been a terrible shock, but Maresciallo Perillo needs your help."

"First, he needs to let Nora's daughters know their mother has been murdered. I don't know Adriana's or Clara's telephone numbers. Nora's address book will tell you."

Nico translated for Perillo, who had stayed by the door.

"Grazie." Perillo took off.

"Mrs. Barron, can you tell—"

"Miss Barron. I never married. Too many insist on calling me Mrs. Barron as though they find my spinsterhood embarrassing. Please do not make that mistake. It annoys me no end." Her hands fluttered in the lamplight. "Do sit down. There's a davenport behind you."

Nico assumed that meant a place to sit. He stretched his leg back a few inches, felt something hard and sat down.

"Miss Barron, can I turn on another lamp so we can see each other?"

"Please indulge me and allow me a few more minutes, Mr. Doyle. I am finding comfort in the dark." Her hands rested back on her lap.

"As you wish. What can you tell me about Mrs. Lamberti?"

"Lamberti was her husband's name. Nora went back to her maiden name, Salviati. She was a very proud woman, at times quite unpleasant to others. Not to me, oddly enough. I considered her a not particularly close friend. She's the one who sought me out. She claimed she enjoyed my company. I think she liked showing off her Queen's English. It was quite good."

Nico leaned forward. "You called the carabi—"

Miss Barron's lifted hand stopped him from going further. "Yes but allow me to continue. Stories need to follow their own rhythm for them to make sense."

"The truth is what we are after." Nico wondered if she was avoiding painful questions or taking time to make up a story.

"We met on a train ride from Bath, where I live, to London four years ago." She spoke in a clear, light voice. "Nora noticed we were reading the same book and started asking questions. She had spent a month in London and had come down to Bath to visit the Roman ruins before going back to Italy. She wanted to know all about me and my interests. I was a bit surprised she found me so interesting. A bit nosy, I thought, but she convinced me to visit this charming area and I will be forever grateful to her. I have been spending two months of every summer in a hotel not far from here."

As he listened, Nico smelled coffee. Perillo had tiptoed back to the doorway.

"This year," Miss Barron continued, "quite unexpectedly, Nora invited me to spend a week with her. We used to see each other only when I came down for the summer. I had plans to go to London to see a few plays, but she was quite insistent. Nora was used to getting her way and it had been raining for days at home. I let her convince me." Miss Barron paused.

"She was playing the piano when her life was taken. Beethoven's *Moonlight Sonata*. The music awakened me. My room is just above."

"What time was this?"

Miss Barron leaned into the lamplight. Her face was thin, bare of makeup, her cheeks flushed. Perfectly arranged gray-blond curls crowned her small head. Nico placed her age on the late side of fifty. Sharp, deep-blue eyes peered at him, then shifted to the shadow Perillo was casting on the carpet.

Miss Barron lifted her eyes to study this short stocky man in the doorway. His face was in shadow now, but she remembered she'd been surprised by his strong, appealing face, the striking dark eyes looking at her from under a shock of black hair. His looks had helped calm her. She felt she was in good hands until she realized he couldn't understand a word of what she was saying. "Why is the mahrayshallow hovering by the door?" she asked. He'd been shifting his weight impatiently, the light from the adjacent room casting a long shadow. "He would be of more use seeking clues, I should think."

Nico translated for Perillo, summarizing what Miss Barron had told him so far, adding, "I hope you enjoyed your coffee."

"And yours. Handing it to you would have been rude. I didn't have tea for her." Perillo turned back to Nico. "Ask her some questions. What are you waiting for?"

"For you to get her some tea."

"Okay, but I'm counting on you, Nico. Find me when you're through." Perillo bowed his head toward Miss Barron and walked away.

Miss Barron waited for Perillo's footsteps to fade into silence. "You are fluent in Italian."

"I had an Italian American mother, an Italian wife and I've lived here for two years," he explained, hoping to put her at ease. "I still make a lot of mistakes and I can't get rid of my accent."

"I envy you, Mr. Doyle. I have tried to speak this country's beautiful language, but my xenophobic ear refuses to hear and learn." She turned off the lamp next to her, rose from her chair and walked to the heavily curtained window. Nico was surprised by how tall she was.

"The sun must be coming up soon," she said. "It's a lovely sight on this side of the house." She threw open the curtains, revealing a tall, paned French window. A pale light poured into the room.

Nico joined Miss Barron to look out. A long blanket of dark grass spotted with wildflowers dipped down and disappeared into the horizon. The sky had turned a blue-tinged gray. A thin pink thread ran along the bottom edge. Birds had begun their morning chatter.

"It must have broken Nora's heart to have to let go of this beautiful place," Miss Barron said.

"She was selling?"

"Yes. She told me last night over dinner. The surprise left me speechless. It's been in her family for over a century."

"Did she say why she was selling?"

"It would have been improper to ask as I assumed she was in economic straits." Miss Barron sat back down. "Why else would she sell?"

To start a new life, Nico thought as he also sat down. That's why he'd sold his very modest Bronx apartment. "To go back to the music you heard last night. Can you tell me what time it woke you up?"

"I lay there listening for a few minutes. When I rose from

the bed and checked my watch, it was eighteen past three in the morning. Nora loved the piano. She had hoped to be a concert pianist when she was young, but her father told her she didn't have enough talent and refused to pay for any more lessons. Parents can be so incredibly cruel. She played the adagio from Brahms's first piano concerto beautifully the first night I came."

"When was that?"

"Wednesday. Five days ago. Where was I?"

"You were checking the time. What happened after that?"

"I left my room and stopped at the top of the stairs." She glanced at the door as Vince walked in sideways holding a large tray with two cups, a silver teapot and a slice of cake on a plate.

"It is my wife's pinoli cake," Vince said. "The signora needs it more than I do. For you, coffee. Sorry, I only had one slice."

"Good thinking, thanks," Nico said, his annoyance at the interruption mitigated by the arrival of much-needed coffee.

Miss Barron clasped her hands together as Vince lowered the tray onto a long bench that acted as a coffee table. "Grazie molto, Signore. Grazie."

Vince stood up and bobbed his head with pleasure. "Tanke you, lady." He walked out backward, adding, "Gianconi and the forensic team are at the gate." That meant they would be taking over the place in a few minutes.

"How very kind," Miss Barron said, sitting back down and pouring milk into her cup, followed by the tea. "Who is Gianconi?"

"The medical examiner."

"He will take Nora away?"

"Yes, to his lab in Florence."

"God bless her. I have already said my goodbye to her. She was a sad woman, at times angry and difficult, but intriguing, full of fascinating stories. I have a weakness for stories." Miss Barron broke off the tip of the thick slice and took a bite. She closed her eyes for a moment as she chewed. "This is lovely." She held out the plate.

"For me?" Nico asked.

"Yes, please share it with me."

Nico noticed a hint of a smile, took a small piece and popped it in his mouth. "Thank you." Maybe he was making headway in the trust department.

Miss Barron sat back in the armchair and took a long sip of her tea. "Where was I in the story?"

"You stopped at the top of the stairs."

"When I reached the top of the stairs, she had finished the adagio. I waited for her to start the second movement. She didn't. I stood still for a few minutes, debating whether I should disturb her or if I should go back to bed. Unfortunately, curiosity got the better of me."

"You could see the door to the music room from the top of the stairs?"

Miss Barron gave Nico a piercing look. "You obviously find interruptions necessary. Since I have a tendency to stray from the topic, which can be annoying, I will consider us even. To answer your question, from where I stood, I saw only the two bottom halves of the door. They were closed. Nora didn't come out or play again, and I wondered if she might like a cup of tea or company. Now you will ask how long I waited before going down. Maybe three or four minutes. Perhaps more. When I reached the closed door, I called out to her. 'That was lovely, Nora.' Of course, she didn't answer. The room was dark when I walked in. I turned on the light and found her collapsed over the piano. I ran to her and saw the cord hanging from her neck." Miss Barron paused for a moment before saying, "I checked her pulse. She had left our world."

"Did you move anything?"

"Checking her pulse, I might have moved her hand a little. It was resting on the keys. I noticed the opal ring she wore on her little finger was missing. She'd won it from her bridge-playing friend in a wager. Do you think whoever killed her took it? Opals can be valuable, although it was very small."

"Maybe. Did you touch anything else?"

"I touched the light switch again. I sat down on the sofa in the dark and prayed for Nora."

"You weren't scared?"

"I think I was too overwhelmed to be scared. After I don't know how long, I got up and went upstairs to check my phone for the closest carabinieri station. Wherever I go I always write down the telephone number of the local police. Here in Chianti, it's the carabinieri. It is best to be prepared."

Nico heard heavy footsteps approaching.

Miss Barron rose from her chair. "No more questions, please. It's time for me to go upstairs to pack."

"The maresciallo needs to take your fingerprints and DNA for elimination purposes."

"I know. Nora and I both liked mystery books. Agatha Christie's *The Mirror Crack'd from Side to Side* is what brought us together on that train ride. Tell him I'll come to the carabinieri station tomorrow morning."

"You will also need to stay in the area for a few days."

"To have you ask more questions, I suppose. You must find it a burden."

"I'm used to it. Back in New York I was a homicide detective."

Miss Barron peered at him for a few seconds. "I misplaced you. I'm not often wrong. I saw you as a teacher."

"I take that as a compliment."

"Good." She walked out of the room with Nico following. "I already booked a room at Hotel Bella Vista, where I have stayed for the past few summers."

A surprised "oh" slipped out of Nico's mouth.

She turned to look at him. "You know the hotel?"

"Yes, I do." It had played an important part in the previous year's murder investigation.

"Then you'll know where to find me." She stopped in front of the stairs and held out her hand. "Goodbye, Mr. Doyle. Do tell the mahrayshallow to look for Nora's ring. If he doesn't find it, then you'll know whoever killed her stole it. That might help."

A male voice in the next room cursed. Other voices spoke in low voices. The forensics team had arrived. Perillo would have his hands full now.

Nico shook her hand. "Will you need a ride to the hotel, Miss Barron?"

"That would be very kind. I don't drive a car here. The Chianti roads are hair-raising. I won't take long."

Nico followed Miss Barron up the stairs to check the view from the second-floor landing. The doors of the music room were now open, but as Miss Barron had said, only the bottom half of the opening was visible. The murderer must have escaped from one of the two windows.

Nico ran down the stairs and popped his head into the music room. Four men in white coveralls were working the room, going over books, music sheets, art objects. A photographer was taking pictures. Standing to one side the piano, a short rotund man was tapping his foot impatiently. Gianconi, Nico presumed. No Perillo.

Suddenly feeling very tired, Nico turned away and headed back the way he had first come. In the living room, a towering portrait of a stunning bejeweled woman in an evening gown stopped him. On the mantel below the painting, a 5x7-inch silver-framed photograph showed a young woman in her wedding dress. The yellow patina told him the photo was an old one. He assumed the bride was Nora. As beautiful as the woman in the portrait. The same dark hair and eyes and a pale oval face. What struck Nico was the expression on her face. She was staring at the camera with defiance, her lips tight, jaws set. *An angry bride*, Nico thought as he walked on.

At the front door, he stepped aside to let two men pass with a stretcher. In the driveway the ambulance was parked in front of a row of cars. He walked out of the villa and across the driveway to the large circle of grass surrounded by flowering rhododendrons. Nico slowly inhaled the mild air heavy with the smell of grass and flowers. *What a sad way to start the week*, he thought. The sweet smell in the air was suddenly tainted by a different odor.

He found Perillo leaning against the carabinieri Alfa with a cigarette in his mouth.

Nico shook his head.

Perillo raised his hand. "I've quit, Nico. I have, you know I have, but good God, another murder merits a few exceptions."

"How many so far?"

"Only three. This is the last one."

Nico had been surprised at how well Perillo had done with breaking a two-pack-a-day habit. He'd taken up chocolate instead, which now showed on his girth. "I thought you'd be in the music room with Dottor Gianconi and the forensics team."

"They know what they're doing and don't need me to get in their way." Perillo threw the cigarette butt on the white gravel next to the other two and stepped on it.

"How did the killer get in?" Nico asked. "A place this grand must have a good security system."

"It does. It was turned off."

"She let him in?"

"Or someone from inside turned it off."

"You mean the English guest."

"Who else?"

"Whoever had a key must also have known how to turn off

the system," Nico said. "Signorina Barron is leaving now. I'm giving her a ride to Hotel Bella Vista. I'll bring her to the station tomorrow morning. She wants you to search for a small opal ring the victim wore on her little finger. It's gone and Signorina Barron thinks the killer took it."

"We'll look for it. Every detail helps although it's probably on Nora's bedside table or in the bathroom."

"Were you able to get hold of the daughters?"

"They didn't answer their phones."

"Where do they live?"

"One lives in Lucca, the other in Florence. I need fortification before calling them again."

Daniele walked up, immediately noticing three crushed cigarette stubs lying on the white gravel.

Perillo caught him frowning. "Don't worry, Dani. I'll pick them up. Any news from the music room?"

Daniele blushed. It was an embarrassing affliction he was trying hard to control. He'd noticed the cigarettes, but his mind had been elsewhere. "Gianconi didn't add anything to what we already know. The poor woman was strangled. If anything of interest shows up after the autopsy, he will let you know. He places the time of death somewhere between eleven last night and four this morning."

"We can narrow that down," Nico said. "Nora Salviati was playing the piano at three-eighteen. A few minutes later she stopped." He mentioned checking the view of the music room doors from the stairs. "Whoever killed her must have escaped from the windows."

"But the two windows in the room were locked from the inside." Perillo let out an "ah." He was looking beyond Nico and Daniele to the entrance of the villa. "Signora Barron is ready to leave, Nico."

"She prefers Signorina Barron. She's not married." Nico

started walking back up the drive with Perillo. Daniele stayed by the Alfa.

"Interesting how calm she was when we arrived," Perillo said. "Dry-eyed and composed. I suppose it's the English way."

"You must have been relieved," Nico said. In his old job back in New York, he had witnessed many reactions to a loved one's violent death. He'd been slapped, even spit on. The hardest to deal with was prolonged silence, as the news trickled in like a slow, lethal poison.

"I was, but it raised a question or two."

"There you are, Mr. Doyle." Miss Barron looked very stylish in a soft burgundy coat belted at the waist and a paler burgundy cloche hat straight out of the 1920s. "Did you see?" Nico followed her gaze. The pink thread of light they had seen from the back side of the villa had spread west and grown thicker. In the trees, birds were belting out their songs.

Miss Barron shook her head slowly. "Nature doesn't give a penny about our deaths. That is how it should be, of course, but still, I find it disconcerting."

"Yes, it is," Nico agreed. After Rita died the plants she had cherished on her windowsills had continued to grow. He had ended up throwing them out. And instantly regretted it. Nico picked up Miss Barron's small leather suitcase. "My car is this way."

"Arrivederci, Signorina Barron," Perillo said, bowing his head.

"Yes, we must see each other again," Miss Barron said with a nod. "Mr. Doyle told me. I'll see you again in the morning at half past ten. I am usually punctual unless I get lost in a good story. Stories keep me company."

Nico translated only the time. Perillo answered with a smiling nod and turned to Nico. "After you've driven her to the hotel, can you come to the station? I'd like to go over what she told you and discuss the next step."

"I'll come but not for long. I'm working today."

"Ah, I didn't know Sotto Il Fico had full service again."

"The tourists are coming back." Tilde had promoted him to sous-chef and insisted on paying him a salary. Nice, but not important to him. He loved helping his adopted family. Tilde, Rita's cousin, and her husband, Enzo, had welcomed him with open arms when he had brought his wife back to be buried in her hometown. Their friendship helped him decide to leave New York and start over in Gravigna. Even Elvira, the crotchety owner of Sotto Il Fico and Enzo's mother, had finally accepted him into the family.

"It won't take long," Perillo said. "I'm going back in, Dani. Lie down on the grass somewhere and grab some rest. Your face is the color of my cigarette ash."

Daniele waited a few minutes, in case the maresciallo came back. It wasn't rest he needed. He was ashamed of himself. The first feeling that had come to him when he saw the dead woman slumped over the piano was a flash of anger followed by shame. No feeling for the dead woman, no sense of horror at the ugliness of murder. He had become selfish.

Daniele leaned against the wall, closed his eyes and said a prayer for Nora Salviati.

His cell phone woke him up.

"Ciao, Dani." Stella's voice was still groggy from sleep. "I know it's early. I just needed to hear your voice."

Daniele felt a clutch in his stomach. "Are you okay?"

"I'm fine," she said with a breathy laugh. "You're just a nice way to start the morning. I didn't wake you, did I?"

His stomach relaxed. "No, no. I've been up since four-thirty. There's been another murder."

"Oh my God, who?"

"A woman, Nora Salviati. She was strangled."

"Oh, the woman who owns that beautiful villa."

"You know her?"

"I never met her. I'm so sorry, Dani. Are you all right?"

"I'm not very proud of myself. My first thought was I wouldn't be able to visit you this weekend." He had finally mustered the courage to declare his feelings to Stella. They had started having wonderful sex during the Christmas holidays, but they did not speak of how they felt for each other. He did not ask. For all he knew Stella was seeing someone else in Florence. Now he needed to know where he stood with her. A sexual relationship was no longer enough.

"Oh, Dani, I'm sorry," Stella said. "I'll come down this weekend and cheer you up."

"How can you? The museum is open."

"I'll find a way," Stella said with a breathy laugh. "I also need to talk to Mamma."

Oh, Daniele thought.

"I'll let you know which bus I'm on. Give a hug to Zio Nico and say hello to Salvatore. I know the three of you will find that killer. Ciao, amore."

Real amore, the kind he was looking for and needed, or was it just a sweet way of getting off the phone? Daniele hoped this coming weekend would let him know.

TWO

After seeing Miss Barron safely inside the Hotel Bella Vista, Nico walked back to the parking lot, got into the car and took his phone out. Nelli took a long time to answer. "Sorry, I couldn't find my phone. Are you okay? I was getting worried."

"It's murder, I'm afraid."

"Who?"

"Nora Salviati."

"Oh. Oh, I'm so sorry. How did she die?"

"She was strangled. You know her?"

"From years ago. She commissioned me to paint her daughters when they were young. Adriana must have been thirteen, Clara eleven. They were a handful. They must be devastated."

"They didn't answer their phones."

"Let me tell them first. They know me. They buy their wine from me at Querciabella. Last summer I painted a portrait of Luca, Adriana's boy. The news would be easier coming from someone they know."

"No, Nelli, please. It's enough that I'm involved. Perillo is the one to give them the bad news. It's part of his job."

"It's so sad. Was it a thief, do you think? The paintings in the villa are an art dealer's dream."

"Everything looked to be in order according to Perillo's men. He'll know more when the daughters check the villa."

"It has to be a thief," Nelli said. "Why would anyone else want to kill her?"

"That's what we need to find out. I'm going to Greve now to meet with Perillo. I won't be long."

"And I have to go to work."

"Please, not a word about this."

"Of course not. I'm sorry, but I can't take OneWag to work with me."

"I'll swing by and pick him up." OneWag liked to express his anger at being stuck at home by chewing the furniture. "Wait for me."

"I can't. I have to open up the wine store. If you need me, you'll find me at the studio in the afternoon."

"I always need you."

"Thank God you don't. Tell Perillo he owes me a good night's sleep. Ciao." Nelli clicked off.

Nico stared at his phone. *Nelli knew the victim. Knows her family. Maybe she has useful information.* He wished Nelli had never met the Lambertis, Salviatis or whatever their name was. *I'll hold off telling Perillo. I don't want Nelli involved with finding a murderer.*

As Nico drove to pick up OneWag at the small stone farmhouse that was now home, he realized Gogol would be waiting for him for their usual weekly breakfast. A ritual he had not abandoned even with Nelli now sleeping over most nights. He called Sandro at Bar All'Angolo. "Ciao. It's Nico. Please tell Gogol when he gets there that I can't make it today. I'll see him tomorrow."

"Done. I'll make sure he gets breakfast."

"Thanks."

"Everything okay?"

"For now. Ciao."

"NICO!" PERILLO HOLLERED AS Nico was about to walk into the Greve Carabinieri Station. "Up here."

Nico and OneWag both turned to look at the small park across the street. Perillo and Daniele were sitting on a sunny bench between two large oak trees. They had changed into civilian clothes. Between them Nico noticed a very welcome sight: a large thermos and three cups.

Perillo waved. "Come on, there's plenty."

Nico followed OneWag up the slope. "Good thinking, you two. I need some of your black poison to give me another jolt. My eyelids are beginning to sag." OneWag headed straight for the basket sitting on Perillo's lap.

"Ehi, Rocco, careful." Perillo lifted the basket in the air. "Nico, for you. My thank you for helping out with Signorina Barron. It's nicer here than in the station. The day is turning out to be a warm one. Perfect for a breakfast picnic."

Nico stepped closer and looked inside the small basket. "One cornetto. Very generous of you. Thanks."

"My bar, unfortunately, does not have whole wheat ones."

"I wouldn't have minded two."

"Ivana has put me on a diet."

"I see. You would have ended up eating mine too."

"It was a risk," Perillo admitted.

Nico filled a too-small cup with pitch-black espresso from the thermos, grabbed the lone cornetto and sat down on the opposite bench. "Come here, buddy. Let's consider ourselves lucky we have one. We'll share."

OneWag lay down a few feet from Nico with his head held high. Nico tore the cornetto apart and tossed half to the dog. OneWag watched it fall onto the grass in front of him, waited a moment, then stretched out his neck to sniff it carefully. Noticing that all three men were watching, he rested his head on a paw.

Perillo looked away, smiling. *Good for Rocco. A proud dog.* "Nico, tell me in detail what Signorina Barron told you."

"I wrote it all out in English and in my Italian. Daniele, I'm counting on you to clean it up."

"I'm sure there will be no need," Daniele said.

"Don't count on that." Nico finished his cornetto half, drank his espresso and repeated what he had heard. While Nico talked, OneWag quietly ate his share of breakfast.

"Assuming Signorina Barron told you the truth—"

"If she was lying, she's very good at it."

"Nico, you forget the British are the best actors in the world."

Nico lifted his empty cup. "Is there any more coffee?"

Daniele shook the thermos. "Yes. Here, let me." He reached over, poured and whispered, "He's not on a diet. The café bar only had one cornetto left."

"Thank you, Dani. I thought so." Nico downed the espresso with two gulps. Daniele shook the thermos to show it was empty and sat back down.

Perillo leaned forward on the bench, resting his elbows on his knees. "There are two things to ponder in what you have just told me." He raised his right thumb. "One, if the music Signorina Barron heard was being played by Nora Lamberti—"

"Nora Salviati," Nico corrected. "She dropped her husband's name."

Perillo gave Nico a forgiving smile, despite hating to be interrupted. "Signora Salviati's murderer did not have much time to kill her and get away before Signorina Barron entered the music room. Strangling isn't the fastest way to kill someone."

"She could be a little off on her timing," Daniele said. "She had just woken up."

Perillo shook his head. "Or the piano player was the murderer, not the victim."

"Why would the murderer call attention to himself?" Nico asked.

"He or she may not have known there was a guest in the villa. Or the killer is the guest."

"Excuse me," Daniele interjected, "did you notice Signorina Barron's hands? There is no strength in them."

"Ah, our defender of women," Perillo announced. "You may be right, Dani, but remember, we need to keep our mind free of any preconceived notions. I know that Signorina Barron lied to Nico. The murderer left the villa either from the front door or the back door. The two windows in the music room, the only exit besides the music room's double doors, were firmly closed from the inside, which means Signorina Barron was not on the staircase when she says she was."

Nico sat back. The wooden slats of the bench creaked. "I slipped up. I didn't check her watch. It could have been off by five, ten minutes. Even more. I have to reset mine every three or four days."

"Perhaps." Perillo's index finger came up to indicate the second point he wanted to ponder. "Why did she wait until four-fifteen to call the carabinieri?"

"She told me she stayed in the room for a time to pray for her friend. Any signs of forced entry?"

Perillo rubbed his bad knee. "None that we could see. The Florence team will tell us more. If they don't find anything, the killer either had a key or Nora let him in or he was already in place."

"Was the opal ring found?"

"Not yet."

"The sale of the estate could be a possible motive for the murder," Daniele offered, hoping to stop his boss from concentrating blame on the English lady.

"Her daughters will tell us more. Adriana Meloni did not pick up. I called Clara's number and spoke to a Marco Zanelli, who said he was Clara's fiancé. She's the younger daughter, according to the birthdate written in a leather-bound address book we found on Nora's night table. After I introduced myself and asked to speak to her, he claimed she wasn't in, which is doubtful as he answered her cell phone. I asked him to have her call me. He insisted on knowing why I was calling. I reiterated my request and clicked off."

"Have you been able to find out who worked at the villa?" Nico asked. "Salviati must have had a big staff to take care of the place."

"Only three people," Daniele said. His face had gone back to its usual Venetian pallor. "I found them in the address book, listed alphabetically by job-title description. Gardener, house-keeper, laundress. I'll try to reach them after the daughters have been informed."

"Let them enjoy their ignorance." Perillo ran his hands down his face. "For me this is the worst part of dealing with murder. Telling the family. Adriana lives in Florence, Clara in Lucca. Holy Heaven, how do you give news like that over the phone? *Buongiorno Signora, I call to convey the news your mother was strangled last night!*" Perillo let out a long breath.

"Not easy," Nico acknowledged. He had hated that part too, although at times the reactions had provided useful informa-tion. "Florence is only an hour away. You know most domestic murders are committed by people close to the victim. Adriana could end up being a suspect. It's important to watch her reac-tions and those of the people who are with her. Reactions can tell you so much."

An exasperated expression crossed Perillo's face. "I have to call first, no? To check if I will find her. Next, I have to tell her why I called. At that point what more does going accomplish?"

"Come on, Perillo, you just don't want to deal with the emo-tions involved."

Perillo's hand covered his heart. "You are correct, Nico." His eyes shifted to Daniele who was standing a few feet away. "We will discuss this matter of emotions further, best with a glass of your good whiskey in our hands."

Nico understood Perillo's reluctance to share personal feelings in front of his brigadiere.

"I wish I could go in your place," Daniele said, clearly chagrined.

"Thank you, Dani. This is a job I can delegate only if the receiver does not speak Italian." Perillo turned to address Nico with a look of satisfaction. "I saw something in Salviati's bedroom that I think would have surprised you. Actually it was Daniele who pointed it out. He is getting a keen eye for art thanks to Stella."

Nico spared Daniele embarrassment by not looking at him blushing. "A famous painting?"

"Certainly a charming one. Two girls sitting on the grass holding hands. No signature, but Daniele is convinced it is a Nelli Corsi painting."

"I know it is," Daniele insisted. "It has her bright colors and her wide, flat strokes. Stella pointed out her work at Gravigna's art show last summer. Nico, can you ask her?"

Nico did a mental shrug. No holding back now. "I don't have to. When I called Nelli before coming here, she told me she had done a painting of the daughters."

Daniele sat up taller. No blush followed his satisfaction.

"Good news then." Perillo dropped his elbow back onto his knees. "I'm going to drive myself to Florence now."

Daniele protested. "Maresciallo, driving is my job."

"It is your job when I want it to be. If you drive, you'll insist on finding a legal parking space, which in Florence is impossible, and maybe find an excuse to catch a glimpse of Stella. I need you here. What I am about to say is as obvious as the sun coming up every day, but I will say it anyway. We need to find out everything we can about our victim. Lawyer, banker, doctor, friends. See what you can find out without getting in touch with anyone until after I've spoken to the daughters. As for you, Nico, I leave it to you to ask Nelli what she knows about the family."

"I'll ask," Nico said, shrugging off his reluctance to involve her. Nelli was a strong and very capable woman. She would only resent his trying to protect her. He turned to Daniele. "Did Salviati have a computer?"

"No desktop. A cell phone and an iPad Pro," Daniele said. "This time I'll have no trouble with passcodes and passwords. Signora Salviati wrote them both down in her address book under the letter *P*. She didn't write what they stood for, but they were easy to spot."

"She must not have had anything to hide, which is too bad," Perillo said. "Tomorrow will be a busy day. Signorina Barron is coming at ten-thirty. I need you here."

"I'm picking her up."

"Good. Tell Chef Tilde not to protest if I need you during your work hours. She owes me."

"What does she owe you?"

"Tilde will tell you."

Nico looked at his watch. "I have to go." He stood up. "Speaking of owing, next time you get me out of bed in the middle of the night, I expect a full bag of whole wheat cornetti and a full thermos of coffee."

"Let's hope there won't be a next time."

"Agreed," Nico said. "Call me tonight. I'm curious to know how the daughters react to the news."

"STAY OUT OF TROUBLE, buddy," Nico said as he and OneWag reached the restaurant. The dog trotted up to Sant'Agnese and stretched himself out on one of the church steps, where he could keep an eye on the comings and goings of the neighborhood. As OneWag had been roaming the streets of Gravigna for at least two years before he found a home, Nico trusted him to be wise.

"Here I am," Nico announced as he walked into Sotto Il Fico with the big bag of bread he'd picked up from Enrico's salumeria down the road. "Ciao, Enzo."

Enzo came out from behind the small bar just beyond the entrance with open arms. "Mamma was worried."

Nico handed the bag over. "I'm not that late."

"You tell her. Thanks for hauling the bread up the slope."

Enzo's thank-you puzzled Nico. "You're welcome, but I've been doing it almost daily for over a year."

"I know but today you look like it was hard going."

"Didn't get enough sleep, that's all." Nico walked to the back where the plates and silverware were kept in a couple of hutches. Elvira was seated in her gilded armchair, folding napkins, her daily task. She liked to wear a different-colored housedress each day of the week. For Monday she had picked a new color, yellow, convinced that it would bring good fortune to the coming week.

"You shine," Nico said and bent down to kiss her wrinkled cheek.

Her hawk eyes examined his face. "You are twelve minutes late and you look terrible. If it were from lack of sleep, you would have been here on time. Something unpleasant has happened. Your eyes give you away. Whatever it is I hope it has nothing to do with Nelli. Or that hound of yours."

"They are both fine." He knew no battle could be won against Elvira, but he did enjoy trying. He held out his watch for her to see. "You need to reset your watch."

Elvira grunted and went back to folding.

Nico left her and walked into the narrow kitchen he

considered his second home. He loved its thick wooden counters, the copper and steel pots and pans hanging from the wall. The window over the sink allowed a view of the dining terrace with its enormous fig tree. Tilde was the best part of it. Tilde, with her long white apron tied over a blue dress, a green kerchief covering her chestnut hair wrapped around her head. She was in front of the sink, stripping the hard leaves from a fist-sized artichoke. A large bowl of water filled with floating lemon slices and cleaned artichokes sat in the sink.

"Are you going to fry them?"

"I'm going to slice and sauté them, add bechamel and layer them on puff pastry that's now thawing."

"Let me clean them."

Tilde didn't look up. "I need you to dice onions, celery and carrots."

"For minestrone?"

"For carabaccia, a Renaissance minestrone with no added broth. We're serving it for dinner." She kept pulling leaves as she spoke. "The vegetables are cooked very slowly so they end up with their own liquid. I'll show you later."

"Sounds good." Nico picked up a knife, went to the counter along the far wall and started dicing the onions.

Tilde stopped for a moment and turned to look at Nico's back. "I heard what my sweet mother-in-law said." Tilde and Elvira had a difficult relationship. "Is she right? Has something upset you?"

"I'm not upset." He went back to chopping. "Any news from Stella?"

Tilde sighed and went back to her artichokes. Since she'd known Nico, he'd been stubborn about sharing what hurt or bothered him. "Stella's very busy. The tourists are pouring into the museum again. If Daniele wants to see her, he will have to go to Florence."

"That's not going to happen anytime soon," Nico said before he could stop himself.

"Something did happen, didn't it? Please tell me. I'll find out soon enough."

Nico knew she was right. The town had a grapevine that could compete with the internet. He resisted telling her because the victim's daughters had the right to be the first to know. And even if they already knew, talk of murder didn't belong in this room that always held warmth and friendship for him.

Reluctantly Nico turned to meet Tilde's concerned gaze. "I'm sorry. Something has happened, but I can't tell you yet."

"But you will tell me?"

"When I can, yes. Not here though."

"You remind me of Ivana who won't allow talk about the unpleasant part of Salvatore's work in their home."

"It's a good policy."

"It must make it hard on him."

"That reminds me." Nico put down his knife and turned around. "Perillo said you owe him."

Tilde laughed. "I guess I owe Salvatore the fantastic lunches Ivana makes for him."

"Go on."

"You'll have to ask Ivana."

"I get it." He turned back to the stack of vegetables waiting for him on the counter. "I don't tell, you don't tell."

"Wrong. You know I'm not that mean-spirited. It's Ivana's story. She should tell it."

ADRIANA LAMBERTI MELONI REACHED for her husband's hand after Perillo gave her the news of her mother's murder. Fabio Meloni stroked it a few times but kept looking at Perillo with clear distaste.

Perillo took advantage of the silence that followed to observe the couple. The slender woman had the bland face one would have to encounter a few times before remembering who she was. Her light-brown hair was pulled back in a low bun. In contrast her clothes were notable—a textured tobacco-colored suit that matched her hair, dark-brown crocodile flats, tasteful gold jewelry. Her husband, equally slender, had more character to his face, perhaps because of his trim red beard and rimless glasses. He wore gray flannel slacks and a brown tweed jacket. He was a dentist, Daniele had discovered, with an office on Via de' Tornabuoni, one of the most elegant streets in Florence.

"What was stolen?" Adriana asked in a nasally voice.

"We don't know if anything was stolen," Perillo said. "Everything looked to be in order. Nothing was disturbed that we could see. No traces of missing paintings on the walls. Her guest, Signorina Barron, did mention that your mother's opal ring is missing."

"What was that silly woman doing there?"

The Englishwoman had not struck him as the least bit silly. "Your mother invited her to spend the week with her."

Fabio Meloni let go of his wife's hand. "I hope you checked her luggage before she left."

Perillo's fists tightened. "If something was stolen, we will do what is necessary to recover the stolen item."

"Certainly something was stolen," Meloni said. "The opal ring for one thing, not that it had any value. The villa is full of valuable things: silver, jewelry, paintings. That's why Nora was killed. Didn't you ask the housekeeper?"

"Only Signora Salviati and Signorina Barron were at the house."

"My God, why didn't you call the housekeeper?"

Perillo released his fists to give a distracting tug at his uniform jacket. "Now that you have been informed," his tone was icy, "I will question everyone involved in any way with Signora

Salviati." He looked at Adriana. "Signora Meloni—" He noticed one stockinged leg start shaking. "I will now go to Lucca to inform your sister unless you prefer to tell her yourself?"

"I'm sure Clara would rather I tell her than a carabiniere she's never met before."

"One of you will have to go to identify the body, and then I will need both of you to come to the carabiniere station in Greve."

"What for?" Fabio asked.

"Don't be stupid, Fabio." Adriana kept her eyes on Perillo. Her leg had stopped shaking. "This man knows nothing about my mother. We do. We'll go down to the villa tomorrow with Clara. You will find us there. The maid will now see you out."

Perillo's jaw tightened. He took a few seconds to control the bile forming in his throat before responding. "No, Signora. You will come to my office at the Greve Carabinieri Station tomorrow after you have ascertained if anything was taken from Signora Salviati's villa. We need to have your fingerprints and DNA for elimination purposes."

"Maresciallo," Adriana said, smiling, "it's our villa now."

Perillo put his hat on with clenched teeth. "I will see myself out without disturbing your maid. Buongiorno." With an upward tilt of his chin, Perillo strode out of the Meloni living room.

"Who the devil does he think he is?" Fabio asked in a voice loud enough for Perillo to hear in the foyer.

"An idiot, darling, but unfortunately, a carabiniere."

IVANA STUDIED HER HUSBAND'S face as he sat down for lunch at the round table in their kitchen. He looked tired and angry. "I'm sorry you didn't get enough sleep. It must be a very upsetting situation."

"I cannot talk about any work unpleasantness in our home, remember? Your rule."

Ivana was surprised by the harshness in his voice. Maybe it was her fault. She picked up the bowl of spaghetti and roasted broccoli florets, made sure the meat sauce was well spread and filled her husband's bowl. "Are you still upset with me?" she asked as she grated Parmigiano-Reggiano over the pasta.

Perillo twirled his fork around the pasta over and over. "I'm not." He had made peace with her decision to work outside the home. It was Adriana and Fabio Meloni's insulting behavior that had riled him.

Ivana served herself a small portion and sat down across from him. "I want to feel useful." During the past couple of years, she had slowly grown tired of dedicating her mornings to shopping and cooking. Dinner was easier as she served easily digestible food. A soup followed by braised vegetables, or a frittata embellished by whatever vegetable she had found at the Coop that morning. "You work at helping people. I only help you."

Perillo stopped twirling and rested his eyes on his wife. Her vibrant looks had blurred, but her black eyes still held him rapt. They'd been married for twenty-four years. A good marriage with some intervening lulls that had done little to endanger their relationship. "I thought you were happy helping me."

Ivana's shoulders slumped. "I am, but now I also want to help me."

"By working eight hours a day?" Perillo slipped the fork with the perfectly wound spaghetti into his mouth and chewed.

"Only six, paid in euros. It will do you good to eat a schiacciata from the bar. It will slim you down."

Perillo knew he'd end up eating at least three. Two slabs of flatbread filled with mortadella, caciotta, prosciutto, or salame were all good but poor substitutes for anything his wife offered. "I just had a thought, Ivana. Why not cook some dishes this week and freeze them? I'll unfreeze them in the microwave. It's the perfect solution."

For you, Ivana thought and did not say out of love for this man for whom she had indeed considered cooking and freezing a week's worth of meals. She was feeling guilty, she'd told Tilde. "Get rid of it," was Tilde's answer. She'd try. No frozen meals. She had enough work planning, shopping and cooking for this week's meals.

Under the table, Perillo's foot nudged Ivana's. "By the way, bella mia, your spaghetti are a delicious gift to remember you by during the dark weeks ahead."

"Nice of you to say." Ivana gently lifted a few strands of pasta with her fork and wound them into a perfect small bundle. "Buon appetito." The bundle went into her mouth.

FOR THE THREE TO five afternoon break, Nico and OneWag walked down to the scrappy park that spread above the new part of town. There were no benches to sit on, so he threw his windbreaker down on the grass, spread it out to make room for both of them, sat down and called Perillo. "Ciao, I'm on break right now."

OneWag, getting no attention from the boss, went off on a grass-sniffing exploration.

"Have you gotten any helpful news?"

"I'll start with the unhelpful," Perillo said. "The substitute prosecutor on this one is going to be, once again, Riccardo Della Langhe. According to him, the Salviati family goes back at least two centuries. Her murder is deplorable and a black mark on Tuscany. He will send down someone from the Nucleo Investigativo to oversee the case. I quote, '*It is of utmost importance for our good name that the case be solved quickly.*' It took a great deal of effort not to cut him off."

"You'll be all right if it's Capitano Tarani. He didn't get in your way with the Mantelli murder. Now give me the helpful news."

"I'm not through yet. Adriana Lamberti Meloni wasn't in the least fazed by her mother's death."

"For some people it hits later."

Perillo barked, "Let me finish!"

Whoa, amico. "Sorry."

"The first words out of her husband were, '*What was stolen?*' not '*Was anything stolen?*' And then they dismissed me. And please don't find excuses for that."

"There are none." He felt for Perillo. He'd been humiliated.

"I come from nothing. I have worked hard to be someone I'm proud of."

"From what I've witnessed, you have every right to be proud. You even stopped smoking."

Perillo let out a forced laugh. "This morning was a necessary exception. Today, I walked out of the Meloni place and didn't even think of lighting a cigarette. I was too angry." He took a deep breath before continuing.

"We have to wait for a warrant to discover Nora's financial situation. Her lawyer wants one before he'll give us any information about the will and the property."

"And the helpful news?"

"Daniele has reached the three people who worked for Nora Salviati. They are all coming in tomorrow to get swabbed and fingerprinted. The results will be sent to Florence for forensics to start the elimination process. That will show Della Langhe how efficient we are."

"Do you plan to question everyone in one day?"

"No. Vince and Dino will handle the preliminaries. I will question the four employees later. First I have Signorina Barron with you, then the Lamberti family is coming in. Until I know who the Investigative Unit is sending over and when, I am going to keep on questioning whomever I think has something helpful to say."

Nico worried about Perillo's anger. Sometimes it could motivate action, but Nico feared that in Perillo's case, it would fog up his thinking. "Sounds like a good plan. By the way, I don't work the dinner shift tomorrow, and Nelli is dining with her Querciabella friends. Why don't you come over for that glass of whiskey?"

"Thanks. I will certainly need it after dealing with Adriana and her husband. I hope her sister is nothing like her. I will see you first at ten-thirty tomorrow morning."

"I'll be there."

From the other side of the park, OneWag watched Nico slip his phone into a pocket of his slacks. The dog sauntered over and sat on the windbreaker next to the boss. Nico put his arm around him. They sat together looking at the bright-green leaves of the trees, enjoying the sight and smell of Nature renewing itself.

THREE

"'He vanished like an arrow from the bow,'" Gogol quoted as Nico walked into a crowded Bar All'Angolo.

"A buongiorno to you, Gogol." Nico waved hello to Jimmy and Sandro and sat down at his usual table across from Gogol. OneWag wove between legs to check the tile floor for tasty tidbits. "Didn't Sandro tell you I couldn't come yesterday?"

"He did, but 'we have no hope and yet we live in longing.'"

"That's a Dante quote I like. I missed you too, amico. How are you?"

Gogol pointed to the empty table. "Hungry." He usually arrived with one salame and one lard crostino he got from Sergio, the butcher.

"They weren't ready yet?"

Gogol wrapped his overcoat tightly around his body. The unusually cold air from the half-open French door helped mitigate the strong smell of the cologne Gogol always wore. "I gave them up for Lent. A coffee, yes."

"Lent was last month. You have to eat something."

"It feels like this month."

"A cornetto or a ciambella?"

Gogol's watery blue eyes smiled. "If the good God permits, a cornetto, please. It is not my favorite, therefore Purgatory, not Hell."

"Nothing but Heaven for you when the time comes. I'll get it." Nico walked to the end of the bar, where Jimmy manned the espresso machine.

"I guess yesterday Gogol remembered it wasn't Lent," Jimmy said as he plated Gogol's cornetto and the two freshly baked whole wheat cornettos Nico always had. "He ate two ciambellas." Jimmy added one Americano and an espresso to the tray. "Is it true?"

"What?"

"The owner of Villa Salviati was murdered?"

"What makes you think that?"

"The Salviati gardener, Lapo. He came in last night saying he'd gone to the villa to put in some new plants. The place was sealed off and carabiniere told him to go home without telling him what had happened. I thought you might know something since you didn't show up yesterday morning."

The murder hadn't been released to the media yet, but Nico was surprised the Gravigna grapevine hadn't picked it up. "Thanks, Jimmy." Nico took the tray and walked way.

"Ehi, Nico, you didn't answer me. Does that mean you don't know?"

"You decide," Nico shot back.

"Okay. I'll ask Gogol. He knows." Jimmy was convinced Gogol had ESP.

"Go ahead," Nico said. He set the tray on the table, sat back down and took an eager bite of his cornetto. He hated playing games with his friends, but Perillo was the man in charge. It was up to him to spread the news.

Gogol was munching happily on his cornetto when Jimmy came over. "What is it, Gogol? Murder or a theft?"

Sandro, making change behind the cash register, frowned. He shared Nico's view on ESP. "Come on, Jimmy. Six people are waiting for their coffees."

Jimmy ignored his husband. "Tell me, please. I want to sleep tonight." He still hadn't gotten over last year's murder.

Jimmy's tense voice made OneWag look up from a tasty-smelling piece of cornetto that had fallen on the floor. He abandoned the piece and made his way to Nico's table.

Gogol put his half-eaten cornetto back on the plate and slowly lifted his withered face to look at Jimmy. "Look out on the sun 'that heals all anxious thought.'"

"Come on, Gogol. What is it?"

OneWag sat down next to Gogol.

"'For some silence is best.'"

Jimmy shook his head in annoyance. "All right, do as you wish."

"Come on, Jimmy," Nico said. "He's telling you he doesn't know."

"Oh, he knows. He's not telling because he knows you don't want him to."

Gogol lifted watery blue eyes at Jimmy. "'People should not be too sure of their judgments.'"

"Ciao." Jimmy stomped back to his post with hunched shoulders.

Sandro went over to Jimmy and hugged him. They had both suffered last year. The six townspeople expecting their coffees waited patiently for the hugging to be over.

Gogol rewarded OneWag by sharing the rest of his cornetto.

"Nico!" Beppe called out as he shot into the bar with a face flushed with excitement. Nico sank in his chair. The news shop owner's son was a nice enough kid, but he had the persistence of a mosquito.

"I just heard someone got murdered." Beppe pulled out a

chair at Nico's table and sat down. "Who is it?" Last year Beppe had started BeppeInfo, a gossip blog.

Jimmy untangled himself from Sandro. "Where did you hear that?"

"On Twitter."

"'Why care what there is whispered?'" Gogol asked in a mutter.

Beppe ignored the comment. "Come on, Nico, give. I'm losing followers. Who is it?"

The aggressive voice made OneWag stop eating.

Nico wanted to swat the question away. "If there was a murder, Maresciallo Perillo is the one to ask."

"He'll never tell me. Come on, who got murdered?"

"If I knew I wouldn't tell you. Now I would like to enjoy my breakfast."

OneWag growled.

"Oh, mamma, he's going to bite me." Beppe stood up quickly, almost kicking the chair to the floor. "Sorry. I'll leave. I'll find out on my own."

"Bravo, young man," Gogol said as Beppe hurried to the door. "'If you follow your star you cannot fail to reach a glorious harbor.'"

Beppe popped his head back inside with a grin on his face. "Thanks, Gogol. I will."

Nico stood up. He wanted to visit Rita before picking up Miss Barron in Panzano. "I need to get going. See you tomorrow."

"If I live."

"I'm counting on it." Nico walked to the counter, paid and waved goodbye.

NICO WALKED OVER TO the pump to fill Rita's vase with fresh water. OneWag lay down next to the grave. Before putting the flowers back in the vase, Nico examined the roses, pulled off the tired petals. A few drooped their heads and needed to be replaced. He'd have to wait until Luciana opened her shop.

"Oh, how sweet of you," a female voice said. "Maso, look, he's lying next to his mistress's grave. It's so sad."

When Nico turned around, a woman was caressing OneWag, who was now on his back, offering his stomach.

As Nico approached Rita's grave, a man brushed against his arm and hurried down the path and out of the gate.

"That was rude," the woman called out to the disappearing back. She went back to rubbing OneWag's stomach.

Nico crossed the path and stopped in front of her. She was young, with thick dark hair falling to her shoulders and a pretty face. "My dog is shameless."

Hearing Nico, OneWag rolled over and started smelling the tiny daisies that had cropped up in the grass.

She stood up. "He's adorable. What's his name?"

"OneWag for English speakers, Rocco for the rest."

"English was drummed into me as a child," she said in accented English. "Ciao, OneWag." She flashed a sun-bright smile at Nico and walked away.

Nico found himself stupidly charmed. He dropped down on one knee and placed the vase of roses on the grave. "Forgive me, Rita."

"GOOD MORNING, MR. DOYLE." Miss Barron looked pleased to see him. She was sitting with Laura in one of the hotel's front rooms wearing a gray cashmere knit dress with a large multi-colored silk shawl tossed around her small shoulders. Gray pearl earrings hung from her ears. Her head was bare. "Having a homicide detective as an escort is rather thrilling. You must have interesting stories to tell." She picked up her handbag and rose from the armchair. "I collect stories. I'm ready to face the mahrayshallow. Thank you, Laura, for keeping me company. I know I'm in good hands."

Laura was also on her feet. "You are. If you need anything when you get back, you'll find me here. Take good care of my favorite guest, Nico."

"I will. Ciao."

Miss Barron hooked her arm in Nico's. Together they left the room. "I hope you will recount a few of your adventures, over dinner one night. The restaurant here serves an excellent meal."

"They are not pretty stories." They had reached his red Fiat 500.

"What interests me is the psychology of the people involved." She waited for him to open the door. "I'm sure you'll want to know more about me. After all, I could be the one who killed poor Nora." She tucked her head and slipped down into the passenger seat.

Nico got into the car. *Was she teasing him, making a bid for attention?* "Did you kill her, Miss Barron?"

"No, I didn't. You don't kill someone for being bossy. Last night when I was having my Pimm's at the hotel bar, I had a think and decided that if I wanted to do away with someone, I would bash them over the head with something hard like that brass poker in the fireplace of the music room. Much easier than strangling, I should think."

"Yes, it would be," Nico said as he started the motor. He was going to have a talk with Laura about Miss Barron.

AT THE STATION NICO took Miss Barron over to Dino's room, where she was fingerprinted and swabbed for DNA.

That done, Miss Barron followed Nico into the maresciallo's office.

"Welcome," Perillo said, a word he had just learned from

Daniele. Daniele stood at his desk in the back of the room, his finger on the tape recorder.

"I suppose I am welcome," Miss Barron said, "although perhaps I will disappoint. I don't have a great deal more information to give you about Nora and her family." She sat in one of the two chairs in front of Perillo's desk and waited, her cleaned hands folded on her lap.

Nico translated and sat next to her. "Miss Barron, the maresciallo has read the report I wrote down of what you told me yesterday at Villa Salviati. He has a few more questions to ask you. I hope you won't object to being recorded."

"I see no use in objecting. Besides, I don't mind being in the spotlight. I used to belong to an amateur theatre group when I was a girl." She straightened her back and turned her head to face Perillo. "I was rather good."

Nico looked at Daniele to start recording. Daniele stated the date, time and people present and pushed the record button. A disgruntled Perillo crossed his arms over his chest and sat back in his armchair. Losing control did not sit well with him. Miss Barron sat up in her chair, eyes gleaming. "Tell her the only way the murderer could have left the music room was by the double doors. If she was at the top of the stairs when she says she was, she would have seen him."

Nico translated.

Miss Barron looked at her small gold Cartier watch, a beloved gift. "My watch keeps perfect time and I find lying unnecessary." Her lips trembled. "The man must have left by one of the windows."

"The windows were latched from the inside," Nico said.

"I see. Then the logical conclusion is that he did not leave the room until after I went to call the carabinieri." Hadn't she smelled something unusual walking into the room? She'd tried to place it before seeing poor Nora slumped over the piano. *What could it be?* she wondered. She smelled it now.

Nico translated for Perillo, adding, "It's possible."

Daniele joined in. "There was a high-backed sofa not far from the piano. He could have slipped behind it."

Perillo did not look convinced.

Miss Barron had been sniffing the air. "Tobacco!" she called out with an excited voice. "The odor in this room reminded me of what I smelled when I first walked into the music room. I am sensitive to the smell. I have never smoked. I never saw Nora smoke. A smoker was in the room."

"Or had been," Nico said.

Miss Barron's face sagged with disappointment. "Oh, Mr. Doyle, do believe me when I say I was on top of the stairs when I said I was."

"Did Mrs. Salviati ever mention any difficulties with a member of her family or her staff?" Nico asked.

Miss Barron perked up. "Nora was very pleased with the people who worked for her. She said they were very devoted. She called them her real family. They acquiesced to all her demands, which seemed to surprise her. I did point out that they really had no choice if they wanted to keep their jobs. My remark was not well received. Her daughters, from what I gathered during our chats, did not show any love or respect for her once her husband died."

"How long ago was that?"

"Ten years ago. Nora told me she had married their father for his money. It's a reverse *Downton Abbey* story. She had the land, he had the euros. I believe he had made his money in construction. I only met her daughters two, at the most three, times during my visits. I detected no overt animosity between the three women. Tension, yes, a certain unnatural holding back." Miss Barron shook her head, her gaze directed at the wall behind Nico. *How very sad to be in a family without love*, she thought. Having a family had been her dream. A man she loved who loved her back, two or three, even four boys and girls. She had expected that for herself.

Turning to face Nico again, Miss Barron said, "I'm afraid the problem stemmed from Nora, not the girls. She was very blunt about not loving her husband and I don't think she loved her children. She liked to control people, have them do her bidding. Well, that's very well with your staff, but not with your children."

"Did she try to control you?"

"No, she was surprisingly gentle. Always let me decide what we would do, what I wished to eat. She wanted to know everything about me. I gave her only impersonal answers. I did ask Nora why she was so interested. She said she wanted to understand who I was, without explaining why. I confess somewhat reluctantly that I was flattered and intrigued."

Color had come to Miss Barron's pale face and there was a sparkle in her eyes. She was enjoying herself, Nico suspected. "Did Nora talk to you about her life?"

"She was an only child. Her mother died when she was eight years old, leaving her valuable jewelry. Her father adored his wife but had less interest in his daughter. Nora claimed her mother's death hardened her, made her selfish. She considered herself rich and beautiful. Men flocked around her. She took some of them as lovers but didn't care for any of them. She decided she would never marry. She liked her freedom too much. Her father died when she turned twenty-two, leaving enormous debts and no money. When her father's lawyers told her she had to sell everything, she asked the creditors to give her six months to pay them back. She married the richest of her lovers without telling him about the debts. A year later she gave birth to Adriana and the debts were paid." Miss Barron relaxed her shoulders and folded her hands on her lap. "That is Nora Salviati's story, as told to me by her the night I arrived."

"Did you ask her for her story?"

"No. She surprised me with it. I have a question for you. Have you found Nora's ring?"

Nico asked Perillo, who shook his head.

Miss Barron looked pleased. "Find the ring, find the killer."

Nico translated.

Perillo turned skeptical eyes on his translator. "Adriana's husband thinks the woman sitting next to you stole it."

"What did he say?" Miss Barron asked.

"Maresciallo Perillo doesn't think finding the killer will be that simple."

Miss Barron frowned at Perillo. "Certainly not with negative thinking. You, with your American positivism should lead the investigation. Are there more questions? I am wearying."

Nico asked Perillo if he had a particular question to ask her.

"How the devil should I know?"

Daniele stopped the recording in case the maresciallo went into one of his temper fits.

"I expected you to translate every sentence or so," Perillo said in an aggrieved voice.

"That would have taken us into tomorrow. You'll have to trust me."

Perillo shrugged his shoulders. "Erase my last comments, Dani."

"Done, Maresciallo." Daniele started recording again.

Nico turned back to face Miss Barron. She did look tired. The color had drained from her cheeks. "One last thing, Miss Barron. We may need to ask you more questions. You will continue to stay at Hotel Bella Vista."

"I have already said I would. I want to see how this story ends. It's not every day one walks into a murder. I know that sounds heartless, but it's the truth."

"Reporters may want to talk to you."

"Not to worry, Mr. Doyle. They won't get their story from me. May I go now?"

Nico asked Perillo, who stood up with a forced smile on his face. "Tanke you, Miss Barron."

"No thanks are needed, Mahrayshallow. I will thank you when you find who killed my friend."

Perillo nodded as if he'd understood. "Tell her to stay in the area. I might need to talk to her again."

"I already told her."

"Well, good for you."

Daniele announced the time of the end of the interview, stopped the recording and brought the statement Nico had prepared yesterday with his corrected translation for Miss Barron to sign.

Perillo watched Nico escort Miss Barron out of his office. "Daniele, I think you should sign up for English lessons. With all the English and Americans who come here, we need to be able to communicate without outside help."

"Nico is one of us," Daniele said, knowing his boss was just sounding out his frustration.

Perillo sat back down heavily. His stupid pride saddened him. Nico deserved an apology. "Erase what I have just said, Daniele. Let's go to the café bar and treat ourselves."

NICO WAS IN ENRICO'S store picking up bread for the restaurant when Ivana parted the beaded curtain and walked in. A short woman in her early forties with a pretty face, she had slimmed down since he'd last seen her. She wore a dark gray A-line skirt and matching sweater, a large handbag hanging from one arm. And sneakers.

That's a first, Nico thought. He'd only seen her in short-heeled pumps. "Buongiorno, Ivana," Nico said. "How nice to see you."

"Thank you, Nico. Buongiorno, Signor Enrico. I've already said hello to Rocco." OneWag was lying on the street just outside the store, munching on a piece of a prosciutto haunch between his paws.

"I didn't know you shopped here," Nico said.

"It's a bit far for me. Alba brought me." She turned to face the counter. "Signor Enrico, I wanted to introduce myself so you would know who was working in your bakery. I'm Ivana, Salvatore Perillo's wife."

Here was another surprise, Nico thought, leaning against the shelves instead of picking up the bags of bread and going to his own job. Ivana had gotten herself a job outside her home. With Tilde's encouragement for sure. No wonder Perillo had said Tilde owed him.

"I know who you are, Signora," Enrico said. He was a small, thin man with tired eyes who had to stand on a platform to be seen over the tall glass counter. "You are welcome to use my bakery. The sins of the husband do not taint the wife."

"What did Salvatore do?" Ivana asked in a worried voice. *Had he already interfered with this transition in her life?* she wondered. *Please, Salva, be good.*

"Salvatore only did his duty," Enrico said. "He fined me for opening the salumeria too early. My grudge is like a mold on cheese and should be cut." He raised his hands in surrender. "Please forgive an aging man. Can I make you a sandwich for your lunch? One for Alba too?"

Ivana laughed and patted her handbag. "No, thank you. I made food for all of us." She gave Enrico a radiant smile.

"All of you?" Nico asked. He hadn't paid much attention to the project Alba had started during the winter: baking and packaging her cantuccini and selling them all over Italy. "How many are working on this?"

"Three women. I don't know what Alba wants me to do yet." Ivana flushed with pride. "Tilde needs Alba back at the restaurant now that tourists are coming back."

"Congratulations, then," Nico said. "Enjoy the work."

"Thank you. Arrivederci."

Enrico raised his hand to wave, a wide grin on his face.

"Ciao," Nico said as Ivana walked out of the store with a nod to him.

Nico picked up the two big bags, bread for lunch and dinner. "You look happy too."

"I'm in on this production. I gave them a space in the bakery for free in exchange for a small cut of the company. Alba's Cantuccini are extraordinary. They are going to sell very well."

"I'm sure they are," Nico said. "Good luck, then. Rocco thanks you. See you tomorrow."

When Nico walked out on the street, OneWag had finished his treat and was examining Ivana's new sneakers.

"Are you waiting for Alba?" Nico asked.

"No, for you. I ran into Sonia Rossi in Piazza Matteoti. She's Signora Salviati's housekeeper."

He put the bread bags down on the sidewalk. "She told you?"

Ivana nodded and crossed herself. "I know Sonia from bingo nights at the church in Greve. She is of course very upset. Sonia claims she has helpful information, but she's afraid if she reveals what she knows, the daughters will not pay her the pension that is due her."

"You have to tell Perillo."

She raised her hand as if to ward off a blow. "I want no talk of murder between Salva and me. Please, you tell him." Ivana reached into her purse. "Sonia gave me her address. She won't come to the station."

Nico said nothing about Perillo already having the address. "Thank you, Ivana." He took the piece of paper she handed him. "I'll tell him."

"Thank *you*, I'm grateful."

"No need to be. Again congratulations on your new job. It

will be quite a change." Standing for hours churning out cantuccini and packaging them in a hot bakery had to be grueling work.

Ivana graced him with a beaming smile. "A new adventure. I feel like a child on her first day of school. Scared and excited. I haven't had a real job since I was selling my father's fish in Pozzuoli." Her hand reached out for Nico's arm. Worried eyes replaced her smile. "Be patient with Salvatore. He's not happy with my doing this."

Nico took her hand. "He likes to grumble, but you know he will end up being very proud of you."

"May God will it," Ivana said with a quick smile.

Someone honked. A tan car was coming up the slope. OneWag ran down to meet it.

"There's Alba. Ciao, Nico."

"Ciao." Nico watched Ivana hurry to the car and waved at Alba, who answered with a honk. After they drove off, he whistled to his dog and called Perillo.

"Madonna! Why the hell did that woman have to bother my wife?" Before Nico could say anything, Perillo hung up.

Nico slipped his phone back into his pocket, picked up the bread bags again and followed OneWag up the slope to Sotto Il Fico. A grumpy Perillo wasn't going to make solving this murder any easier.

SONIA ROSSI LIVED IN a three-room apartment two floors above the big Greve Coop.

"A convenient address," Perillo remarked after introducing himself and Daniele at the front door. Small talk sometimes proved helpful in relaxing the interviewee. He needed to relax too.

"Convenient for shopping but not for the mice," Sonia Rossi said. She had a square face with strong jaws, narrow tea-colored eyes, and a long nose dipping into fleshy lips. Her short graying brown hair was cut straight across, helmet style. Her tall sturdy body was covered in a floral housedress that contrasted with her stern looks.

She doesn't look like she would be afraid of anything, Perillo thought. And yet she hadn't shown up at the station to be fingerprinted and swabbed.

Daniele looked at Sonia's strong arms and hands and wished he could hand over the heavy office tape recorder Perillo had insisted they bring since he was no longer satisfied recording with a cell phone. This wasn't even an official interview. There was no need to record the conversation. He'd offered to take notes. Today nothing seemed to satisfy.

"Can we sit down?" Perillo asked in a gruff voice.

"Of course, please." Sonia stepped aside. Against a beige wall a two-seater sofa covered in plastic faced a television on the opposite wall. Next to the sofa was a floral armchair holding a basket with what looked like knitting. Above the armchair a cross made of dried palm leaves hung below an old black-and-white photograph of what Daniele thought must be the housekeeper's parents. An open door showed part of the kitchen.

Perillo headed to the table in the middle of the room covered with a lace tablecloth and a basket of dried flowers. He pulled out a chair and sat down.

Daniele looked for an outlet. There was one occupied by a standing lamp next to the sofa.

"You're not going to blow a fuse, are you?" Sonia asked.

Daniele offered her a placating smile as he unplugged the lamp. "I don't think so."

"This is all for your benefit," Perillo said, trying not to show his anger at Sonia for burdening Ivana.

"Can I offer an espresso? I have lemon cookies I made for Signora Nora." Sonia lifted her shoulders high for a few seconds, then let them drop. Her face remained neutral.

"No, thank you," Perillo said. "Please sit down. I will now ask you some questions, but you must come to the station for fingerprinting, a DNA swab and to sign your statement."

"Will Signora Salviati's family know what I tell you?"

"I cannot answer as I don't know what you are going to tell me. What you say here will be recorded by my brigadiere. You understand?"

Sonia stared hard at Perillo. "What I say here will not change overnight, if that is what you mean by understanding." Sonia walked over to the armchair, put the knitting basket on the floor and sat down.

After plugging in the tape recorder, Daniele fetched the free chair from the table, placed it next to the recorder and sat down. The thought of sitting on a plastic sofa and hearing it squeak like a mouse under his weight gave him the chills. Daniele pushed the record button and announced the time, the place and the people present.

"Please state your name, place of birth and birthdate," Perillo said.

"Sonia Maria Filomena Rossi, born in Greve-in-Chianti, February third, fifty-three years ago." Her words mixed with the sounds of traffic and someone laughing coming from the open window.

"What was your relationship to Signora Nora?"

"I have been her housekeeper since her husband died ten years ago. She fired the old housekeeper and hired me. Signora Nora was an impatient and demanding employer, but"—Sonia pushed her chin forward—"she appreciated good work. Just a few days ago she told me how much she had always depended on me."

"Were you leaving her?"

"Oh no! I would have worked for her until my legs gave way. I love the house, the beauty of it. The garden. The birds. I wanted to live there. There were two servants' rooms next to the kitchen, but she didn't want anyone staying over."

"Didn't she have guests stay over?"

"If she did, they came after four in the afternoon and left before I walked in at eight in the morning."

"Miss Barron was staying there."

"No one else had before her. A very nice signora." Her face opened into a smile. "She brought me a wool lace scarf from England and offered me a cup of tea when I came in. It was clear she wasn't used to having a housekeeper. Her bed was always made."

"Was this the first time you met her?"

"Oh, no. She came for lunch a few times during the summers. Maybe for dinner on the weekends."

"Do you know any of Signora Nora's friends besides Signorina Barron?"

"The Rosatis. They live across the road. Signora Rosati and Signora Nora liked to play bridge on Thursday afternoons. Sometimes the husband would come, and they would stay for dinner. The food was brought in from Oltre Il Giardino in Panzano. In the summer I would set everything up on the west patio so they could watch the sunset. I offered to stay and serve, but she didn't want me to."

"Did the Rosatis stay for dinner often?"

"Once or twice a month. When she had no guests, I prepared a simple dinner for Signora Nora, which she would reheat in the microwave. In the morning all I had to do was empty the dishwasher. Signora Nora was a very neat woman." Sonia tilted her head to one side, as if she needed to reflect a moment before going on.

"Too neat if a housekeeper is allowed an opinion. It was like she was afraid her world would fall apart if she didn't keep order. I learned quickly to put everything back exactly as I found it.

What a mess when the daughters came to visit, which was thankfully not often. Signora Adriana was the bad one. She would laugh and move things just a few centimeters. Signorina Clara would try to put them back, but their mother always noticed. Had Signora Adriana been my daughter, I would have given her a good slap in the face. Not Signora Nora. She would just put things back."

"Did you notice any change in her behavior in the weeks before her death?"

"She was nervous. I thought it was because the English lady was coming over. The only other people who stayed at the villa were her daughters the few times they bothered to come." Sonia sniffed her disapproval. "Last week, before the English lady came, I heard her laughing. She must have been on the phone. I was surprised because Signora Nora wasn't one for laughing. She was a sad lady."

"You told my wife you had information that would help us with the investigation."

"Yes, I do." Sonia sat up tall in her armchair, a grim expression on her face. "Signora Adriana and her husband are trying to sell the villa and the land to that Swiss company, you know the one. They've been busy buying up all the hotels and pensiones in this area."

Perillo felt a spark of excitement and leaned forward. "Where and when did you get this information?"

"I overheard it the last time they visited Signora Nora. Three weeks ago. Signor Fabio was on the phone in the little studio next to the library. Signora Nora never goes in there. I was in the library dusting the books. I heard him say something about knowing that the company was buying a lot of properties in the area. He listened for a bit then asked if they had any interest in Villa Salviati and the grounds. Then Lapo, he's the gardener, turned on his infernal leaf blower just outside the windows.

He drives me crazy turning on that thing. I missed the rest of the conversation with the company, but I did hear what Signor Fabio told his wife. '*They've made an offer.*' That's my information."

"Very interesting, Signora Sonia." This time he remembered to deepen his voice. He was convinced he sounded like a castrato in a recording. "Did Signora Nora ever say anything about her relationship with her daughters?"

"Only once, after I witnessed Signora Adriana yell at her mother, accusing la signora of never having loved her father. After Adriana left, she came into the kitchen and said, '*Adriana is right. I never did love him. I hope you were lucky enough to have a lovable one.*' I answered I was very lucky except I lost him too soon."

"Did you ever have any problems with Signora Nora?"

"I was angry only once: when she rearranged the pantry, and I could no longer find what I needed. I told her if she wanted me to keep working for her, she had to let me be in charge of the kitchen area. Her face made it clear she wasn't happy, but she never touched the pantry again. It took me hours to put everything back the way I like it."

"What can you tell me about the gardener?"

"I can tell you Lapo comes into the kitchen and tries to swipe my lemon cookies when I'm not looking. For anything else you will have to ask him."

Perillo looked at his watch and announced the time. "End of interview with Sonia Rossi." He stood up. "I expect you at the station at nine in the morning tomorrow."

Sonia gave Perillo a reluctant nod.

Daniele unplugged the recorder and bent over to lift the machine.

"That looks heavy," Sonia said. "Do you want to use my shopping cart? I'll pick it up in the morning."

Daniele blushed as he shook his head. Did he look that weak? "Very kind, thank you. The car is nearby."

"Make life easy for yourself," Sonia said, striding over to Daniele. She took the tape recorder from his arms, walked it over to the kitchen and came out with the recorder in the shopping cart. "Here." She pushed the cart in Daniele's direction. "Save your show of muscles for a girl your age."

Perillo was smiling and Daniele was still blushing as Sonia walked them to the door. "Please find who killed her, Maresciallo."

Perillo lifted his hat. "I will try hard, but I can offer no guarantees. Thank you. Buongiorno."

FOUR

Nico was dishing out heapfuls of rigatoni with sausage and mushrooms when Tilde let out a low whistle. She was looking out of the narrow window that faced part of the terrace.

"I bet he expects a free lunch," she said.

Nico joined her at the window. Alba, dressed in a short skirt and a breast-hugging sweater was showing the menu to a civilian-clothed maresciallo of the carabinieri.

"Ivana working is your doing?"

"No, her own. I just found her the job."

Nico went back to the counter to fill the last plate Alba had asked for. "I'll be right back."

"Tell him he's perfectly capable of making his own lunch, but the first course is on me." Tilde went back to cutting paper-thin slices of beef to make stracci con rughetta—rags with arugula. "Today only!" She called out to Nico's back.

"The rigatoni are great," Nico said as a hello to Perillo after handing Alba the dish she'd requested.

Perillo kept his eyes on the menu. "Is that what you cooked?"

"I made the sauce."

"What did Tilde cook?"

"Eggplant lasagne to start."

Perillo shook his head. "Northerners don't know how to

make lasagne. Not enough layers. No ricotta. I'll take yours."
He looked up at Nico. "The woman you sent me to," he said in
a low voice, "has long ears full of interesting information."

Nico understood he meant Sonia, the housekeeper.

"I'm going to need some Super Tuscan with your rigatoni.
This afternoon I have the family. You still want me tonight?"

"More than ever." Nico was curious to know what the housekeeper and the family had to say. He also knew that Perillo
would need bolstering. "You decide the time."

"Seven. I won't stay long. I'm anxious to hear about Ivana's
first day at work. I don't know if I hope she loves it or if she's
ready to quit tomorrow. Not that she ever would. Too proud
like her husband. You'd better get back in the kitchen. I can feel
Tilde's eyes burrowing into me from that window."

"Your first course is on her."

"As it should be." Perillo raised his empty wine glass at the
window.

"Buon appetito and give me a call when you're on your way."
Nico walked back into the kitchen and prepared Perillo's order,
adding an extra sausage for his friend.

HAVING EATEN AN EXCELLENT and discounted lunch at
Sotto Il Fico, Perillo sat behind his desk, ready to face Nora's
family. Daniele, who hadn't been able to reach Stella during her
lunch hour, was glumly arranging four chairs in a semicircle in
front of Perillo's desk.

"That was not pleasant," Adriana said as she walked into the
room, dressed in a silk red-floral dress and pink blazer. Her husband, sister and sister's boyfriend were being fingerprinted and
swabbed for DNA.

Perillo blinked at the colors she was wearing. *She's celebrating
her mother's murder.* "Identifying a body never is."

"Oh, that." Adriana checked her hands for cleanliness. "Well, we knew what to expect. It's the journalists. They won't leave us alone. Who knows what stories they will invent. Can't you do something?"

"They have worn out our patience here also. I'm afraid there's nothing I can do."

Adriana sat down in one of the chairs, crossed her legs and declared, "Well, I hope you catch the thief who killed my mother."

Perillo sat up. "You did not find the opal ring?"

"Forget about that stupid ring. What's missing is my mother's very valuable jewelry. Seven pieces in all. I prepared a list for you." Adriana flipped open a tiny pink purse and handed Perillo a folded sheet of paper. "The thief left the art—too hard to fence, I suppose."

Perillo unfolded the note and read:

> *Missing: a 3-carat Art Deco diamond ring set in platinum, an oval cabochon ruby ring set in gold, a 12-carat graduated round diamond necklace set in white gold with matching drop earrings, a diamond broach depicting a bird in flight, a two-strand pearl-and-diamond choker and a thin single-strand diamond bracelet.*

"Do you have photographs of the jewelry?"

"We didn't find any. Fabio called the insurance company to see if they had photos. My mother canceled the insurance on the jewelry months ago. The agent said they sent the photos back. It would have been just like her to tear them up."

"Where did your mother keep this jewelry?" Perillo asked. "And when was the last time you saw any of it?"

"She kept it in the garden shed," Fabio Meloni said. He'd been standing at the door with Clara while Perillo read the list. Today he wore dark green corduroy slacks and a mustard-colored knit jacket. "I recently had some business to take care of in the area and used the opportunity to visit Nora and convince her to get a safe-deposit box at her bank." He sat down next to his wife.

"We all told her it was crazy to keep it in the shed," Clara said as she came in and sat on the other side of her sister. "Mamma was stubborn. She never wore any of the jewelry, but she liked to look at it."

Daniele had been observing Clara from the minute she walked into the room. With her espresso-dark eyes and sensual mouth, she was very attractive, dynamic looking. Dark messy hair grazed her shoulders, and she was wearing a knit tunic that stopped mid-thigh over thin ribbed gray leggings that tucked into matching gray ankle boots. Daniele felt heat rise to his cheeks as his eyes stared at her long shapely legs.

"When was this visit, Signor Meloni?" Perillo asked.

"Nine days ago."

"You saw the jewelry then?"

For a moment Fabio looked flustered. "No, I didn't, but she would have told me if she had sold it."

"Certainly she would have told my husband," Adriana said, looking very annoyed. "They had an excellent rapport."

"Maresciallo," Clara said after a quick look at her sister. "Mamma showed me the diamond ring about a month ago. She took it out of the plastic bag that held all the jewelry."

"What?" Adriana asked with narrowed eyes before Perillo could ask his question.

Clara glared at her sister. "Don't be a bitch. She just showed me the ring and put it back in the bag and back into the potting mix."

Daniele quietly took out his notebook and started taking notes.

Perillo crossed his arms and watched the interesting family dynamics.

"Oh, I'm not the bitch here!"

Fabio tugged Adriana's arm. It didn't stop her.

"I know what you did. You brought your handsome Marco over to show him off to Mamma, telling her the two of you were going to get married and I can just hear you hinting that her ring would make a wonderful engagement ring. But our mother put it right back in a bag of dirt. Exactly like she did with our father."

Clara gave her sister a condescending smile. "You always think you know everything. Mamma showed it to me because she wanted me to know she was going to sell it to help the Syrian refugees."

"Ha!" Adriana exclaimed. "That's a really good one."

Perillo had had enough. "Maybe Signora Salviati did donate the jewelry."

"Never," Adriana said calmly. "She was either lying to Clara or Clara is lying now." She waved her hand as if to clear the air. "Stolen, Maresciallo. Gone. Understood?"

Under the desk Perillo's right hand tightened into a fist. "We will look into the theft of your mother's jewelry, but it may not be the reason she was killed." The theft was too convenient. He didn't trust these people.

"What other reason can there be?" Fabio Meloni asked, craning his thin neck out toward the maresciallo. "Nora knew who stole the jewelry, confronted the person and got strangled. You should start by carefully examining the Barron woman's possessions."

"We will do all that is necessary to try to recover the stolen items. Now I would like to get back to your mother-in-law's murder."

Adriana recrossed her legs, readjusted her pink jacket. "I thought that's what we were talking about, Maresciallo."

Perillo scratched his palm to suppress the urge to slap this smug woman. "Signorina Barron heard the *Moonlight Sonata* being played on the piano shortly before she entered the music room and discovered your mother's body. Does that sonata have any special significance in your family?"

"Oh, yes, at least for the two of us," Clara said. "Our piano teacher had us play it for hours, and days. We could never play it to his satisfaction. I always ended up in tears."

"We were both hopeless with music," Adriana added. "I finally convinced Babbo we would be considered proper young signorine without knowing how to play the piano. Our mother, always negative, said we'd regret it. We never did."

"I did," Clara said. "It would have been fun at parties."

Adriana dismissed her sister with a shrug.

"The *Moonlight Sonata* had no special meaning for your mother?" Perillo asked.

"Not that I know of." Adriana looked at her sister for confirmation. Clara shook her head.

Perillo felt he was getting nowhere. The theft of the jewelry was an added headache, and he wasn't sure it was the motive for the murder. Last night he'd tried to listen to the *Moonlight Sonata* on YouTube with Ivana, and he'd been so tired, he fell asleep. This morning he asked her what she thought of the music. "Those beautiful notes come from a pained heart," she said.

Perillo now asked, "Do you know if your mother was in a romantic relationship with someone?"

Adrian snorted. "With herself."

"You're being unfair, Adriana," Clara protested. "Mamma was self-involved because she was unhappy. You didn't love her. I didn't pay much attention to her. Babbo had lots of affairs."

Adriana's spine went iron-rod straight as she glared at her sister.

Clara faced Perillo. "I don't know of any romantic relationship."

Listening to the Lamberti sisters, Perillo was reminded of the good cop/bad cop he'd seen on American shows. He wondered if the two women were putting on an act. Or was he showing his prejudice against upper-class people?

Perillo picked up the phone and buzzed Dino. "What's taking so long with Marco Zanelli?" Dino's answer was short. "Ah," Perillo said and put down the phone. The good feeling lunch had given him was long gone. "I asked for Marco Zanelli to be present and you, Signora Meloni, told him to go home?"

"I did," Adriana said. "He's not family and has no business being part of this meeting. I assumed you only wanted him for his fingerprints and saliva."

Perillo banged his fist on the desk. "Never assume anything about me!"

Adriana shrugged. "There's no need to be upset. He's not going to know anything. You can call him in again if you insist."

"He's waiting for me in my car," Clara said. "Should I call him?"

"No." He needed to get away from this family. He needed a cigarette or a coffee or a mouthful of air. He needed to calm down. "I will interview him separately, as I will interview the three of you separately. Your statements will be recorded and typed up. You will then come back and after checking for inaccuracies, you will sign your statements." Perillo stood up. "Daniele, please set up the interviews. Buonasera. We will meet again." He bowed to the two women and walked out of the room.

As soon as Perillo stepped outside, he regretted his show of temper. Regret brought more anger. He clenched and unclenched his fist. "*Never lose control on the job*," his adoptive carabiniere father had told him countless times. "*It is a sign of weakness*." He called Nico. "I could come over in half an hour." He wanted to calm down first.

"Whenever you want."

"Thanks." He slipped the phone back into his jacket pocket.

Dino made a timid appearance at the door of the station. The rigid set of the maresciallo's shoulders signaled a warning. "Excuse me, Maresciallo."

"What?" Perillo snapped as he patted down his uniform pants pockets for a pack of cigarettes.

"Avvocato Sbarra, Signora Salviati's lawyer, is on the phone."

"Get his number. I'll call him back." *Where are my damn cigarettes?*

"Yes, Maresciallo." Dino happily retreated into the safety of the station.

You quit, idiot. Remember? Perillo strode to the café bar and savored an espresso with grappa. His anger retreated as he watched the Lamberti Meloni family leave the station. Once their cars were out of sight, he walked across the street and sat on a bench in the small park he often used as an office. He called Dino. "What's the number?" He jotted it down. "Thanks."

"Ah, Maresciallo, I'm glad you called," Sbarra said after Perillo introduced himself. "I was about to leave the office. I decided not to wait for the warrant. The sooner you are informed, the faster you will solve the signora's terrible murder. I have Signora Salviati's new will in front of me."

"How new?"

"Fifteen days ago. Do you want to come by to read a copy? My secretary can let you in."

"No, please read it over the phone."

It didn't take long.

"How different is it from the previous will?" Perillo asked.

"Very." The lawyer went on to explain the differences. "There's another document you should know about."

This news was cigarette worthy. "Does the family know?"

"I'm going to the villa now to read the will and show them the document."

WHEN PERILLO WALKED IN, still in uniform, Nico took one look at his friend's face, went directly to the small hutch Nelli had suggested he buy and took out the whiskey bottle.

Perillo dropped down in a new armchair opposite Nico's old one. OneWag, always sensitive to moods, gave his boss's friend a friendly nudge with his snout. "Ciao, Rocco." Perillo patted the dog's head and looked around the room that acted as a small living room, a dining room and a kitchen. "Nelli has made changes," he observed. OneWag settled down at his feet. "Just a few now that she spends three or four nights a week here." Nico put the two glasses on the table next to a dish filled with chunks of Parmigiano-Reggiano. "I liked her suggestions so no arguments. Ice?"

"Smooth, thanks."

Nico poured two inches of whiskey into each glass. They raised them, clinked and wished each other health. Nico sat in his old armchair and offered the cheese dish to Perillo.

"No, thanks. I need my whiskey full strength."

"How did it go with the family?" Nico placed the dish on the floor between them. OneWag didn't like parmigiano.

"Not well. We now have a new complication in the case. It seems Nora's valuable jewelry was stolen. She kept it in the garden shed, according to the daughters. The forensics team is already on the way to see what they can discover in that shed and its immediate surroundings. In the morning, Dani and I are going over there to talk to the gardener and his son. I need you to—"

Nico didn't let him finish. "I can guess—pay a visit to Nora's English guest."

"Right. The family immediately suspected her."

"Who will come with me to go through Signorina Barron's things?"

"Dino."

"Do you have a search warrant?"

"I'm not sure I can get one. I think you, with Laura Benati's help, can explain how it is to Signorina Barron's advantage to clear her name quickly."

"You think Nora was killed for the jewelry?"

"That's what they think but Clara mentioned that Nora was planning to sell the jewelry to help Syrian refugees, which could have given someone in the family the idea to steal it before Nora gave it away. Adriana was adamant about the Syrian thing being a lie."

"She could have been eliminating a motive for killing Nora."

"Those diamonds are certainly worth a great deal of money, but there are other possible motives." Perillo took another sip. "Nora's lawyer called. She changed her will fifteen days ago and left her daughters a sizable amount of money divided equally. Her gardener gets a surprisingly large amount in both the old and new wills. In the new one Lapo's son gets ten thousand euros, instead of five thousand when he turns eighteen. The bequests to her housekeeper and the laundress didn't change."

"What about the property and the jewelry?"

"The daughters inherited both under the old will. There's no mention of either in the new one. According to her lawyer, Nora refused to sign a residuary clause."

"Then what happens to the jewelry and the property?"

"For the jewelry the probate court has to first determine who are the next of kin. Nora's daughters will eventually get it, unless there's a hidden child somewhere, but it will take some time before they do." Perillo emptied his glass and picked up a chunk of the cheese. He was beginning to feel better.

"And the property?"

"Nora signed an agreement to sell to BelPosto, a Swiss hotel company, the same company that is buying up small hotels all over Chianti, according to the lawyer. Their goal is to turn Chianti into a paradise for the very rich. To hell with anyone else. The villa would become a five-star hotel. BelPosto sent her a hefty down payment last week." Perillo leaned back in the armchair. "Three weeks ago, Sonia, the housekeeper, overheard Fabio Meloni talking to a Swiss company and then telling his wife, '*They made an offer.*' Meloni must have suspected she was planning to sell. The prospect of losing that property might give one or more of the family members a solid motive."

"Why risk waiting three weeks to kill her?"

"Well, Fabio only knew that BelPosto had made an offer. He didn't necessarily know she wanted to go through with it at that point, but maybe he heard or saw something that confirmed she was selling."

"Did you ask the BelPosto people about Meloni's call?"

"It was on my list. Now that I know about the sale, there's no need. I have no doubt the family will fight it in court. They might win, but it will take years. I can just see Fabio Meloni wanting to play the important Chianti vintner."

"Why not the daughters?" Nico asked. "Antinori is run by three sisters, Castello di Volpaia by a mother and daughter. I'm sure there are countless others."

"I accept the slap on the wrist, Nico. To be fair, I can also see Adriana wanting that role. Salviati wines were apparently considered the very best the Chianti region produced."

"Maybe they won't want to fight it. The sale of that property would bring in a lot of money. Have you looked into the family's finances?"

"I asked for a warrant. Daniele is trying to see what he can find out without one. He can do magic with the internet."

Nico got up and poured another inch of whiskey into Perillo's glass. "I know you are hoping someone in the family killed Nora, but so far you've got nothing on them."

Perillo frowned and swished the whiskey in his glass.

Nico sat back down. "Who else was Nora involved with?"

Perillo repeated what the housekeeper had told him about the Rosatis. "I'll pay them a visit with Daniele." He drank and let a satisfied smile cross his lips. "You are a piece of bread, Nico, but your whiskey is gold."

"The whiskey mellows. I listen."

"I know you do. And you notice too. So does Rocco. Look at him asleep at my feet."

OneWag lifted his sleepy head a few inches at the sound of his name. Seeing nothing had changed, his head went back down between his paws.

"It's the first time he hasn't sniffed my boots. How does a dog know? How did you know I needed an ear?"

"It showed in your face."

"I guess it did, still does probably. Ivana thinks I'm upset with her." Perillo pointed a finger at his chest. "I am upset with me. I never imagined she wanted to have a life outside of the house. She never said and I never asked." Shame is what he felt. He turned his head to look out at the small terrace where he and Daniele had eaten Nico's good food, where he had smoked too many cigarettes. He was glad Dani wasn't with him this time. Glad the smoking was over. "Have the swallows come back?"

"Yes, a month ago. The ceiling beams are holding three nests." Nico waited, hoping his friend would open up to him, tell him what was weighing him down. Six months ago, with his fiftieth birthday looming, Perillo had come to him worried about aging. This time, Nico sensed there was more than Ivana weighing his friend down.

Perillo stood up and put his empty glass down on the kitchen table. He pulled out one of the chairs and sat down, wanting to feel the straight back hard against his spine. "I have decided that I cannot be impartial investigating Nora's murder. I will tell the substitute prosecutor the Investigative Unit can take over without my help."

Nico didn't try to hide his surprise. Perillo willingly giving up control was unheard of. This was bad news for his friend. "Why do you feel you can't be impartial?"

"Because I have a long-lived bias against the rich, the entitled, the people who think they own the world. The kind of people who can walk by in their Gucci shoes and Prada handbags full of money and not even notice the famished beggar holding out his hand. People like Adriana and Fabio Meloni. In America, I read you call them the one percent. I hate them."

"I didn't live my boyhood on the streets like you did," Nico said, "but I don't like the one percent either. Before you call the prosecutor, why don't you think of what your carabiniere father would say to you now." Last year Perillo had told him how Capitano Perillo had caught him stealing and instead of taking him to jail, had offered him a home and a new life.

"Oh, il Capitano would fill my ears with duty, justice, and the carabinieri motto *Faithful Through the Centuries.*"

"And what about Nora who, by not leaving her jewelry to her daughters, must have been planning to donate it to help the Syrian refugees? She doesn't deserve your help in finding her killer?"

"Certainly Nora deserves justice," Perillo answered. "Even bastards do—at least their families do, but I fear I will not be fair. It would give me great satisfaction to pin the murder on Adriana and Fabio just to justify my prejudices. You heard my bias. I don't trust myself anymore."

"You'll have Dani and me with you. And whoever the prosecutor sends down. Daniele was the one who found our guilty party last time."

Perillo thought back to their last case for a moment. His face relaxed. "Yes, he did. And I was convinced the killer was someone else. I guess I'm a pompous jerk. But, may my father forgive me, I really can't stand that woman and her husband."

"Who knows?" Nico said. "One or both could be the killer. What's your impression of the sister and the boyfriend?"

"I got only a glimpse of the boyfriend." Perillo explained the reason for losing his temper. "I don't know about Clara. She told her sister not to be a bitch, which I enjoyed." He sat back down on the comfortable armchair and looked at his watch. "I should go now, or Ivana is going to worry, but before I do . . ." He reached down, took three pieces of parmigiano from the dish on the floor, popped one into his mouth and chewed. "Mmm, this is very good. Where did you get it?"

Maybe the crisis is over, Nico thought. "Enrico's salumeria."

"He still hasn't forgiven me for fining him that one time." Perillo bent over and placed a piece of the cheese in front of OneWag's mouth. The dog sniffed and looked up to find his boss's friend peering down at him. Gently he took the cheese into his mouth.

"You are a lucky bastard, Rocco," Perillo said. "And also, molto simpatico." He stood up, popped another piece of cheese into his mouth, pulled down his uniform jacket, checked the crease of his trousers and walked to the door. "Thank you, amico and buonasera. Call me after your visit to Signorina Barron."

"I'll send pictures of the stash."

"Luck be with us."

"Do me a favor and call the BelPosto people. I think we should know what exactly was said during the phone call."

"I agree. Ciao and thanks."

"Anytime. Buonanotte." Nico closed the door.

OneWag opened his mouth. The parmigiano piece fell to the floor.

"AH, HERE YOU ARE," Ivana said when she heard the front door opening. She turned up the gas on the stracciatella soup, quickly took off her apron and fluffed up her hair. The table was already set with the new floral tablecloth she had bought at the Saturday market. She was exhausted, happy and worried, a combination of feelings that was new to her.

"Ciao, bella mia." Perillo gave Ivana a long hug. "I missed you."

"Not just my food?" Tilde had tipped her off that he'd eaten a big meal at Sotto Il Fico.

"I missed your beautiful face." Perillo meant it. Looking at her face across the table at lunch made the ugly aspects of his work recede. She gave him peace, made him feel blessed. "You must be tired. Sit down, Ivana. I'll serve."

Ivana hid her surprise and did as he asked. She was happy to get off her feet.

Perillo lifted the lid to the only pot on the stove. "Ah, stracciatella. My favorite."

She enjoyed his effort to please her. His favorite was pasta and potato soup. "Then a salad and fruit. You can turn off the burner now."

With a smile, Perillo did as told and ladled the soup in shallow bowls and sat down opposite her. "How did your first day go?" he asked.

"Alba put me in charge of supervising the making of the dough. She bought this huge kneading machine. We are three women, working as a team. I had fun, Salva. I really did, but my feet hurt."

"If you're enjoying yourself, your feet will adjust." He half-filled two glasses with Chianti. "Cin cin, cara. I'm happy for you. And you are right. I do need to slim down."

Ivana raised her glass and silently thanked Sant'Antonio for giving her such a good husband.

FIVE

When Perillo and Daniele reached the shed at the southern end of the eight-hectare property, they were hit by a strong smell of coffee. A long-legged, muscled man in jeans, a dirt-streaked T-shirt and bare feet ignored them as he spread fistfuls of dark grounds along the bed of a row of climbing hydrangeas leaning against the stone wall of the shed.

"Are those coffee grounds?" Daniele asked, curiosity getting the better of him. The maresciallo liked to be the one to speak first.

"Turns them blue," the man said. He had a handsome, strong-jawed face, already dark from the sun. His large eyes and his mass of wavy hair were the same color as the coffee grounds he was spreading. He looked to be in his mid-to-late forties.

"Signor Angelini?" Perillo asked.

The gardener put the large can of coffee grounds down, wiped his hands down his jeans and spoke before Perillo had a chance to introduce himself and Daniele. "Lapo Angelini. I didn't kill her if that's why you're here, and I have no use for fancy stuff. Nora and me got along. Ask anyone. She had no interest in changing anything on the land, so I take care of things as I see best. Only thing we argued over was my wanting to plant a vegetable garden and some grape vines along that stretch." He pointed a thumb behind him. "The land dips there. The slope gets sun all day long.

"The wine would have been good. All this land is just a banquet for the eyes. '*The eye needs to be fed*,' she'd repeat. '*So does the stomach*,' was my reply. I don't care how rich you are, land is meant to feed you. She should have had her own wine. She said she was tired of being pestered about turning the place into a vineyard again. I got the idea she wasn't talking about me. The whole place had been a vineyard a long time ago. Mine was a good idea that went nowhere. So we argued about that. Nothing else. She was good to me. Hired Cecco to help me out last year. He's my son. He's out buying some badly needed sod. Nora said our work kept her eyes happy. That's how she put it." Lapo put his hands on his hips and looked directly at Perillo. "That's all I've got to say, Maresciallo."

"Maresciallo Perillo"—he extended his arm toward Daniele—"and Brigadiere Daniele Donato." They had missed seeing the gardener yesterday. Vince had taken care of the fingerprinting and DNA swab. "I do have some questions. Is there someplace we can sit?" On waking up, Perillo had been greeted with a sunny, warm Wednesday and a throbbing knee, a reminder of an old cycling fall. The walk from the car to the shed had been at least a kilometer long.

"I'd say the grass is as good a place as any," Lapo said. "The sun has already dried it out."

"A bench or a couple of chairs would be better," Daniele suggested. He had noticed the slight limp. Besides the maresciallo was fussy about his uniform.

"The fingerprint people came and left," Lapo said. "They turned my stuff upside down and sealed the shed. There's a couple of old sarcophagi behind the shed you can sit on."

Perillo shuddered. Pain be damned. He wasn't about to sit on a coffin no matter how ancient it was. He took out his handkerchief, shook it open, and prepared to spread it carefully over the grass. Lowering himself was going to be difficult.

"Maresciallo, wait!" Daniele picked up the can full of coffee grounds, punched the lid down on it and placed it on the grass. "Try this."

Perillo gave his brigadiere a grateful nod, covered the rusty lid with his handkerchief and gingerly sat down. Relieved the bucket didn't buckle, Daniele crossed his legs and sat on the grass next to Perillo. Lapo looked at them with an amused expression Daniele hoped the maresciallo wouldn't catch.

Perillo was too preoccupied with finding the best position for his leg. Once found he asked, "You call your employer by her first name. That's unusual."

Lapo shrugged. "That's the way she wanted it. The day after Signor Lamberti's heart quit on him, she told me she wouldn't answer to Signora Lamberti anymore."

Daniele took out his trusted pocket notebook and pen, ready to write, grateful that this time his boss hadn't insisted on lugging the tape recorder.

"Please sit down, Lapo," Perillo said. It would make him feel less ridiculous.

Lapo shrugged again and folded himself down onto the grass.

"Thank you," Perillo said. "Did the Lambertis not get along?"

"His pants had a loose zipper. Wives don't like that."

Ah! Maybe not relevant but interesting. Perillo stretched out his leg. "Are you married?"

"Cecco has a mother. She lives in Siena."

"And you and your son?"

"We are in the old gatehouse at the north end of the property. The entrance road to the villa got moved way before I got hired."

"How long have you worked here?"

"Signor Lamberti hired me fifteen years ago as his head

gardener. When he was alive, I oversaw a team of four men. It's a big place."

"And after his death?"

"Nora said they weren't necessary. I got a big raise so I didn't mind being on my own. These trees and bushes have been here for many years. They mostly take care of themselves."

Perillo noticed Daniele seemed eager to say something. "Go ahead, Brigadiere. Ask your questions."

Daniele's heart did a jump. Perillo willingly ceding control was rare. To his great relief, his cheeks stayed pale. "Did you know Signora Salviati's jewelry was kept in the shed?"

"Yes. She brought it over about a month ago, wanting to hide it there. She usually kept it in a safe in her bedroom."

Interesting that he should know that, Perillo thought.

"I suggested a bag of manure," Lapo said. "No one was going to stick their hand in that. She didn't want the stuff to smell so it ended up in mulch."

Daniele asked, "Did she say why she wanted to hide it all of a sudden?"

"No, and I didn't ask. If she wanted me to know she would have told me."

"Do you know if Signora Salviati had a falling out with anyone?"

"I don't know anything about her life outside this villa."

Perillo jumped in. "What about her family? Did you notice any animosity between them?"

"It wasn't my business to notice."

"It may not be your business," Perillo insisted, "but perhaps you witnessed the daughters fighting with their mother."

Daniele picked up his pen and notebook again.

Lapo raised his thick eyebrows. "You think they hated their mother so much, one of them or both killed her? I can't help you with that. The girls fought with their mother like all spoiled kids, but killing her? No."

"Did you witness Nora showing Clara a diamond ring a month ago?"

"I did. Clara is getting engaged."

"Did you overhear their conversation?"

"I couldn't help it. I was standing right there. Nora told Clara she planned to donate her jewelry to help the Syrian refugees."

Perillo caught the sudden flicker of disapproval in the gardener's eyes. "Was Clara's fiancé with her?"

"No."

"Do you think Nora's daughters loved her?"

Lapo's expression went blank. "I'm only the gardener. I watch over plants, not people."

"Indeed, and you have done a very good job of it from what I have seen." Perillo wondered if Lapo was telling the truth. "Did you meet Nora's guest, the English signorina?"

"Yes. Nora brought her over to the shed and introduced me, although we could not communicate. Nora showed her the bag of mulch. She was speaking English, so I don't know what she said."

"Do you have the keys to the villa?"

"I didn't want them, but Nora insisted in case she needed help. At night she was alone in there."

Daniele watched as the maresciallo put his weight on his good leg and slowly stood up. His help would not have been welcome.

"Thank you, Lapo," Perillo said, as Daniele and Lapo quickly got on their feet too. Daniele brushed off the seat of his pants.

"One last question for now. Where were you the night between this past Sunday and Monday?"

"I wasn't strangling Nora. I was sleeping off two bottles of wine I drank at dinner with Cecco. Ask Cecco. He had to sleep it off too."

"Where and what were you celebrating?"

"At Gino's in Gravigna. His eighteenth birthday."

"I will have to speak to him too. We will talk again. Arrivederci." Perillo started to walk away but his knee stopped him. "Is there a way to drive up here?"

"Sure. You mean you walked here from the villa? I told the carabiniere who called me yesterday how to get to the shed by car."

Perillo snapped his eyes at his brigadiere. "Not me," Daniele said. The maresciallo would find out soon enough that Vince had made the call.

Lapo pointed to his left. "The service road starts at the old entrance, next to the gatehouse where I live. Let me drive you down to your car in my mini truck. It's better than walking back on that bad leg of yours."

First he felt ridiculous, now humiliated. "Not a bad leg," Perillo corrected. "Just the knee being temperamental."

"Happens to me too," Daniele said for the maresciallo's sake. For a man who hated lying he was getting pretty good at it.

LAURA BENATI LEFT THE reception desk when Nico and Dino entered the vast foyer of Hotel Bella Vista. "Buongiorno."

"Ciao, Laura." She looked lovely as she walked across the dark terra-cotta tiles, wearing tan slacks and a matching tan silk blouse with a dark blue wool cardigan draped over her shoulders, the sleeves tied over her chest. Her long blond hair was loosely tied behind her neck. She wore no jewelry and only a trace of lipstick.

"You've brought—" Laura stopped when she saw a carabiniere following Nico. "I was about to say that you've brought a beautiful day with you, but now I wonder." She had had enough of the carabinieri last year.

"You are right to wonder. Have you met Dino?"

"I've seen you with the maresciallo," Laura said, reminding herself she was in the hospitality business. "Buongiorno."

Dino stepped forward and clicked his heels. "The pleasure is mine, Signorina."

Laura acknowledged the greeting with a polite smile. "You must be here to see Signorina Barron. She is having breakfast in her room. Can I offer you an espresso while you wait?"

"No, thank you, Laura. What is her room number?"

"You can't go up there. She's probably still in her nightgown."

"I'll explain later. Please give me her room number."

Laura's jaw tightened. "No." Friends or no friends, it was her job to protect her guests. "If you need to talk to her, I will let her know you are here."

Nico turned to see if anyone else had walked in. "I'll explain now then." He told her about the stolen jewelry, the Lamberti family's insistence that Miss Barron be searched. "If Perillo needs to wait for a search warrant he will, but she might want to get this over with as quickly as possible."

"It's what I would wish." She couldn't just let them go up there without warning. But if she warned Miss Barron and they found nothing, they would think she managed to hide the jewelry outside her room. Then they would turn the hotel upside down, looking for jewelry that she hadn't stolen in the first place. "Here's what we'll do, Nico. I will stand by the door of her room to make sure she doesn't leave, and you will call her on the house phone and tell her what you need to do. If she insists on a search warrant, you will tell her to open her door and let me know. Does that sound acceptable?"

"You won't warn her?"

"You'll have to trust me."

"I do."

"By the way, the hotel has twenty-three rooms, seven of which are occupied today. Please don't go barging in any of them looking for Miss Barron's. And the house number to her room has no relationship to her room number. I'm walking up. Give

me five minutes and dial room 311. The phone is over there."
Laura pointed to a long heavy table underneath a window and
walked away.

MISS BARRON OPENED THE door with a smile on her face.
"Good morning, Signor Doyle." She was wrapped in the light-
blue dressing gown she wore when he had first seen her. Her hair
was perfectly combed.

Nico was happy to see she didn't look in the least upset.
"Good morning. I'm sorry we're barging in on you so early. The
maresciallo wanted to clear you as quickly as possible. Thank
you for understanding." He introduced Dino.

She acknowledged Dino with a tilt of her head. "I thought
the suspicion of theft usually rests first on the servants, not the
guest, but you are welcome to search every nook and corner."
She stepped aside to let them in. The corner room was large
with two windows overlooking the entrance of the hotel and the
view of Vignamaggio in the distance. Another window framed
a stand of chestnut trees. Nico made a mental note to check
the ground below the windows. Dino slipped on gloves and
patted and checked Miss Barron's empty suitcase. He moved
on, opening the drawers of an antique-looking bureau between
the two windows.

Miss Barron watched him calmly. "Should I wait outside
while you go through my things?"

"No, please, Miss Barron," Nico said. "I need you to witness
our search."

"Then I won't be able to accuse you of planting a diamond
necklace in my suitcase, should you find one."

"Will I find one?" Nico asked.

"No. I think diamonds are gaudy. And you won't find the
opal ring."

"I'm glad to hear that." He didn't like this job. It had to be demeaning for Miss Barron. He hoped they would not find anything. If they did, Miss Barron would jump to the top of the suspect list. He couldn't picture her as a thief or a murderer.

Nico crossed the room to the open suitcase sitting on a luggage rack next to a handsome oak armoire.

Laura appeared at the still-open door. "Would you like me to stay with you, Miss Barron?"

"Heavens no, Laura, thank you. You have a hotel to run. I trust Mr. Doyle and Mr. Dino will behave like gentlemen, but please pat me down before you go. I might have pocketed a pair of earrings."

"That's absurd," Laura protested.

"Laura"—Nico looked up from rummaging through the suitcase—"if you don't, I'll have to."

Laura laughed when she saw the twinkle in Miss Barron's eyes. "You're enjoying this, aren't you?"

"Immensely." Miss Barron spread out her arms. "I haven't been paid this much male attention in years."

Laura patted her down and found only a balled-up tissue in one bathrobe pocket. Dino took it from her and crushed it in his hand. Nothing there. He hadn't found any jewelry in the drawers.

Laura stayed by the door with Miss Barron while Nico and Dino finished searching the luggage, then moved on to the bed, the clothes hanging in the armoire, her three pairs of shoes. They checked the night table, stripped the bed, lifted the mattress, pummeled the two pillows, Dino lay down on the floor and checked the springs. The floor revealed a dropped bookmark.

No jewelry was found in the bathroom. Nico walked back into the bedroom with a grin on his face. "We're done. You are not a jewelry thief I'm glad to say. Thank you for putting up with us." Dino bowed his thanks with his head and started to remake the bed.

"Leave that," Laura told Dino. "We'll take care of putting everything back in order."

"Thank you, Laura," Nico said with relief. He was eager to leave so he could stop feeling embarrassed. Dino flickered a shy smile at both women and left the room.

With a mischievous look on her face, Miss Barron held out her fisted hand. "What about this?" She opened her fist, revealing a curled-up gold chain.

"Oh, no," was Laura's reaction. "How did I miss it?"

Nico plucked the chain from Miss Barron's hand. It was heavy. A small gold seal with the initial P hung from the middle of the chain. He'd never seen anything like it. "What is it?"

"A watch fob. It's an English one from the Victorian period. Her daughters will tell you it belonged to Nora. Adriana will accuse me of stealing it." The expression on her face was now serious. "For some reason she is not well-disposed toward me, but then she isn't toward most people."

"Did you steal it?"

"I admired it and Nora gave it to me. I'm afraid I can't prove that."

"Why didn't you show it to us right away?"

"And spoil the fun?"

"We would have gone ahead with the search."

"Without the same fervor, I think. I do hope I will be able to keep Nora's gift. It has a great deal of meaning for me."

"I hope so too."

"Now I would like to get dressed and start my day."

"Of course," Nico said. "Goodbye, Miss Barron."

"Oh, I'm sure we'll see each other again. I suspect the mah-rayshallow will put me at the top of the suspect list."

She's hungry for attention, Nico decided. "Then I look forward to seeing you again. And again, thank you for being such a good sport." Miss Barron's smile followed him out.

Dino was outside the hotel wiping his hands clean on his jeans. "I dug around in the ground underneath her windows. All I found were cigarette butts and three snails. Nothing worth any money."

Nico handed Dino the watch fob. "Come on, Dino, I'll drive you back to the station. Then I must get to work."

"You think la signorina stole that chain?" Dino asked as they walked to the car park.

"I don't know. She says Nora gave it to her."

"My aunt liked to steal tulip bulbs. She never planted them. She liked to hold them in her hands, said they made her feel good. La signorina reminded me of my aunt. People do crazy things."

PERILLO SCRAMBLED TO HIS feet when Capitano Carlo Tarani of the Florence Nucleo Investigativo walked into his office. Daniele, already standing, saluted. There had been no warning. Luckily this time they were both in uniform.

"We meet again, Maresciallo Perillo." Tarani took off his hat and gave them both a broad smile. "Brigadiere Donato." He was a tall, trim man with a thin face, small eyes and slicked-back hair that had, since they had last seen him, changed from dust-colored brown to a darker brown.

"Benvenuto, Capitano." With his arm, Perillo indicated the armchair he'd just been sitting in. "Please, make yourself comfortable."

"No, no. I am here only to listen, not to take over."

Tarani strode over to the chair facing Perillo's desk and sat down, placing his hat in his lap. "Maresciallo Perillo, Brigadiere Donato, please sit down. There is no need for formalities. We are colleagues. I am here because Prosecutor Della Langhe feels this case is more delicate than the previous one. I must say I don't agree although my opinion should stay in this room. All victims

deserve the same investigative fervor, something you, the brigadiere and Signor Doyle are endowed with. I am assuming he is
also involved in this case."

"More than ever. The Englishwoman who found Signora Salviati's body, Signorina Barron, speaks no Italian."

"Thank heaven then that you are blessed with Mr. Doyle's
assistance. My English is only rudimentary. Now give me the
facts as you know them."

Perillo raised his eyebrows. "Should we order coffees before
I start?"

"Excellent idea. Cane sugar for me."

Perillo picked up the phone. "Vince, two espressos, one cane
sugar and an apricot juice."

Vince quickly removed the cracker he was about to bite into
from his mouth. "Already done, Maresciallo." He hadn't ordered
the cane sugar, but he had a supply in his desk drawer.

"Bravo, Vince."

While Perillo was on the phone, Daniele slipped the report
he had typed out last night onto his desk.

Perillo looked down and started reading. "At four-fifteen
Monday morning, April—"

Tarani cut him off. "No, talk to me. You can send me that
report later. Has the autopsy been done? What did it reveal?"

"The report came in this morning. She died by strangulation
with a meter of curtain cord that came from the victim's bedroom. Her stomach contents so far show no immediate traces of
drugs, but more testing is being done. Along with blood anal-
ysis. She must have known her attacker as she had no defensive
wounds."

"No helpful DNA under her fingernails then," Tarani said in
a matter-of-fact voice. "Still, you don't let a friend strangle you
without protesting, which leads me to think she must have been
drugged. What's the time range?"

"Six hours and fifteen minutes. The victim and her guest said good night to each other Sunday night around ten o'clock. The guest called us at four-fifteen Monday morning."

"What about the victim's financial records? Was she taking out large sums or vice versa?"

"We're waiting for warrants for her financial records and the family's."

"I'll see if I can speed that along. What about phone records? Any help there?"

Perillo turned to Daniele who stepped forward. "The villa's landline was used only to place orders with the butcher, the baker and the florist."

"Calls made by her housekeeper, I'm sure," Tarani said. "What about her cell phone?"

"Signora Salviati made personal calls on her cell. Mostly texts to her two daughters, to Signora Rosati—a neighbor—and several to the Italian part of Switzerland. The number belongs to a company called BelPosto."

"That sounds like a retirement village. How old is our victim?"

"She would have been fifty-five in April," Daniele said. "The company buys properties and turns them into five-star hotels."

He was interrupted by the arrival of the coffees and apricot juice. Daniele saved his apricot juice for later. He wanted to keep looking at Tarani. The capitano looked different and not just because he had dyed his hair. The superior-officer stiffness he had displayed the last time they worked together was gone. His face had softened.

Perillo waited until Tarani had put his coffee cup back on the tray to add, "Signora Salviati signed an agreement to sell the property to BelPosto two weeks ago and was paid a large deposit."

Tarani let out a long whistle.

"The reading of the will was last night," Perillo said. "I'm sure the lawyer told them about the sale agreement at the same time. I am interviewing them today. To complicate matters, the family claims valuable jewelry is missing."

Daniele added, "This morning Signor Doyle is searching Signorina Barron's room and belongings in case she has the missing jewelry."

Tarani put his coffee cup back on the tray. "Very well. The jewelry may have been stolen as they say, but keep in mind that if the jewelry is as valuable as they claim, it would add heavily to the already-onerous estate taxes."

Perillo grinned. "Why not make it disappear until the time it can be sold piece by piece without the Revenue Agency finding out? Now I should ask for a warrant to search Adriana's and Clara's homes."

"You would never get it. No evidence." Tarani looked at his watch. "You will forgive me, but I will watch over this case from a distance. I know it is in very capable hands. I will need almost daily reports, which I will then refer to Della Langhe." He stood up. Perillo and Daniele stood also. "I am about to become a father for the first time. My wife is having a difficult pregnancy. She needs all the help I can give her."

Perillo and Daniele congratulated him. Perillo added an out-dated wish, "Figli maschi!"

Tarani laughed. "Thank you, but I will be just as happy with a daughter. I trust my personal information will also stay between the four of us."

"Of course," Perillo and Daniele said in tandem, both glad Nico had been included. Tarani stood up and noticed the cumbersome tape recorder sitting next to Daniele's desk. "Is that World War II relic recording your interviews?"

Daniele nodded.

"Put in a request for a new one."

"We did, Capitano. Six months ago," Daniele said. "Nothing yet."

"Ah, our excellent bureaucracy never disappoints." The three men shook hands.

Perillo walked Tarani to the front door of the station. "Let us know," he said, feeling a stab of regret for his departure.

TWENTY MINUTES LATER Marco Zanelli, a nice-looking man with broad shoulders, wavy dark hair falling over his forehead and a wide smiling face showed up at the Greve station. He was wearing a dark-blue suit jacket over jeans and a white T-shirt. Perillo, seated back at his desk, watched the young man walk in with assurance and an apology.

"Buongiorno, Maresciallo. I shouldn't have listened to Adriana yesterday but disagreeing with her is not usually worth the effort." He sat down in the chair Perillo indicated and pushed his hair back. "My name is Marco Zanelli. I was born in Lucca in—"

Perillo held up his hand to stop him. "We will record this meeting."

"Am I a suspect?"

"At this moment everyone tied to the victim is a possible suspect. Daniele?"

Daniele pressed record on the cumbersome tape machine and announced the date, time and people present.

Perillo raised his hand. "Continue, Signor Zanelli."

"Marco, please. Not even my students call me by my last name. I'm Marco Zanelli, born in Lucca." He'd raised his voice as though afraid his words would not get picked up. "I'm thirty-one years old. I graduated from the Cherubini Music Conservatory in Florence and now teach piano to school-aged children. On weekends I earn some extra money by playing at parties. My parents own a bicycle-repair shop in Lucca. I met Clara three years ago. Our bicycles ran into each other on the city walls. I offered to fix hers in Babbo's shop. I fell in love with her instantly. She took a little longer. I'm not that great a catch for someone like her. She disappeared for a while and I thought that was it, but I found her again, bicycling on the city walls." He grinned and beat a light fist against his chest. "We became engaged three months ago. I admit I had no love for Clara's mother, but I didn't kill her."

"Why did you dislike her?"

"She made it clear to Clara that I was acceptable only as a sex object, an object she would soon be bored with. As a husband I was unthinkable—that's what she hissed at me when Clara told her we had gotten engaged. I would never earn enough money to keep Clara in the style she was used to. I was after the money Clara would one day inherit. I was too low-class. I was also too young. Clara is three years older than I am. That's why I disliked Nora Salviati; may her soul finally find peace. She was a very angry, unhappy woman."

"When was this visit?"

Marco thought for a moment. "About a month ago."

"Did you meet again?"

"My God, no! I think she would have slammed the door in my face. I'd only seen her two times before that."

"At the villa?"

"The first two times in Lucca. She came up to see Clara and walk the ramparts with her. Nora assumed I was just a friend. The second time the three of us had lunch together. She asked who my parents were, not what they did." Marco's eyes widened in disbelief. "Who they are? I was about to say something Clara wasn't going to like. My luck that she answered for me. '*They're good people*,' she said, which they are.

"The last time we'd gone to Siena for a weekend and on the way back, stopped at the villa. Clara hoped her mother would accept me because I teach piano. We'd have something in common since her mother loved playing the piano."

"You were shown the music room?"

"Yes. And she asked me to play."

"The *Moonlight Sonata*?"

"I wish. That's a piece I teach my students. No, she handed me a sheet of music and said, '*Let's see how you play this.*' Liszt's 'La Campanella,' an impossibly difficult piece. I put all of me into my playing, but halfway through she sat down next to me on the piano bench and took over the keyboard. Not a friendly act but she was a better player than I am."

"She insulted you. Weren't you angry?"

"I was taken aback, but when I listened to her playing, I was envious of her ability. She should have been playing in concert halls."

"Did you know she possessed valuable jewelry?"

"Clara told me."

"Did she tell you where her mother kept the jewelry?"

"Yes, she did. In a bag of dirt in the garden shed, and she was going to sell some of it to help Syrian refugees. I think she was having fun with her daughters. Nora Salviati didn't have an ounce of generosity in her blood. I'll save you the trouble of asking if I stole her jewelry. I never saw any of it and I did not steal even a single piece."

Perillo opened his desk drawer and took out the watch fob Dino had brought back. "Have you seen this before?"

Marco leaned closer to Perillo's desk. "That's a watch fob. One of my piano teachers wore one. His had a seal on it too. A lion's head. Is it Nora's?"

"Have you seen it before?" Perillo repeated.

"Oh, sorry. No. I haven't. I thought the stolen stuff was all diamonds."

Perillo announced, "End of interview with Marco Zanelli."

Daniele added the date, the time and turned off the tape recorder.

Perillo stood up. Marco did the same. "Thank you, Signor Zanelli. Brigadiere Donato here will type up the interview, and when it's ready you will need to come back to sign it."

"I'll do whatever needs to be done. Clara is very upset about her mother's death. I know you'll be seeing her later. Please be gentle with her."

Perillo straightened his back. "I do not believe I was harsh with you."

With a short laugh, Marco said, "You were much kinder than some of my piano teachers at the conservatory. I just find it difficult to see her suffering."

Daniele walked to the door and said, "Please follow me."

Marco raised his hand in a salute and followed Daniele out of the office. Perillo picked up the office phone.

BY TEN O'CLOCK, the sun had taken the early morning chill away. The sole linden tree in Gravigna's main piazza was showing bright-green leaves. Two of the four benches were occupied by the Bench Boys as Perillo liked to call them. Weather permitting the four old friends spent mornings and afternoons discussing, arguing, complaining. Nico parked his Fiat 500 at the far end of the piazza and crossed it with OneWag. They were on his way to Enrico's salumeria. "Buongiorno, Signori. Beautiful day, isn't it?"

Gustavo looked up from reading the Florentine newspaper, *La Nazione.* "Ah, Nico, I was waiting for you." The other three pensioners nodded their salute.

Nico's cell phone rang. He held up his hand at Gustavo and stopped to answer. OneWag kept going, eager for Enrico's treat.

"Ciao, Perillo. You got the watch fob?"

"Yes, thanks. I showed it to Clara's fiancé. He didn't recognize it."

"Did he have anything interesting to say?"

"Yes. He hated Nora Salviati. She made it clear he wasn't worthy of Clara. That's not the reason I called. Della Langhe assigned Tarani to our investigation. He showed up without letting me know beforehand."

"Unfortunately, that's the privilege of those who outrank us. You must be relieved, though. You managed to warm up Tarani the last time. He pretty much left us alone."

"Thanks to you. This time the investigation is completely ours. Tarani needs to be with his wife, who is having a difficult pregnancy. It's their first baby. He wanted to make sure you were still helping me."

"I hope you don't—"

"I don't. Come on, Nico. I'm the one who asked for your help with the Gerardi murder so how can I resent you? I assured him you're still part of the team. I must send him daily reports he can relay to Della Langhe without the prosecutor being any wiser. What's your impression of Signorina Barron? Is she lying about Nora giving her that watch fob?"

"I don't know, Perillo." He noticed Gustavo waving at him to come over. Nico held up his finger to indicate un minuto. "There's something not quite real about her."

"I told you. The English are great actors." Perillo sounded pleased, Nico thought. He did enjoy being right.

"If she's acting, I'm not sure she's acting for our sake. Anyway, I plan to ask Laura about her."

"She could have hidden the jewelry somewhere else. We might have to search the whole hotel."

"To get a search warrant you're going to need a better reason than an old watch fob. Maybe I should get Daniele to come with me to spend some time with her. He's great at understanding women. Just look at the patience he has with Stella."

"You think he sees that in her heart Stella is in love with him? I think he's deluding himself. I asked Ivana to talk to him."

Thin-faced, long-nosed, fluffy white-haired Gustavo was now staring at Nico with his arms crossed over his chest, his thick eyebrows meeting in a scowl. Sitting next to him, Ettore, his bald head hidden by a squashed fedora, was sneaking a look at his friend's newspaper.

"We'll talk again," Perillo said. "Daniele is calling BelPosto now. I'm interviewing Adriana again, her husband right after. Is Nelli with you tonight?"

"I'm working. I'll be done by ten if you and Daniele want to meet for a where-are-we session."

"I'll let you know. Ciao."

Nico clicked off. Gustavo slapped his hands loudly on his knees. Nico read that as meaning era ora! "Sorry. I was talking to Maresciallo Perillo. I'm all yours."

"Good. Ettore, go sit with Simone and Pippo. I have a story to tell Nico."

Ettore aimed kind eyes at Nico. "For you I move. Not for him." Ettore grabbed Gustavo's paper and moved to a third bench.

"Don't mess it up," Gustavo yelled at Ettore as he patted the emptied space next to him. "Sit, sit. I want to tell you about the Salviati family. It could help you with the murder."

"Did you know Nora?"

"Never met her, but my wife's cousin used to work at the villa when Signor Lamberti was alive. She didn't like him. Thought a lot of himself. He insisted his name be added to the plaque at the gate. He wanted the property to be referred to as Villa Salviati Lamberti. Some old families in the area weren't happy about that. The Salviatis entered the local history records in the early eighteenth century, when Chianti wine became a legal entity thanks to Cosimo III de' Medici. The property was a successful vineyard until 1972, when Nora's mother died. Edoardo, her father, was so upset he had all the vines torn out. In a letter to his buyers he wrote, 'There can be no joy coming from a house of mourning.'"

"How awful for Nora." He was going to be late picking up the bread and getting it to Sotto Il Fico, but he was hooked by this story.

"The man was crazy. When I was growing up, people said that Salviati blood was tainted, that several Salviatis ended up in insane asylums."

"Were there or are there any rumors about Nora?" Nico asked.

"Well, she was a little strange. The day after her husband died, Nora fired everyone who worked for her husband except her gardener, Lapo Angelini. You have to ask yourself why was he spared, eh? He's a handsome man. It's something to think about."

"Yes. Thank you." Nico started to stand. Gustavo pushed him back down.

"Adriana, the oldest daughter—have you met her?"

"No."

"She was conceived before Nora married Lamberti. Nora hated him, hated the baby too. I understand hating him. She was forced to marry him to keep her good name and he liked to share what made him a man with many women, but to hate your own child, that's crazy. The child, now a woman, hated her back, I hear. I also hear the dentist husband, Fabio Meloni, is not as rich as he pretends to be."

"You hear a lot," Nico said, not sure how much of what Gustavo had told him was true.

"Always have. I was born with big ears, now assisted by a good hearing aid. Listening has always taken me elsewhere. Sometimes elsewhere is better than here. I've told you all I know about the Salviati Lambertis. Now you tell Salvatore Perillo there's no need to come up to Gravigna to reassure us. We're not scared this time. Our wives are sleeping soundly. Nora Salviati's murder has nothing to do with Gravigna. I've kept you long enough. Rocco has been calling you."

Nico heard the barking only now. It was coming from La Salita della Chiesa, the road that led to Enrico's, to the restaurant and to the church. "He's telling me I'm late." He shook hands with Gustavo. "Thank you for the information."

"Put it to good use and catch the bastard."

As Nico walked toward La Salita he heard, "Ettore, give me back my newspaper!"

DANIELE DROPPED THE OFFICE phone handset back on its cradle.

Perillo looked up from the sudoku he was working on. It was a game Vince had shown him. He'd happily discovered he was good at it. "Maybe I should have been a mathematician, Dani. I could have bought myself my own Alfa Romeo." He put his pencil down. "So, what did BelPosto have to say that we don't already know?"

Daniele walked to the maresciallo's desk and sat down in the interview chair. "The man Fabio Meloni spoke with is in charge of acquisitions for Tuscany. He said that Fabio Meloni did not ask if Nora was trying to sell the property. He asked if BelPosto would be interested in buying it."

Perillo took a moment to digest the news. Looking up at his brigadiere, he asked, "When does a man try to sell a property he doesn't own?"

"When he knows the owner will die soon?"

"Exactly."

SIX

Adriana marched into Perillo's office with her husband in tow. She wore the same hard, haughty face as the last time he had seen her, but today she had dressed down in a navy T-shirt, a bright-yellow biker jacket, jeans with a large Gucci tag sewn at the bottom of one leg and black ankle boots. Fabio wore jeans, a purple-and-white-striped shirt with a purple sweater clinging to his shoulders.

Perillo was too exhilarated by the news Daniele had given him to lose his temper. "Please leave my office, Signor Meloni. I will interrogate you after your wife. You agreed to this."

"I don't want my wife to go through this by herself."

Adriana sat down in the interview chair, crossed her legs, and offered Perillo a patient smile. Daniele, watching from his post by the tape recorder, was reminded of a purring cat.

"I won't answer any questions without him, Maresciallo."

"Why not, Signora? Haven't the two of you gotten your story straight yet?"

"We don't have a story." Fabio was still by the door. "We're not suspects."

"Signor Meloni, please leave. If you don't, I will have to charge you with obstruction of justice."

"Wait outside, Fabio," Adriana ordered, without turning around. "I can handle this alone."

Fabio slammed the door behind him.

Daniele turned on the tape recorder and made the required announcement.

Perillo had decided to start with the watch fob. Now he reached for it in the desk drawer and lay it out on the desk. "This is the only jewelry of your mother's we found in Signorina Barron's possession. She claims your mother gave it to her."

Adriana reached out her hand.

Who killed Nora? Perillo asked himself. *One or both?* He lifted the fob and let it drop into her hand. *Maybe a family affair with Marco doing the dirty work.*

Adriana looked at it briefly. "Is this all you found on her?"

"That is all. Did it belong to your mother?"

"I don't remember ever seeing it. Despite having precious jewels she inherited from her mother, the only jewelry I ever saw her wear was that ugly opal ring."

"Signorina Barron didn't have it."

"Mamma probably threw it away." Adriana's face softened. "When Clara and I were small, Mamma would take different pieces out of the safe and let us play with them. Sometimes she'd play with us and tell us stories about our grandmother. Mamma was nine or ten when her mother died. I used to try to attribute her meanness to that one loss. More than one loss, according to the old servants. Her father drowned in grief." She looked up at Perillo. "I'm not trying to distract you, Maresciallo. Sometimes bits and pieces slip out uncalled for."

She tossed the watch fob back on Perillo's desk. "It can't be worth that much. If it is my mother's, she was probably trying to get rid of it. Stolen or not, Signorina Barron can keep it, as far as I'm concerned."

"BelPosto has informed me that your husband made a call

to them regarding the property. Were you present when Signor Meloni made that call?"

Adriana gave a small tug at her biker jacket. "When was this?"

"Three weeks before your mother died."

"I don't know. Fabio makes a lot of calls. If I'm with him, I usually don't listen. You'll have to ask him."

Her slippery answer disappointed Perillo. He wasn't quite sure what answer he'd expected.

Adriana looked at the thin gold watch on her wrist. "Do you have more questions for me?"

"Can you think of anyone who had reason to hate your mother?"

"I got close to that at times. Marco probably does. According to Clara, Mamma disparaged her fiancé to his face."

"It must have upset your sister."

"What anyone says doesn't matter to my sister. She will do whatever she wants. She always has."

"You can think of no one else?"

"Maresciallo, hate has nothing to do with Mamma's murder. Whoever killed Nora Salviati wanted her jewelry. Find the thief, you have your killer."

"Did you steal it?"

Adriana leaned closer. "No. I have plenty of my own, and I didn't for one second believe she was going to give it away to help refugees. Have you searched Sonia the housekeeper's place? Lapo's? The laundress's home? Have you?" She dismissed the question with a wave of her hand. "Too late. By now one of them has passed it on to an accomplice."

Perillo readjusted the papers on his desk. "May I remind you that you and your husband were convinced Signorina Barron was the thief. The jewelry stores and pawnshops in all of Tuscany have been alerted." Perillo sat back in his armchair and looked at her. She stared at him. "Signora Meloni, were you aware your mother was selling the property?"

Adriana looked down and checked her red nails.

"Signora Meloni, please answer the question."

Adriana looked up from her nails. "Did I know? In a rare moment of regard, Mamma asked us if we would mind. I wasn't happy about it, but Fabio thought it an excellent idea. The taxes on the place were eating into our inheritance. What were we going to do with the place after she died? We live in Florence. The idea of renting it out to foreigners was unthinkable. We told her to go ahead."

"When did she ask you?"

"Over a month ago. I don't remember the exact date."

Daniele had kept his eyes on Adriana. He was trying to see whether he could tell if she was lying. Instinctively he didn't believe her, but her body gave nothing away. She sat up with a straight back, her hands quiet on her lap, one ankle crossed over the other. Why did he doubt her? Because she was unpleasant? Was he picking up Perillo's bias? He hoped not.

Perillo leaned his forearms on his desk. "When you say your mother asked you, does 'you' include your sister?"

"By the way she reacted to the news last night, I don't think so."

"How did she react?"

"You'll have to ask her. I'm not going to rat on my sister."

That was exactly what she just did, thought Perillo. "Were you satisfied with the contents of your mother's will?"

Adriana's smile was genuine. "I was surprised at how much of my father's money she still had. She married him for his money, everyone knows that. The villa was falling apart. My father spent a lot of money restoring it."

Her comment made Daniele step forward. "Why did your father marry her?"

Perillo looked at Daniele in surprise. Daniele quickly stepped back, fighting the heat rising in his cheeks.

Adriana's hands clenched. "Everyone thinks he wanted the property. It's not true. He told me countless times how much he loved her. He wanted me to love her too. I pretended I did for his sake. Can I go now?"

"In a few minutes. Where were you between the hours of midnight and four o'clock this past Monday morning?"

"Home in Florence, in bed with my husband."

"Do you have a sleep-in housekeeper?"

"No. If you need corroboration, you can ask Luca, my two-year-old son, although I hope he was asleep too."

Perillo nodded to Daniele who announced the time and turned the old tape recorder off.

"Thank you. Daniele, please escort Signora Meloni out and her husband in. Make sure they don't speak to each other."

"No need." She stood up and took her cell phone out of her jacket pocket. "He'll just repeat what I said." She followed Daniele out, digging her boot heels hard on the floor.

Perillo waited for Daniele to come back. "What prompted you to ask that question?"

"I'm sorry, Maresciallo. I should have better control of myself."

"No, it was a legitimate question. I was curious too. I'm also curious what made you ask? You were a little aggressive, which is not like you. You have not yet spoken to Stella?"

Daniele blushed. "No."

"Dani, stop putting it off. Tell her how you feel using the same intensity I heard when you asked Adriana that question."

Daniele shook his head. "Maresciallo, that question came out of anger."

"Love has its own intensity. You got angry because Adriana is despicable, am I right?"

"She kept insulting her mother. It made me angry."

"I see." Daniele greatly loved his own mother. "Maybe Adriana has good reason to dislike her mother."

"Then she should keep it to herself."

"I'm glad she didn't. Honesty pays off during a murder investigation. Now go find out what happened to her husband."

"I GOT ALL THE vegetables you asked for," Enzo said as he took the bread bag from Nico. "Carrots, baby onions, artichokes, zucchini, peppers. We already had celery. They're in the kitchen."

"Thanks, Enzo."

At the far end, Elvira, ensconced in her gilded armchair, protested, "My son is not your lackey."

Enzo huffed. "Mamma, I offered!"

"Buongiorno, Elvira." Nico walked past the few tables in the room. "Enzo did me a favor. I can't tell a good vegetable from a bad one." He was learning with his now-neglected vegetable garden.

Elvira, dressed in a new spring-green housecoat, offered up her cheeks to be kissed. "The bad ones are soft, you should know that much, and I will not let you or my daughter-in-law turn my restaurant into a vegetarian one. I hope that is understood."

He kissed both her cheeks. "Perfectly understood. I like your new dress."

Elvira shrugged off the compliment.

"What if I add chicken thighs floured and browned until they are crisp, put them aside while I scrape up the bits in the pan with wine, simmer the vegetables until softened, pour over the chicken and finish the dish in the oven? Does that meet your approval?"

"I would have to taste it first." Elvira looked up at him with her piercing eyes. "You finally look happy, Nico. Nelli is with you now and you're getting paid for rattling pans in Tilde's kitchen. Isn't it time to let Salvatore solve his own murders?"

"If you think a dish needs a missing ingredient to make it good, wouldn't you look for that ingredient?"

"That's Tilde's job and yours now."

"It's what I try to do for Tilde and Salvatore. I look for the missing ingredient. Justice must be good too."

"Psssha!" Elvira flapped her hand at Nico. "Get to work. You're talking gibberish."

When he walked into the kitchen Tilde welcomed him with, "Passing by my mother-in-law is like walking through fire."

Nico laughed. "I enjoy it. I bet she does too."

"She loves it. The vegetables are on the back counter. Your dish, your work." Tilde retied her long white apron over a burgundy-and-gray-striped dress. Her long hair was tied in a bright orange scarf. Her face was tight, her jaw clenched as she started cutting leeks.

Nico went to the sink and washed his hands. "What are you preparing?" To find out what was bothering Tilde, Nico knew he had to take the long road.

"A leek, butter and parmigiano sauce for spaghetti."

"Sounds delicious. Need help?"

"My dish, my work," she snapped.

"Right." Nico dried his hands, retreated to the back counter and started cutting carrots, zucchini, celery and bell peppers into strips. They worked in silence. Tilde finished first, then washed her leeks in a colander and left it in the sink to drain. Without asking, she did the same with Nico's vegetables.

"What about my dish, my work?" Nico joked.

"A present for snapping at you. Don't get used to it."

"I don't plan to." He needed to start sautéing the chicken thighs. He was going to botch this new dish if he didn't find out what was going on with Tilde. Rita's cousin had become a sister to him. "Whatever it is, Tilde, I'd like to help."

Tilde shook her head. "Not now. I need to get over my bad mood first."

Nico pecked her cheek just as Alba bounced into the kitchen with her usual big smile. "Ciao! Great day out." She blew two kisses and reached for a short white apron hanging behind the door. She was wearing a denim skirt that showed off good legs and a fluffy white blouse half covered by a traditional Albanian men's red and orange vest. She looked at Tilde's headscarf and dress. "We match! It will bring good luck to both of us."

Tilde offered Alba a wan smile. "That would be nice."

Alba tugged at Nico's shirtsleeve. "You should have been here last night. A couple at table seven was talking about Nora Salviati. I heard the man mention your name. She asked me if you were working here last night. I told her you would be here today. I looked up the reservation. Signora and Signor Rosati. Do you know them?"

"No, but I've heard the name."

Alba reached into her skirt's back pocket and extracted a piece of paper. "That's their number."

"Thank you." He tucked the paper into the pocket of his jeans. He would let Perillo know.

Tilde banged the colander on the porcelain sink with more strength than draining required. "The tables don't set themselves, Alba."

"They need *me*." Alba rushed out with a wave of her hand.

Tilde reached up and took down a large copper-bottomed skillet hanging from the wall above the sink and wiped it clean. "According to Enzo, the whole restaurant was talking about what happened to that poor woman. Murder has become a tourist attraction. It's terrible."

"Has my working with Perillo become a problem for the restaurant? The locals all know I'm involved."

Tilde swept some vegetable oil into the skillet and set it on the gas burner. "The tourists find out too. Knowing that the food they are eating might have been cooked by a New York ex-homicide detective who is working on a local murder probably adds spice to the meal. Since we started opening for both meals, the number of diners has only increased." Tilde held her hand over the skillet to know when to toss in the leeks. She watched Nico drying the chicken thighs with a clean dish towel. Paper towels had been designated tree killers. "You do want to keep working here, don't you?"

Nico looked up in surprise. "Absolutely. I love working with you. I have from the start."

"Good. Don't ever listen to my mother-in-law. Keep looking for the missing ingredient for me and Salvatore."

Nico spread flour on a plate, generously salted and peppered the thighs and watched Tilde stir the leeks. "Have you lost your bad temper yet?" he asked.

"It's on low now, but we've got too much work to start churning out worries."

"You're right. I want Elvira to lick her whiskers when she tastes my dish."

FABIO MELONI SAT BACK in the interview chair with the look of a man who knew he'd aced the test.

That look pleased Perillo. He couldn't wait to wipe it off Meloni's face.

"I'm listening, Maresciallo."

Perillo unclenched his fingers and spread them out on the desk. "Did your mother-in-law tell you she was selling the property?"

"I had suggested it many times. She was spending enormous amounts of money on property taxes and running the place. She didn't need all those fancy rooms. I was certain Nora would have been happier and less stressed living in a smaller place. She needed to think of her daughters. By the time she died there wouldn't have been any inheritance to speak of."

"Except for the property that has now fetched a very good price."

"I would have asked for more."

Perillo looked down at his hands. He was listening to a man

who had no idea of the ugly impression his words were giving. "And the jewels are worth a great deal of money."

"Well, they're gone, thanks to your inefficiency."

"Did you steal them?"

Daniele, with one eye checking that the old tape recorder didn't jam, watched disbelief grip Fabio's face.

"Really, Maresciallo, you are clutching air. Why would I deprive Nora of her jewelry, jewelry that rightfully belongs to my wife and Clara?"

"A *no* would have been enough," Perillo said. "I want to go back to a question you didn't answer directly. Did Nora tell you she was selling the property?"

"Yes, of course."

"When did she tell you?"

"At least a month ago. I told her it was the best decision she could make."

Perillo glued his eyes on Fabio's face to catch every lying twitch. "What made you call BelPosto four weeks ago?"

Fabio didn't flinch. "I wanted to check if Nora was selling."

"You didn't believe her?"

"My mother-in-law wasn't always truthful."

Perillo squared his shoulders, the way the boxers did on television before stepping into the ring. "You spoke with the acquisition manager for Tuscany."

Fabio shifted in his chair. "I don't remember who I spoke to."

"The manager remembers you. Your offer surprised him. He told you he had already been in contact with the property owner and submitted a bid. That's when you found out Nora was selling. Nora never told you. How can you offer to sell a property you don't own?"

"Easily. You pretend you own it to find out if Nora was really selling."

"Why not ask directly?"

"The manager wouldn't have told me."

"He told you the company had made a bid."

Fabio released a sigh of patience. "He told me they made a bid on a similar property, that's all. From that I understood Nora had told the truth. She was selling."

"I find it interesting," Perillo said, "that you needed to make sure your mother-in-law was selling. Why was that?"

Fabio took a moment to answer. "Adriana was upset. She wanted the property to stay in the family. I wanted to be sure Nora wasn't playing games with my wife."

"Perhaps the real reason you needed to make sure was so that Nora's murder didn't end up being useless."

"Maresciallo, do plant your boots back on earth. I understand that, however incompetently, you are desperate to discover who killed my mother-in-law. I appreciate how difficult that is. As I have already said, I was in favor of the sale. Once Nora died, taking care of the property would have fallen on my shoulders, something I dreaded.

"As to where I was Sunday night and Monday morning, I will be specific. Adriana and I went to bed together around ten o'clock Sunday. We made love and went to sleep. The alarm woke me at seven Monday morning. We both got up. Now go ahead and ask me the final question."

Perillo would have preferred to tell Meloni to take it in the rear end, but the tape was running, and the question had to be asked. "Did you kill Nora Salviati?"

"I did not." Fabio stood up. "I'll see myself out."

When the office door closed behind Fabio Meloni's back, Perillo slumped back in his armchair.

Daniele walked toward his defeated-looking boss. "Maresciallo, would you like a coffee?"

Perillo looked up at his young brigadiere. "That man slipped out of my hand like an eel."

"He's good at lying, at defending himself. I don't believe he was in favor of the sale."

"Why do you think that?"

"He kept underlining it. He wants you to believe he knew about the sale, and he was in favor of it, therefore he had no reason to kill Nora."

"I know," Perillo said. Meloni had humiliated him more than once. Why hadn't he fought back? What had happened to the grit he'd acquired on the streets of Naples? It had served him well until now.

"Should I call the bar for a coffee?" An espresso strengthened with grappa would make the maresciallo feel better.

"No. I'm agitated enough as it is. Sit down."

Daniele sat in the chair Meloni had just vacated. He would have loved an apricot juice.

"How is Stella?" Perillo asked. The thought of young love was soothing.

"Stella is going to try to come down this weekend. I'm hoping we can spend some time together."

"Even more reason to get this murder solved by then." Perillo stared at the sudoku grid and picked up his pencil.

"Maresciallo, the warrant came through for their finances. The report should come in soon."

"If we're in luck, the Melonis are desperate for money."

ALBA SLIPPED ON THICK oven gloves, opened the oven at Enrico's bakery and pulled out a large, long tray filled with her twice-baked cantuccini.

Ivana was sitting on a stool next to an open window at the far end of a row of tables running along the length of the bakery wall. She was helping lavender-haired Carletta stuff the early morning batch of cantuccini into cellophane bags. Her own short dark hair was covered by a net. Over her sleeveless summer dress, she wore a floral apron she had brought from home.

Alba slid the tray onto a table. Ivana watched as Alba blew on a cantuccino to cool it. She felt a nervous churning in her chest. This was only her second day. Alba had put her in charge of mixing the batch of dough while Alba was working at Sotto Il Fico. Last night's batch had gone well. Ivana now held her breath.

Alba munched, swallowed, took a second bite, a third. The cantuccino was gone. "I madh!" Alba declared to the big room and blew Ivana a kiss.

Ivana didn't know what *i madh* meant, but the blown kiss was enough. She smiled, feeling a glow rise inside her.

"It means *great* in Albanian," Carletta said. She was wearing jeans torn at the knee and a red Trattoria Da Gino T-shirt.

"Good for you," Alba said.

Carletta smiled at the compliment. "I know something else. It's about the murdered woman."

Ivana prayed it was nothing ugly.

"I used to wait on Nora Salviati at Babbo's restaurant," Carletta said. Her father owned Da Gino in Gravigna's main square. "She used to come for dinner with a man and a little boy. They always ate inside even when it was boiling hot. Babbo told me to always put them at the table in the back corner. I guess she called ahead to tell him she was coming. I guess she didn't want people to see her. The man wasn't at all classy like she was. I liked her because she was very sweet with the boy. I think he had some kind of problem. Maybe the kid was hers. She always tipped me which only tourists do. She stopped coming last year. I don't know why."

Ivana was relieved nothing unpleasant had come up. If anything, the opposite. Did Salva know about the boy? Maybe not. She should break her own rule of not getting involved and tell him.

THERE WAS A KNOCK on the door, followed by Vince announcing Clara Lamberti. Perillo stood up, closed his notebook and pulled down his uniform jacket. "Send her in."

Daniele scuttled to his post in the back of the room.

Clara had a smile on her face when she walked in. "Buongiorno, Maresciallo, Brigadiere. Marco has reassured me you don't bite." She crossed the room with long legs covered by loose cropped red slacks over which she wore a black oversize jersey top cut on a bias. She wore no makeup. "But then of course you have no reason to bite him. He's a sweet, honorable person."

"You are not?" Perillo extended his arm toward the chair in front of his desk.

Clara sat down. "Certainly not sweet. Marco mentioned Signorina Barron took my mother's watch fob. May I see it?"

Perillo turned to Daniele, who had his eyes closed, rehearsing what he was going to say to Stella.

"Brigadiere Donato, the tape recorder, please."

Daniele popped open his eyes. He quickly pushed the record button and managed to say what was required without mumbling. He could do nothing about the wash of red sweeping over his face.

Perillo turned back to Clara and showed her the watch fob. "Have you seen it before?"

"Yes. I remember when Mamma came home with it. She went on a trip to England sometime after Babbo died and came back with it around her neck. When she stopped wearing it, I asked if I could have it. She said no because it belonged to someone who had made her happy."

"You know of no reason why she would give it to Signorina Barron?"

"I think they met on that trip. That could be a reason." Clara lifted her shoulders as though she didn't care. Her expression said otherwise. "I guess there's no way to know if she stole it?"

"I'm afraid not. Who were your mother's friends besides the Rosatis?"

"She didn't have any and I doubt that Gianna Rosati and Mamma were really friends, not in the sense that they confided in each other. Mamma didn't know how to do that, and Gianna Rosati can only talk bridge or how successful her two sons are."

"They live here?"

"No. Tommaso runs a *very successful* tech company in San Francisco according to Gianna. Gorgeous Stefano"—Clara laughed—"I had a crush on him until he tried to kiss me. I was only ten. I thought it was disgusting. After that I wouldn't let him get near me. He went to South Africa on a safari and never came back. According to what Gianna told my mother, he owns a big vineyard down there. A Tuscan going to South Africa to make wine is weird, but he probably wanted to get away from his mother. She can suck oxygen right out of your lungs if you get too close."

"What can you tell me of Signor Rosati?"

"Federico is boring, Mamma's words. Apparently, Gianna finds him boring too. She came on to Lapo more than once, even tried to get him to leave Mamma and work for her. Lapo and Mamma had a good laugh over that one. I guess Lapo is the one friend my mother had."

"Could they have been romantically involved?"

Clara's face brightened. "Oh, I hope so. She needed some tenderness. She was such an unhappy woman."

"Why?"

"She lost her mother early on and the loss turned her father into an angry, nasty man. That's what Babbo told me." Mentioning her father brought a smile. "Babbo was the opposite, full of fun and charm. That's exactly what she needed. It should have been a good marriage." The smile was gone.

"Why wasn't it?" As Perillo asked the question, he thought of his own marriage. There was work he needed to do.

Daniele was now listening intently. There was something magnetic about Clara Lamberti. It pulled him in. He knew the maresciallo was feeling it too. His boss was sitting back in his armchair, shoulders relaxed. His voice was soft, not the baritone voice he used when the tape recorder was running. Daniele decided he didn't trust Clara.

Clara came up with another smile, a rueful one this time. "My father loved women very much and did nothing to hide it."

"I see." Perillo had been tempted only once, during the month Ivana had gone back to Naples to take care of her mother. He had come to his senses quickly.

Perillo leaned over his desk. "Signorina Lamberti, do you have any idea who killed your mother?"

Clara met Perillo's gaze with unblinking eyes. "If I knew, I'm not sure I would tell you."

"Why not?"

"Because whoever killed her did my mother a favor. She's no longer miserable now."

"You don't believe she deserves justice?"

"Justice won't change anything. Mamma deserves peace now. So do we." If Perillo had another question to ask, Clara's statement wiped it away.

"Are we through?"

Perillo turned to look at his stunned brigadiere. Daniele announced the end of the interview and the time and pushed the stop button.

Perillo stood up. "I may need to talk to you again."

Clara uncrossed her legs and stood up. "You'll find me at the villa. I can lead my yoga classes from there by Zoom until this is over. Marco was right. You don't bite. Ciao." She stepped away from Perillo and beamed Daniele a beautiful smile. "Ciao to you too."

Daniele lifted a hand in salute. He was too surprised to blush.

After the office door closed behind Clara, Perillo asked Daniele, "What do you think?"

"The murderer did her and her sister a great favor, not her mother."

Perillo cocked an eyebrow at Daniele. "I'm surprised she didn't convince you. You usually have a soft spot for attractive women."

"Not her."

"Why?"

"I don't know." He did know. Clara's sexiness had stirred a surprising desire in him. That scared him.

Daniele's face was turning red, Perillo noticed. "Well, the family's bank statements will tell us more. It's time to restore our energy. Come upstairs with me. Ivana has taken pity on us and left lunch in the microwave."

SEVEN

Three o'clock. Time for his afternoon break. Nico found OneWag asleep on the sunny church steps just above the restaurant. His legs were twitching.

"Come on, buddy. We've got some work to do."

The dog's response was half a wag. The rabbit was so close.

Nico waited. OneWag's legs started twitching again. "Dream away. I'll be back." Nico went to his Fiat 500 just beyond the steps. The parking spot was reserved for Don Alfonso, but after a small donation to the church, the multi-parish priest let him park in his spot except on Sundays. He turned on the motor and reached over to open the passenger door, just in case. OneWag never missed an adventure.

But the dog didn't budge. Nico closed the passenger door, reversed, swung around and drove halfway down the road. One eye caught motion in his rearview mirror. He looked again. "Cazzo!" He slammed on the breaks. Swearing in Italian came more easily than in English, he'd just discovered. It also made him feel more like a native.

He opened the passenger door. OneWag, tongue hanging out, chest heaving, jumped up on the seat and turned to Nico with his *Where to?* look.

"OneWag, don't you ever do that again, you hear me?"

OneWag curled himself up on the forbidden passenger seat.

By the time they reached Hotel Bella Vista, OneWag's lungs had calmed down, but Nico went looking for a water source. OneWag lay down on a patch of grass and waited.

"Good boy. Stay there. I'll be right back with water." Nico walked into the hotel looking for Laura. He found her in the hotel bar making herself an espresso.

"Hi, Nico. Want one?" she asked in her almost accentless English.

"No, thanks. My dog needs water. Do you have a bowl or something I can use? He's out in front."

Laura looked beyond Nico's shoulder. "Hi, OneWag. I'll get you water."

The dog did his one wag, sat down by the door and carefully avoided looking at his boss. Nico had to suppress a smile. Bawling out the mutt would have been a waste of time. OneWag was a firm believer in personal independence.

Laura filled a small ice bucket with water. Nico reached for the bucket.

"No, let me." She came out from behind the bar. She was wearing dark-green slacks and a turquoise knit top. Her wavy blond hair hung loose on her shoulders. *She looks good*, Nico thought. *Last year's sadness gone, at least from her face. What she holds inside is unknowable.*

OneWag met Laura halfway. She put the ice bucket on the tile floor in front of him. "He's always welcome here. Are you looking for Miss Barron?" she asked as she watched OneWag lap eagerly.

"No. If you have a minute, I'd like to ask you a few questions about her."

Laura gave him a straight look. "She's a suspect, is she?" Her tone wasn't friendly.

Nico sat down on a barstool. "Look. She found the body and we don't know anything about her."

OneWag stopped lapping, gave Laura's shoes a quick sniff and walked back out.

"Why don't you ask her? She's on the patio reading a book."

"Come on, Laura, give me a hand. She's been coming here how long?"

Laura picked up her espresso and sat on a barstool next to Nico. "I don't like going behind someone's back, but the idea of her killing that woman is so preposterous, I'll tell you the little I know. She started coming here four summers ago. She keeps to herself, reading or taking walks in inappropriate shoes. She obviously cares more about looking good than comfort. She rarely eats out. After dinner she goes to the bar, has a Pimm's and sits quietly watching the other guests. Two or three times a summer, Nora Salviati would join her for dinner here."

"You knew Nora Salviati?"

"Only because Miss Barron introduced me to her. I assumed Miss Barron was a widow. She had—has an aura of sadness around her that made me think that. I always called her Mrs. Barron. Yesterday she asked me to call her Miss Barron. She explained she had almost become a Mrs., but her fiancé died in a car accident weeks before the wedding."

Odd, Nico thought. *She seemed quite proud of being single.* "Miss Barron corrected me right away," he said. "Did you wonder why she didn't correct you before?"

"I asked her. She admitted she had enjoyed the illusion of having had a husband, but Nora's murder has shaken all her illusions."

Nico wondered what other illusions Miss Barron gave up that morning. "Do you think her capable of stealing?"

"Why would she? She is wealthy. Spending two and a half months in this hotel costs a great deal and she fills her suitcases with designer clothes she gets at the mall."

"Those clothes are discounted."

"And still very expensive. Besides, I've never seen her wear any jewelry. I don't know how you and Perillo can stand your jobs, always having to think the worst of people."

"That's not fair, Laura. We're trying to find a murderer."

"Of course."

"Good afternoon." Miss Barron stood at the entrance of the bar, her face partially hidden by large sunglasses. "How nice to see you, Mr. Doyle." OneWag followed her in.

Nico smiled. "How are you?"

"The sun has made me quite warm. This sweet dog was keeping me company. He seems to be fascinated by shoes. Is he yours?"

"Yes. I call him OneWag."

"I like unusual names for pets. It shows the owner has character."

Laura slipped off the stool and went behind the bar. "Can I get you anything, Miss Barron?"

"A glass of water, thank you, and a cappuccino." Miss Barron took her place on the stool. She was wearing a Peter Pan–collared pearl-gray light wool dress that draped softly over her knees. Small mother-of-pearl buttons ran down the center from collar to waist. "Did you know, Mr. Doyle, that Italians never have a cappuccino after eleven in the morning? It's a silly deprivation, don't you think? I'm more of a tea drinker, but an afternoon cappuccino gives me a much-needed boost."

OneWag sniffed the air. No food. He turned around and went off to see what he could find besides sweet-smelling shoes.

"Nico was asking questions about you," Laura said as she poured milk into a metal jug.

Nico shot her a look she ignored.

Miss Barron saw it. "Please don't be annoyed with Laura. I should think you need to ask a bucketful of questions about anyone involved with Nora. How else will you and the mah-rayshallow find the culprit? Laura has no reason to fabricate stories about me, so believe whatever she has told you." Miss Barron raised her eyebrows. "I have a question for you."

"Go ahead."

"Will Nora's daughters let me keep the watch fob?"

"I hope so, but I'll have to ask the maresciallo."

"It would be a nice reminder of Nora. I was quite surprised when she offered it to me. I asked her why. She said it meant nothing to her anymore." Miss Barron tilted her head to one side and peered at Nico with her bright blue eyes. "I suspect it belonged to a lover. Isn't there anything you wish to ask me?" She looked hopeful.

Nico relaxed. He was getting fond of this woman who was like no one he had ever known. "Actually, there is. Did Nora tell you anything about her friends, the Rosatis?"

"Oh!" Miss Barron pulled her eyebrows together in a dis-approving frown. "Gianna Rosati had the gall to call me here at the hotel yesterday. I'd only met her once last summer. She wanted to know all the details, declaring she was overcome with sorrow. '*Dear, dear Nora, she was my very best friend. I'm utterly devastated. Is it true she was slumped over the piano?*' Her rudeness is difficult to forgive. There was no thought to my own feelings at finding Nora."

Laura placed the cappuccino on the counter. Miss Barron clasped the cup and drank. "Thank you, dear." She put the cup down on its saucer and wiped foam from her lips with a napkin.

Nico waited until Laura had tiptoed out of the room to ask, "Did you see Gianna Rosati during this visit?"

"The Rosatis were leaving just as I arrived. They had been playing bridge, and Nora was a little put out because she had lost. After they left she told me Mr. Rosati was a terrible bridge player and she let him play with them sometimes only because

Gianna insisted. She liked to play with Gianna because she was an excellent player, but obviously she didn't like losing." She picked up the cup again and finished her cappuccino. "Do you know why they call it a cappuccino?" she asked Nico.

"I don't."

"It's the same color of the robes worn by the Capuchin friars. I hope they get to enjoy their cappuccino any time they feel like it." She slipped off the stool. "I think I need to rest a bit before dinner."

Nico looked at this watch and stood up. "And time for me to get back to work."

"That's right. You're a detective and a chef in a restaurant. Quite extraordinary."

"I'm an ex-detective and a sous-chef."

"I'll have to come. Laura says the view is beautiful and the food delicious. Goodbye, Mr. Doyle."

"Call me Nico."

"Then you would have to call me Laetitia. As a possible suspect in Nora's murder, I would find that awkward. If you want to know more about Nora, the man to ask is her gardener. She once told me he was the only person she trusted. I find it extremely sad for a mother of two children to say that, but she said it and meant it. I'm sure we will see each other again soon."

"I would enjoy that," Nico said. He meant it.

THE TURNOFF TO the Rosatis' was just before Villa Salviati. The two-story stone house was at the end of a short driveway flanked by flowering laurel bushes.

"A very plain house," Perillo said as Daniele parked the Alfa next to a red Smart car. "I expected something closer in grandeur to the villa."

Daniele turned off the motor. "If I had a choice, I would take this one. It doesn't have any pretensions."

"Let's go see if the Rosatis have any."

Gianna Rosati was waiting for them at the door. She was a short, plump woman, with an attractive angled face, pale skin, and narrow hazel eyes that gave her a feline look. Her short hair, worn slicked back, was dyed henna. Daniele had looked her up online. She was sixty-one years old, seven years older than Nora.

Perillo introduced himself and Daniele. "Forgive my attire, Maresciallo." She was dressed in jeans and an oversized striped blue and white shirt frayed at the collar. "I was in the back weeding my flower beds; they give me peace. I lost all sense of time. The sound of your car brought me back. Please come in. I'll call Federico."

Daniele and Perillo followed her into a small foyer. A line of floral majolica plates ran along the walls painted a summer sky blue. Against one wall stood a long table with many framed photographs and two brass candlesticks holding blue candles.

"Such a tragedy," Gianna said, walking into a large square living room with a wide fireplace framed in dark-green tiles. "Can I offer you a coffee?"

Both men declined.

"Please sit down." She indicated a light-green corduroy sofa facing the spent fireplace. On each side of the sofa were two armchairs in faded contrasting colors. At the far end a row of large windows faced the garden. "Nora's death is an incredible loss for the whole family. My sons are very sad. Nora always let them play on the property whenever they wanted."

"Are these your sons?" Daniele asked, looking at the framed photos of two men at various ages displayed on one side of the coffee table.

"Yes. Tommaso owns a technology company in San Francisco. Stefano owns a vineyard in South Africa. They're so far away. I miss them terribly, but I'm proud to say they have been very successful. Tommaso . . ."

"Would you please call your husband, Signora Rosati?" Perillo said.

"Oh!" Gianna pulled back her chin and mumbled, "Of course."

"We know how successful your sons are," he said to placate her. "They visit often?"

Gianna quickly ran a hand down her short hair. "Yes, yes. Do sit. I'll get Federico." She hurried out of the room, her rubber boots squeaking on the waxed tile floor.

"That question flustered her," Daniele said.

"I think my interrupting her did that."

Daniele took out his notebook and pen, grateful the tape recorder had stayed at the station. His boss considered this interview with the Rosatis a preliminary one. Taking notes would suffice.

Gianna walked back in, now wearing flat shoes and an olive-green knit top over her jeans. Her husband followed her, wearing tan slacks and a blue quilted jacket over a collared white shirt.

"I'm sorry I kept you waiting," Federico Rosati said. "I was writing down a few thoughts about Nora in case her daughters ask me to speak at the funeral." He was extremely tall, which made him stoop. He had a narrow, bland face with small blue eyes, a long nose and surprisingly full lips. He shook Perillo's hand, nodded at Daniele. Federico Rosati, Daniele had discovered, was fifty-five years old and the account manager of Vigneto Tre Cipressi, a medium-sized vineyard just south of Radda-in-Chianti.

"Please, make yourself comfortable. We will do anything to help." He took the lead by sitting in the armchair closest to the fireplace. Perillo sat at one end of the sofa, Daniele at the other.

Gianna looked at the seating options with a trembling head.

"Do sit down, dear," Federico said. He pulled an armchair closer to his. "Here, next to me."

"Yes, I will. I'll make coffee first."

"My wife has taken Nora's death very badly. I have too, but not in the same way." He straightened his back with what Daniele thought was a proud look on his face.

"You were both good friends of Signora Salviati?" Perillo asked.

"I grew up with Nora," Federico said.

Perillo leaned forward. "How so?"

"My father managed the Salviati vineyards for Nora's father, Edoardo Salviati. We lived in Panzano then and on weekends my father would bring me up to the villa to play. Nora and I were only a few years apart. It took her a long time to warm up to me. She was very shy then. We ended up being good friends."

"Here we are." Gianna walked in carrying a tray with four espresso cups designed with flowers and a matching coffeepot. She put the tray down on a side table. "I'm sure you were just being polite when you said no."

Daniele and Perillo smiled and thanked her. In Perillo's case, Gianna was right. Daniele never had coffee after breakfast. He wouldn't sleep tonight. Not that he had slept that much in the past few nights thanks to his impending talk with Stella. They both thanked her and picked up their cups.

Perillo finished his in two sips. "Wasn't the Salviati vineyard destroyed?" Nico had phoned and relayed Gustavo's comments.

Federico drank his coffee before answering. He handed his empty cup and saucer to his wife. "It had to be. The roots were being attacked by a deadly parasite, the phylloxera aphid. If my father hadn't convinced Nora's father to destroy every plant, the aphids would have spread to the other vineyards."

"It must have been very hard for your father." Perillo set his empty cup and saucer on the floor. The side table was at the other end of the sofa on Daniele's side. Before Gianna could swoop down, Daniele picked them up and placed them on the tray. "Did he stay on?"

Federico's shoulders shivered, the expression on his face frozen. Seconds passed and Federico rested his head on the back of his armchair. "He did not. My father blamed himself for not catching the disease in time and hung himself from an oak tree on the property."

"Poor Federico was only a young boy," Gianna said, with her hand resting over her heart. "It was worse for his mother, may her soul rest in peace."

"Nora's father was very kind."

Daniele looked up from writing. Federico's voice was now loud as if the sound would somehow muffle his feelings.

"He gave my mother this house and the garden, which gave her much happiness." Federico looked at his wife with what seemed like tenderness to Daniele. "And now my wife."

Gianna's face came alive. "Oh, yes, I love taking care of flowers. I'm a little obsessed with them. I kept telling Nora she should get Lapo to plant more flowers." She clutched the cup she was holding on her lap and squeezed her eyes shut, before quickly opening them again. "I won the last game of bridge we played. It was an easy win. Nora was distracted, edgy. I regret it so. Nora hated losing."

"She's hated it since she was a little girl," Federico said. "She'd throw temper tantrums. I started letting her win the games we played then."

Gianna shook her head. "When I tried that she caught me. The only reason she didn't ditch us as she did her husband's friends was because I play bridge very well. She thrived on the challenge."

Gianna puzzled Perillo. She didn't match his idea of an ace bridge player. Playing cards requires paying attention. "You were friends with her husband?"

"We weren't close," Federico said. "Alberto would invite us for one of his dinners every few months."

"Because of Federico's father," Gianna added.

Perillo looked at Federico. "But weren't you still friends with Nora?"

"She barely spoke to us at those dinners," Gianna answered for him. "Sometimes she didn't show up."

Federico's hands clasped the arms of his chair. "Alberto was a handsome, charming man who liked to have his way. Nora was a beautiful, strong-headed woman. The combination was not a good one."

Daniele looked up a moment from writing to see Gianna tilt her head to one side like a sparrow eyeing a crumb. He'd been too busy taking notes to watch the Rosatis' body language, but he'd heard the tone of their words. Gianna's voice kept changing in pitch. She wasn't at ease.

"She was forced to marry Alberto," Gianna said.

Daniele stopped writing. This was not new information.

"Now, Gianna—" Federico crossed his legs, revealing a hairy strip of flesh above his short sock. "There's no need to go into what happened a long time ago."

Gianna's face puckered.

"No, please," Perillo said. "Every bit of information helps." He was interested in listening to whatever the two had to say about Nora. One of them or both could have a reason to kill her.

Gianna gave Perillo a satisfied nod. "Poor Nora, two months after she and Alberto got married, she lost the baby. She was furious."

Daniele started writing again.

Federico dropped his leg down with a thump. "Gianna, you don't know that!"

"Yes, I do, Federico. Fury has been on her face ever since. You look surprised, Maresciallo?"

"I thought Adriana was the result of that pregnancy."

Gianna preened. "Adriana was adopted a few months later. It

seems Alberto was devastated by the miscarriage. I would have thought a man like Alberto would want a son to carry on his name, but then he did have a weakness for women."

"The miscarried baby was a girl," Federico said, clearly not happy with his wife's disclosures.

Now that's interesting news, Perillo thought. "Does Adriana know she was adopted?"

Gianna shook both her hands. "Does she ever. Clara was born two years later, and I don't think there's a day gone by that Adriana doesn't resent it. I can understand why. She must feel replaced, an adoptee not able to compete with a birth daughter."

Federico's forehead crunched in a frown. "Maresciallo, my wife has a vivid imagination."

"That can be useful," Perillo said with a placating smile. "Adriana has made her negative feelings toward her mother very clear. Signora Rosati is providing a possible reason."

Gianna beamed. "Thank you, Maresciallo. I studied psychology at the university in Siena. I have always thought Adriana's angry claim that Nora didn't love her own husband was just a cover-up for feeling that she was the one Nora didn't love."

Federico looked at his wife with one raised eyebrow. "With your astute knowledge of psychology, are you claiming that Nora loved her husband?"

"She might have if Alberto had loved her back," Gianna snapped. Her face stayed turned toward Perillo. "Love makes all the difference, don't you think?"

Daniele found himself nodding.

"Certainly, Signora Rosati," Perillo said, eager to change the course of the conversation. "I'd like to go back to the last time you played bridge with Nora Salviati. When was it?"

"A week ago. She refused a rematch because the English-woman was coming in a few hours. Nora said they were old friends, but I've been playing bridge with Nora ever since her husband died and not once did she mention this good friend. I find that rather odd, don't you?"

Federico jumped in. "Nora always kept secrets. Remember when she would disappear for two weeks or a month without telling her daughters? The last time she went off she came back with a floral scarf for you from the Victoria and Albert Museum."

"That was five or six years ago, I think. I love that Liberty scarf," Gianna said. "Adriana was very angry with her mother for going off like that."

"Adriana is always angry," Federico said with the air of a man satisfied with his own opinions.

"Clara is easier going than her sister," Gianna said. "I think she just shrugged her shoulders at her mother's disappearances."

"When was this?"

"She started taking trips a few months after Alberto died." Gianna stretched her neck out toward Perillo, this time reminding Daniele of a bird about to peck. "Is it true that Nora's jewelry has been stolen?"

"It is. Had she ever shown it to you?"

Gianna's neck retreated. "She used to wear the diamond and sapphire ring when her husband entertained. I never saw it again after Alberto died. I know there are more pieces, but I've only seen them in a portrait. There's a lovely painting in the villa's main hall of Nora's mother in an evening gown, practically covered in jewelry. Nora pointed it out to me once saying, '*I wonder how poor Mamma managed to stand with all that weight on her.*' Nora told me she sometimes would take some of the pieces out of the safe and imagine her mother wearing them." Her face puckered. "I find that incredibly sad. It's appalling to think it was the reason she was killed."

Federico sniffed loudly. "It's appalling whatever the reason."

Gianna responded to her husband's reprimand with a quick nod. "There is the possibility that jewelry theft and the murder might not be connected," Perillo said to Gianna. "We need to keep that in mind."

Gianna gasped. "That's a terrible possibility. Are you saying someone hated her enough to kill her?"

"It's possible. Thank you for the coffee and your patience, Signora." Perillo started to stand up.

"The opal ring," Daniele said in a low voice.

"Ah, yes." Perillo sat back down. "I almost forgot. Signorina Barron told us Nora wore a small opal ring she had won from you. Is that so, Signora Rosati?"

"Nora didn't win it. I bought the ring years ago at an antique shop in Florence. It didn't cost very much, but the minute Nora saw it, she fell in love with it, as I had."

"She wasn't very subtle about wanting it," Federico said.

"There was nothing subtle about Nora," Gianna said. "She kept looking at it, saying how pretty it was, asking to try it on. I confess I got tired of her hints. I finally gave it to her last year for her birthday."

"Would you have a picture of it?" Perillo asked.

"Federico does."

"I have it on my phone," Federico said, reaching into the pocket of his jacket and taking out his phone. Once he found the photo, he handed the phone to Perillo. "Is the ring important to your investigation?" he asked.

Perillo looked at the close-up of the ring. He couldn't understand why a woman with diamonds available to her would want that trinket. Daniele, looking over Perillo's shoulder, thought it was pretty, a sweet ring a young girl would love.

"I wouldn't say important," Perillo said, "but she wasn't wearing it when she died and we haven't found it."

"Oh," Gianna's trembling hand covered her mouth.

Federico leaned forward in his chair. "Should you find it, Maresciallo, could you give it back to my wife? With Nora's children's approval, of course. I know she regrets having given it away."

"Oh, Federico, the maresciallo is now going to think I took it back." Gianna clutched her hand to stop the trembling. "I didn't. I would never. A gift is forever."

"Take a hold of yourself, Gianna," Federico said gently. "Maresciallo, please reassure her."

"Signora Rosati, please don't worry. I think no such thing." Perillo stood up, thinking Gianna's killing Nora and taking the ring was a possibility, but Signorina Barron's killing Nora and taking the ring to confuse matters was more likely. "I will need both of you to come down to the Greve station for finger-printing and a DNA sample for elimination purposes."

Federico unfolded his long frame from the chair. "Of course. Anything that will help find Nora's murderer. We'll come in the morning."

"Yes, in the morning." Gianna rose from her chair with a reassured expression on her face. "I must remember to pick up the book waiting for me at the bookshop while I'm in Greve." She took a step. "Let me walk you to the door."

Perillo stopped her with, "One last question." He liked to pop this question at the very end, hoping the reaction would tell him something useful.

Gianna looked startled. "Oh, I'm sorry."

"Where were you Sunday night from ten o'clock until four Monday morning?"

Federico put his arm around his wife. "We had retired to our bedroom by then. You can't possibly think—"

Giana interrupted him. "No, no, he doesn't. The maresciallo must ask everyone who knew Nora. Federico turned off his lamp by ten-thirty and quickly fell into his usual blissful, snoring sleep. I studied my seed catalogs for a while. I'm afraid I can't tell you what time I turned off my lamp."

"Thank you," Perillo said. "I may need to ask more questions as the investigation proceeds. Please stay in the area. Arrivederci."

Federico nodded. "We'll be here."

"I'll see you out," Gianna said with evident relief on her face. Perillo and Daniele followed her out.

Walking to the car, Perillo asked, "What do you think?"

"He seems straightforward. She confused me."

Perillo got in the passenger seat. "Me too. Now drive to Lapo's house just up ahead. It's time we meet his son. He's eighteen years old and he's yours."

"Thank you." Daniele's cheeks had only a hint of a blush.

NICO WALKED INTO Sotto Il Fico at five, greeted Enzo dusting bottles behind the bar and stopped to kiss Elvira's withered cheeks. As he straightened his back, she grabbed his shirt sleeve. "I have something to tell you."

"You loved my chicken and vegetables."

"No. Alberto Lamberti used to bring his women two doors down from my house. I suppose he thought he wouldn't run into his fancy rich friends in old town Gravigna."

"You knew him?"

"I recognized him from the picture in the paper when he died. I used to sit in front of my house to watch people come and go. Alberto stood out because he reminded me of Cary Grant."

"Nico," Tilde called out from the kitchen. She always tried to save him from Elvira. "You have work to do."

Which was true, but he wanted to hear what Elvira had to say. She was still holding on to his shirt sleeve. "I'll be right there."

Elvira peered at him with her dark, penetrating eyes. "He'd park his car under the chestnut tree fifteen meters from my house. Walk right by me without even a nod of acknowledgement. I stopped him once with a '*Buonasera, Cary.*' I got a laugh out of him." Elvira closed her eyes with a long sigh.

Her eyes snapped open. "His children knew about his love nest. A couple of times, I saw a boy take a girl up there. They couldn't have been more than fifteen. I was tempted to let him know, but once that itch starts in a young man or a girl, a locked door isn't going to stop it. His women didn't last long, except the last one. It wasn't his wife. I saw her picture yesterday in *La Nazione*. Whoever she is or was, that woman lasted until he died."

"Do you remember what she looked like?" Nico asked, although he doubted Elvira's information had any relevance to the case.

"Of course, I remember. There's no gray in my brain." The gray in her hair was dyed boot black. "Plain face. Wore flowery dresses that didn't become her. Lovely long chestnut-colored hair she kept tied in a ribbon. Whoever she is or was, she managed to win his heart besides his loins. I think I envied her and I was sorry he died, which shows you what a foolish woman I am." She let go of his sleeve. "Off with you. Make a good dish tonight too."

"Thank you!"

In the kitchen, Nico gave Tilde a hug. "I just won an Oscar."

Tilde pushed him away. "They don't give those out for food."

"Well, they should."

Tilde pushed a button on the huge food processor. The blades whirred loudly.

"Are those my leftovers?" he asked with a raised voice. They hadn't had a crowd at lunch. With the leftovers of his chicken with vegetables dish he planned to make a hearty soup and serve it at room temperature.

"No, it's my veal and mushroom filling for cannelloni. Your

soup is better chopped. The food processor would just make mush out of it."

"Meaning use your man muscles?" Tilde's mood had not improved. Nico wanted to know why.

"Exactly."

They worked to the sound of Nico's rhythmic chopping and the food processor turning spinach, egg and cheeses into a homogenous mixture. When done, Tilde turned off the machine. Nico kept his cleaver working until his cell phone rang.

"Ciao, Nico," Nelli said. "Do you have a minute?"

"For you, always. Ciao!" Nico's shoulders relaxed. "Just about a minute though."

"I'd like to come over tonight, spend the night. I'll be at the studio when you get off work."

"I'd love for you to stay with me tonight, but Perillo called earlier. We're getting together to go over what we have so far. I don't know how long it will take."

"At your home?"

"That's where we usually meet. I'm sorry." Damn. He would so much rather be with soft, warm, lovely Nelli. "Tomorrow night?"

"I guess the interesting tidbit I found out today can wait."

"Nelli, you're teasing."

"Maybe, maybe not. Have fun with your men friends. Give Dani a hug for me. He needs one. I'll be having breakfast with Gogol in the morning if you care to join us."

"You're annoyed with me. I'm sorry."

Her wonderful laugh filled his ear. "Not enough to worry about. Ciao, amore. See you in the morning."

Silence followed. Nico picked up his cleaver and chopped hard into the chicken.

Tilde took out the square sheets of pasta from the refrigerator. "Is everything okay with Nelli?"

"I'll tell you if you tell me. You first."

"I guess you'll find out from Stella." She dropped a full table-spoon of filling on the pasta sheet, tucked in two ends and rolled.

Nico turned around. "Find out what?"

"She wants to quit her job. She says she's tired of showing great art to people who take photos instead of looking. Enzo says he'll back her whatever she wants to do. I should too, but I keep thinking of all the work she put into her art studies. The museum director spotted her talent and promoted her to guide right away. Now she's willing to throw all that away. I can't stand it."

"Do you know what she wants to do next?"

"Hah! Why should a mother know something like that? Enough. I'll make a mess of this dish if I don't stop. Tell me about you and Nelli."

"I'll be quick. We're happy together. The only hitch is that this new murder is going to get in the way until we find who did it."

"You can have time off if that will help you find the man, but when you're here, I want your full attention."

"You'll have it. A murderer is automatically a man?"

"Women knife, shoot, suffocate, even drown. They don't strangle."

Nico raised a hand. "The oracle has spoken."

"Then go and prove me wrong, but now start chopping again. Your soup is printed in ink on the dinner menu."

Nico picked up the cleaver again. Tilde went back to her can-nelloni.

LAPO'S SON WAS KICKING a soccer ball on the lawn next to a small square stone gatehouse. Daniele stopped the car at the end of the short driveway and got out. "Ciao."

"He's not here." Cecco aimed the ball at the car and kicked.

When it hit the front tire, Daniele shouted, "Goal!"

Cecco grinned. He had his father's long legs without the muscles, the same strong jaw and the same mass of wavy hair except he had shaved it on the sides, making him look as though he had a dark mop on his head. He was wearing baggy jeans, new-looking Adidas sneakers and a purple Fiorentina soccer team T-shirt.

Daniele kicked the ball back to Cecco. "I'm Daniele Donato. I'm here with my boss, Maresciallo Perillo. We're here to talk to you, not your father."

"About the murder?"

"Yes. Is that all right?"

"Sure."

Perillo joined Daniele. "Buonasera, I heard you just had an important birthday."

Cecco grinned. "I got these sneakers." He lifted one foot to show them off.

"Congratulations," Perillo said. "You are legally an adult."

Cecco nodded. "I get my liceo diploma in June." He picked up the ball and wrapped his arms around it.

"You must be on the school's soccer team," Daniele said.

"I wanted to be, but Babbo won't let me. Something's wrong with my heart."

"I'm sorry to hear that."

Cecco shrugged. "I'm used to it. Are you going to find who killed Nora?"

"We'll find whoever it was, but we need your help."

"I don't know anything, but I'll try to help. She was nice to me. She gave me three hundred euros for my birthday."

"When was this?" Daniele asked.

"Sunday morning. She came down to the west lawn with the money in an envelope. I was checking the watering system. I guess she saw me from a window. She couldn't come to dinner with us because of the English lady and she was angry with Babbo for making me work on my birthday. I told her it was my idea." He shrugged again. "I lied."

"Why?"

"Is there a place we can sit?" Perillo asked before Cecco could answer.

"The grass is pretty soft," Cecco said. Daniele had a hard time concealing a smile.

"I'll sit in the car," Perillo said, not hiding his annoyance. "Talk loudly."

Cecco watched Perillo's short walk to the car. "Is his heart bad too?"

"Bad knee. He used to do a lot of cycling."

"Did he do L'Eroica? Babbo did it lots of times. Two hundred and nine kilometers on vintage bikes. It must be great. I'd love to do it."

From the car Perillo shouted, "A maresciallo of the carabinieri does not have the time to do L'Eroica." He had left the car door open.

"Have you?" Cecco asked Daniele.

"I find driving on these impossible hills hard enough."

Cecco knitted his eyebrows together. "You speak funny. Where are you from?"

"Venice."

"Ah. Flat and wet."

"And no cars."

Cecco dropped down on the grass with crossed legs, his arms firmly hugging the soccer ball.

Daniele dropped down too. To hell with the grass stains on his white trousers. "Why did you lie to Nora about whose idea it was to work on your birthday?"

"I don't like people to be angry with each other."

"Was Nora angry with your father a lot?"

Cecco shook his head, frowning. "Nooo! She loved us."

Daniele remembered Cecco's missing mother. "You can love someone and still have a reason to be angry with that person."

"I'm not sure, but okay, she did get angry once. Babbo wanted to plant grapevines and also have a vegetable garden for me to take care of." He shook his head. "Oh mamma, she didn't like that idea at all. Told him not to ever bring it up again."

"Did she say why?" Perillo asked from the car.

The interruption annoyed Daniele. He was about to ask the same question.

"No, she didn't," Cecco shouted as if Perillo were much farther away.

"Too bad," Perillo said. "Back to you, Dani."

Daniele relaxed his shoulders, changed the cross of his legs. "After your birthday dinner Sunday night did you come home with your father?"

"Where else was I going to go? I can see the villa from my bedroom. It's high up, above the kitchen. No lights were on." Cecco looked down at the ball. "Babbo kept me up half the night with his snoring."

He's setting up an alibi for his father, Daniele thought. He was learning to be cynical and not proud of it. "The curtains would have been drawn."

"I saw lights up there a lot of times. I stay up late playing games on my iPhone. Nora gave me her old one."

"You know her jewelry was stolen?"

Cecco threw the ball up in the air, caught it. "Uh huh. She put it in a dumb place. Babbo told her. I told her." The ball went up again, got caught again. "She was stubborn. Big pliers could easily break the lock on the shed."

"But you had to know the jewelry was there."

"Clara knew and I bet Fabio knew too."

"Why?"

Cecco put the ball aside and straightened up. "A couple of weeks ago I was in the shed getting bags of soil for Babbo. Fabio walked in and was nosing around. I was in the back playing with my phone. He didn't see me right away." A gleam lit up in his eyes. "I heard a rustling sound from the other end. That's where we keep sacks of mulch. '*Looking for something, Signor Meloni?*' I said. No, not really. That's what I wanted to say. All I came up with was '*Ciao.*'

"'*Just checking the supplies your father buys,*' he said and walked out. I told Babbo. He just nodded like he already knew."

"What about Nora's neighbors, the Rosatis? Did you ever see them in or around the shed?"

"Signora Rosati was always around Babbo. I haven't seen her in a while though. Whenever I run into Signor Rosati, he always asks how I'm feeling. I guess he's being nice, but I don't like it. It reminds me I'm not at a hundred percent."

"I think I would feel that way too," Daniele said. Having a weak heart had to be very frightening. "Do you run into him often?"

"Not a lot."

"Alone?"

"Yeah, except last week. Nora was with him on the front lawn. It looked like he was giving her a lecture. He was talk, talk, talking about traditional values or something like that. They didn't see me."

"Did he sound angry?"

"Sort of. You know like a teacher when he knows your head's empty?"

Daniele laughed. "Happens to you too, eh?"

Cecco rolled his eyes. "All the time."

Perillo swung his legs out of the car and asked, "Your father and Nora were really good friends, weren't they?"

"Sure."

Daniele scrambled to his feet. He was afraid of what the maresciallo was going to ask next.

Perillo held out his hand. "Don't worry, Dani." He stood up and walked over to them. "I think we've asked this young man enough questions. Thank you for your help and patience."

Cecco got to his feet with a quick laugh. "I got to have patience with my condition."

Perillo wondered what Cecco's condition really was. He acted younger than any eighteen-year-old he'd met. "Thanks for talking to us."

"I talked to Daniele."

"That's right." The position of the sun and his empty stomach told Perillo it was late. He and Dani needed a good meal before writing the daily report for Tarani and meeting Nico later. "We need your fingerprints and DNA in order to spot the ones that don't belong."

"I've got school."

"Now you have an excuse to be late. One of my men will write you a note."

"You'll find my prints all over the piano. Nora was trying to teach me how to play."

Perillo felt a twitch in his chest. "How was it going?"

Cecco grinned, his cheeks puffing up. "I'm a lot better with a ball."

"Good," Perillo said, the twitch in his chest gone, replaced by relief. Cecco seemed like a nice young man. He wouldn't relish putting him on the suspect list.

ONEWAG GREETED DANIELE at the door with a triple body wiggle.

"Make room, Rocco." Perillo walked past Daniele, holding up a bottle of limoncello. He was wearing slacks and a light cotton dress shirt, his suede jacket that was beginning to show signs of wear slung over one shoulder. "Ivana made this when she still had time to spoil her hardworking husband."

Daniele bent down and gave the dog a back scratch. "Sorry, Rocco, no present this time." OneWag plopped his backside down on the floor and stared.

Nico took the bottle. He was wearing his after-work uniform, a New York Yankees sweatshirt and jeans. "Stop whining, Perillo. Who ironed that shirt and slacks you're wearing?"

Perillo turned back to Nico and pointed a finger at his own chest. "I did."

Nico stopped himself from laughing out loud. Perillo at the ironing board was pure comedy. "You want to start with limoncello?"

"Maybe a good whiskey chaser? I have interesting information."

"Inside or outside?" Nico had left the balcony door open. The swallows were already tucked in between ceiling and wooden beams. They'd gotten used to visitors.

"The wind is picking up."

"Inside, then." Glasses, small plates and forks were already on the table, along with a bottle of white wine for Daniele if he decided to drink something besides water and an open bottle of Johnnie Walker Black Label, which Nelli had bought him the night she parked her toothbrush next to his for the long run.

"You don't believe me, do you, Rocco?" Daniele slapped his hands on his empty pockets. He'd changed into jeans and a black long-sleeved polo shirt. "See? Empty."

OneWag continued to stare.

"Come on, Dani," Nico said. "He'll forgive you. Let's sit down and go over what we've got." He sat down, followed by Perillo.

Daniele pulled out a wrapped beef jerky from his back pocket, slipped it behind the sofa and joined them.

"Please pour yourself a drink. I'm too tired to play host. Nelli left us a small lemon ricotta cake in the fridge with a good luck note. Help yourself."

"Aaah," Perillo said. "A gift to the stomach is a gift of true love."

Daniele thought of the first time Stella had let him pay for her meal. That had been a gift of trust.

Perillo went on to say, "Tarani called right after we got back from talking to Lapo's son. He'd just received the result of the drug tests on Nora. It explains why she had no defensive wounds. She'd been drugged with over fifty milligrams of diazepam. Probably in liquid form."

Perillo's comment reminded Nico to pour himself some white wine. He would only drink the whiskey with Nelli. "Whoever administered the drug was a friend, someone she would accept a drink or some food from in the music room."

"The curtain cord she was strangled with came from her bedroom," Daniele said. "Maybe that's where she was drugged."

Perillo shook his head. "No. She'd have to be carried down those stairs."

"Not necessarily," Nico said. "Even that heavy a dose wouldn't take effect immediately. How close is Nora's bedroom to the one Signorina Barron stayed in?"

"At the other end of a long corridor," Daniele said. "She would only have heard very loud sounds."

"Did you check with Nora's doctor if he'd prescribed the drug?"

"I did." Dani was half listening to cellophane paper being ripped apart under the sofa. "The only thing he'd prescribed was an anti-acid medicine for her stomach."

Nico caught Perillo eyeing the whiskey bottle. He'd hoped his friend would go for Ivana's limoncello. Nico picked up a glass and poured two fingers' worth. "Were any glasses found in Nora's bedroom or the music room?"

"No and none in the kitchen," Perillo answered. "The drug could have been injected, but they didn't find any needle marks."

"Those can easily be missed," Nico said after taking a long sip of wine. "Did you find out anything about the family's finances?"

"Yes." Daniele was eager to get his report over with so he could ask for a slice of the ricotta cake. "Fabio Meloni's dental practice is not going well. The bank statements show an almost forty percent loss of income in the last eighteen months."

"Tell Nico why," Perillo said, sniffing his whiskey glass as if it held vintage wine.

"I did some internet sleuthing. Twenty months ago, a patient filed a complaint with the police about being subjected to 'improper behavior' by Dr. Fabio Meloni." When the police did nothing, the woman started posting angry comments on her Twitter account about the police and Fabio. She already had a big following and now it's huge. Her #MeToo campaign has cost him a lot of female patients. His private bank account is small. All the money was in the practice. Adriana Meloni has her own account. When her father died, she and Clara each inherited, after taxes, just over five hundred thousand euros. Now Adriana is down to eighty thousand. Clara has twenty-two thousand euros left. Two months ago, Clara requested a bank loan to purchase an all-cash apartment in Lucca's fashionable center for six-hundred-fifty-thousand euros. She gave the Salviati property as collateral signed by her mother. Clara's fiancé, Marco Zanelli, has very little money in his bank account."

"Thank you. I'm impressed," Nico said. "How did you remember all that?"

There was no way he could not turn red after a compliment from Nico. "I looked at my notes before coming."

"Nora didn't have enough cash to loan the money to Clara?"

"She did. I guess she didn't want to." Daniele's voice was unusually harsh. A bad mother was inconceivable to him.

"Wine? Water? A slice of ricotta cake?"

"A slice, thank you."

While Nico got the cake from the refrigerator and cut out three slices, Perillo started telling him about their visit to the Rosatis'.

Nico slipped the slices onto the plates on the table and sat down to listen. "Destroying a productive vineyard because of disease makes more sense than the reason Gustavo gave me."

Perillo eyed the ricotta cake. "Gustavo is a romantic." Perillo's full spoon disappeared in his mouth. After a few seconds his eyes widened.

"Good?" Nico asked.

Perillo swallowed. "Heavenly. This is Migliaccio, a traditional Neapolitan cake. Find out where she bought it."

"Nelli made it."

"A Tuscan woman making Migliaccio? Incredible. You are truly blessed, Nico." Perillo dug up more cake with his spoon.

"I agree." Nico took a small bite of his slice. It felt as if he'd bitten into a lemony sugar cloud. "Could one or both of the Rosatis have a reason to kill Nora?"

Daniele took advantage of Perillo's full mouth to answer. "If Federico knew Nora was selling the land, he could have resented it, maybe even harbored dreams of convincing Nora to replant a vineyard."

"Nora definitely said no when Lapo suggested it," Perillo countered with a full mouth.

"According to what Cecco overheard, Federico is a believer in tradition and his father killed himself on that land."

Perillo put his spoon down and sat back. "Now you're the one who is being a romantic, Dani. Federico's father killed himself years ago, but I do trust your instinct, so I won't rule it out as a possible motive. What do you think, Nico?"

"I wouldn't rule it out either." Nico smiled at Dani, glad Perillo hadn't dismissed his brigadiere's thinking.

Daniele concentrated on eating his slice of Migliaccio.

"I'd like to meet the Rosatis," Nico said. "They asked for me at the restaurant the other night. Gave Alba their telephone number."

Perillo slapped a hand on the table. "Wonderful. Pay them a visit."

"I will." Nico pushed his now-empty plate aside to remove any temptation to have another slice. "What about the wife?"

"I don't think getting the opal ring back is a strong enough motive," Perillo said after licking his lips. "They were card-playing friends. She seemed genuinely upset Nora was dead. She did find it 'odd' that Nora had never mentioned Signorina Barron before her visit. I think she was not very subtly pointing the finger. When you and Dino went through Signorina Barron's things, did you find sleeping pills?"

"You'll have to ask Dino. He's the one who searched the bathroom."

"I will."

"She didn't answer when you asked if her sons were still abroad," Daniele said. "I think the question upset her."

Perillo shook his head in disagreement. "I cut her off. She claims Nora never showed her the jewelry. She says it was kept in the safe. And listen to this. Much to her husband's displeasure, Gianna also informed us that Nora miscarried the baby that forced her to get married. Adriana was adopted to replace her. That's helpful news." Perillo finished off his slice of Migliaccio.

"Adriana being adopted is a surprise," Nico said.

Daniele again took advantage of Perillo's full mouth to say, "Nora then gave birth to Clara two years later. According to Gianna, Clara's birth made Adriana feel unloved. An adopted daughter wasn't as good as a real one."

Nico took a long sip of his wine. "Let me think this through

out loud. That Adriana was angry with her mother is abun-
dantly clear from what you've told me. Feeling unloved made
her angry, then enraged. So much so, she wanted to kill her
mother? Maybe, but why now?"

Perillo swallowed. "Because Nora was going to sell the land."

"Did Adriana know that? Fabio only found out that BelPosto
had made a bid. That doesn't mean Nora accepted."

"She claims her mother told her she was selling. The husband
said the same thing." Perillo kept turning his empty whiskey
glass. He was tired. The movement helped him stay focused.
"Whether they found out from Nora or BelPosto, they knew
Nora was selling."

Daniele felt a nudge on his leg. "Wouldn't the money they
would inherit, sale or no sale, be enough of a motive?" Daniele
asked. His arm reached down to scratch OneWag's head. The
dog was now sniffing his pockets for more beef jerky.

Nico noticed Daniele leaning to one side. "OneWag, leave
Dani alone."

"No, please. We're pals."

"Don't worry. He never listens."

Perillo peered under the table. "Ehi, Rocco, I'm a pal too."

"An empty-handed pal," Nico said, his attention still on
Daniele. "When you were looking into Fabio's finances, did you
see either his personal account or the dental office receive any
money from Adriana's account?"

"Once. Two months ago. Seventy-five hundred euros into his
office account. It's the amount he paid out every month."

"The rent?"

"Yes."

"Adriana is a stingy wife. Fabio might not get a cent from the
inheritance. That makes him a more likely jewelry thief than
a murderer. Do you both agree?" Nico knew that Perillo welcomed his help but got huffy when he took over.

"Seems right," said a lopsided Daniele. He was now kneading the dog's ears. OneWag moaned with pleasure.

Perillo nodded his agreement. "Clara had a high stake in the property staying in her mother's possession. No property, no mortgage on the six-hundred-and-fifty-thousand-euro apartment."

Daniele put his kneading hand back on the table. Something wasn't adding up. "Why would Nora offer the property as collateral when she knew she was selling it?"

"Maybe giving her spoiled daughter a lesson on excessive consumption." The thought gave Perillo a kick. Clara seemed nice, but holy heaven, spending that kind of money for an apartment was indecent. Another possibility dropped into his head. He stopped turning his glass. "Maybe Nora didn't offer the property as collateral."

"You think Clara forged her mother's signature?" Nico asked.

"It's possible. As Dani said, why would she sign a collateral agreement if she was going to sell the place?"

Daniele stepped in. "The agreement was signed two months ago. We don't know that Nora knew she was selling at that time."

Perillo dropped his arms in surrender. "Suppositions, possibilities. We're on quicksand here. Was Nora killed for her property? Did Fabio kill for the jewelry? Did Adriana or Clara kill for the property? For both? And Signorina Barron? She's still high on my list. And there's Lapo and Marco."

"And the Rosatis," Daniele added.

Perillo's arms went up in the air. "Yes, why not the Rosatis, and let's add Cecco. Throw the whole lot into the suspect cauldron. We're going to have to do a lot of stirring to come up with the murderer."

Nico reached over and gave Perillo's shoulder a friendly slap. "We'll stir slowly and thoroughly, and we'll get there." Nico stood up. "It's late and we're tired."

Perillo and Daniele got on their feet. "Thanks for the hospitality," Perillo said, "and tell Nelli her Migliaccio proves she has Neapolitan blood in her veins."

OneWag scurried over to the door. The men followed.

"We'll touch base tomorrow," Nico said.

"Glad to hear it," Perillo said.

Daniele gave OneWag one last pat. "Ciao, Rocco. Buonanotte, Nico."

"Notte." Nico closed the door and went to clear the table. OneWag hit the bed.

EIGHT

"There you are," Nelli said as OneWag ran through the open door of Bar All'Angolo. Nelli picked him up. "I missed you, Rocco." The dog covered her cheek with licks. She was dressed for work. Pressed burgundy slacks, a matching knit top that now was covered with blond dog hair. She didn't care.

Gogol looked up from his ciambella and nodded his approval. "'Neither creator nor creature was ever without love.'"

Nico walked in wearing jeans, a red polo shirt and a thin down jacket he didn't need. At eight o'clock in the morning the sun had already absorbed any chill. "Buongiorno to all."

Nelli smiled at Nico. Sandro, busy giving change to a customer, lifted his chin up from behind the cash register.

"Ciao, Nico," Jimmy called out from the far end of the counter where the hulking espresso machine dominated in all its shiny glory. "My stack of whole wheat cornetti got wiped out by the schoolkids. Sorry."

Nico clutched his heart and moaned.

Gogol looked up from his ciambella and nodded his approval. "Sergio, the butcher, made no crostini." He looked down at his half-empty plate. "I resort to the ciambella Nelli has with her generous heart offered me."

"I thought you gave up salame and lard crostini to atone for your sins." Nico kissed the top of Nelli's head and sat down next to her. Nelli pecked his cheek.

"Ah, yes. I allow sad events, such as my sins, to float in and out of mind. It helps preserve my serenity."

"Not a bad idea," Nico said. "Your ricotta cake was a great success, Nelli. Did you know it was a Neapolitan specialty?"

"I guessed it was since Ivana made it when she found out the three of you were getting together."

"Oh, and here I was rejoicing to discover your baking talents."

Nelli laughed as she put OneWag down. "Panna cotta is the extent of my culinary talents." The dog started his usual periscope search. "Don't tell him, please."

"I won't, but be prepared to come up with a Neapolitan in your family tree the next time you see Perillo."

"I'll ask Ivana for a suitable one. How did the meeting of the Three Musketeers go?"

"There were four," Gogol corrected. "Athos, Porthos, Aramis and D'Artagnan."

Nelli gave Gogol's hand a squeeze. She was worried about him. His face was drained of color and his hands trembled. "D'Artagnan joins them later, doesn't he?"

"Indeed." Gogol looked at Nelli with tired blue eyes. "And now there are four."

Nelli understood. "No, Gogol, I want no part in their investigation, only their friendship."

"I hear talk of friendship." Perillo strode to the table, raising a hand at Sandro and Jimmy. Several men having their breakfasts at the counter acknowledged the maresciallo's presence with nods or full-mouthed hellos. He was in uniform. "Ciao, Nelli, Signor Gogol. May I join you for the time it takes to have a double espresso?" Perillo never felt at ease in Gogol's presence.

"'His face was the face of an honest man,'" Gogol quoted.

"I assume that's a yes even if in the past tense."

"Oh, sit down," Nelli said with a trace of impatience, annoyed by the interruption.

"Nelli, congratulations. Your Migliaccio was superior." Perillo sat down. "Would you share the recipe? I would like to surprise Ivana with it."

Nico stared at Perillo. "You cook?"

Perillo puffed up his chest. "All Italian men cook."

"I make good omelettes," Gogol said. "Excellent ones if porcini are in season."

"Your omelettes are delicious, Gogol," Nelli said. "He made one for my birthday last year."

Nico continued to stare at Perillo. "If you know how to cook, why does Ivana do all the cooking?"

"I work hard."

"Now she does too," Nelli said. "I can give you lots of my mother's recipes. They are fail-safe." She was grinning.

Perillo looked at both Nico and Nelli. "Why are you ganging up on me?"

"We're not," Nelli said. "You said you work hard. We're just saying that she does too."

"All right. You made your point. Now I have one to make too. This one is for Nico." Perillo leaned across the table. "Dino—" He stopped when he saw Sandro approach with Nico's breakfast and his double espresso. "Ah, thanks, Sandro, that was quick."

"It always is." Sandro put the cornetti and the coffees on the table. "Enjoy."

"What did Dino say?" Nico asked after Sandro walked away.

Perillo took a quick sip of his coffee and leaned across the table again. "He noticed a bottle with the same contents that are in a bottle his mother keeps in her medicine cabinet."

"The contents the same as what was found in Florence?"

"The same."

"I keep a small bottle of gin in mine," Gogol said. "In wise quantities it gives the tired heart a kick."

"Remember to be wise," Nelli said. "I don't want you to fall."

"I would float, Nelli dear, not fall."

Nelli laughed and kissed Gogol's withered cheek. "Yes, you probably would."

Nico was thinking of what Perillo had just implied. Miss Barron had a bottle of diazepam. Suspicious. But he just couldn't see Miss Barron as a murderer. "I'll look into it."

"Please do." Perillo finished his coffee and stood up. "Thank you for letting me join you. I enjoyed it. Gogol, stay heathy. A pleasure. Nelli, I look forward to receiving the recipe."

"I'll give it to Nico," Nelli said. "Please say hello to Daniele for me."

"I will. We have an appointment with a woman named Marta not far from here."

"Ah that explains the uniform," Nelli said.

"Nico, we'll be in touch."

"Sure."

Perillo paid at the cash register and walked out.

"He paid for your breakfasts," Sandro announced in a surprised voice.

"That's a first," Nico said, not liking it. He usually ended up paying for his friend, who would settle the debt at the end of the month. Perillo paying for all of them meant he was feeling guilty about something.

Nico picked up his phone and texted Daniele:

PLEASE FIND OUT IF SIGNORINA BARRON'S FINGERPRINTS WERE FOUND IN NORA'S BEDROOM. THANK YOU

He put the phone down and attacked his first cornetto.

Nelli had been watching him. His mind was elsewhere. She wanted him back. "You're not curious what interesting bit I wanted to tell you last night?"

Nico swallowed his bite of cornetto. "I thought you were kidding."

"I just said that because you didn't seem interested. For all I know it's not important to the case."

"Go on." He took another bite, his eyes on her.

"Yesterday morning I was alone at the sale shop at Querciabella. A young man comes in with an incredible tan, handsome too. Anyway, he asks to speak to the owner. I tell him the owner is with a client, which wasn't true, but that's what I'm supposed to say if it's someone we don't know." A light snore came from Gogol.

"The man tells me he came back ten days ago and has been visiting the vintners in the area trying to interest them in a South African varietal, Pinotage."

"Yes?" Nico started on the second cornetto, wondering where Nelli was going with her story. She was enjoying herself.

"He had a light Tuscan inflection in his speech. I asked him if he was Tuscan. It turns out I knew him when he was Adriana's age. He came over a couple of times while I was painting her and Clara. Isn't that incredible?"

"It is. He's tanned, handsome and *young*."

Nelli laughed. "Don't worry, I like old men."

Nelli's laugh woke Gogol. "Brava! The old have wisdom youth finds frivolous. Gogol, not Dante." Gogol lowered his chin to his chest and went back to sleep.

"If you're not telling me about this young man to make me jealous, why are you?"

"Stefano is the son of Nora's good friends, the Rosatis."

Nico leaned over and kissed her forehead. "Thank you. That *is* interesting."

Gogol's chest heaved with each noisy breath.

I don't think he's well, Nelli mouthed as she checked Gogol's forehead for fever. It was warm but so was the room. *He's never fallen asleep.*

Did you ask him? Nico mouthed back.

Nelli took a pen out of her bag and wrote on her napkin: *I told him that he didn't look his usual grouchy self. Was he okay? He laughed at grouchy and said he had no power over Fortune. She turns her wheel as she likes.*

"I'll walk him home," Nico said in his normal voice.

"I'll come with you." Nelli stroked Gogol's cheek, shook him gently. "Breakfast is over. We're taking you home."

Gogol raised his head and rubbed his eyes, then chuckled to himself. "'I have come, but I don't stay.'" He slowly stood up. "That is Gogol's way as it is with all of us." He picked up what was left of his ciambella and dropped it to the floor for OneWag, whose periscoping rounds had given meagre results.

OneWag gave Gogol a wag and ate.

Gogol said his usual goodbye, "Tomorrow if I live," and ambled to the door.

Nico gave his usual answer. "You will."

Nelli joined Gogol, linking her arm in his. Nico and OneWag followed.

Sandro and Jimmy watched them leave. For the past two years, six mornings a week, they had served Nico and Gogol breakfast. The two had become an institution.

"Gogol must be close to ninety," Sandro said.

"He claims seventy-nine," Jimmy said. "He'll be fine."

NORA'S LAUNDRESS LIVED IN the new section of Gravigna on the top floor of a three-family house. As Daniele led Perillo slowly up the stairs, he spotted a young woman on a long, narrow terrace hanging laundry. A baby with a pink hat was strapped to her chest.

"I think that's her," Daniele said.

Perillo stopped climbing to look at the terrace. He needed to pause. His knee was throbbing. "Marta Macchi?" he called out.

The woman leaned over the parapet, a hand covering the baby's head. "Here I am. I'll open the door."

"Thank you," Daniele said. He had been the one to make the appointment. He waited for Perillo to pass him. It was only right that the maresciallo be the first to enter.

Perillo nodded and carefully walked up the last seven steps.

Marta was standing at the open door in bare feet, denim tights and a loose white shirt, a small towel flung over her shoulder. She was short and thin, not at all Daniele's idea of a laundress. He'd imagined someone much older and hefty. Marta had a full, pleasant face and tired hazel eyes. Her long blond hair was tied in a ponytail that hung between her shoulder blades.

Perillo introduced himself and Daniele.

"Come in, come in," she said in a nervous voice.

They followed her into a room that tripled as a living room, dining room, and kitchen. A two-seater sofa sat against one wall. In the middle of the room was a small rectangular table with four straw chairs and a baby cradle sitting on top. At one end, a small hallway led to what must be the bedroom and bathroom. *A sweet cozy space*, Daniele thought, his mind having lately taken a domestic turn.

"Would you like a coffee or a glass of water?"

"No, thank you," they both said.

"What's the baby's name?" Daniele asked.

"Celestina. It's my mother's middle name. It's warm in here," Marta said. "You could sit outside under the awning?"

"Good idea," Perillo said. The day had turned out to be a hot one. No clouds. No breeze.

They reached the terrace by going out on the landing and opening a gate. Two bamboo armchairs sat underneath a small dark-green awning. "I'll stand," Daniele said.

"No, please sit," Marta said. Perillo had already dropped down on the closest chair, one leg stretched out to relieve his knee. "I need to finish hanging the laundry. With the baby . . ." She left the rest unsaid, picked up a wet towel from a wicker basket and clipped it onto one of many strings running across half the length of the terrace. "How can I help you?"

"I'm curious about one thing that has nothing to do with the investigation." Perillo was feeling much better now that he was seated. "Nora Salviati lived alone. A housekeeper would have met all her needs. Why employ a laundress?"

"Tradition," Marta said. "She came from an old family. Thank you." Instead of sitting, Daniele was bending down, picking up an item and handing it to her. He noticed Marta wasn't wearing a wedding ring. That didn't mean anything. Marriage had gone out of style. He hoped at least she had a partner for the baby's sake.

Perillo made himself more comfortable by resting his head back on the chair. "She didn't have a cook."

"Signora Salviati wasn't interested in food," Marta said. "Whatever bland food Sonia fed her was fine with her. Her lace-trimmed linen sheets and towels, she cared very much about those." She glanced down at the basket and quickly said to Daniele, "It's very sweet of you to help, but please sit down."

Daniele sat down, his cheeks picking up color. Marta's panties would have been next.

Marta dug deeper into the basket. "She cared about the things that had been handed down from her side of the family." She pulled out baby pajamas.

"Even the jewelry?" Perillo asked.

"I would think so. If she still had all the stuff her mother was wearing in the portrait, it would be very valuable."

"Did you ever see any of it?"

"No, and I didn't steal it. You don't need a warrant. Go ahead and search if you want." The basket was now empty except for her underwear.

"Do you know where she kept it?"

"I imagine in a safe."

"Where did you do the laundry?"

"The villa has a large windowless room behind the pantry with a washing machine, a dryer and an ironing table. La signora let me do my own stuff there. And she didn't mind my bringing the baby." Marta looked at the hanging laundry dripping onto the tiles and shook her head. "Now we have to buy a washing machine. I don't know where we'll put it."

"You won't be working there anymore?" Daniele asked.

"No. Signora Adriana told me there was no need for me."

"Have you found other work?" Daniele asked in a hopeful voice.

"My partner doesn't want me to. He says we can manage. He works at the hardware store in Panzano. I'll go back to work when Celestina is older." She smiled shyly. "Unless . . ." She didn't finish her sentence.

Daniele returned her smile.

The mention of a partner made Perillo say, "You must have had a key to the villa."

"Never. Sonia would let me in."

"The name of your partner?"

Marta frowned. "Max Vitale." Daniele jotted down this new information. Marta started rocking the sleeping baby, her frown more pronounced. "You can't think Max had anything to do with what happened. He never set foot in the villa."

"It's just routine," Daniele reassured her.

Perillo sat up. He was getting drowsy. "How long had you worked for la signora?"

Marta stopped rocking the baby. "Since I was sixteen. That was twelve years ago."

Interesting, Perillo thought. "When her husband died, she fired the housekeeper but kept you."

"I didn't let him into my bed."

"You're attractive. He must have tried."

"My father is Sergio, the butcher. I let Signor Alberto know what my father would do to him if he ever even touched me. And I told the signora too."

"Good for you," slipped out of Daniele's mouth.

Perillo gave his brigadiere a stern look that Daniele ignored. He was too busy admiring Marta's courage.

"Now tell me about the sheets you washed and ironed," Perillo said. "Did they show any signs of amorous activities?"

The baby started fussing, pushing against Marta's chest. "Shh, shh." Marta started swaying. "Do you really need to know that?"

"We are trying to discover who killed her. If she had a lover, it gives us someone to look into."

"It makes me feel disloyal."

"That's a yes, then?"

Marta nodded and shifted her weight from one foot to the other while she patted Celestina's back.

"Every week?"

"Soon after her husband died, yes. For a while. Then nothing for a long time. A couple of years ago it started again."

"Do you know who the man was?"

Daniele wished the maresciallo would stop. Marta was clearly uncomfortable.

"Maresciallo, how would I know? He didn't sign his name."

"Could it be Lapo?"

"I don't know who it was." Celestina started whimpering. "I have to feed Celestina now. I would go ahead, but Max doesn't want me to feed her in front of other men. I hope you understand."

Perillo and Daniele both stood up. "Of course," Perillo said. "We'll leave." Watching women feed their babies in public always made him uncomfortable. "I'll call if I have any more questions. Thank you."

"Thank you," Daniele said.

Celestina let out a howl.

The men hurried to the gate.

Celestina's hungry howl accompanied them down the stairs and to the car.

"WE HAD A GOOD crowd today," Tilde said. She was scraping off the stuck bits of cheese, mushrooms and rigatoni from a large baking dish. The lunch service was over. "Good weather always brings them in."

"And good food," Nico said. "I made that dish. I should be the one to wash it off."

"I'm sure you have something better to do."

"Thanks. I have an appointment." Nico took his apron off. Signora Rosati had sounded excited to see him. He had no idea why unless it was to pump him for information. His involvement in murder investigations was by now a well-known fact in the area. "I might be a little late tonight."

"Take the night off. I won't need you. It's supposed to start raining hard around six, so no terrace dining. If we're lucky the five inside tables will fill up but that's all."

Alba walked in with a tray of dirty dishes. "Everyone's gone except for a foreign woman who just asked for you, Nico."

"Miss Barron?" He needed to talk to her, but this was not the right time.

"Yes, something like that," Alba said. "Go talk to her so she'll leave, and I can finish up out there."

"At your command," Nico said.

Miss Barron was sitting at a table by the parapet, gazing out at the hills drenched in sunlight. She was dressed in a flowing floral dress and heels.

"What a surprise, Miss Barron," Nico said as he approached. "What brings you here?"

"Hello, Mr. Doyle. I woke up this morning needing an adventure. Laura spoke very highly of this restaurant, and I was curious to see where you worked. I thoroughly enjoyed the mozzarella in a carriage the young waitress suggested after translating the menu for me. A wonderful dish and a wonderful name. A carriage made of bread, egg and breadcrumbs."

"Exactly. Did Laura bring you here?"

"No, she was far too busy. The hotel is filling up. The young man who brings the newspapers to the hotel offered to pick me up in his mother's car and drive me here."

Nico groaned in silence. "Beppe."

"Yes. He's a very inquisitive young man. Wanted to know all about the murder. I reproached him for being insensitive. He did tell me he was helpful in solving last year's murder. Was he?"

"He did help," Nico admitted, "but we'd like to keep the details of this murder to ourselves."

"I revealed nothing."

"I'm glad. I do need to talk with you some more, Miss Barron, but I have an appointment now. Can we have dinner tonight?"

Miss Barron's cheeks puffed up with her smile, making her look years younger. "That would be lovely. Here?"

"It's going to rain."

Alba started noisily readjusting chairs. All the tables had been cleared except Miss Barron's.

"My hotel then." She gracefully stood up, flinging a tan Prada bag over one shoulder. "Seven-thirty."

"I'll drive you back to the hotel now. It's on my way."

"Thank you, but Beppe has been patiently waiting for me outside. I will try to keep him happy with a description of the villa. It's already been written about in books. I don't think there's any harm in that."

"There shouldn't be." With Beppe's love of exaggeration, he would probably make the Salviatis' villa unrecognizable. Together they walked out of the restaurant.

BEFORE ENTERING THE ROSATIS' short driveway, Nico called Perillo. "I'm just outside the Rosatis'. Their son Stefano is in the area. Nelli met him at Querciabella."

"Do his parents know? When I asked Gianna if the sons were still away, she didn't answer."

"I'll find out. How did it go with Marta?"

"Nice woman. She saw signs of lovemaking on the bedsheets. Nora had a lover for a couple of years after her husband died, then none in her bed until two years ago. She claims she didn't know who he or they could be."

"Claims?"

"Well, she seems honest enough, but I'm not good at reading women anymore. They've gotten too smart."

"They've always been smart. Dani's a sharp observer. What does he think?"

"Marta has a baby so now she's purity itself. Talk to you later. Lapo just walked in." Perillo clicked off. Nico drove into the Rosatis' driveway.

AS SOON AS LAPO'S jeans hit the chair, Perillo shot out, "Were you Nora's lover?"

Lapo laughed. Daniele coughed to warn Perillo. He hadn't turned on the tape recorder yet.

"And a buonasera to you too, Maresciallo." Lapo hitched one leg over the other and crossed his arms. "How do you know she had a lover?"

Perillo waited until Daniele made his recording announcement and pushed the record button. "We have evidence that she had a weekly lover."

"Good for her."

Perillo heard resentment in his tone. "You didn't know?"

"She didn't share her sex life with me."

"But you were very close."

"Before we get into my relationship with my employer, I'd like you to know I don't appreciate you questioning my son."

"I hope he wasn't upset," Daniele said.

"It's hard to say with Cecco."

"He mentioned that he caught Fabio in the garden shed looking at the mulch sacks. He said he told you. What do you make of it?"

"Fabio likes to stick his nose in everything. He'd been trying to take over the running of the villa from Nora. He complained she spent too much money running the place. He tried to get me to side with him, help him convince Nora to put him in charge of the property. I just walked away."

"When was this?"

"Four or five months ago."

"Now back to your relationship with Nora. You were very close?"

"We were once."

"As close as lovers?"

Lapo unhitched his leg, pulled on his nose. He looked over at Daniele in the back of the room. "I don't want my son to know."

"There's no reason to tell him that I can see," Perillo answered.

"Well, keep it that way. Nora meant the world to him." Lapo leaned back. "While her husband was alive, she'd flirt with me. After a while I decided to flirt back. There was no harm in it because we both knew we weren't going to take it any further. Cecco's mother was still with me." Lapo looked beyond Perillo's shoulder, his mind off somewhere.

"Then Alberto died," Perillo prompted.

"He died and Cecco's mother found herself another man. There was nothing to hold us back."

"Did you love each other?" Perillo asked. Love could turn to hate so quickly.

"No. It was a carnal thing, nothing more."

"When was the last time you had sex together?"

A short laugh came out of Lapo's throat. "I'd say about five years ago. She'd just come back from a trip to England. The exact date isn't written on my heart. She stopped it."

"Did she give a reason?"

"Why would she? She was the boss, I was only the laborer."

"You must have been angry."

"Oh, yes, she pissed me off all right, but not enough to kill her."

"Do you have any idea who replaced you?"

"I knew she had another lover just by looking at her at certain times. She'd go away for a few days and come back with the smiling look of a cat with a mouse in her belly. I could have found out by nosing around, but why bother? I didn't think he was from around here."

"Come on, Lapo. You had to be curious."

"Maybe I didn't want to know. I might have been tempted to smash his face."

Ah, got you! Perillo stretched his torso over the desk. "You *are* angry that Nora dumped you! Maybe so angry that you drugged her, cut off the curtain cord from her bedroom and strangled her."

Lapo sat up straight, his face alert. "She was drugged?"

"Come on, you know she was. There was a guest in the house. You couldn't have Nora make noise." Perillo settled back in his armchair and narrowed his eyes at Lapo. "I will ask you again. Lapo Angelini, did you kill Nora Salviati?"

"No, I did not. I was angry at being kicked out of Nora's

bed with no reason given. Any man would have been. Sure, punching the other guy's face would have made me feel good. But five years have gone by. If I was going to kill her, I'd have done it then."

"Can you prove it was five years ago?"

"No. Now listen to me, Maresciallo Perillo." With a face tight with controlled anger, Lapo pulled his chair closer and leaned over the desk. He was spitting distance from his accuser. "Even if she had kicked me out of her bed last week, I would never harm Nora. She has been a lifesaver to my son, covering him with love his own mother is incapable of giving."

Perillo met Lapo's gaze with tight fists. "She left you and your son a great deal of money."

Lapo pulled himself back, his face softening. "Yes, God bless her. She told me she would, but I did not kill her. Any other questions?"

"Did you know she was selling the property? It was going to put you out of work."

Not a blink, not a flicker in his eyes. "I did not. That came as a surprise."

Perillo, with tension gone, loosened his hands. "No more questions for now. Interview is over."

Daniele happily made the end-of-interview announcement. For a dreadful moment he'd thought Lapo was going to punch Perillo's face in.

Lapo stood up. "Let me know when you want me to sign the statement. I'm not going anywhere. Arrivederci." He walked out, hands stuffed in his jean pockets.

Perillo swiveled his armchair around to face Daniele. "What do you think?"

"He told the truth about the affair. I'm not sure about not knowing she was selling."

"If he did know, he had a double reason to kill her. Do we know anything about his finances?"

"Nora annotated his monthly salary in her account book. It came to sixty thousand euros a year with an added three-thousand-euro bonus in December."

Perillo whistled. "That's a lot of money. Not an amount you'd be happy to lose."

"Lapo inherits a lot."

"Yes. And he let us know he knew about it. I don't think a guilty man would reveal that fact."

"A clever man might," Daniele said.

Perillo slumped back in his armchair, unhappy with the way the interrogation had gone, feeling like fool. He was too eager to find the murderer and go back to normal life. Lapo had kept the upper hand throughout.

NINE

"You have a very beautiful garden," Nico said. He was sitting with the Rosatis on the wide stone-paved patio in the back of their house. OneWag was at his feet. They were surrounded by a vast array of terra-cotta pots filled with peonies and roses and plants Nico couldn't name.

Gianna pressed her hand to her chest. She was wearing a floral skirt with a frilly white blouse. "Thank you." An armada of clouds was now floating in from the north, mitigating the sun's heat. Gianna had offered him a coffee he'd turned down. She had brought out a bowl of water the dog ignored.

"He just drank," Nico somehow felt compelled to say.

"Well, just in case," Gianna said in a chipper voice. "We greatly appreciate you taking the time to see us." Her husband sat a few feet apart from her with what Nico thought was a patient expression on his face.

"My wife is extremely upset by Nora's death, which is understandable as they were great friends, but it has led her to worry that Maresciallo Perillo will not find the killer."

Nico looked at Federico. "Do you have the same worry?"

"I have full faith in the maresciallo, but we have heard that you have helped him in the past and Gianna—"

Gianna reached over and tapped his knee. "Please let me

speak for myself." She turned to Nico with an eager face. "A New York detective obviously has much more experience in solving murders than a maresciallo of the carabinieri in charge of a rural area. Please reassure me that you are involved in the investigation."

"I have no legal status here. I can only give advice. I do have a question for you, Signor Rosati, if you don't mind."

"Please ask whatever you wish," Federico said. "We are here to help."

"Thank you. Last week you were overheard on the grounds of the villa giving Nora what our witness said sounded like a lecture. Something about tradition?"

"Ah, yes, I was quite upset with Nora. I would say it was more of a sermon than a lecture. She had just told me she was selling the property. I was aghast at first and then I tried to have her see reason. Yes, I spoke about the value of tradition, about the joy the land and the villa had given generations of her family, how it had fed them.

"She didn't need to sell the property. She had enough money. I bombarded her with my self-righteous words. I was quite upset. Nora could have walked away, but she listened patiently. When I finally asked her to give me a reason for selling, she said what she did with her property was none of my business."

"That was a bit rough." Nico was perplexed by Federico. His retelling of what clearly had been an emotional moment seemed to have no feeling behind it.

"Nora was not tenderhearted, Signor Doyle. She was right. It was none of my business."

Gianna reached behind her and stroked her husband's knee. "You were upset for your father. He died there. His spirit is still hanging from that tree."

Federico smiled at his wife and moved his knee. Gianna let her hand hang. "My wife has a fervid imagination. I'm not one to believe in spirits lingering anywhere. Whether the land stays in Salviati Lamberti hands or is sold to the highest bidder, my father is still dead. No, I'm an old-fashioned man. I dislike change."

"I understand," Nico said.

Gianna retrieved her hand. "I'm sure you do. You came all the way from America." She craned her neck toward Nico. "Have you come any closer to finding out who killed her?"

"I'm not allowed to say. Maybe you can help us. Who do you think could have killed her?"

Gianna retreated into her chair. "I don't know. The girls had a difficult relationship with their mother, but they wouldn't hurt her. Adriana's husband can be very unpleasant, arrogant and rude. He didn't like his mother-in-law and he detests me."

"Now don't exaggerate," Federico said. "I will agree that he is not a nice man. He suggested to Gianna—"

Gianna raised her hand to stop him. "That's private. I do think the sudden appearance of Signorina Barron is a bit of a mystery. Nora never uttered even one word about her and all of a sudden she is staying for a week. No one except the girls have ever spent the night in the villa since Alberto died. Never."

"Gianna, stop prevaricating. Nothing can be private if you want to help solve a murder." Federico glanced at Nico. "Isn't that right?"

Nico nodded. "Every little bit helps."

"Then I'll tell you," Gianna said. "This was maybe a year ago. Fabio stopped me as I left the villa, saying that instead of playing bridge with Nora, I should concentrate on who my husband was playing with." Gianna ran both hands down her hennaed hair, a look of fury on her face. "I stood there looking at him for I don't know how long. Then he smirked and I slapped him with all the strength I had in me."

Federico looked impassive. "When Gianna told me I was ready to bloody his face, but Gianna begged me not to."

"It's true," she said. "I regretted slapping him. It gave Fabio's lie too much credit."

"What Fabio implied never happened," Federico said, with an indignant expression on his face.

"There's evidence that she did have a romantic partner for many years."

Federico gave his wife a questioning look. "Lapo?"

Gianna's laugh shook her chest. "Why not? The holder of the grand old Salviati name hopping in bed with her gardener. Just the idea of it would have given Nora a kick. Her father and husband must be swallowing their teeth in their graves. What about Claudio Nardi?"

"I don't remember him," Federico said.

"I guess you wouldn't. Nora used to talk about him a lot when we were alone. We'd find a room during one of Alberto's fancy parties and just chat. Claudio had been her sweetheart at the liceo. She wanted to marry him, but Alberto charmed her for one night and poor Nora got pregnant. She was too honest to pretend the baby was Claudio's."

Nico took out a small notebook with pen attached and wrote down *Claudio Nardi*. "Would you have an address for him?"

"Nora mentioned he owns a restaurant in Gaiole. Il Cestino, I think it's called."

"When did she say this?"

"Oh, at least a year ago."

Federico crossed his long legs. "How do you remember this trivia?"

"I remember because I wanted us to go there for dinner so I could see what he looked like, but you complained that a thirty-kilometer drive was too far for a mediocre meal, so we had a mediocre meal at home."

Nico was looking up at the sky. OneWag followed Nico's lead and sniffed the air. The clouds had turned dark gray. Nico realized he had better hurry before they burst open.

"Thank you. You have been very helpful. You must be very happy your son Stefano is here from Africa."

Nico thought he saw Gianna gulp before she asked, "How do you know he's here?"

"He introduced himself to a friend of mine at the Querciabella vineyard."

"He wants to introduce a different varietal of grapes to this area. One that works well in South Africa," Federico said. "I told him he'll have a hard time convincing anyone. Tre Cipressi, that's where I work, has no interest whatsoever."

"I'm sure they'll regret it," Gianna said. She turned a proud face toward Nico. "Stefano has been very successful with that grape in South Africa."

"Is he staying with you?"

Gianna joined her hands together as if she was going to pray. "I wish he were, but he prefers to stay with friends in Florence. Do you have children, Nico?"

"I do not."

"They can give you heartache."

"Our sons love us very much," Federico said, after a reproachful glance at his wife. "As grown men they are free to do as they wish. That is as it should be."

"How long has your son been back here?"

Nico saw Gianna's hand clutch her skirt.

Federico's face stiffened. "I hope you're not thinking my son is involved in any way with Nora's death?"

"Not at all, but Maresciallo Perillo is trying to understand the dynamics of the Salviati Lamberti family. Living so close by, your sons and Nora's daughters must have grown up together."

"Well." Federico readjusted himself in the wicker chair as

though his bones were aching. Nico understood he had worn out his welcome. "They did spend some time together when they were quite young. By the time they were teenagers our boys preferred to play with their school friends."

The light in the garden darkened. Nico looked up at the sky. The clouds were now one dark blanket. OneWag sniffed the air. He hated getting wet.

"Clara did have a crush on Tommaso," Gianna said. "They spent quite a bit of time together. They are close in age. I thought maybe they would . . ." She shook her head and didn't finish.

"It's going to rain any minute." Nico stood up. OneWag scampered quickly out of the gate. "It's time I stopped bothering you."

A high pitched "oh" came out of Gianna. She jumped up. "No bother at all. We enjoy visitors, even if the reason is a sad one, don't we, Federico?"

"Of course."

"Thank you for being so helpful."

"You're welcome." Still seated, Federico held out his hand.

Nico shook it and as he walked away, big raindrops clattered onto the roof of the car. OneWag barked a protest. Nico didn't hear him. He was pondering the Rosatis. He had the distinct impression he'd been lied to, but he couldn't pinpoint what moment, what phrase had given him that impression. At least he had a new lead: Claudio Nardi.

By the time Nico opened the car door, he and OneWag were soaked. The dog made sure to vigorously shake off a lot of the water onto Nico.

NELLI WAS BENT OVER a table, drawing intersecting swoops of graphite on a roll of rice paper when OneWag rushed into the studio, trailing raindrops.

"Oh, you poor thing." Nelli reached for the large shirt she

wore when painting and rubbed the dog down. OneWag licked her hand.

"What about me?" Nico asked as he stepped inside the small room and closed the door behind him.

"You're a big boy." Nelli threw him one of the rags she used to clean her brushes.

"Thanks." Nico caught it, sat down on the only chair in the small room and smelled the rag for turpentine.

"It's clean." Behind Nelli, water streamed down the one window, softening the view of the yard beyond. She picked up her pencil again as OneWag curled himself down next to her feet. "Where do the two of you come from in this weather?"

Nico wiped his face and hair with the rag. "The Rosatis'. Odd couple."

Nelli started slowly adding swoops to the rice paper. "Gianna likes to play the devoted and ditzy mamma, that was Nora's opinion of her, at least the one she gave me. She thought it was an act."

"Nora discussed the Rosatis with you?"

"Yes, while I was painting the girls. That's at least eighteen years ago. Gianna would come over and watch me paint, something I don't like. It interferes with my concentration. I had to get Nora to stop her from coming. After my painting session Nora would offer me lunch, just the two of us."

"No lunch for the girls?"

"The housekeeper would feed them in the kitchen. Nora claimed she wanted grown-up talk with me. I suspect she was a terrible mother and from what she said about Gianna, not a very good friend."

"Did she say anything about Federico Rosati?"

"I remember only one time. He'd come by with a case of wine from the vineyard he managed. After he left, she remarked that he was a sad, dull, deluded man. She let him play bridge with her and Gianna out of pity."

"Eighteen years ago, and you remember the words?"

Nelli put her pencil down. "I've worked hard to remember. I knew you didn't want me to get involved, but I was and am involved. I've been with this family. I was hoping to remember something that might help you."

"You're helping me right now and I apologize for trying to shut you out."

"Shutting women out is a male genetic flaw. It's okay since I didn't listen."

Nico chuckled. "What are you working on?"

"I'll tell you later. What did they say about Stefano?"

"When I asked how long he'd been here, Federico got upset. '*I hope you're not thinking my son is involved,*' etcetera."

"Are you thinking he could be involved?"

"I'm just trying to dot all the *i*'s that come up. Here's something that puzzles me. Federico insisted Gianna tell me Fabio had implied that her husband was playing around."

"How sweet of Fabio. There's a man who thinks he's God's gift to the world. Adriana should be the one to worry. Fabio groped me when I was painting his son. I squirted cadmium red on his white shirt and told him that if he tried that again I'd tell Adriana. He backed off like a frightened turtle."

"Good for you."

"I agree. I'd guess that Federico was only trying to disparage Fabio, maybe even hinting he could be Nora's killer. I wouldn't be surprised if he's the one, but my opinion is strongly colored by the weight of his hands on my body." Nelli took a step back to examine her drawing.

Nico stood up to look. He saw a jumble of dark lines curving in various directions. "What is that?"

"An outline of vine leaves. This morning my boss at Querciabella commissioned me to do a mural for the wineshop."

"Congratulations." He leaned over the table and kissed the

top of her bent head. OneWag stretched up to her thigh and nudged her elbow.

Nelli looked at both of them with a proud smile. "Thank you, both. I'll celebrate tonight."

"I'm sorry," Nico said after a loud sigh. "I'm taking our key witness and possible suspect out to dinner."

"I know. The elegant Signorina Barron. Laura told me. She and I are going off to Radda for pizza. You and I will celebrate another time. Now I need to concentrate." She went back to studying her drawing.

Nico kissed the top of her head again. "I'll miss you." Nelli was lost in her drawing. Nico looked down at OneWag. "Come on, buster."

The dog curled himself back down at Nelli's feet.

"Let's go. It stopped raining."

OneWag curled himself tighter.

"You go." Nelli didn't look up. "Rocco stays with me. He loves pizza."

"Ciao, then."

Nelli was too immersed in her work to answer.

Nico felt rebuffed, which he decided, while walking back to the car, was dumb. What he needed was a hot shower and dry clothes.

AFTER ARRIVING AT THE hotel ten minutes early, Nico parked his small Fiat and called Perillo to fill him in on what he'd gleaned from the Rosatis. "They did know Stefano was here."

"Hm. Gianna didn't want me to know that. Maybe I will have a chat with him. What else?"

Nico told him about Fabio's nasty comment to Gianna.

"Federico, having an affair?" Perillo sounded skeptical.

"That was Fabio's implication."

"Who with? His old friend and neighbor?"

"Maybe." Nico looked at his watch. He suspected that Miss Barron prized punctuality and tonight he needed to be on her good side. He had another five minutes.

"Lapo did get kicked out of Nora's bed five years ago," Perillo said. "Then clean sheets for a long while."

"She could have chosen someone else's bed."

"True enough. Lapo mentioned she had done some traveling. Two years ago she takes her lover back into her bed. If it is Federico that could give Gianna a motive."

"Let's remember that Fabio could be lying. Thanks to Gianna we have someone else to look into—Nora's old sweetheart, Claudio Nardi. He owns a restaurant in Gaiole."

"Let's go for lunch tomorrow."

"I can't. Sotto Il Fico is fully booked for lunch tomorrow. I have to help."

"What about tonight?"

I'm out with Miss Barron tonight. We can go to Gaiole during my break."

"That's too far from now." Perillo's sigh came through clearly. "Tilde has to understand you are part of the investigation. I know Tilde pays you, and if I could, I would, but please hook your apron on a nail for a while. I don't know which way to turn."

"I'll talk to Tilde. Any news on the jewelry?"

"None. Whoever stole it is holding on to it. Tarani is talking to Clara's bank about the collateral agreement Nora supposedly signed."

"Good. I have to go."

"So do I. Ivana just got back from work. Don't let la signorina's charm cloud your judgment. She's still on top of the list."

"Your list. Not mine."

"Her fingerprints were found in Nora's bedroom."

"On the curtain cord?"

"Unfortunately, the material is too rough to pick up any readable fingerprints. Ciao."

Nico clicked off. Even if Miss Barron's fingerprints had been on the cord, he would still have a hard time believing she killed Nora. What motive could there be?

MISS BARRON GREETED HIM at the entrance to the patio in the rear of the hotel. "Good evening, Mr. Doyle."

"Buonasera, Miss Barron." She was beautifully dressed in impeccably ironed beige wide-leg linen pants and a coffee-brown linen top. Soft graying curls framed her lightly made-up face, making her look years younger than fifty-two. A deep green shawl covered her shoulders. Nico wanted to compliment her but held back. He was there as an investigator, not a date.

"I hope you don't mind if we eat under the sky. The rain has mercifully stopped. The sun has reappeared. The staff has wiped the tables and chairs dry. It is so much lovelier here." She gestured at the deep-pink azaleas surrounding the patio.

"I couldn't agree more." Nico felt a pang of guilt. Now that the weather had changed Tilde and Alba would have their hands full at Sotto Il Fico.

Miss Barron hooked her arm in Nico's and together they walked out onto the patio. "I hope you don't mind. It's been years since I've felt the warmth of a man's arm. Don't worry. I am perfectly aware of why you are here. You want information that will help find Nora's killer, and I will give you the little I know as best I can."

"I have a job to do," Nico said as an apology.

"And Nora deserves justice despite not being just in life." Miss Barron stopped at a table next to an azalea bush at one end of the patio, far from the other diners. Nico pushed back a chair. Miss Barron sat down.

A waiter rushed over, placed two glasses of prosecco on the table and greeted Miss Barron with a wide smile.

"Bona sehra, Leo," she answered. "Grahzye."

Leo offered them menus, filled their water glasses and walked to another table.

Miss Barron picked up her menu. "The chef here makes a wonderful veal stew with garlic, tomatoes and red wine. I highly recommend it. That's what I fancy tonight."

"I'll join you."

"Should we share an antipasto plate?"

"Good idea. What wine would you like?"

Miss Barron fingered the stem of her prosecco flute. "This will be enough. I need to keep my wits about me." She gave a coy laugh. "A wrong answer and I might get arrested."

"Only if you confess."

"I can only confess to killing the weeds in my garden—and the occasional pesky fly." She raised her prosecco flute. "Cin cin?"

Nico clicked his glass against hers. This was a novel way to start an interrogation. Was she softening him up? Not that she needed to. He was already partial.

"Fire away, Mr. Doyle."

"Tell me more about how your friendship with Nora started. You said you met on a train from Bath to London?"

"Yes. As I believe I already told you, she was sitting across from me. I was happily lost in my mystery book when she interrupted me by asking what I was reading. I thought that was a bit rude of her, but I did catch her slight accent and I answered her. Foreigners have their own code of manners."

"When was this?"

"Four years ago, February. I was going to London to hear a new opera, *A Winter's Tale*. I showed her the cover of my book, Nora introduced herself, said she'd come to Bath to see the Roman ruins. She then wanted to know if I worked, was I married, had I always lived in Bath, why was I going to London."

Leo appeared. "Cosa desiderate mangiare stasera?"

Nico gave him their order, adding a glass of Panzanello Riserva for himself.

Miss Barron waited for Leo to be out of hearing before resuming. "A complete stranger's being so curious about me was odd, but she had such a sad and hungry face, I answered her. She thanked me and started telling me about herself. Widow, reluctant mother, owner of an old villa. She took out her phone and showed me a picture of her home, the land surrounding it, the hills covered with vineyards. It looked like a dreamland to me. '*Come in the summer*,' she said. '*Chianti will nourish your heart.*' How right she was."

"Did you come here the following summer?"

"Yes and have happily been back every summer since."

"Do you still feel it's a dreamland after what you've been through?"

"Yes, I do. I've been through difficult times, so have you from what Beppe has told me. Laura too. He was telling the truth, wasn't he?"

"Yes. I lost my wife. As for what Beppe told you about Laura, you'll need to ask her."

"I have. I was here when it happened."

"Can I ask about your difficult times?"

"You may. When I was forty, I finally met a man with whom I fell deeply in love. We were very happy together for seven beautiful years, but then I lost him."

"He died?" Nico asked.

"Yes, he did and I buffered my heart with expensive clothes, a habit I can't seem to lose."

"You wear them well."

"Thank you. Luckily I have the money for it." She turned

to watch Leo lower a large wooden cutting board covered with slices of mortadella, prosciutto, various salami, crostini, grilled red peppers and eggplant. "Perfect timing, Leo."

The waiter set down Nico's wine glass with a puzzled look on his face. Nico translated.

Leo bent his head. "Grazie."

"This is enough food for six people," Nico said.

"I suspect this is Laura's doing. She thinks I'm much too thin."

They both helped themselves.

"What do you think of Nora's daughters?" Nico asked after they had eaten a few slices.

"I've only been with them a few times. They never stayed long, and I got the feeling they didn't appreciate my presence. Last summer Clara asked me if her mother had shown me her jewelry. The only jewelry I had seen was painted on a canvas." Miss Barron speared half of a glistening charred red pepper and placed it on her plate. "She must have worried I might run away with it." She looked at Nico. "This visit Nora did tell me where she kept it. I didn't steal it, in case you were thinking of asking me again."

"I wasn't going to."

"Good." She cut the half into quarters and ate them with a satisfied smile.

Nico ate in silence, waiting for her to continue.

Miss Barron put her fork down on the plate. "I suppose a difficult mother usually produces difficult children. I think Nora's daughters both disliked her. Adriana lets it show. Clara is more devious. In Adriana's presence she was very loving to Nora, but without her sister around, she was cold with Nora, annoyed, dismissive. Of the two, she'd be the one I wouldn't trust."

Miss Barron certainly has strong opinions, Nico thought. Did those opinions reflect the truth or was she trying to shift suspicion off herself? He hoped the former. "Do you think Clara is capable of murdering her mother?" he asked.

"Why not? There was no love in that family. I think both daughters are capable of it. Probably we all are if pushed hard enough." She took a sip of her prosecco. "Pushed hard enough by greed, by a long ago hurt or love that has turned into hate." Her tone was light, impersonal. "The road leading to murder can be miles long or just steps away."

"You left out revenge."

"Did I? Maybe revenge should be on top of the list." She drank the last drops of prosecco. "It must feel deliciously satisfying to feel avenged of a wrong, perceived or not, don't you think so?"

"I don't know. It's a feeling I don't think I've ever had." When he'd finally hit his violent drunk father after years of his beating his wife and son, he had felt only sadness and shame. His father had left them soon after.

"Eccomi," Leo said as he approached the table with their entrees. Nico tucked thoughts of his father away and welcomed the waiter's arrival. A busboy preceded him and quickly cleared the antipasti plates. Once Leo had served them, wished them "Buon appetito" and walked away, Nico asked, "Did Nora talk to you about her daughters?"

Miss Barron inhaled the tantalizing smell of the veal spezzatino, which had been served on a thick slice of garlic-brushed toast. "You are relentless with your questions, Mr. Doyle. Do enjoy what has been placed before you."

Nico looked down on the glistening dish dotted with basil leaves. Leo had placed a side dish of roasted asparagus next to it. "I apologize. This dish does merit attention."

"I'm glad you agree."

They ate in silence, with Nico pausing only to drink some wine.

When Miss Barron's dish was half empty, she pressed her napkin to her mouth and finally answered Nico's question. "She did complain about the men they had chosen. She thought both Fabio and Clara's young men were only after the Lamberti money and the Salviati prestige. I thought Marco seemed rather sweet, clearly adoring Clara." She went back to her spezzatino. When she had finished, she placed her knife and fork at five o'clock on the plate and sat back.

Nico had also finished, both his plates barely showing signs of having had anything on them. Tomorrow he would add twenty minutes to his run.

"Now, that was enjoyable, wasn't it, Mr. Doyle?"

The busboy removed the plates and left them a dessert menu. Miss Barron pushed it to one side. "Next?"

Nico laughed. "I am relentless, aren't I?"

"We'll celebrate the end of the questions with a scrumptious dessert."

"You've already told me you met the Rosatis briefly when you arrived. Did Nora say anything about them after they left?"

"I was the curious one. She explained she'd known Federico since she was a child. His is an intriguing story. Do you know it?"

"I know two different versions. Tell me the one Nora gave you."

"Federico's father worked for Nora's father as his vineyard manager. When Nora's mother died, her father seems to have gone mad with grief, accusing his manager of having been his dead wife's lover. He fired him and had the vineyard destroyed. Federico's father then hung himself on one of the oak trees on the property."

"That's a third version of the story," Nico said.

"Which one is the true one, do you think? Or does the truth matter in this case?"

"It depends on what effect each version has had on whoever was left behind."

"Surely not a good one for the Rosatis. Nora thought Gianna was a stupid woman who happened to play bridge well and her husband thought far too much of himself."

"Nora doesn't sound like a very pleasant woman and earlier you said she wasn't just in life."

"She wasn't."

Nico caught her eyeing the dessert menu without moving her head. He had one last question. "If she wasn't pleasant, why were you friends with her?"

"I believe I've said it before. She was an intriguing woman. I had never met anyone like her. She was unpleasant to me a few times, but once I protested, she looked at me in surprise and asked me why I was upset. She had no idea of the power of her words or actions. She simply said and did what she felt like saying and doing, without any idea of the consequences."

"You don't think that could have been just an act?" *And was Miss Barron telling the truth about her friendship with Nora?* Nico wondered.

"I don't think so, but then I would have had to study years of psychology to determine whether it was an act or not. It's only my opinion."

"Which is what I wanted. Thank you. No more questions."

"Good." Miss Barron straightened her back, drank some water and picked up the dessert menu. "Now what shall we have?"

Nico was stuffed. "Nothing for me."

"No, you owe me a watch fob. We'll share. Fried apples with vanilla gelato. Will I ever get it back?"

"Tomorrow. The family has agreed to let you keep it."

Miss Barron clapped her hands. "Double gelato then."

Nico smiled at her, despite wondering what her answers had left out.

AS SOON AS IVANA got home, loaded down by two full bags of groceries, the smell of onions caramelizing made her rush to the kitchen. What she saw stopped her in the doorway. The table was set for dinner. The small glass vase she kept in the bedroom now stood in the center holding a small bunch of anemones. Her husband, wearing her checked apron, was standing next to the stove beating eggs. A skillet filled with sliced onions was on the stove over low flames.

"Salva, what happened?" she asked.

Perillo stopped beating and looked at his wife. She was wearing what she called her work outfit. A woman who had always dressed in well-pressed skirts, tailored tops and small heeled pumps now wore sneakers, slacks, an old knit top and a denim jacket she had bought at the Saturday market. There was a dusting of flour on the jacket and on the sneakers. He'd expected to see a tired woman, but her face brimmed with energy and surprise. With time her figure had broadened, and her face was no longer as smooth as new soap, but to him she was as beautiful as the first time he saw her.

"What happened?" she repeated.

Perillo smiled. "Nothing. How was work?"

"Don't tell me nothing. The only time you stand anywhere near that stove is to fill the moka in the morning or to taste what I'm cooking." Ivana dropped the grocery bags on the counter, pulled out a chair and sat down. "So tell me. You solved the murder?"

"I did not. I wanted to surprise you. You work hard now."

Ivana eyed Perillo with twist of her head. "I believe I worked hard before."

"I know. I know. I'm sorry." He leaned the egg-wet fork against the rim of the bowl of eggs, gave the onions a turn around with a wooden spoon and sat down next to his wife. "I pay attention to what you say, don't I?"

"Most of the time. Why are you asking?"

"Have I been a good husband?"

Ivana patted Perillo's hand. He looked so dejected.

"I'm still here, aren't I?" She sniffed. "I think your onions are done. I bought some spinach at the Coop. Do you want to add that to the frittata?"

"Thanks." Perillo reached over to the stove and turned off the burner. "What would I do without you? I'd be lost."

His sincerity struck her, made her feel uncomfortable. "No, you'd be fine, Salva. What's wrong? Do you think I went to work because I'm unhappy with you? I'm not at all. Housework got boring."

"It's not your job. It's the people involved with this murder that started me reflecting on what kind of husband I've been."

Relieved her work wasn't the main culprit, Ivana took the spinach out of her grocery bag and walked to the sink. "Tell me about these people."

"You don't want me to bring a murder case inside our home."

"You're right. Mamma taught me that a home should be an oasis. The ugly things that happen outside should stay outside." Ivana filled the sink with water and plunged the spinach inside. While she swished the spinach, she turned to look at Perillo. "Now I think I've been unfair all these years. I'm the one who should have been listening to your worries. Who knows?" She lifted her shoulders with a smile. "A female point of view might have helped you." She released the water, refilled the sink. "So talk to me about Nora Salviati and the people around her." At the bakery, Carletta kept gossiping about the dead woman and her stolen jewelry. Her incessant chatter had reminded Ivana of the birds in the park waking her up at dawn.

"Let me," Perillo said as he stood up and took his wife's place at the sink. She put the rest of the groceries in their proper place and sat back down.

While Perillo added the shaken-dry spinach to the hot onions and mixed the two until the spinach had wilted, he told Ivana about Nora's sumptuous villa and the land she had inherited along with a lot of money and precious jewelry, now stolen. How she had planned to sell the jewelry to help Syrian refugees, how she had sold the villa and the land from under her daughters' noses. "There were and are only bad feelings in that family. No love whatsoever that I could see."

"Is that what got you worried about us?" Ivana said, watching Perillo's movements. He'd never cooked an omelette.

"It got me wondering what kind of person I am."

"The best." She stood up and clasped her husband's hand. "You're just frustrated because you haven't found the culprit yet. And I'm tired from work. Let's get some rest. The omelette can wait."

Perillo hugged Ivana. "You're the one who's the best."

DANIELE WAS HALFWAY THROUGH his margherita pizza when his cell phone rang. He swallowed quickly and swiped. "Ciao, Stella. I was going to call you later."

"I'm going out to eat with a friend in a few minutes."

What friend? Daniele's heartbeat picked up speed. "You're still coming on Saturday, aren't you?"

"Yes. I need to talk to my parents about something."

Dani swallowed and said, "I also need to talk to you."

"Fine. Dinner at Oltre il Giardino in Panzano? It will be my treat."

"Stella, I'll have dinner wherever you want, but I will pay." He was going to pour his heart out to her finally. If his courage held up. No, he had to. Even at the risk of losing her friendship. Loving her and not knowing how she felt about him had become unbearable.

"Since I also have something to tell you," Stella said, "we'll argue about who feels like paying when the bill shows up."

Daniele's stomach clenched. "Why not tell me now or when you come home later? I'll be up."

"It's not something I want to tell you over the phone. I'll take care of the reservation. Eight o'clock?"

"Eight it is." After he clicked off, Daniele threw the rest of his pizza in the garbage can. He'd completely lost his appetite.

NICO OPENED THE FRONT door and was happy to hear the radio playing and to see the bedroom light on. Nelli had come to spend the night. "Ciao, Nelli. I'm so glad you're here." OneWag, stretched out on the sofa, lifted his tail once in greeting. "Hey, buddy." Dropping his keys on the table, Nico walked toward the bedroom and saw that Nelli wasn't in bed. *Of course not. It's only nine-thirty. She's in the bathroom.*

He sat down on one of the table chairs to take off the uncomfortable lace-up shoes he'd worn for Miss Barron's sake. As he bent down, his elbow nudged a piece of paper, which fell to the floor. Once the shoes were off, he picked it up.

I hope you won't mind my raising your electric bill, but I didn't want to leave Rocco in dark silence. Too scary. I hope you had a good time with Miss Barron. I'm off to work early tomorrow morning so it's just you and Gogol for breakfast. Make sure he's all right, please, and please excuse old-fashioned note. Forgot phone in the studio. Buonanotte. Baci

Nico sat back in the chair with slumped shoulders. The note floated back to the floor.

OneWag, sensing a change in the weather of the room, jumped off the sofa, padded over to Nico's socked feet and looked up at his boss.

Nico, with an ache in his chest, ruffled the silky fur on

OneWag's head. "It's just us tonight, buddy." He picked up the dog and sat him on his lap. "What do you say we ask her to stay with us? Day and night?"

OneWag licked Nico's chin. Nico took it as a yes. Nelli's yes was going to be far less certain.

TEN

Aldo Ferri called out, "Buongiorno!" as Nico went past the Ferriello vineyard on his daily run. The small stone farm-house Nico rented from Aldo was just two kilometers west.

Nico stopped and raised a hand to indicate *let me catch my breath*, then, breath restored, walked over to where Aldo was standing next to a big metal contraption. "Ciao, Aldo, what are you doing up so early in the morning?" The sun was just edging over the hills in the distance, dressing them in a pale glow.

Aldo, wearing jeans and his usual burgundy Ferriello T-shirt that barely made it over his large stomach, grinned and tapped the metal contraption. "I had to greet our new bottling machine. She's an expensive beauty, but she'll earn her keep. After twenty-two years the old one finally broke down. Come and have dinner with us tonight to celebrate the new arrival. Nelli and Rocco too, of course."

Nico wiped his forehead with the back of his hand. "Thanks, but I'm busy tonight." Off to Gaiole with Perillo and Dani. After a lot of muttering, Tilde had agreed to let him go.

"Nelli and the dog are welcome without you. I have a couple of sausages left over from last night's grilling that Rocco will heartily appreciate. How's the murder investigation going?"

"We're working on it. Did you know Nora Salviati?"

"Not personally. My mother knew her father, Edoardo. He had an extremely successful vineyard. I remember her crying when she found out he had destroyed every vine shortly after his wife died. This was forty years or so ago. I was just a kid then and started crying with her. I'd never seen Mamma cry before."

"Do you know Federico Rosati?"

"Yes. He's the accounts manager at the Tre Cipressi vineyard. A dour, conceited man, if you'll excuse my frankness."

To Nico, Rosati had come across as a stiff and sad man. "His father managed the Salviati vineyard. Federico told me the vineyard was destroyed to stop the spread of some terrible aphid, phyllox something."

Aldo shook his head. "That can't be true. We would have known about it. The phylloxera aphid is deadly and spreads very quickly. It almost destroyed the wine business in Europe back in the nineteenth century. I've studied the history of wine-growing in Chianti going back a hundred years. There is no mention of phylloxera aphid attacking any of our vineyards."

Nico started jogging in place to stop his legs from cramping. "Odd he would lie about it."

"It's a wild lie. Didn't his father kill himself?"

"He did. According to Rosati, his father blamed himself for having to destroy the vineyard."

Aldo stroked his belly with a satisfied look. "Reason for the lie resolved. Your father killing himself over a dreaded vine disease he didn't catch in time is better than your father killing himself for reasons you were too young to understand."

"You could be right. Rosati's son is here from South Africa where he has a vineyard. He's going around trying to interest the local vintners in growing a South African grape. Has he approached you?"

"Yes, Pinotage. Stefano is coming over at three o'clock. Come over if you want to meet him."

"Perillo might."

Aldo jerked his head back. "Stefano's not a suspect, is he?"

"No, but he grew up with Nora Salviati's daughters and might know something helpful."

Aldo relaxed. "Well, good luck. I must get to work. Ask Nelli to let Cinzia know if she's coming. Eight o'clock. You too. Tilde can let you go for one night." Aldo headed toward the Wine Center, waving goodbye.

Nico followed him. "Wait, Aldo, have you ever eaten at Il Cestino in Gaiole?"

Aldo turned around. "More than once. Small space, but excellent food, and a very welcoming owner. If you go, order the risotto dell'orto served in an emptied parmigiano crust."

"Thanks, Aldo. I'll tell Nelli about tonight. Ciao." Nico spun around and ran home to shower and change.

"THERE'S NO NEWS ON the jewelry," Daniele said as soon as a uniformed Perillo walked into the office with an unusual morning smile on his face.

Perillo stopped midstep and raised his arms as if to defend himself. "What happened? You swallowed your '*Buongiorno, Maresciallo*' with your breakfast? If you need to report something first thing, let it be today's weather."

Daniele stood at attention. "I'm sorry, Maresciallo. Buongiorno, Maresciallo."

"Buongiorno to you too, Dani. Now you can drop the maresciallo. My knee is telling me it's going to be a very nice day." Perillo sat down. "You were telling me what?"

"Jewelers and pawnshops haven't seen anything that resembles the list we sent them."

"I find it hard to believe there are no photos of the actual jewelry, don't you?"

"Yes. It makes it much harder to find. I wonder . . ." Daniele hesitated, not sure how the maresciallo would react.

Perillo wished Daniele would regain the courage his friend-ship with Stella had given him in the past year. Lately he'd reverted to being the obedient brigadiere. "Go on, Dani."

"I wonder if the thief has no intention of selling the jewelry."

"Because it was taken to cover up the real motive for the murder? I thought that at first after Fabio Meloni immediately assumed something had been stolen."

"You've changed your mind?"

"Let's say I'm not convinced. Nora removed the jewelry from the safe in her bedroom to the shed about a month ago. Why did she do that?"

"To make it easy to steal it?"

"She told her family about the move. Even Lapo and Cecco knew."

"She trusted them, Maresciallo."

"I wonder if she was tempting someone."

"Who?"

"Marco Zanelli. A month ago Nora found out about his engagement to Clara. She was very much against it. Being a snob, she considered him too low-class for Clara."

"You think she was hoping Marco would steal so Clara would break the engagement?"

"It is possible."

Daniele's face paled. "That's terrible."

"Yes, it is. I will ask Nico what he thinks. And now we are off to Panzano to visit the hardware store."

Daniele had looked into Massimo Vitale, known as Max. At fifty-two he was seventeen years older than Marta. *Too old*, Daniele had thought immediately. He had a clean record, not even a parking ticket. He was the sole employee of the store and had worked there for fifteen years. A good citizen, then. Daniele thought the man should be spared an unasked-for visit by the carabinieri.

"What could Max Vitale know?" Daniele dared to ask. The image of Marta holding Celestina had moved him.

"That's what we need to find out, Dani. If we determine he knows nothing, I'll cross him off the list. Let's go."

A muted "O Sole Mio" rang out as they walked out of the station. Perillo reached into his pocket and answered. "Three o'clock. Thanks. We'll be there."

NICO STUDIED GOGOL'S FACE. Some color had come back to his cheeks. His eyes had lost their dullness. "I'm glad you're feeling better. Nelli was worried and so was I." Nico clasped Gogol's free hand. The other held what was left of his second ciambella. The crostini had been eaten before Nico got to the café. "You mean a lot to both of us."

Gogol bowed his head. "The caring you show has grown my confidence like the sun that opens the rose. My Dante adaptation to this heartfelt moment."

"Well, keep blooming, Gogol." Nico got his phone out and texted Nelli. Private phone calls were frowned upon at Querciabella.

GOGOL LOOKS HEALTHY. CALL ME ON YOUR LUNCH BREAK. ALDO INVITED YOU AND ONEWAG FOR DINNER TONIGHT AT 8. CINZIA NEEDS TO KNOW. I'M OUT WITH PERILLO AND DANI. TWO NIGHTS IN A ROW. FORGIVE ME. ONEWAG AND I MISSED YOU LAST NIGHT.

Nico slipped the phone back into his pocket and went over to the counter to pay for their brief breakfast. "Getting any closer to a solution?" Sandro asked in a low voice. Nearby four locals were having their espressos and discussing the upcoming soccer matches. Nico answered Sandro with a shake of his head and paid.

As soon as Nico stepped away, OneWag nudged Gogol's knee with his head, his eyes fixed on the piece of ciambella in the old man's hand.

Gogol's chest started shaking with silent laughter. "'What good is it to bash your head against the fates?' The fates decree that this last piece of sweetness is mine." He popped the ciambella in his mouth.

Nico walked back to the table. "Come on, buddy, we're off. See you tomorrow, Gogol."

"Tomorrow."

Nico turned away and walked to the front door, not wanting to show his surprise. It was the first time in the two years they'd breakfasted together that his "See you tomorrow" wasn't followed by Gogol's "If I live." Nico wasn't sure if that was a good thing or not.

DANIELE WAS RELIEVED THERE were no customers when he followed Perillo into the hardware store. A hefty man with a round face, thin lips, deep-set eyes and a wide bald spot on top of his head stood behind the counter. He greeted them with a smile and a "Buongiorno," surprising Daniele. When in uniform, he was used to being met with questioning faces or slight frowns.

"Buongiorno," Perillo said. "Are you Max Vitale, by any chance?"

"I am. Marta said you might come by." The smile remained. It was his only attractive feature, Daniele decided. "I'm not sure I can be of any help to you. I'm sorry Signora Nora met such an ugly death, but I am glad Marta will stay home now. I asked her to quit countless times, but she liked working in such a beautiful place. I admit that didn't make me feel good. I will never be able to afford more than what we have now."

"You have a very nice home," Daniele said. He would happily live in a similar home with Stella. And he liked the store.

The large window let a great deal of light come in. The stock was neatly displayed on shelves or gathered in small drawers with handwritten labels. Behind him, there was a second room that he had seen before entering, filled with all sizes of olive wood bowls, salad spoons and painted dishes that would appeal to tourists.

Perillo leaned his forearms on the counter. "Did Marta ever take you inside the villa?"

Max chuckled. "Oh, no. I asked her countless times. I was curious. She wouldn't, claiming Signora Nora would be angry, but I think Marta wanted the place to be her private castle. Marta can be very childish at times and always stubborn."

Daniele heard the affection in Max's voice and reconsidered his bad opinion of the man.

"So you never saw the inside of the place?" Perillo asked with the tone of a man just asking for curiosity's sake.

"Oh, I did. Only once, but I'll never forget it."

Perillo withdrew his forearms from the counter. Daniele quickly took his notebook and pen out of his pocket.

"Incredible, don't you think, Maresciallo?" Max asked. "I felt like I'd walked back two hundred years."

"How did you get in?"

"Years ago, a man came in here to buy a whole new set of dishes and some pots and pans. Usually, it's the women who buy those. I was curious and so helped him select what he needed. We got to talking and he told me he was the villa's gardener. Ever since then, Lapo comes in here to buy nails or grommets, whatever. We've shared a few glasses of wine from time to time. When I found out where he worked, I asked him if he could show me around and he did."

"When was this?"

Max thought for a moment, lips puckered. "Oh, about four years ago. Signora Nora had gone to England again."

"What do you mean by *again*?"

"That's what Lapo said. He said she'd been traveling a lot. You'll have to ask him."

"Did Lapo have to unlock the security system?" *Max could have seen the combination.*

"No, the main door was open. The housekeeper must have been there. I could hear a vacuum cleaner working. Lapo just took me around the ground floor. He seemed angry the whole time we were in there. I thought he regretted taking me, but he said he was angry about something else."

"You went there only once?"

"Didn't need to go again. I wanted to know why Marta wouldn't quit the job when I asked her to. I saw the place; I understood and didn't ask her again."

A man in cutoff jeans and a sleeveless T-shirt opened the door, eyed the two carabinieri and with a frown asked, "Want me to come back, Max? I need a new handsaw."

Max aimed a questioning look at Perillo.

Perillo waved the man in. "We're leaving. Thanks for your time, Signor Vitale. I need you to come to the station to make and sign a statement." He omitted mentioning finger-printing and DNA swabbing in front of Max's customer.

As Daniele closed the store door behind him, he heard, "Are you in trouble, Max?" To his relief, Max's answer was a laugh.

NICO AND TILDE HAD just finished cleaning up the kitchen when Nico's phone rang. As he fumbled to retrieve it from underneath his apron, Tilde said, "I'll tell Enzo to wait."

"I'll be right there."

Having coffee together on the terrace was a ritual the three of them had as soon as the lunch service was over. While Elvira snoozed in her armchair, they would drop down on the chairs facing the view of the hills, prop their legs up on the balustrade and enjoy an after-hard-work espresso.

"Ciao," Nico said into the phone. "Are you angry with me?"

"No," Nelli answered. "Should I be?"

Nico clasped the phone tighter against his ear. He loved her low, soft voice. "When you didn't call at lunchtime, I thought you were upset I was taking time off from work tonight again for Perillo instead of for you."

"I'm sorry. I got your text and I should have answered, but I haven't had a second. A big shipment going out to America had to be labeled and boxed. Two of our men are out sick so I had to pitch in. Nico, listen to me, I am not a petulant or needy woman. Right now the murder investigation is far more important than the two of us dining together. Don't be so nervous about us."

"Will you come and sleep over tonight?"

"You'll probably be home before me. Aldo and Cinzia's dinners are long affairs. I'll call Cinzia now and accept. Enjoy your dinner in Gaiole. Don't wait up."

"I won't," he lied. "Have fun."

"Ciao, amore." Nelli clicked off.

Nico stood in the kitchen for a few minutes.

"Ehi, Nico," Tilde called out, "are you coming?"

"Yes." Nico untied his apron and walked out with a grin on his face.

Enzo noticed first. "This cat has swallowed the mouse. You have your killer?"

Tilde looked up from her empty coffee cup as Nico sat down. Seconds later she laughed and squeezed her husband's hand. "Oh, dearest Enzo, you've forgotten what it's like."

Nico's grin got wider.

PERILLO FOUND ALDO ON the vast covered terrace of the Ferriello Wine Center, sitting in front of a man who had to be Stefano Rosati. He was wearing an orange shirt with patches of stripes going in varied directions. Three wine glasses and three open bottles were on the table.

Aldo looked up and waved Perillo over. "Stefano, let me introduce you to Salvatore Perillo, our estimable maresciallo. Don't let his civilian clothes fool you. He's always on duty." Aldo hadn't completely forgiven Perillo for what he'd put him through last year.

Perillo had changed into jeans and a white shirt. "Not true. Always curious though." He reached the table and held out his hand.

Stefano stood up and shook it. "Stefano Rosati."

Not a bad-looking man, Perillo decided. His mother's angled face with the same narrow hazel eyes, but his deep tan rendered them remarkable. Long chestnut-colored hair tied in the back with a leather string. And that eye-popping shirt. Thirty-five years old, Daniele had said. Now that Perillo was close, he could see the black stitching on one shoulder: MVEMVE VEINI. "Am I interrupting?"

"No, I've done my pitch. Now I'm tasting Aldo's excellent wines."

"I'm trying to convince him to be my distributor down there," Aldo said. "With his own, he sells mine. No extra work needed."

Stefano laughed. "And risk my clients buying yours instead of mine? No, thank you. Maresciallo, why don't you join me. I have three different wines to taste."

Aldo pushed himself up from the table. "To taste, not drink. I'll bring more glasses."

"I know you talked to my parents on Wednesday," Stefano said. "I understand that you must investigate everyone connected to Nora, that's your job, but please go easy on them." Stefano sat back as Aldo placed a glass in front of Perillo and poured two fingers' worth of his regular Chianti Classico. "I'll let the two of you talk. I'll be inside."

Stefano poured himself the same amount of wine. "My parents are incapable of stealing, much less killing. I don't say that as a devoted son. I'm not devoted. I don't have much love for them. My mother clung so hard to us, she left us gasping for air. My father believes life can only be lived by following his rules."

"His father died by suicide."

"Yes, and he has made us pay for it. They are the reason I grow vines in South Africa and my brother has a technology company in San Francisco."

"And yet you're defending them."

Stefano took a long drink of wine. "They don't need defending. They are incapable of change, therefore they cannot have stolen anything or killed anyone."

The expression "The tunic does not make the monk" slipped into Perillo's head as he listened. Stefano's dispassionate voice was upending Perillo's first impression of him.

"Once we left, my mother devoted herself to two things. Growing flowers and bridge. Nora was the only bridge partner she wanted to play with. Why would she kill her or steal her jewelry? My parents don't need money. I send them enough." Stefano lifted his shoulders.

Perillo had been swirling the wine glass, watching the movement of the wine, listening. Stefano was convincing. "And your father?"

"He lives a life of unbreakable rules, ones that don't include theft or murder."

Perillo remembered what Clara had said about Stefano. "As children you and your brother must have played often with Clara and Adriana. You lived so close by."

"Oh, yes, we did. Every Sunday after church and almost every day during summer. I fell in love with Clara. She was prettier and more fun than her mopey sister. I kissed her once. She didn't like it. My father unfortunately saw me kissing her and that was the end of our playing with the Lamberti sisters."

"Your brother too?"

"He's two years older. Who knows what carnal sin he would have committed."

"How old were the two of you?"

"Eleven and thirteen. Hormones beginning to churn, parent horrified." Stefano checked his cell phone and frowned. "I'm sorry. I have to go. If you have questions you think I can answer, here, let me give you my number." He tore off a piece from the paper placemat under the bottles and jotted the number down.

"When I asked your mother if her sons were here, she didn't answer me."

"She was probably upset with me. I wasn't playing the devoted son and cradling her grief. I hope you find whoever killed Nora. She was Mamma's only friend. Arrivederci."

Interesting man, Perillo thought, taking a sip of Aldo's wine. What he'd said about his parents was sad, but he did care. He did a good job of defending them, but it didn't cross them off the suspect list. He took out his phone and texted Daniele.

SEE WHAT YOU CAN FIND OUT ABOUT STEFANO ROSATI'S WINE BUSINESS.

Stefano had let him know he had enough money to help his parents. Maybe he was telling the truth, but young men liked to boast.

ON THE DRIVE TO Gaiole, Daniele took out his notebook and filled Nico in on what he had learned about Claudio Nardi. "Fifty-five years old, born in Panzano, has a degree in classical studies from the University of Floreeee—" Daniele swayed toward the rear door, his seat belt nearly choking him as Perillo took one of the many *S* curves too quickly.

"Slow down," Nico said. He was in the suicide seat. "Dani and I want to get there with hearts still pumping."

Perillo slowed down a fraction.

Daniele went back to his notes. "His wife died eight years ago. No children. Lived in Florence until he stopped teaching four and a half years ago. He moved to Bologna and apprenticed at Osteria Bartolini. He moved to Gaiole two years ago. Il Cestino opened April of last year. Gambero Rosso gives it a good review."

"So does Tripadvisor." Nico didn't quite see the point of this visit. Daniele had reserved for seven o'clock, the restaurant's opening. Even so it was unlikely that Nardi would have the time or the desire to answer questions while serving dinner. "Is Ivana busy tonight?"

"Church bingo with pizza."

That explained it. "How are we approaching Nardi? You picked me up wearing civilian clothes, driving your own car and explaining 'don't want to give in the eye,' which I take to mean you don't want to be noticed."

"That is correct," Perillo said as the car swooped down into the town. "People get stiff around carabinieri. They immediately think something is wrong. We will improvise."

They walked by the huge metal black rooster, emblem of Chianti Classico wines, and entered the heart of the town, a long oblong piazza that had once been the marketplace. The treeless piazza was lined with cafés and their scruffy outside tables. Large terra-cotta pots filled with roses made the space festive. They walked in the shade—the day had been a hot one—but a retreating sun still dropped a now-softer light on half the piazza.

The restaurant was at the narrower far end.

"Elegant," Perillo commented as they reached it. Its

unoccupied outside tables were covered with linen place mats and long-stemmed glasses.

A well-built square-faced man with a thick mop of curly gray hair appeared at the entrance. He was wearing a white linen shirt over rumpled gray slacks and black Crocs. "Buonasera and welcome."

"Buonasera," Perillo said. "Donato, we reserved." Out of precaution he had used Daniele's last name.

The man gestured toward the tables on each side of the entrance. "Your choice of outside or inside tables. My next reservations aren't until seven-forty-five." He moved aside to let the three men enter Il Cestino-Vino e Cucina.

It was a small L-shaped room, with a tall counter in front of the back wall, behind which were shelves filled with wine bottles. At the far right was the opening to the kitchen. Nico could see the backs of two women, hair wrapped in scarves.

"I'd say inside," Perillo said. He chose a corner table near the window and sat down. Daniele and Nico sat on either side of him, facing the room. "You are the owner?" Perillo asked.

"Claudio Nardi, Maresciallo. I was expecting you."

Perillo's eyebrows shot up. Daniele bent his head to hide a smile. Nico enjoyed the moment with a blank face.

"I meant to come to the station, but I had no time."

Perillo sat taller in his chair, his composure regained. "You have something to tell me?"

"No, but I am sure you have questions. Before you start"— Nardi reached over toward the counter and picked up three menus and a wine list—"decide what you want to eat and drink first." He left them on the table and walked away.

The menus were printed on thick paper stock, the three pages held together by a silk ribbon. *Elegant indeed*, Nico thought, surprised the prices were affordable. He eyed what he wanted right away.

A few minutes later, Nardi came back with three flutes filled with prosecco. "I offer this to all my guests, Maresciallo. I don't want you to think I am trying to soften you."

"It would take much more than prosecco." Perillo parked a smile on his face to cover his annoyance at having been recognized.

Nardi smiled back. "What have you chosen?"

For starters Perillo and Daniele chose the lemon risotto. Nico got the farro salad, curious to test it against his own. Nico and Perillo picked lamb ribs scottadito, called *burns fingers* because they were meant to be eaten by hand. Daniele ordered dandelion greens in phyllo dough and melted pecorino.

Wishing Nelli were with him, Nico picked a 2016 bottle of Querciabella Riserva.

"You made good choices," Nardi said.

"They always say that," Perillo grumbled while Nardi gave their orders to the kitchen.

Two minutes later he was back and sat down in the empty chair facing Perillo, filled his flute with prosecco, took a sip and sat back. "Please introduce me to your team."

"Brigadiere Daniele Donato and New York homicide detective Nico Doyle."

"Ex-detective," Nico corrected. "Here to have a good meal."

"And to assess." Nardi's eyes met Perillo's. "What is it you wish to know?"

Daniele took out his phone.

"My brigadiere will record our conversation on his iPhone."

Daniele checked the charge—86 percent—and announced the time, place and people present.

Perillo straightened his back. "What was your relationship with Nora Salviati?"

"Nora and I were very much in love when we were young. We planned to elope, but Alberto Lamberti took advantage of her, and she became pregnant. I still wanted to marry her. I would have raised her child as my own, but she refused. She believed I would grow to hate her and her child, that I would think of her as soiled goods. She was the one who believed that, not I. She got married and I went away."

"When did you meet again?"

"She found me on Facebook two years ago."

Perillo raised his eyebrows at Daniele.

"I looked, Maresciallo. There was no social media on her computer."

"She erased her page immediately afterward," Nardi said. "She claimed she put herself on Facebook to look for me. I was in Bologna learning the restaurant business. She asked to be friends. I'd grown a thick rind around my heart by then, but I was curious and accepted. She would message. I would answer. We saw each other when I came back to Gaiole to start this restaurant. From having coffee together, to aperitivos, to dinners, we ended up in her bed. I became a regular late-night visitor to the villa once or twice a week. There was no love anymore. It was simply sex."

How sad, Daniele thought, his expression mirroring his thought.

Nardi read him. "Time brings change. Nora was still in love with someone else, and she was no longer the person I had loved years ago."

"When did you last see her?" Perillo asked.

"Ten days ago."

Daniele quickly calculated backward. "Tuesday." He didn't want the maresciallo to have to ask what day it was.

"Tuesday, of course," Perillo said.

"An English friend was coming to stay with her the next day, and I was not to show up again until the English guest left."

Perillo wet his mouth with some prosecco before asking. "How did you get in?"

Nardi reached into his shirt and pulled out a black cord with a key hanging from it. He pulled the cord over his head and handed it to Perillo.

A bell rang out from the kitchen.

Nardi stood up. "Your dinner is ready."

When Nardi stepped into the kitchen, Perillo turned to Daniele. "I was perfectly aware it was Tuesday, Dani."

"Of course, Maresciallo." He stopped recording.

Perillo sighed loudly to express his impatience with Daniele's stubbornness. "Salvatore, Dani. Salvatore amongst us. Maresciallo with others."

Daniele said nothing. His cheeks stayed pale—a victory.

"What do you think of Nardi's speech, Nico?" Perillo asked.

"It's a very smooth narrative."

"Am I missing something?"

"Later," Nico answered as Nardi walked back into the dining room with their first courses.

Nardi served them and left to greet a young, impeccably dressed Asian couple who had just walked in.

Perillo watched as Nardi showed the couple to a table at the far end. "Revelations over."

"You sound pleased." Nico started dressing his colorful salad. Italian restaurants assumed everyone knew how to dress a salad. Rita used to dress his. He'd asked for Ivana's help since he was ashamed to show his ignorance with Nelli. Ivana's formula was one part vinegar, three parts oil, and salt "to your pleasure."

Perillo knocked lightly on the Parmigiano-Reggiano crust holding the risotto. "I am happy with anticipation. Look at what I have before me, Nico. Behold the individual grains embraced by the melting butter and cheese, smell the tang of lemon."

"It does look good. Enjoy."

The food deserved the silence they fell into. Both courses

were worthy of four stars. The wine was good. Not the best, Nico thought, but he would never let Nelli know. More diners came in, keeping Nardi busy.

Perillo was biting into his last lamb rib when "O Sole Mio" rang out. "Madonna!" He flung his rib down on the plate, lifted himself to get his phone out of his tight pants pocket and clicked it off.

Daniele took the last bite and wiped his mouth. He wondered if Stella would have enjoyed the phyllo dough–wrapped dandelion greens as much as he had. Probably not. She was a meat eater.

Nico heard the music. "Vivaldi's ringing, Dani."

"Oh, sorry." Being slim, Daniele managed to get his phone out without having to lift himself up. He clasped it to his ear without checking who was calling.

"Yes, he's here." Daniele handed the phone to Perillo. "It's Dino."

"Yes, Dino? We're in the middle of dinner."

Daniele and Nico eyed each other. Whatever it was, it had to be something serious.

"Put him on."

"Maresciallo, you nee—"

"We're in Gaiole. It will take us an hour to get to the station. Okay, okay. We're coming. Let me talk to Dino." Seconds later he said, "Ask the boy if he wants anything. A drink, ice cream, whatever. Lapo too. We're leaving right now." Perillo clicked off and raised his hand to catch Nardi's attention.

"What happened?" Nico asked.

Daniele silently prayed they hadn't found another body.

Nardi walked over. "Would you like to see the dessert menu?"

"The check please," Perillo said. "We need to leave."

"I hope you will sample our excellent desserts when you come back."

"I'm afraid we will have to resume our conversation at the station. I expect you tomorrow morning at nine-thirty. Now the check."

"Since you are in a hurry," Nardi said, pulling their table back to give them more room, "I'll bring the check in the morning. That way you can be rest assured I will show up."

Nico slipped out first. "Call before you come in case the maresciallo has been called away." Lapo's bringing his son to the station sounded serious.

"Is Cecco all right?" Daniele asked the minute they stepped outside.

"Proud and excited, I would think," Perillo said, walking quickly down the piazza. "He just found a diamond bracelet."

CECCO WAS SITTING WITH his father on the bench next to the station entrance, dangling a plastic grocery bag between his legs. Dino sat behind the reception desk. All three stood up as Perillo walked in, followed by Daniele and Nico.

"Bravo, Cecco," Perillo announced. He was back in his arm-chair. Lapo and Cecco sat across the desk. Daniele was at his desk in the back, the tape recorder at his elbow. Nico sat to one side of Perillo. He was here only to listen.

Perillo pointed to the plastic bag Cecco was now clutching tight against his chest. "Is it in there?"

Cecco nodded vigorously. "It was covered with dirt, but I didn't wash it. The bag was dirty too, so I wrapped it with one of Babbo's handkerchiefs. A clean one. And I only touched the catch, I think."

"That was good thinking, Cecco."

"Thank you. I like American detective shows." He stole a glance at Nico.

Nico responded with a smile. That people he'd never met knew about him always surprised him.

"Daniele," Perillo called out, without turning.

Daniele pressed the record button on the old tape recorder and made his usual announcement.

"Ehi, wait a minute." Lapo half rose from his chair, his face flushed with anger. "Tape recorders get turned on for suspects. My son did nothing wrong. Turn it off!"

"Your son has a story to tell, has he not?" Perillo asked.

"Yes, I do, I do," Cecco said, with great eagerness, his eyes on Daniele. "It's all right, Babbo."

He trusts Daniele, Nico thought, just as Daniele stepped in. "Signor Lapo, it is vital that what Cecco wants to tell us be recorded correctly. He has made a very important discovery."

Cecco beamed, nodded. "It is! I might have to testify in court."

"Cecco!" Lapo warned.

"I might. It's not just about what I found, Babbo."

Lapo narrowed his eyes. "Tell the truth, Cecco. For Nora's sake."

"I don't lie anymore. I'm eighteen now."

A very young eighteen, Nico thought. Perillo had mentioned the boy had a health problem.

Cecco shifted his body to fully face Perillo. "Do you want to see the bracelet first or hear how I found it?"

"Let's start with the bracelet." He held out his hand and waited as Cecco slowly hooked the grocery bag over the maresciallo's fingers. He opened the bag, carefully lifted the handkerchief out, unknotted it, touching only the ends, and spread it open. A thin strand of diamonds embedded with dirt lay curled on the handkerchief. Perillo reached into his desk drawer and took out a copy of the Salviati jewelry list the insurance company had sent.

Nico leaned forward to try to see, but a fold of the handkerchief hid the bracelet. Daniele stepped closer to the desk, craning his neck. The maresciallo's back blocked the view.

The platinum bracelet with six cushion-cut diamonds was last on the list, insured for twenty-five thousand euros. Perillo crossed his arms, then finally took a step forward. This was far better than dessert. "Where did you find this?"

Cecco stopped jiggling in his chair. "It was buried in a big mound of dirt from the hole Babbo dug up to plant a tree. I was trying to see how far I could kick the soccer ball."

Lapo shook his head. "How many times have I . . ."

"I wasn't running," Cecco protested, "just kicking. Come on, that can't hurt me."

"You kicked the ball into the mound," Perillo said, his impatience barely veiled. "When did you do that?"

Cecco turned to Perillo, eyes bright with excitement. "The mound was my goal, Maresciallo."

"When?"

"Tonight, before dinner. I was about thirty meters away and I put my whole soul, heart and body into that kick." He threw back his head. "A perfect kick! The ball torpedoed straight into the center of the mound. I threw myself on the grass and rolled, I was so happy. When I lifted the ball out, my thumb hit something hard. I pushed some dirt away and there it was. Do you think they'll give me a reward?"

Lapo shook his head at his son.

"They should," Perillo said, not sure who to include in that *they*. Who put that bracelet in the mound, and why? It was the least-valuable item of the stolen lot.

Nico was asking himself the same questions. Daniele was praying there weren't going to be any more surprises before Monday.

Perillo reknotted the handkerchief around the bracelet and put it in his drawer, along with the insurance list. Cecco's discovery was confusing him. He turned his head sideways.

Nico looked back at him and understood. "Cecco, the mound of dirt was exactly where on the property?"

"Behind the shed."

"Did you see anyone go near it in the last few days?"

Cecco eyed his father.

"It's all right."

"Sometimes my legs get cramps in bed. It wakes me up and I have to take a walk to make them go away. Outside, not to wake Babbo. I like that the crickets go silent when I walk past them. It's like they respect me. This morning it was still dark. I started to walk up to the shed because I'd left the light on and wanted to turn it off before Babbo found out. He doesn't like me to forget things. The shed is not that far. I saw him."

Perillo took over. "Who did you see?"

"Signor Rosati. He walked in front of the windows."

"The shed has three long narrow windows," Lapo explained.

"Did he stop in front of any of them?" Perillo asked.

"No, just walked in front of them."

"How far away were you?"

"Halfway up the hill. Easy kicking distance."

"About twenty-five meters," Lapo said. "Cecco showed me."

Perillo fixed his eyes back on Lapo's son. "I realize you have young eyes, but that's a good distance. How can you be sure it was Signor Rosati?"

"Easy. He's really tall and he stoops when he walks. He was walking fast, but it was him."

"Have the two of you seen anyone else on the property?"

Cecco shook his head. "It's just us."

"Yesterday morning, Signorina Clara went back to Lucca," Lapo said. "Only for a few days. She wanted me to take extra care watching the villa. She gave the housekeeper time off, so now it's just Cecco and me."

Cecco made a face. "It's a lot of work."

"Not for much longer," Lapo reminded him, regret heavy in his voice. He turned toward Perillo, shifting his weight in the chair. "Maresciallo, it's late. Cecco has school tomorrow morning. He's told you everything he knows."

"I have for now," Cecco said. "I'm going to start searching the rest of the place tomorrow. I bet he's hidden stuff all over."

"You best leave that to the special search team." Perillo stood up and held out his hand. "Thank you for bringing the bracelet and answering all my questions."

Cecco stood up and pumped the maresciallo's hand a few times, his attention taken by Daniele announcing the end of the meeting.

Perillo tugged his hand back. "What you have told us has to stay in this room, you understand?"

Cecco zipped his fingers across his lips. "For Nora."

"You can trust him." Lapo put an arm around his son's shoulder. "Buonanotte."

Daniele walked down to the boy. "Have fun at school tomorrow."

Cecco scrunched up his face.

As Cecco walked by him, Nico said, "You might be surprised."

With a grin, Cecco pointed his finger at Nico. "Hold 'em up or I'll shoot!"

"That's enough," Lapo said. "Home."

The office door clicked shut behind them. Nico and Daniele joined Perillo at his desk. Nico unknotted Lapo's handkerchief and spread it out.

Daniele's eyes went wide. "How beautiful."

How many refugee mouths would it feed? Nico wondered.

"Take a photo, Dani," Perillo said, joining them in staring, "then lock it up in the safe."

Daniele hurried out of the room. Nico dropped down on Cecco's vacated chair. "Why get rid of the jewelry piecemeal?"

"Something or someone scared the thief, but I'm too tired

to think anything out. I need Tarani to put in a request to get the Salviati grounds searched, every plant, every clump of dirt upturned. Without the substitute prosecutor's approval my men can only search for drugs and weapons. What I can do is interrogate Rosati."

Daniele came back with the station's digital camera and took front and back photos, lifting the bracelet with gloved hands. He then rewrapped it.

"Is Miss Barron's watch fob in the safe?" Nico asked. "We need to give it back to her."

Daniele looked over at Perillo. "Take it out, Dani."

Waiting for Daniele to come back, Nico found his mind wandering away from the night's events. *Maybe Nelli will already be there when I get home. If not, I'll wait for her. There is no way I am going to fall asleep anytime soon.*

Perillo looked at his watch, a birthday gift from his adoptive father: 10:37. His cell phone showed the same. *His old Bulova still keeps perfect time. Ivana must be home by now, taking her nightly bath. I have never told her the perfumed soap she loves makes my nose itch.*

"Done," Daniele said, walking back in. He handed Nico the watch fob in an envelope.

Nico thanked him and pushed it into his pants pocket. "I'll give it to her tomorrow. Are you going to talk to Nardi in the morning?"

"No. The Rosatis are more important."

"There's something you should ask Nardi."

"What?"

"Ask him if he knows who Nora was in love with."

"Dani, make a note. I know I'll forget."

"I'll remember."

"That's right. You're young. Tomorrow . . ." Perillo put his hands down flat on the desk and closed his eyes.

Daniele held his breath. Tarani's nightly report would be a long one and he also had to look into Stefano's wine business. He was aching to go to his room and read over the many notes he'd taken for his talk with Stella.

"Yes, tomorrow," Perillo said slowly. He readjusted his stiff body on the armchair and opened his eyes. "I'll put in my request. Dani, Tarani's report can wait until morning."

Daniele's exhale was a quiet one.

"In the morning a visit to the Rosatis."

"Why not bring them in?" Daniele asked, not looking forward to lugging the heavy tape recorder.

"Because I prefer to be in their garden than here."

Nico laughed. "You can't be serious."

"I am. Dani and his iPhone got us our last killer. He can do it again." Perillo pointed his index finger at his brigadiere. "Make sure it's fully charged."

"Certainly, Salvatore," Daniele said, not hiding his relief. He'd bring the extra charger he'd bought to make sure he wouldn't miss a call from Stella afterward. Not that she called that often, but it was best to be prepared.

"I'd like you with me at this meeting, Nico."

"Tilde needs me and you don't. You'll tell me about it later."

"No, please come. I want them scared so they'll tell the truth. Your presence will help. Ten o'clock. Meet you there." Perillo stood up. "Buonanotte to you both."

ELEVEN

Perillo and Daniele sat in the Alfa with the four windows down. Daniele had parked the car some distance from the entrance to the Rosati home. The cypress-flanked road that led uphill to Villa Salviati was just ahead. The air was light and smelled of new leaves and blooming flowers.

"It is going to be a good day," Perillo declared. When he'd finally gone home last night, he'd found Ivana delighted with her twenty-euro win at bingo, which she'd immediately given to the parish priest, Don Alfonso. With his nose itching, Perillo had fallen asleep holding her hand. A sound sleep with no dreams. He felt invigorated, optimistic.

Daniele had slept badly. After writing the report, he'd only managed to doodle nonsense last night. "Thanks to Cecco's discovery, the investigation has taken a promising turn." He hoped it would all be over by lunchtime. Movement in his rearview mirror made him look up. Nico's red 500 was stopping behind them.

Perillo swung out of the car. Daniele followed.

"I'm sorry I'm late," Nico said. Knowing Perillo and Daniele would be in uniform, he'd asked Nelli to pick his clothes: light wool tan slacks and a white dress shirt with sleeves she'd neatly rolled up for him.

Daniele observed Nico's face as he approached them. "Nico, are you all right?"

"Yes," Perillo joined in. "What's wrong?"

"Gogol fainted at breakfast. I carried him back to his room. Nelli called the ambulance. She's staying with him. Let's go and get this over with."

The wooden gate was closed. Perillo pressed the intercom button. Gianna Rosati asked who it was. He told her. They waited. Nico was in the car with Daniele. After a minute had gone by, Perillo lost his patience and kept his finger pressed on the button. The gate finally opened slowly. Perillo strode down the path, arms swinging. Daniele drove the Alfa in.

Gianna stood at the half-open front door with a trembling smile. "You are a surprise, Maresciallo. I was getting dressed."

Perillo glanced at her outfit: a floral shirt tucked into old slacks with fresh dirt at the knee. When he looked back at her, she was looking beyond his shoulder.

"Brigadiere and Detective Doyle are with me."

She lifted her neck, straightened her shoulders and gave him a clearly forced smile. "You must have news for us then. I'll call Federico. Make yourself at home on the patio. It's such a lovely day. I'll bring coffee." She hurried away.

"No coffee," Perillo called after her.

"Since when?" Nico asked, walking up to him with Daniele.

"She'll use the time to confabulate with her husband."

"He's coming," Daniele said. Rosati was walking to the door.

"Buongiorno, Maresciallo." Federico nodded to Nico and Daniele. He walked past them, his long legs scissoring across the grass to a semicircle of six chairs facing the flowering garden. "Let's sit here. The sun is not yet hot." He folded himself down in the same chair he had sat in before, a chair whose seat was higher than the other chairs. "We must owe this Saturday morning visit to some important news."

Perillo moved a chair so he could sit facing Rosati. "Yes." Nico and Dani sat to one side.

"Let's hear," Federico said.

Perillo stretched out his bad knee. "I prefer to wait for your wife."

Nico leaned forward. "The signora has kindly offered to make us coffee."

A flicker of annoyance crossed Rosati's face.

He doesn't know the bracelet has been found, Daniele thought. He had his iPhone out.

"Here I am. Coffee for everyone." Gianna placed the tray on the table next to her husband. "Who takes sugar?"

"Gianna, sit down," Rosati snapped. "The maresciallo has news about Nora's murder."

"Not the murder for now." Perillo got up and picked up one of the coffee cups. He looked around the gathering. "Anyone else?"

Nico and Daniele shook their heads. Gianna sat down next to her husband and mumbled, "No, thank you."

Perillo drank the espresso in one sip and put the cup back on the tray. All eyes were on him. An enjoyable sensation, he decided. "My brigadiere is recording our conversation."

"Whatever for?" Federico asked.

"To spare you the first trip to the station. I'm sure you will agree it is more pleasant here."

"How nice of you," Gianna said, her cheeks pink with pleasure.

Federico looked puzzled. "What do you mean by *first*?"

Perillo didn't answer.

Daniele pressed record and stated the time, place and people present.

"I have news about Nora's jewelry." Perillo sat down and told the Rosatis about the diamond bracelet found in a mound of dirt on the Salviati property.

"Who found it?" Federico's impassive face finally showed an emotion Nico couldn't read. He was trying to pay attention, but Gogol was foremost on his mind. His cell phone sat on one knee.

"The property will be searched in case more pieces were hidden," Perillo said, "but it would save us a great deal of time and money if you told us where they are."

"I hid nothing!" Anger splashed across his face. "Nothing!"

"You were seen crossing in front of the lit window of the shed in the early evening yesterday."

"That boy is not right in his head. He's lying."

"I didn't say he was the one who told me."

"His father's no better. Telling people his son has a heart disease when the disease is in the boy's head."

"No, Federico," Gianna pleaded, half rising from her chair. "Don't be cruel."

"Be quiet, Gianna."

"I won't be quiet. Please stop telling me to be silent. Denial isn't going to help." She turned to face Perillo. "It is all my fault, Maresciallo. Federico wanted to call you immediately, but I panicked and begged him not to. You were going to think I or Federico stole the jewelry and maybe even that we murdered poor Nora. You were, weren't you?"

Perillo said nothing, waiting for her to untangle her story.

Gianna turned to Nico with a face corrugated by fear. "He was, wasn't he? We didn't steal anything. We could never kill her. She was our friend. You must believe us."

"The bracelet just appeared?" Nico asked. Gianna had kept her eyes on him.

"Oh, yes, yes. Coming home yesterday afternoon from shopping I noticed one of the laurel bushes along the driveway was crooked."

"If you had for once remembered to get out of the car and

close the gate." Federico was drumming his fingers on the arm of the chair, looking up at the sky.

"If you had bothered to listen to me for once," she snapped at him. "I asked Federico to bury it somewhere far away from here. Let some poor man find it and get a reward. But here they are, thinking we're thieves, maybe even murderers."

"Signora," Daniele said, hating the bickering. It was ugly and a terrible waste of time. "You came home to a crooked laurel bush."

"Oh, yes." She eagerly turned toward Daniele. "Come see. I'll show you."

"You go," Perillo said, tapping his knee.

Nico didn't move. He was annoyed with himself. He should have stayed with Gogol, let Nelli go to work. He was useless here.

Daniele handed Nico his cell phone in case Perillo questioned Federico in his absence, and followed Gianna down the driveway. She stopped in front of a bush that was as straight as the others. "I like them to line up like soldiers at attention." She tapped her foot at the base of the plant. "I looked down and saw the soil around the trunk was in disorder." She moved aside to let him look at the spot.

Daniele bent down to see. The soil around the trunk showed neat rake marks.

"The bracelet was here?"

"Underneath. I was worried the animal had buried something nasty. Just a few flicks of my hand spade and there it was. There's nothing to see now. I tidied it up, but I thought you should see the spot."

Daniele straightened up. "Yes, of course."

She turned and headed back to the others. Daniele walked at her side.

"Whoever left it didn't bother to bury it very deep," she said.

"Maybe he wanted it found or he was in a hurry, what do you think?"

"I don't know." Turning the corner, Daniele found the maresciallo standing, having another cup of coffee.

"Signora Rosati," Perillo said, returning the empty cup to the tray, "you claim you found the bracelet under a laurel."

Gianna answered with a vigorous nod.

"Maybe there are earrings under a rose, a necklace between the geraniums."

"Go ahead," Federico said. "Send your team to search our garden, our house."

Gianna clasped her hands to her chest. "Please forgive us, Maresciallo. When I saw the bracelet, I immediately knew it was Nora's. Sense went flying out of my head."

"Like a startled bird," Federico said in a softer voice. "My wife's courage works best in front of her flowers or a pack of cards. In this case her fear was too painful to witness, and I indulged her. In this instance a mistake, but I think you will agree that placating a hysterical wife is a husband's duty."

Gianna aimed pleading eyes at Perillo. "I hope you will find it in your heart to forgive us, Maresciallo."

"As a man I have the freedom to forgive you, as an officer of the law, I cannot. Even if I were to believe your story, by hiding the bracelet you have interfered with the investigation."

"I told you the truth," Gianna protested, the word *truth* hitting a high note.

"Obstruction of justice is a crime. I will have to denounce you to the public prosecutor. He will start an investigation."

Gianna gasped. Federico shrugged one shoulder. "Nonsense."

Perillo stood up slowly, pulled down his uniform jacket and looked at Gianna. "Gianna Rosati, did you steal the diamond bracelet that was found on the Salviati property last night?"

"Of course not."

"Just say no, please."

"No."

"Did you kill Nora Salviati?"

"No!"

Perillo turned to Federico and asked the same questions. He got the same answers. "Brigadiere Donato."

Daniele took the phone from Nico, announced the time and stopped recording.

"I need you to come down to the station this afternoon to sign your statements. Do not think of leaving the area. You will be watched."

Federico lowered his head and looked at Perillo. "Spare your men. We have no desire to leave Chianti."

"Where would we go?" Gianna asked no one in particular.

"Arrivederla, then," Perillo said.

Daniele and Nico said their goodbyes and followed Perillo back to their cars.

Perillo leaned against the hood of the Alfa and asked Nico, "Do you believe them?"

"I do." Nico looked down at his phone.

"Any news?" Daniele asked.

"Not yet."

"I believe their story," Perillo said, "but I don't really know why."

Nico held onto his phone. Nelli's silence scared him. "Their story is dumb enough to be true. If they stole Nora's jewels why get rid of only one piece?"

"Maybe Rosati hid jewelry here and there," Daniele said.

"What does he gain by dumping it piecemeal? I think they are being . . ." Nico heard the ping.

WE'RE AT CAREGGI. GOGOL'S BLOOD PRESSURE IS TOO LOW. THEY ARE CHECKING OUT HIS HEART. HE ASKED

ME TO TELL YOU 'DO NOT LET YOUR FEAR HARM YOU.'
INF., C7, L4. BECAUSE HIS DYING IS NOT NEAR. HE
KNOWS HOW MUCH YOU CARE. DON'T COME. I THINK
IT WOULD SCARE HIM.

Daniele noticed Nico blinking quickly. "How is he?"

"He's in the hospital in Florence. His blood pressure was too low. Let me answer this."

TELL HIM I'LL SEE HIM TOMORROW MORNING AT
BREAKFAST. I'LL GET THE CROSTINI. LOVE YOU.

Nico put his phone away.

Perillo noticed the emotion on Nico's face. "They'll pump him up with stuff and he'll be fine."

"I hope so."

"He means a great deal to you, doesn't he?"

"Yes. He's my first Gravigna friend outside of Rita's family."

"I'm the second." Perillo gave Nico a light punch in the arm.

"No. OneWag is."

Perillo spread out his arms in amazement. "A mutt favored over me? Scandalous." The arms came down. "So where is Rocco?"

"Sandro and Jimmy offered to take care of him until Luciana opens up her florist shop. OneWag and Luciana go way back. I think whoever left that bracelet wants us to believe we've found the thief and our killer. The Rosatis are being used as scapegoats."

Perillo did a slow nod. "Yes, possible."

Nico leaned against the car. He was tired; it was hard to concentrate. He wanted to be at the hospital with Nelli, watching Gogol's chest lift and fall, lift and fall.

"I have it." Perillo grinned with satisfaction. "I'll denounce the Rosatis this afternoon for obstruction of justice and let the media know. Then we let it slip out that we have a suspect. They will assume it's one of the Rosatis or both."

How unfair to them, Daniele thought. "Maybe it's better to make the murderer worry that we haven't fallen for his ruse," he said. "He'll get nervous and make a mistake."

"Let's think about it over lunch?" Perillo suggested. To think the brain needed food.

"Who is going to watch the Rosatis?" Daniele assumed he'd be stuck with that duty, which was okay. As long as he was free tonight for dinner with Stella.

"Don't bother," Nico said. "They won't go anywhere." He checked his watch: 11:45. In fifteen minutes, Sotto Il Fico would start serving lunch. That's where he should go. He would feel better. "I'm going."

"But we haven't decided anything," Perillo protested.

"Get in touch with Tarani."

Perillo agreed. "He's the one who has to denounce them." For once he had no regrets about not being in charge. "It's up to him to get in touch with the prosecutor."

"Daniele is right. Don't say a word to the press or anyone else about that or the bracelet," Nico said. "Let me know how it goes."

Perillo watched the Fiat 500 drive off. "Gogol fainted, needed help and Nico came here anyway. That should make me feel better, but it doesn't. He wanted to stay with Gogol."

"You're his good friend too."

"Thank the heavens Rocco didn't need him. Now let's go. My knee is yelling at me to get off my feet."

Once Daniele got the Alfa on the road back to Greve, he told Perillo that he'd looked up Stefano Rosati's wine business.

Perillo gave his brigadiere a sideways glance. "You couldn't sleep, eh?"

"I slept perfectly well." Daniele clutched the steering wheel to stop the heat from rising to his cheeks. "I just woke up early."

"I bet you also wrote the report for Tarani." If Stella rejected this wonderful young man, how in the devil were they going to put him back together?

"It only needs your signature."

"Bravo. Tell me about Stefano."

"His South African wines are selling very well. Since I was up, I got curious about the brother, Tommaso. I found him on LinkedIn. He owns a startup that got funded well but now it's sinking."

"That tells you to stick to what you can eat and drink. And don't worry about tonight. The wind will fill your sails."

This time Daniele let the blush come.

NICO AND ONEWAG WERE sitting in the vegetable garden during his two-hour break. He was proud of the small garden and liked to sit there whenever something worried him. Sitting among life-sustaining plants calmed him. Nelli had sent no more news about Gogol. He wanted them both to come home.

His cell phone started ringing. He saw it was Perillo. He hated the interruption but felt compelled to answer. "News?"

"And a ciao to you too. Were you resting?"

"Rocco and I are sitting in my vegetable garden admiring my gorgeous eggplants. They need another week of sun and then they'll make the best eggplant parmigiana I've ever tasted. I have no Gogol news. What is your news?"

"The Rosatis came in as meek as lambs and signed their statements. Tarani has formally denounced them, but I convinced him to hold off on sending a search team to their home or the villa. Lapo has agreed to do the looking with Cecco. They know every centimeter of the grounds. What do you think?"

"I don't know the man or his son." He had to trust Perillo's instincts, which recently had grown shaky. Daniele was more reliable. "You trust Lapo?"

"I trust both. They could have kept that bracelet."

"And Daniele?"

"It was his idea to ask them."

"You're saving the carabinieri some money. Did Gianna offer to search her garden?"

"How did you know?"

"Don't forget you are dealing with an ex-homicide detective from the Bronx." He was being inane, a sure sign he was worried. "Anything else?"

"No, enjoy your rest. We'll talk tomorrow."

"Ciao." Slipping the phone into the back pocket of his shorts, Nico noticed OneWag giving him his *What's up?* look.

Nico double tapped his thigh. The dog jumped up into his lap. "We both miss them. That's what's up."

IVANA STOPPED EATING FOR a moment to watch her husband plunge his fork into a mound of spaghetti with sautéed crumbs, garlic, arugula and grape tomatoes with a generous sprinkling of grated pecorino. She had come home late from work and once again found the table set for dinner and Salva draining the pasta. Not a light dinner this time. She believed a heavy dinner led to indigestion and bad dreams, but this dish was too good. She too kept plunging the fork, twirling it around, gathering a neat bundle of twisted spaghetti and slipping it into her mouth. It was almost sexy.

"Salva, thank you." She blew him a kiss.

Perillo swallowed. "The follow-up is salad and fruit, so you won't accuse me of giving you bad dreams."

"I appreciate it, but we'll still have to wait at least two hours before going to bed."

"No, two hours to go to sleep."

The wall phone rang. Two rings. Then silence. Thirty seconds later the ringing resumed. That meant the call came from the carabiniere on duty downstairs. Perillo mouthed a vaffa. "I'm not going to answer. Whatever it is they can handle it without me."

"You're the maresciallo at this station, not a child. Answer the phone."

"I'm not a maresciallo when I'm eating."

"I'll cover the pasta to keep it warm."

"It won't be as good."

Ivana pushed her chair back, reached one arm behind her, unhooked the receiver, and dropped it next to Perillo's plate.

"Maresciallo? Are you there?" She recognized Dino's voice pitched high.

Perillo pressed the receiver against his ear. "Uh-huh." His mouth was full.

Ivana went back to eating the pasta. She was used to these interruptions. A too-loud party, a stolen wallet, a home break-in, a fight on the streets or in a home. Everyone always wanted to deal with the maresciallo, the top man. She hoped it was something that could be taken care of in the morning. Salva was tired, worn down by this new murder. He had aged recently while she felt younger. It made her feel guilty.

Perillo pulled his napkin down, swallowed. "Where?" He scraped the chair back and got on his feet. "Call 118 and the Stradale. Tell the woman to stay where she is. I'm coming." He hung up and called Daniele, praying his brigadiere hadn't turned off his phone.

Ivana questioned him with her eyes.

"There's been a hit-and-run. Come on, Dani, answer the phone."

"Can't you ask Dino or Vince to go with you?"

"No." He knew he was being unfair, but Dani was his right-hand man. He didn't think clearly without him or Nico.

After ten rings and no answer he clicked off. He turned to her. Ivana held her breath. *Please don't ask.*

"Did Dani tell you where he was taking Stella tonight?"

Dani, forgive me. I can't lie to my husband. "Panzano."

"Did he mention which restaurant?"

She fingered the flower pattern on the tablecloth. "Oltre Il Giardino. I think."

Perillo kissed the top of her head. "Thank you. I know that cost you."

Ivana stood up and picked up both of their still-full plates. Salva had to leave, and she wasn't hungry anymore. She covered the plates with plastic wrap and put them on the counter.

Perillo called Nico. "A woman called in a hit-and-run about three kilometers before the Rosatis' house. The man isn't moving.

"No. She didn't want to touch him. I'm getting Daniele. See you there."

"Don't forget to take your apron off," Ivana said.

"Don't wait up."

"I won't. Be careful." Ivana walked out of the kitchen. *How could she ever make it up to Dani?*

DANIELE AND STELLA LOOKED out at the view of the small park below and beyond to the vast patchwork of vineyards. The sun had dropped out of view in front of them, leaving an orange vein along the horizon almost the same color as the Aperol spritz they were drinking. When the waitress appeared, Daniele was happy to let Stella order for him: bruschetta, grilled vegetables, sautéed zucchini and a bottle of Vermentino.

"How did your talk with your parents go?" Daniele was no longer nervous. After writing countless sentences, crossing them off, rewriting, he'd stopped and just thought about what she meant to him. That's what he was going to say when the right moment came. After a few glasses of wine.

"That's what I wanted to talk to you about. I'm making a big change in my life. In September . . ." She waved. "Buonasera."

Daniele turned around. The maresciallo was walking toward them with a grim look on his face.

No. Please no.

"Buonasera, Stella, Daniele. I'm sorry, but I need Daniele to come with me."

Under the table Stella squeezed Daniele's knee. "I understand."

"I don't," Daniele protested.

"I'll explain in the car. We need to hurry."

"It's okay, Dani. Call me when you get home. Even in the middle of the night. Be safe."

No. Daniele didn't move. He'd waited too long for this.

Perillo noticed Daniele's rigid stance, the resolve in his face. "I'm parked in the piazza. Buonasera, Stella. Again, forgive me." He left them.

Stella clasped Daniele's hand. "What is it, Dani?"

He took a deep breath and the words slipped out. "I love you. That's what I was going to tell you tonight. I love you very much."

Stella started laughing. "Dani, I've been waiting for you to say that since forever. I love you too. Very much."

Daniele turned the color of beets.

"Now go before you lose your job."

Daniele bent over, kissed her quickly and ran to join the maresciallo.

"How did you find me?" he asked as he buckled his seat belt.

"I asked Tilde," Perillo lied. "You must never, ever again turn off your phone. You are an officer of the law, and you must be reachable at all times. The reason I interrupted—"

Daniele put his head against the headrest, closed his eyes and didn't hear a word of what came next.

NICO APPROACHED THE CAR parked on the side of the road. "Buonasera. Are you Erica who called the carabinieri?" he asked the woman behind the wheel.

She stuck her head out of the window. "Yes. Can I go home now?"

"I'm sorry. You'll have to wait for the maresciallo." Nico raised his hand. "I'll be right back." The sky was darkening but he could make out something white on the side of the road just ahead. Nico turned on his cell phone light. The girl must have been watching him because she turned on her car's headlights. He raised his hand in thanks and ran, careful to stay on the very edge of the road to avoid messing up any tire tracks. Bending down, he checked the man's pulse. Nothing.

Nico straightened up and shined his light across the body. The white-shirted victim was lying with the front wheel of a black motorcycle pinning down his hips. His legs were splayed out on the road; from the waist up, he lay on the side of the road. One arm rested on his chest, the other twisted into a sharp angle. His head rested on a blood-soaked rock, face looking at the sky with open eyes.

Erica was texting on her phone when Nico walked back. She stuck her head out again. A girl really, barely eighteen. A plain face surrounded by thick blond curls. Nico introduced himself. "The maresciallo will be here soon."

She made a face. "Awful isn't it? Poor man."

"Are you all right?"

"I'm lucky, that's what I am. The truck could have hit me. About two kilometers back just before that nasty curve, he raced right past me, almost hit my side mirror. Scared me. I had to stop for a minute to calm down. I turned up the radio and started singing. That helped."

"Did you notice the color of the truck?"

"I was so startled I think I shut my eyes for a second. He zipped around the curve in a blink."

"How much time elapsed between the truck passing you and you finding the man?"

She shook her head, her curls falling over her face. "Oh, I don't know. I was singing along with the radio—I don't remember what song—and then I called my friend Gemma to tell her a truck almost hit me. I didn't call Mamma; she'd freak out. Maybe ten, fifteen minutes."

Perillo and Daniele walked up to the car. "Thank you for alerting us," Perillo said. "Some people would have driven right past. I'm Maresciallo Perillo."

"Can I go now? I have to get home."

"I got some information from her," Nico said.

"Good. Give Brigadiere Donato your full name, address, phone number. When you're done, drive past slowly, staying on the opposite edge of the road from the dead man. I don't want any tire marks. Then drive safely home. Thanks again. Buonanotte." Perillo turned to Nico. "Where is he?"

"Just up ahead." He led the way.

Erica drove her car slowly past them. Nico stopped and shined his phone light on the man's face.

Perillo joined him and looked down. "Good God!"

"I know," Nico said. "I think he got hit by a truck. The girl said a truck sped past her, almost sideswiping her car. She was too shaken to notice the color."

Perillo kept staring. He could hear motorcycles behind him, an ambulance siren in the distance. The girl had driven away. Now they were standing in the dark except for Nico's cell phone light.

Daniele ran over, added his light to the man's face, and made the sign of the cross.

"Nico," Perillo said, "meet Clara's fiancé, Marco Zanelli."

Nico looked again at those lifeless eyes. "Poor guy."

"Quite a coincidence if that's what it is."

"You think it's murder?"

"I wish I knew."

"Move over, please." Two EMTs pushed past them, carrying a stretcher. They had left on the ambulance's headlights, and the scene was again awash with stark light.

Nico and Daniele stepped aside. Perillo didn't move. "Where the devil is the Stradale?"

"Right behind you, Maresciallo." The road policeman stopped in front of Perillo and took off his motorcycle helmet.

"What took you so long?"

"Saturday nights keep us busy, unfortunately." The policeman watched the two EMTs lift the motorcycle away from Marco's body. A car stopped behind him and turned on its headlights. "Looks like a pirate of the road sent this guy flying."

"Maybe a man driving a truck."

"We'll determine that. It's our job now."

"You are welcome to it. I just need his cell phone."

The EMT reached into Marco's pockets and slowly extracted a mangled piece of metal with a few shards of glass clinging to it. "You're not going to get anything out of this."

"I'm afraid he's right, Maresciallo," Daniele said.

"So be it." Perillo didn't know why he'd even asked for it. It wasn't going to tell him who the driver was. "I'll leave you to do your job, Officer. The victim was involved in a murder investigation. His death could be a simple hit-and-run incident or it could be murder. Please let me know of any information that points one way or the other." Perillo walked away, followed by Nico and Daniele.

Nico got back in his car and called Nelli. "How is he?"

"Disgruntled up to ten minutes ago. Now muttering in his sleep. Snippets of Dante, for sure."

"You're wonderful to spend the night with him."

"No, I'm selfish. I need to make sure he wakes up. How are you?"

Nico told her about the hit-and-run. "Perillo thinks it might be murder."

"And you?"

"Too soon to know."

"Rocco?"

"He's fine. I left him with Tilde."

TWELVE

Clara sat in the interview chair, in old jeans and a rumpled shirt she hadn't bothered to tuck in. Her face was splotchy and puffed up from crying. "I don't understand what you're saying. Why would anyone want him dead?"

"I'm sorry," Perillo said. "I realize how painful your fiancé's death is for you, but I need to know if his death was just a matter of chance and bad luck or if he was killed deliberately."

"What difference does it make?" She took a deep breath. "He's gone."

"His death might be linked to your mother's murder."

"What?"

"He may have known who killed her."

"No!" She shook her head hard. "He would have told me. We had no secrets." She kept shaking her head, her long hair slapping her face.

"Can I get you anything from the bar?" Daniele asked. Clara's grief was making him feel guilty about his own happiness.

Clara smiled at him, eyes filling with tears. "A double order of Marco, please?" She started sobbing. Daniele went over to her and stroked her shoulders.

Perillo closed his eyes. Watching a woman cry made him feel powerless. He should have waited. Given Clara at least another day before presenting her with the possibility that Marco was murdered. No, not a possibility. Chance was not involved. He was convinced Marco was run over on purpose.

He opened his eyes. She was blowing her nose. Daniele had stopped stroking her. *He means well, but a woman could take offense.* "Signorina Clara, I apologize for my excessive zeal in trying to understand your fiancé's death—"

"Stop calling him my fiancé!" she shouted. "He has a name: Marco. Marco Zanelli."

Daniele took a step back.

Perillo leaned forward. "Would you like to go home? We can talk when you feel better."

"And when will that be?" Clara snapped. "Tomorrow? The next day? A month from now? How long are you willing to wait? A year? Two?" Her tone was bitter. "No. Let's get it over with now. Ask your questions."

"Marco was killed only a few kilometers from the villa, which at first made me think he was on his way to see you. I went to the villa, but you weren't there." Lapo had to remind him that Clara was in Lucca. He and Daniele had driven to Lucca and told Marco's parents first. The loss of one's child took precedence. They took the news quietly, as though they were used to bad news. Clara had stopped screaming only after he shook her. "Did he know you wouldn't be there?"

"Yes. We had lunch together yesterday in Lucca. He wanted me to come down with him, but the weekends are my busiest days at the gym. I told him I'd join him tonight. He asked if he could go without me." She took a deep, broken breath. "I gave him the key."

"Did he explain why he wanted to go to the villa without you?"

She blew her nose. "He didn't have to. It's a great deal nicer than where he lives."

"You didn't live together?"

"We did, but he liked to spend some nights at home. His mother has been sick."

"Whoever stole your mother's jewelry inexplicably took the trouble of burying one of the pieces."

Clara's eyes widened. "Just one piece?"

"Yes. A diamond bracelet."

"Where did you find it?"

"I can't tell you that. Do you think it's possible—"

She didn't let him finish. "No, not in the least bit possible." She clasped the edge of Perillo's desk, her neck straining forward. "Marco had absolutely no interest in those diamonds. He wouldn't know how to steal a paper clip. You want the thief? Take a good look at my brother-in-law's bank account. He's desperate for money and I know my sister isn't going to bail him out with her inheritance."

"You think he killed your mother?"

"That's for you to find out."

"Before you interrupted me, I was asking if it was possible that Marco knew who the thief was? I wasn't going to accuse him of the theft."

"Oh." She sat back, looking abashed. "I don't know. He didn't say anything to me. If he knew or suspected, he would have told me. We didn't keep things from each other. You really think he was murdered because he knew something?"

"I do. I don't believe in coincidences, but I have no proof."

Clara rose to her feet. "Whether Marco knew something incriminating or not, slamming a truck into a man on a motorcycle and leaving him there is murder. You must find who killed him."

"I agree." Perillo stood up.

"Where is Marco? I want to see him."

"At the Florence morgue. His parents are probably there now, identifying his body."

She squeezed her eyes shut. "I should have been the one to do that."

"They are his parents."

Red, tear-filled eyes flashed Perillo an angry look. "I love him just as much as they do."

"I can arrange for you to see him, if you wish."

"Yes, please. I need to understand he's gone. Let me know when. I'll be staying down here until the Swiss kick me out."

"Thank you for coming, Signorina Clara. I'll let you know about the visit. I hope I won't need to disturb you again."

"I hope you will. To show me the murderer's head on a platter."

Daniele was at the door, holding it open for her.

She turned her head back. "I'm counting on you."

Daniele closed the door behind her. The church bells started ringing.

"Go, Dani, or you'll be late for Mass. Ivana is waiting for you."

Daniele grabbed his phone from his desk. "I'll pray for Clara."

"And us. We could use a little help with this investigation."

Daniele had already left.

NICO FOUND MISS BARRON in one of the side rooms of the hotel, sitting on a leather sofa, a map of Florence spread out on the low table in front of her. She was dressed in a beige pant-suit and brown ankle boots. A gold pin in the shape of a tulip adorned her right lapel.

"Good morning, Miss Barron. Are you going to Florence?"

"Ah, good morning, Mr. Doyle. Yes, last night I decided it was time to venture out into the world again. I'm also beginning to miss my home." She held out her hand. "Come and say hello, OneWag."

The dog padded over, sniffed her sweet-smelling boots first, then gave her hand an obliging lick.

"Thank you. I needed that."

OneWag gave her a tail wag and settled down next to her feet.

Miss Barron turned her attention to Nico, who was sitting in the nearest armchair. "Have you come any closer to finding Nora's killer?"

"No, but has the maresciallo ordered you not to leave?"

"He has not, but I'm sure he would rather I didn't. He must consider me a suspect. Don't you?"

"I guess I should, but what motive would you have?"

"Not the jewelry. You've seen I don't have it." She lifted the map off the table and folded it neatly. "Well, we'll have to think of something."

"You don't seem to mind being suspected of murder."

"Since I'm innocent, I rather enjoy it." She tucked the map into a brown handbag covered with initials. "I heard about the poor young man. How cruel of someone to run him down and then abandon him. Clara must be devastated. Terribly cruel."

"I agree. How did you hear?"

"Beppe told me. I've hired him to drive me to Florence today. I have every intention of dragging him to the Accademia. The art will give him something to write about in his blog instead of inanities." She peered at Nico for a few seconds. "You seem to be brimming with good news. Please tell."

Nico leaned forward and stretched out his arm. "Here you are, Miss Barron." He held out the watch fob. "It's yours. Nora's family wants nothing to do with it."

Miss Barron clasped her hands together, her eyes filling with tears. "Oh, dear." She quickly dabbed her eyes with her fingers. "I didn't think I'd get it back."

Her reaction surprised Nico. "Nora's present means a great deal to you."

"Well, yes. I don't know." Her cheeks had turned bright pink.

She was clearly embarrassed. "It's just that . . . what started as a week of lovely Tuscany has ended rather horribly. And so I cry over Nora's watch fob. It's somehow easier."

"I'm sorry you've had to go through this."

"Oh, I'm not the one you should be sorry for, am I?" She cupped the watch fob with both hands. "I had a thought this morning and I was hoping to see you so I could ask your opinion."

"Go ahead."

"I did something reprehensible at breakfast. I killed a bee. Swatted it ferociously with my map because I was afraid it was going to sting me. Bees should never be killed. They are precious."

"What thought did killing the bee inspire?"

"The young man, Clara's fiancé, perhaps he was killed because someone was afraid of him. Afraid of what he knew or might know." Her blue eyes questioned Nico.

He was tempted to put her off by saying she was reading too many mysteries. He didn't want to encourage her curiosity. "Or he was simply on the wrong road at the wrong time. But I will suggest that possibility to Maresciallo Perillo."

Her eyes smiled. "Thank you."

"I hope you'll forgive me if I ask you something about Nora again."

"It's your job, isn't it?"

"I'm trying to help the maresciallo. Did Nora mention being in love with someone?"

Miss Barron visibly tightened her jaw. "You wish to know who that someone is?"

"You seem uncomfortable with the question."

"It was unexpected."

"We need to investigate everyone who was close to Nora."

She looked down at the watch fob cupped in her hands. "I understand, although one would hope, even in death, that a woman's love life would remain private."

"Nothing remains private in a successful murder investigation."

"Some may wish it not to be successful."

"The murderer, for one."

"Maybe even Nora. I don't think she minded dying. She was that unhappy."

"Nora did mention she was in love with someone, didn't she?"

"Yes, on our last night together." Miss Barron held out the watch fob. "Please, could you fasten it around my neck? I don't want to lose it."

Nico stood up and fumbled with the clasp. "I have thick fingers, I'm afraid." That and impatience. Miss Barron was playing for time. "There." The hook of the clasp caught the chain. "Done. Let me see?"

Miss Barron straightened up and patted the fob against her chest. "Thank you."

Nico sat back down. "It looks very nice. Now tell me about your last night with your hostess."

"Sonia had prepared a light supper out on the patio. It was a lovely Tuscan evening, with a breeze brushing through the tree leaves, the setting sun splashing pink light onto the clouds, the cold zucchini soup delicious. I wanted to enjoy myself, bask in the good fortune of being unexpectedly in Italy again. But Nora clearly wasn't enjoying anything. We ate in silence. I had my glass of wine, Nora finished the bottle and was well into another one when she—" Miss Barron clasped her cheeks with her hands, then slowly dropped them to her lap. "I can quote her verbatim." She looked beyond Nico's shoulder. "'*You knew happiness. The world was yours to cherish. You were about to marry your love.*'" Her eyes found Nico's. "Have you ever felt the world was yours, Mr. Doyle?"

"I have been happily in love. I am again now, but I never allowed myself to think the world was mine."

"It is your good fortune. The letdown is devastating. '*You were about to marry your love*,' she repeated, '*and then one day he is gone. And you discover you are expected to go on living when it is the last thing you want to do.'*

"Since we are revealing secrets, that is exactly what happened to me, Mr. Doyle, but I hadn't told her."

"How did she find out?"

"Nora was talking about herself. She was always the center of every occurrence, every conversation. Nevertheless, I listened. She described their love for each other as too all-consuming to be held back. She was very dramatic and romantic in her telling. I cannot give you the name of her love as she never mentioned it, and I did not ask."

"It must have been a difficult evening for you."

"Yes, extremely so. Nora managed to notice my discomfort and apologized"—her fingers lifted the watch fob from her chest—"by giving me this. It is now inextricably linked to my own love story. Thank you again for bringing it back."

"It belongs to you. What do you think Nora meant when she said the man was gone?"

"Mine is dead." Miss Barron rose from the sofa. "I now must put a few things together for my trip to Florence. I find a good map, which I happen to have, is indispensable. I am sorry I was not of more help to you."

Nico stood up. "You've been wonderful, thank you. Enjoy Florence."

"I always do."

With one last sniff at Miss Barron's boots, OneWag followed Nico out of the room.

"EHI, NICO, WHERE ARE you?" Perillo asked over the phone.

"I was walking up a steep hill with two heavy bags of bread. Now I'm answering my phone while balancing the bags against my legs, hoping they don't fall and send the bread rolling down the hill. Buongiorno."

"You're in an odd mood."

"Yes, I am. Gogol will be released from the hospital, Miss Barron has her watch fob, I have an idea for a new recipe and you're about to tell me more good news, I hope."

"I could use some. Watching Clara's grief this morning was difficult."

"More so for her, I would guess."

"I know. I know. It was a mistake asking her to see me. Marco's parents just called me. They insist on driving down from Lucca to talk to me. I'd like you to be there."

"I've got a lunch shift."

"I told them to come at four."

"Why do you need me?"

"For support. I told Daniele he could continue the conversation he started with Stella last night. The joy on his face almost erased Clara's tears."

"Did Marco's parents say why they want to see you?"

"I spoke to the father. He said they needed to clear something up."

Before Nico could answer, OneWag barked and took off. Nico turned to see the dog chase a ciabatta down the hill. "I'll call you back."

As soon as Nico walked into Sotto Il Fico, Enzo greeted him with open arms. Nico handed over the bread. "One ciabatta escaped."

"We'll survive." Enzo put the bread bags on a table. "You could use the cart."

"I shouldn't answer the phone walking uphill. Excuse me, I have to call Perillo back." Nico stepped back into the street. OneWag, lying on a church step, cocked his ears, the ciabatta uneaten between his paws. "Good catch. It's yours." As OneWag took his first bite, Nico clicked on Perillo's number.

"I'll be there."

"You're a friend."

Nico clicked off before they both started getting sappy and went back into the restaurant.

"I've got an idea for a new dish," he told Elvira after kissing her bent head. He got a grunt in response. She was testing letters for some new word game.

"What new dish?" Tilde asked without the usual smile she gave Nico when he first walked into the kitchen. She was standing in front of a large stainless-steel pot, an apron over her green dress, a matching scarf covering her hair. Stella's presence in town usually had Tilde smiling all day long. Not this time.

Nico wrapped an apron around his waist. "What's yours?"

She was using a wooden spoon to push cooked navy beans through a conical strainer.

"Nothing new. Room-temperature bean soup with fried panko and chopped scallions. You?"

"Fresh taglierini with sauteed onions, leeks and a grating of nutmeg covered with fried prosciutto chips."

"For today? I only have dried spaghetti."

"That would be good too, although it won't pick up the sauce as well. Not today. I need your approval first."

"It's yours. I'll put it on the menu for Tuesday."

"Now that we have that out of the way, please go easier on that spoon, Tilde. You'll dig a hole in the strainer." Nico took the cooked farro out of the refrigerator.

"Leave me alone. It makes me feel better."

"That bad?" He was going to make the farro salad he had eaten at Il Cestino. Tomatoes, yellow peppers, red onions, whole wheat croutons with a plain vinaigrette dressing. "I guess you had the talk with Stella."

Tilde put the strainer down on a plate. "A family reunion. Stella had her say. She's given notice at the museum and in

September, she starts a new job at the lower school here, teaching art to children."

"Why does that upset you?"

"Now she'll be stuck in Gravigna." Tilde held out her hand, palm up to stop Nico from speaking. "Yes, I agree. There's nothing wrong with Gravigna. For us, at our age. But she's young. I wanted more for her."

"She's happy here with her family."

"And with Daniele." Tilde picked up the spoon and started pushing the beans through the strainer again. "It's obvious she's the sun and the moon to him. You remember feeling like that?"

"I don't have to remember."

Tilde let out a throaty laugh. "That's right. You're a lucky man."

"And so is Daniele."

"Lucky doesn't begin to describe it."

The kitchen door opened. "May I interrupt?"

Tilde spun around. "Nelli! How are you?"

"Ciao, Tilde, Nico."

Nico put the bowl down and gave Nelli a big hug. "I'm so glad to see you."

Nelli hugged him back. "I've missed you."

"I couldn't reach you and I was scar—"

"I know, Nico. I'm sorry. Come out on the terrace for a minute, can you?"

"For you," Tilde said, "I'll give him ten."

Nico followed Nelli out to the terrace. A coat-wrapped Gogol was sitting at the table with the best view. OneWag was at his feet, sniffing at the coat. "He wanted to see you before I took him home."

Gogol raised a hand at Nico. "Ehi, amico, I lived."

Nico felt a surge of joy. "Of course, you lived." He walked across the empty terrace and gave Gogol a pat on the arm before sitting down next to him. Gogol shied away from any physical contact that wasn't from Nelli or OneWag. "You look brand-new. So does your coat." The cologne odor was gone.

Nelli joined them. "He let me give him a haircut and I got the coat steam cleaned."

Gogol hung his head. "I felt bereft."

Nelli put an arm around his shoulder. "They wouldn't let him wear it in the hospital bed."

"What did the doctors say?"

Gogol dismissed the question with a grunt. Nico gave Nelli a questioning look.

"He has a blocked artery, and they want to insert a stent. Tell Nico what you said."

"They 'set their opinion before listening to art or reason.'"

"What art or reason didn't they listen to?" Nico asked.

"'Your intellect slumbers.'"

"That's why I want you to tell me what you mean." It was going to be hard to convince his friend to accept the doctors' advice.

Gogol rubbed his nose. "Tomorrow at breakfast."

Nelli stood up. "He's tired. I need to take him home."

"And I have a salad to make."

Her eyes smiled at Nico. "Are we together tonight after work?"

He grinned. "Oh, yes. Very much together."

Gogol pushed himself up from the table.

Nico saw the effort it took. "I'm happy you are back, Gogol. Breakfast without you doesn't satisfy. I missed you. I'll see you at Bar All'Angolo tomorrow."

"Tomorrow. If the heart wills it."

"It will."

"Nelli, accompany me."

Nelli linked her arm in Gogol's. "I'm here."

Nico watched them slowly walk away with OneWag at their

heels and felt a tightness in his chest. Gogol needed to understand that the doctors' words had both art and reason.

DANIELE STROKED STELLA'S HAIR. He was sitting on Elvira's sofa, with Stella's head leaning on the crook of his shoulder. "Your Nonna is nice." Elvira had offered Stella the use of her apartment for the afternoon, saying she had work to do at the restaurant. Next to her bed she had left folded clean sheets and a pillowcase.

"She is wonderful with me always," Stella said, stretching her legs out on the sofa. "With others she likes to be grumpy."

"She wasn't with me."

"I forbade her to be grumpy with you."

Daniele looked at Stella's intense green eyes. He had never felt happier. "You're lovely, Stella."

She lifted her head and kissed him. "So are you. I think I need to stretch out those rumpled sheets again. Don't you?"

Daniele answered with a kiss.

DINO WAS AT THE front desk when Nico walked into the carabinieri station.

"Ciao, Dino, the maresciallo is expecting me. Is he alone?" Nico was ten minutes early.

"No. Signori Zanelli arrived an hour ago. They talked with the maresciallo in his office a long time and now he took them to the bar. He's expecting you there."

"Thanks." The bar was a two-minute walk. As Nico crossed the courtyard in front of the café bar, he spotted Perillo sitting with a couple at an outside table. The man was wearing a tie and coat, despite the warm weather. The woman had on a plain dress.

Perillo gestured for him to join them.

Nico walked over. "Buonasera."

Perillo half rose from his chair. "Let me introduce you to Detective Doyle, assisting me with the investigation. Signora and Signor Zanelli."

Marco's mother, an overly thin woman, looked up at him with a face stunned by grief.

Nico said. "I am so sorry, Signora."

"Marco was a good, honest man."

Nico glanced at Perillo. *What's going on?*

Her husband stroked her arm. "Shh, Maria, shh." He spoke softly, like a parent soothing a crying child. He had a tired, rough face with eyes that looked at Nico blankly. The nails of his stroking hand were embedded with what looked like grease. Nico remembered that he owned a bicycle-repair shop.

Perillo pulled out the chair next to his. "Sit down, Nico. Drink, Signora, the brandy will help."

A glass holding a few drops of red wine sat on the table in front of Signor Zanelli. His wife's brandy glass had not been touched.

"Maybe a coffee?" Perillo asked. "Something to eat?"

Marco's mother clasped a large handbag to her chest and looked at her husband. "Let's go, Pietro."

Her husband looked at Perillo. Nico waited for information.

"Yes, of course, you can go home."

Signora Zanelli stood up. "Not home. We'll be at my sister's until it's over."

"The search team won't come until tomorrow," Perillo said.

Marco's father got on his feet too. They were all standing now. "Maresciallo, please, can you ask them to start with the shop? I'm closed Monday mornings, but the afternoon is always busy. On the weekend people drink, they smash their bicycles."

Signora Zanelli walked away.

"We'll be searching the home and shop at the same time," Perillo said.

"Thank you for your trust."

"Of course, you came to tell me." Perillo waited until both Zanellis were out of earshot to say, "They're good people, they deserve trust. Unfortunately, Tarani couldn't get a search team to Lucca before tomorrow."

"They found some jewelry."

"Come back to the office. You want this brandy?"

"No, thanks."

"I'll take it then." He waved to the waiter. "I'll bring the glass back."

"If you don't," the waiter shot back, "you'll be charged, Maresciallo."

"Bah! Back in Naples I didn't have to pay for anything." They walked the short distance to the station. "They came almost an hour early. Signora Zanelli walked into my office already talking. She was angry. '*What's this doing in my son's belongings? You're trying to frame him. My son is not a thief.*' She was a waterfall of words. Her husband just kept shaking his head. I couldn't wait for you."

Nico grabbed Perillo's arm and stopped. "You're playing games. What did she find?"

"Keep walking, I'll show you."

"I'm not moving."

Perillo gave Nico a resigned look. "A little suspense is good, Nico, stimulates the brain, but you want the American way. Rush rush rush. Now now now."

"Yes." Nico let go of Perillo's arm.

"The Zanellis went to the mortuary this morning to identify Marco. The staff gave them his belongings. A diamond ring was in a bag with his clothes."

They started walking again. "Nora's ring?"

"Yes, unless Marco's piano lessons paid extremely well."

Dino was on the phone when they entered the station. Seeing

Perillo, Dino put a hand over the handset and mouthed *Meloni again. He's now at the villa.*

Perillo shook his head and kept walking. "He has been storming the station with phone calls since early this morning." He closed the office door behind Nico. "Whatever I know about the hit-and-run I told Clara. When I have something to add, I will inform her, not him." Perillo pulled out his keys from his uniform pocket and opened the desk drawer. He took out a small velvet pouch, untied the string and shook the ring out onto the desk.

Nico looked down. It had a large diamond in the center, held by three levels of long baguettes on each side. "A very expensive engagement ring." He'd bought Rita a half-carat diamond that took him a long time to pay off.

"I need to make sure it is part of the stolen jewelry. I don't have the heart to ask Clara. I'll have to face Adriana and Meloni again." He sat down behind his desk and took a long sip of the brandy. "I will call them in the morning. It is Sunday after all. Sit Nico. Where's Rocco?"

"With Nelli." Nico sat down in the interview chair. "She brought Gogol back from the hospital."

Perillo slapped his hands together. "More good news. We have found our thief. You have your love and your friend back."

"I do." Perillo didn't need to know that Gogol needed a stent. "But what makes you so sure Marco is the thief? The ring could have been planted on him."

"What? The driver hits him, gets out of the truck, plants the ring, gets back in the truck, drives off when anyone could have driven by and seen him with Marco's body?"

"You have a point. Too risky. If Marco is the thief, do you think he's also our murderer?"

"For now, let's just think of him as the thief. Only Marco's parents and the two of us know about the ring."

"They must have wanted to spare Clara the bad news."

Perillo took another sip of brandy. "I suppose, which was nice of them. From what they said it was clear they weren't happy about the engagement. The father thought his son was entering a world in which he would never belong. The mother said she didn't like anything about Clara and wouldn't give me a reason."

"Maybe Marco bought the ring on his own to impress his rich bride-to-be," Nico said, "and saddled himself with years of debt."

"It matches the description on the list, but I'll *maybe* you back. Maybe Marco had the ring with him because he planned to give it to Clara."

"And let her know he was the thief?"

"That might have given her a good laugh at her sister's expense. Nora recently showed the ring to Clara and Adriana accused her, in front of me, of trying to convince their mother to give her the ring as an engagement gift. Marco was present when Nora told Clara she was selling all the jewelry to help refugees."

"Okay, that might have given him the idea to steal it for her. But what about the rest of the jewels?"

"Nothing has come up from jewelers or pawnshops. The refugee center in Florence said they did not get any jewelry donation."

"Have you checked if anyone in the family has been taking trips outside of Italy? Amsterdam or New York, for instance?"

"Tarani has asked to take over tracing the jewelry. He has more men at his disposal."

"How is his wife?"

"Still in bed with a month to go, I think." Perillo drank what was left of the brandy and dropped his elbows on the desk.

"Let me ask you something. If Marco is our thief, what reason would anyone have to kill him?"

"He *is* our thief and maybe he knew who killed Nora."

"With the amount of money the jewelry sale would bring in, he didn't need to blackmail anyone."

"You're thinking he was just in the wrong place at the wrong time?" Perillo asked.

"Maybe we're jumping to conclusions."

"Maybe. Maybe not. But coincidences make me suspicious. You?"

"Me too. Has the Stradale told you anything about the accident?"

"They found clear truck tire marks that kept going. No sign of the truck braking. Every farmer and every vintner in Tuscany owns at least one truck. Finding the right one will be almost impossible. But mercifully, it is the Stradale's job, not ours."

"But we need to find Nora's murderer. Maybe tomorrow you'll get a lead. It's now five o'clock and I have some dinners to help prepare." Nico stood up. "Call me tomorrow after you talk to the Melonis. Say hello to Ivana for me."

Perillo spread out his arms in exasperation. "My wife is at work. On a Sunday, can you believe it? She tells me Alba's Cantuccini are flying off the shelves. Enrico and Alba are thinking of building a bigger bakery." He picked up the empty brandy glass and sipped nothing.

"Have dinner at Sotto Il Fico. Peasant soup is on the menu. We open at seven. You'll survive. Ciao."

WHEN NICO WALKED INTO the kitchen, Tilde was chopping Swiss chard, one of the many vegetables that went into a local favorite soup she served at room temperature both winter and summer.

"Ciao, Tilde." Nico reached for his apron. "I'll chop the onions."

"Already done."

The basket of onions was still full. "Carrots? Celery? Potatoes? Cabbage?"

"I don't need you tonight. Go home."

"What did I do?"

Tilde turned to look at him. "Nothing. I think you deserve a night off from cooking and death."

"Nelli got to you."

"She didn't have to. I saw how upset you were about Gogol. He's back and so is Nelli. Go and enjoy the good news. See you tomorrow." She went back to chopping.

Nico put his apron back on the door hook. "I'll make it up to you."

"With that leek and onion taglierini with prosciutto chips on tomorrow night's menu."

"Done."

NELLI WAS SITTING ON the church steps with OneWag when Nico walked out of Sotto Il Fico. She was wearing a light-blue dress that flattered her pale face. The dog gave him a wiggle of recognition. Nelli raised a hand. He sat down next to her and kissed her lightly. "Thanks."

"I had nothing to do with it. Tilde just let me know you weren't staying. Disappointed?"

"Thrilled. What would you like to do?"

"Sit on your balcony with you, Rocco, the swallows and a cold glass of Vernaccia."

"The swallows will be off getting food for their noisy babies, and I don't have any Vernaccia. I hope Rocco and I will be enough."

"They'll come back at dusk." She lifted the straw bag from the step. "I have wine and dinner."

Nico stood up and held out his hand. She took it and lifted herself up. OneWag was already halfway down the street.

"I wrote Clara a condolence note," Nelli said as she cracked eggs in a bowl on Nico's narrow kitchen counter. "I doubt she'll remember me, but I feel so bad for her. And for you. Marco's death must complicate the investigation." She looked up at Nico, who was setting the table. Rocco was curled up on the sofa. "You don't mind my bringing it up, do you?"

"No, as long as you don't try to get involved."

"I won't, but I'll listen if you need to talk about it."

Nico went back in and gave Nelli a hug. "What I need is for you to postpone dinner."

"You'll have to wait. The asparagus and parmigiano are roasting in the oven. I'm going to whip up these eggs, add them to the pan. Ten minutes later we'll eat my omelette. Then we'll decide what to do next."

Nico went back to the table and sat down. "I hope you're not implying I need those eggs."

She started whipping the eggs with a fork. "I am not. I'm sorry, Nico. I do want all of me to be with you tonight. I love you. You make me happy. It's just that part of me is still worrying about our sweet, lovable friend."

Nico started to get up. Nelli held out her hand. "Please. I don't want to start crying."

He sat back down. "We'll convince him to get that stent. I know we will."

"I'll have to reread the *Divine Comedy* to find something to hit him with." She grabbed a pot holder, opened the oven door.

Nico rushed over. "Let me help." He picked up the bowl with the eggs as Nelli pulled the rack with the pan out. The parmigiano had crusted a golden brown over the asparagus. "Pour slowly."

Nico did as he was told. The eggs sizzled as they hit the hot vegetables. Nelli slipped the rack back in, closed the oven door and locked her arms around Nico. "I'm so glad you're in my life."

Nico hugged her hard. "The same goes for me."

THIRTEEN

Perillo and Daniele found the Melonis in their dressing gowns, having breakfast in a small herb garden outside the villa's kitchen. On seeing them approach, Fabio put his coffee cup down on the table. "Ah, Maresciallo, you deign us with your presence, and even brought your trusted brigadiere. Since you are starting early this morning, I presume more jewelry has been found. I hope all of it."

Perillo and Daniele took off their hats and said, "Buongiorno."

Adriana spread a thin layer of jam on a slice of toast. "Clara told me about the bracelet. May I see it?"

Daniele watched her bite into the toast and hold out her hand for the bracelet. *What kind of people are these?* he asked himself. *No respect for the maresciallo. No mention of Marco's death. The jewelry was all that mattered to them.* His revulsion prompted him to ask, "How is Signorina Clara?"

Adriana gave him a quick smile. "Grieving, sulking. She's not used to being deprived of what she wants. And she wanted Marco, not that any of us could see why." She wiggled the fingers of her outstretched hand. "The bracelet, please."

Perillo stepped closer and dropped the ring into her hand. "I think you will find this more interesting."

Adriana fingered the ring, slipped it on her finger. "Much more interesting." She flashed an ecstatic smile at her husband sitting across the table from her. "It's Mamma's ring."

Fabio reached his arm across the table. "Let me see."

She took off the sapphire ring she was wearing on her left hand, slipped on the stolen one and held her hand up next to her cheek. "Doesn't compare, does it?"

"Don't be vulgar," Fabio answered. He withdrew his arm and faced Perillo. "Where did you find it?"

"I'm not at liberty to say." Perillo had shown the ring to Adriana only to make sure it was Nora's ring. He did not look forward to giving Clara the terrible news.

Fabio threw his napkin on the table. "That is not acceptable, Maresciallo." His voice screeched with indignation. "My wife and her sister are the legal owners of that ring and the bracelet."

This is not the time to bring up the probate court, Perillo thought. "As I told you when I gave you the sad news of your mother-in-law's death by strangulation, I am conducting a murder investigation. I have no doubt you recall that terrible meeting."

Daniele looked down at his feet to stop from smiling. The maresciallo was having a good time with his answer.

"On that sad occasion, Signor Meloni, you were convinced the theft was the motive for the murder. Until I have more solid information in my hands, I cannot share how the ring and bracelet were found."

"And how long before more solid information falls into your hands?"

"Don't yell." Adriana slipped the sapphire ring onto the index finger of her right hand. "You'll wake up Clara and her tears."

"I'm awake and cried out." Clara appeared at the open kitchen door with a cup in her hand. She was dressed in artfully torn jeans and an oversized men's shirt. "Hello, Maresciallo. Are you the reason Fabio is shouting?"

"I'm afraid so."

"He doesn't like you. Do you have news for me?"

"Does he ever." Adriana flashed her left hand in the air. "Come look."

Clara walked closer and took the hand Adriana held out to her. Her hand shot back as if she'd been burned. She lifted astonished eyes in Perillo's direction. "Where did you find it?"

"I'm not at liberty to say." He needed to tell her, but not here in front of those two.

"Clara, sit down," Fabio commanded, patting the chair next to him. "We don't need you fainting on us."

Clara broke off a sprig of rosemary and dropped down on the grass next to the plant. "Why would I do that?" She loudly inhaled the smell.

"Because I think I know where the maresciallo found your mother's ring. Poor Marco was killed Saturday night. He was carted off to the morgue, where they examined his body and I presume his belongings. This morning we have the maresciallo showing us the stolen ring, which makes me conclude that Marco is our thief. Am I not right, Maresciallo?"

Please don't let her know, Daniele begged silently. *Not yet.*

Clara narrowed her swollen eyes at her brother-in-law, her torso trembling. "You are a detestable man. I don't know how my sister can stomach you." She took a deep breath. "Tell him he's wrong, Maresciallo."

Perillo decided there was no point in holding back now. "I wish I could, Signorina Clara. I really do. The ring was found among your fiancé's belongings."

Clara shook her head. "No. You're wrong." She scrambled to her feet, threw the coffee cup at the table and ran back into the house.

Adriana watched her sister run off. "She was always excellent at theatrics." She stood up. "I'll try to console her."

"Signora, your mother's ring, please," Perillo said. "Evidence stays with me until the case is closed."

Adriana raised her eyebrows in surprise. "Isn't it closed now? Marco murdered my mother for her jewelry."

"The case is not closed." He held out his hand. She twisted the ring off her finger, threw it down on the table and strode to the open kitchen door.

Daniele quickly picked up the ring and gave it to Perillo.

Fabio was laughing. "When it comes to theatrics, my wife is just as good as Clara. Have a cup of coffee with me, Maresciallo, your brigadiere too, and tell me when you plan to close this case."

"When I have enough evidence against Nora Salviati's murderer."

"Stealing the jewelry is not enough?"

"No. Buongiorno." Perillo put his hat back on and walked away. Daniele followed, his hat forgotten in the crux of his arm.

NELLI AND NICO WERE having breakfast next to the open French door of Bar All'Angolo with Gogol wrapped in his cleaned overcoat, now giving off his signature cologne. After talking their throats raw trying to convince Gogol to have the stent operation, he was still refusing.

"Doctors are 'a people greedy, envious and proud.'" Gogol slipped a salame slice into his mouth and chewed with gusto.

"Ah," Nelli exclaimed. "I was waiting for Dante and I'm going to Dante you right back." Waking up early, she had silently recited what she remembered of the *Inferno*. "'Open your chest to the truth that comes.' If you don't get the stent, 'night will be free to summon all its darkness.'"

Gogol clapped loudly, with a proud gleam in his eyes. "Brava!"

OneWag, who'd been walking the floor, padded over to see what the excitement was all about. Gogol rewarded him with the empty crostino.

"Why do you want to die sooner than later?" Nelli asked.

"My friend," Gogol said.

Nelli took his rough, withered hands in hers. "Your friends, plural. Nelli and Nico."

Sandro, who'd been following the conversation from behind the counter, called out, "Jimmy and Sandro want to see you at that table every morning except Sunday for another twenty years."

"We want you to live as long as possible," Nico said. "For your sake, but also for ours. We love you. Please have the operation."

Gogol grinned. Nelli understood he'd just thought of another quote to match the moment. "'Your prayer is worthy of much praise, therefore I accept it.'"

"Wonderful!" Nelli planted a kiss on top of Gogol's head.

"I guess that's a Dante *yes*," Nico said. "Let's get back to enjoying our food. Gogol, how about a ciambella?"

"With gratitude, yes."

"That's a yes for both stent and ciambella, right?"

Gogol bowed his head. "If it is so decreed by my friends."

"It is," Nico and Nelli said together and hugged the old man. OneWag stood up on his hind legs and nuzzled his head among all three.

AFTER WALKING GOGOL HOME, Nelli rushed off to her job at the Querciabella vineyard. Nico called Perillo. "When is Nardi coming down to you?"

"If he's punctual he should be here in twenty minutes. He said nine-thirty."

"Good. I'd like to hear what he has to say."

"Happy to have you."

PERILLO WAS SITTING AT his desk, drinking his third espresso, when Nico walked into the office. OneWag had gone straight to Vince's room. Daniele stood up from his desk. "Ciao, Nico."

Nico took in Daniele's relaxed, happy face. "Ciao, Dani. I'm glad to see the sun is shining for you. May it always. Forgive my eloquence, but I've just come from a session of Dante quotes."

Daniele's cheeks had turned pink.

"It's all right to blush, Dani. You brighten up this room," Nico said.

Perillo spooned the remaining sugar from the small bowl into his espresso. "Dante explains the relief on your face, Nico. I was hoping you had a lead for us."

Nico took a chair from the back of the room and set it to one side of Perillo's desk. "No lead. Just two questions I'm hoping Nardi can answer."

"How is Gogol?" Daniele asked.

"He has agreed to have the stent operation he badly needs, at least for now. Nelli is going to call the doctor to have them schedule it as soon as possible. That's the reason I'm relieved."

"Glad to hear that." Perillo put his cup down on the bar tray. "Although the thought of a stent in my heart makes me shake like a windblown leaf. Prosecutor Della Langhe has decided not to prosecute the Rosatis. He told Tarani he believes they meant no harm."

"I agree," Nico said.

A knock on the door and Dino's face appeared. "Signor Nardi is here."

Perillo stood up and picked up the bar tray. "Please." Dino hurried to Perillo and relieved him of the tray. As Dino left the room, Nardi walked in wearing sneakers, jeans and a T-shirt advertising the famous bicycle race, L'Eroica.

"Buongiorno, Maresciallo, Brigadiere, Signor Doyle. Swabbed and fingerprinted, I am now at your disposal for the next half hour." Without waiting to be asked, he sat down in the interview chair. "What more do you wish to know about my relationship with Nora?"

"Thank you for coming," Perillo said. "Our conversation will be recorded."

"I will answer with my best, most honest voice."

Perillo lowered his eyebrows and glared at Nardi. "Do you consider the murder of your lover a joking matter?"

"Forgive me, Maresciallo. Making light of what is bad in life helps me accept it. I won't do it again."

"Start the recording please," Perillo said, not appeased by Nardi's answer.

While Daniele pushed the record button and announced the date, the time and who was in the room, Nardi dropped an envelope onto Perillo's desk. "Your dinner bill. You can send me a check."

Perillo nodded. "Where were you the night between Sunday May fifteenth and Monday May sixteenth?"

"Il Cestino is closed on Mondays. I take off at ten Sunday evening and drive to Siena where my ninety-two-year-old mother insists on living. She waits up for me with a tisane she believes will keep me living to at least her age. We drink our tisanes; we go to bed. In the morning, I whip up a zabaglione without alcohol for her and kiss her goodbye. In less than forty-five minutes I am back in Gaiole, attending to the coming week's supplies."

"Today is Monday," Perillo pointed out.

"Today I let her aide make the zabaglione." Nardi reached into his jeans pocket, took out a folded piece of paper and let it fall on Perillo's desk. "I wrote down the aide's name and her cell phone number. Also my mother's home phone number should you want to talk to her. She won't know which Sunday is which, but if you ask her whether I have ever missed a Sunday night, Monday morning with her she will list all the Sundays I was in Siena with the correct dates."

Another dead end, Perillo thought, and turned to Nico. "You had a question for Signor Nardi?"

"Yes." Nico sat up in his chair. "Did you know Nora Salviati had very valuable jewelry in her safe?"

"I did. One night she took out a pearl-and-diamond necklace and asked me to fasten it on her. She wore it all night."

"When was this?"

"I don't know exactly. My guess would be two or three months ago."

"Did she tell you that a month or so ago she removed all the jewelry from the safe and put it somewhere else?"

"I'm afraid that was my fault. I made the mistake of asking her for a loan. Il Cestino hasn't become a go-to restaurant yet. Last summer it didn't bring in enough money to keep me going through the winter. I had to shut down for two months. A lot of high-end restaurants in the area close their doors, but the year-round residents deserve to have an excellent place to eat twelve months of the year. That is my ambition for Il Cestino.

"My request upset her. She accused me of wanting to become her gigolo. I walked out and stayed away for over a week. She called and apologized, told me she would talk to her accountant to see how much she could loan me. I'm not proud to say I went back to her bed. One night she opened her safe in front of me, saying she needed a document for her accountant. She let me see that now the safe held only a small pile of papers. The jewelry was no longer there should I be tempted to steal it. I said nothing. She said nothing."

"You kept seeing her anyway."

"Yes. My mother still accuses me of being a hopeless optimist. I continued to hope."

"Thank you for answering with frankness," Nico said. "I do have another question. Did Nora ever talk about the man she'd loved?"

"Yes, she did when I first came back to Gaiole and we'd meet to catch up on our lives. Before we became intimate, she talked about him. A bit too much, I thought. At first, I wondered if she was trying to make me jealous, but then I realized she was grieving. He'd died just before she contacted me. Maybe by talking to a friend, she was getting the grief out of her system. She said she's never let anyone know about him, not even her daughters."

Nardi's index finger went to his lips, his gaze far off. Half a minute later he looked up with a satisfied smile. "Martin, that's his name. Nora said she started having a Rémy Martin nightcap after he died to wish him good night. I don't think she ever told me his last name. Is he important to the investigation?"

Perillo questioned Nico with his eyes. He'd wanted to ask the same question from the start.

"He could be," Nico said. "Did she say anything else about him?"

"She probably did, but at a certain point I stopped listening. She caught on eventually."

"Thank you," Nico said. "I have no more questions."

"Maresciallo?" Nardi asked.

Perillo held up the piece of paper Nardi had given him. "I will have to question your mother and her aide. Also your neighbors."

"Be prepared. Mamma will inundate you with a torrent of complaints about how badly our government is run, and the neighbors will tell you what a terrible son I am for not living with the woman to whom I owe my life."

"Good. That means they will tell the truth, which might not be the case with your mother and her aide. You are free to go. The interview is over."

Daniele read out the time and stopped the recording. Nardi and Nico stood up. Perillo said, "Thank you for finally taking the time to come, Signor Nardi." Nico mouthed his thanks.

"I hope you will forgive my reluctance," Nardi said. "I have brought dessert, which you were not able to have at the restaurant. Crema Catalana for the three of you. One of your brigadieres kindly offered to store it in his refrigerator."

The thought of Vince with their dessert made Perillo get out of his armchair. "Thank you."

"Consider it an advertisement for Il Cestino, not a bribe."

"Of course not. I will enjoy it."

Nardi shifted his attention to Nico. "You might think it is crème brûlée, but crema Catalana is made with milk instead of cream. Much lighter. Arrivedervi at Il Cestino."

"I look forward to coming again," Nico said. *Nelli would enjoy it.*

As soon at the door closed, Perillo picked up the phone. "Is the crema covered?"

Nico could hear Vince's deep voice answer.

"Three covered dishes. Good." He put the handset back down. "I don't know what Vince keeps in that refrigerator. I don't like my desserts smelling of fish or fried food."

Nico looked at his watch. He needed to pick up the bread from Enrico's. "Time for me to go and do some real work."

Perillo sat back down. "Not amusing, Nico. Sit. Dani, you too. Explain the reason for your questions." Nico sat in the chair Nardi had just vacated. Daniele pulled up a chair and joined them.

Perillo raised a hand. "No, I understand the first one. Why Nora moved the jewelry needed clarifying, but the old lover? Do you think he could be our killer?"

"Even if he could have been our killer, we now know he's dead. I was curious about him because of what Miss Barron told me. There are some similarities that make me think Nora's English guest may not have told us the whole truth."

"Forgive me, Nico," Daniele interjected, "you think Signorina Barron has lied to you? That is hard to believe. To me she is a true signora. A 'lady,' as you say."

"Yes, Dani. Very much a lady. Refined, polite, well-spoken."

"Should I bring her in?" Perillo asked.

"No. Best to meet her where's she's comfortable. At the hotel at three-thirty?"

"There's no point in my coming," Perillo snapped. "The conversation will all be in English. Daniele will go with you as witness and recorder. I will need a verbal translation as soon as you have finished. Then I will know how to proceed with this new information. If there is any."

Nico stood up straight and tapped his heels. "Yessir!"

Perillo looked up with a frown. "What is it?"

"I'm taking time off from a job that pays."

Perillo spread out his arms. "Nico, Nico, your help fills me with joy. However, depending on you totally because I do not know English makes me as prickly as a chestnut burr. Feeling ignorant leaves a harsh taste on my tongue. Nicotine deprivation does not help. Forgive me."

"Done. I'll take my dessert with me if Vince and OneWag haven't gobbled it down."

Perillo's phone rang when Nico reached the door. "Wait." Nico turned around.

Perillo kept nodding as he listened. "The best to you and your wife, Capitano, and whatever sex comes out, rejoice." He put the phone down. "Tarani's wife's feet are very swollen, which he says is bad. He's taking her to the hospital three weeks early. I thought the baby was due in a month. Three weeks premature is better I guess."

"*Whatever sex comes out?*" Nico repeated with an astonished voice.

Perillo looked puzzled. "What's wrong with that? You can't say auguri e figli maschi anymore. I was saying rejoice whatever sex the baby is."

"Auguri e figli maschi o femmine?" Daniele offered.

Perillo blew out his cheeks. "I meant well. Tarani knows that.

He is a good man. Besides taking care of his wife, he's still looking into whether any diamond dealer in New York and Amsterdam has been offered Nora's jewelry. And he says they didn't find any jewelry at the bike-repair shop or Zanelli's home. Clara's place is being searched next, just in case Marco was dumb enough to hide some of it there."

"Unlikely." Nico opened the door. "Dani, I'll confirm our three-thirty meeting after I get hold of Miss Barron. Ciao."

Perillo waited until he heard Nico whistle for Rocco to ask Daniele, "I was bad, eh?"

Yes, Daniele wanted to say. *You have always been temperamental, but lately you are insensitive and self-involved.* Instead, he said, "I think Signor Nardi's crema Catalana has made you hungry."

"Bravo." Perillo smiled at his astute brigadiere. "I am not at my best when my stomach is as desolate as the Gobi Desert. Let us retrieve our desserts before Vince loses control."

Perillo abandoned his armchair and hurried to the door followed by a relieved Daniele.

THE BREAD HADN'T YET arrived at Enrico's. "You have to understand." Enrico was cutting a few ends of ham. OneWag was casually spread out on the sunny sidewalk outside as if the salumiere's treats were of no interest. "Alba and her women have taken over the bakery. I should not complain as we are having an unexpected success. We have plans to expand the bakery, but in the meantime, I struggle to have a free oven. I don't want to lose my bread clients." He came out from behind the counter and stepped out onto the street, holding the beaded curtain open with one hand. OneWag acknowledged him with a raised head and a quick wag.

"Sit up, OneWag," Nico called out. "That's the least you could do. I apologize for my ungrateful mutt, Enrico. He doesn't deserve your treats."

"No, no. It is a game we play. Is that not true, Rocco?"

OneWag answered by gobbling all three pieces, while Nico found the hotel's telephone number in his contacts. "Good morning, Laura, Nico here. Is Miss Barron around? I'd like to speak to her."

OneWag was stroking his head against Enrico's leg. "Nico will say you are asking for more, but I know you are thanking me."

"She went to Siena with Beppe, I see."

"She wants him to see the Duomo." *Nothing wrong with that. Best to ask though.*

"Do you still have her passport?

"She needed it to shop?

"Oh, I see, the shopkeeper needs it to fill out the detax form." *Rita never bought an expensive enough item to need it.*

"Her luggage is still in the hotel." *Good.*

"No, I don't think she's running away. I just asked, old police habits, I guess.

"She reserved dinner at the hotel at seven." *Tilde was going to throw one of her cast-iron pans at him.*

"Please tell her I'll come by, but no need to disturb her in Siena." *And get her worried in advance.* "Thanks. Ciao."

"The bread is here," Enrico announced, coming back in. "Two bags full. Still warm. Can I get you a treat?"

"Thanks, no. See you tomorrow."

"Tell Gogol I'm glad he's better. Tomorrow I'll have a just-baked package of Alba's Cantuccini for him."

"Thanks. He'll like that. Ciao." Out on the street he called Daniele to give him the time change.

TILDE'S HAND WENT TO her hips. "Maremma maiale, Nico! What about the taglierini with prosciutto chips you were going to serve tonight? It's already on the menu, and I just spent a lot of money getting the fresh pasta from our pastaiolo. It will be here at five." She reached for the phone in her apron. "Let's hope I can cancel."

"Don't. I'll prepare everything in advance. All you'll have to do is cook the pasta."

Tilde threw down the dishtowel. "Of course, I have nothing else to do, do I?"

"Get Enzo to help."

"Ha, you tell him."

"What's wrong with asking your mother-in-law?" Elvira said, her body taking up the width of the kitchen door. "Before you came along, who do you think was doing the cooking in the place, eh? What do you think, Nico? Do you trust me not to overcook the pasta?"

Nico glanced at Tilde before answering. Elvira couldn't see her.

Tilde raised her chest and took a deep breath. She nodded with her exhale.

"How can an American not trust an Italian when it comes to cooking pasta?"

"I was being polite. Now, all the ingredients must be cooked and ready. I will take care of assembling and mixing. Alba will serve, Tilde will take care of the rest of the menu." Elvira stepped into the kitchen so Tilde could see her. "Agreed?"

Tilde mustered a smile. "Agreed. Thank you for offering to help."

"Your crisis, my restaurant, my solution." Elvira turned around and walked out.

Nico waited until Elvira was out of earshot to say, "I'm sorry, Tilde. I'll make it up to you."

"Start by solving the murder. Now get to work. We have a lunch to prepare."

MISS BARRON WAS SITTING at a table in a corner of the hotel patio when Nico and Daniele walked out. She looked very elegant in a long navy-blue silk dress with a white wool shawl draped on her shoulders. She raised a hand when she saw Nico.

Six other tables were occupied with couples and one family with two small, very well-behaved children. Passing by them, Nico heard French. "Good evening, Miss Barron. I think you remember Brigadiere Donato."

She smiled, her face soft and younger looking in the table's candlelight. "Yes, I do. He's the mahrayshallow's handsome young man. Laura told me you were coming by. I waited to have dessert, thinking you might enjoy having some too."

"I'm sorry you waited," Nico said, noticing she was still wearing the watch fob around her neck. "I thought you would have finished by now. Go ahead, please. Have your dessert. We'll wait for you in the room we were in yesterday. No hurry."

"I see. We are going to have a serious meeting. I think I'll have a Pimm's for my dessert. I'll get it in the bar on the way."

The hotel waiter, Leo, on bartending duty that night, greeted Miss Barron with a big smile. "Il solito. No, sorry. Usual?"

"Yes, Leo. Although tonight is going to be different, I suspect. Nothing for you, gentlemen?" She didn't wait for an answer. "Of course not. You're on duty. Add a generous splash of gin to my glass, Leo. Molto gin. These gentlemen want me to bare my soul." She took hold of the tall glass of Pimm's Leo offered her and led the way to the room where she had sat with Nico the day before.

Miss Barron lowered herself slowly onto one of the leather sofas, careful not to spill her drink. She indicated the two armchairs facing her. "I suppose you've found me out, Mr. Doyle. I was afraid you would." She took a sip of her drink and put it down with its napkin on the side table.

Daniele took out his cell phone.

She noticed the phone and looked up at Daniele, with what Nico assumed was a forgiving smile. "Of course. I am to be recorded. I will have to be careful with my words."

"Can you—" Nico started to say.

"Please." Miss Barron cupped her hands together, the earlier softness in her face gone. "It is my story, Mr. Doyle. Allow me to be the one to tell it."

"Go ahead, but I will need to ask questions."

"You might not have any." She reached for her Pimm's and this time took a long thirsty drink.

Daniele tapped the record button and made his announcement.

Miss Barron sat back on the sofa, holding the glass with both her hands as if it would give her support. "As I told you that ghastly morning, Nora and I met on a train from Bath to London. She told me she had gone down to Bath to see the Roman ruins. I believed her. She was terribly curious about me and asked all sorts of questions that I answered, stupidly flattered that someone found me interesting. I find it hard to forgive myself for my lapse in judgment, but I was very unhappy at the time. My ex-fiancé, a man I still loved, loved deeply, was dying of cancer and refused to let me see him. I was still carrying the wounds of his rejection the year before. For that one-and-a-half-hour ride to London, Nora kept me captive with her energy, her self-assurance, her conviction that a trip to Italy would rid me of what she defined as the '*paralyzing sorrow*' that was showing on my face—" Miss Barron raised her glass and pressed it against her cheek.

Daniele rose and opened both windows.

"Grazie." She put the drink back on the side table. "I didn't realize my state was that apparent to a complete stranger. It was a shock. One I needed. She wrote out her address when we arrived in London and brashly tucked the paper into the pocket of my coat. '*When you come to my parts come find me.*'

"Martin died a few months after that train trip. On May fifteenth. One month later I came to stay at this hotel, with a new hairdo, new clothes, my paralyzing sadness locked in my heart. Everyone assumed, given my age, that I was a signora. A widow, surely, since no man was at my side. Why not be what I had hoped to be? A woman who had married the man she loved. It was only after my evening with Nora the night before she died—yes, Mr. Doyle, I see the question in your eyes. May fifteenth, the anniversary of Martin's death. Nora had planned my visit with great care, waiting to reveal how cleverly she had duped me on the very night that every year filled me with wrenching pain.

"That night, after a quiet dinner out on the back patio, we went to the music room as we had every night. She had her usual Cognac. I nursed my wine. She asked me if I wanted her to play the *Moonlight Sonata*. She leaned her body toward me with her eyes fixed on my face. I don't think I gasped visibly. I hope not, but the intensity with which she studied my face told me she had not suggested that sonata randomly. A light began to flicker in my head."

Miss Barron readjusted her body on the sofa, smoothed the skirt of her dress and took several sips from her drink. She offered Nico a hesitant smile. "You will find me foolish, but I am reenacting my gestures of discomfort. They take me back."

"*What makes you think I want to listen to the* Moonlight Sonata?*'

"*Martin told me it was his favorite piece of music. You used to play it for him.'

"The flicker steadies into a flame. I ask a question to which I fear I know the answer. *You are the one?*'

"*I am. We met on my first trip to England at a London art gallery. We admired the same painting. I found his Englishness sexy.*' Nora sips between sentences. *It wasn't his fault or yours. I simply showed him a different way of loving, one fed by passion. Have you ever known passion, Laetitia? It is a very irrational emotion. It has no rules.*'

"I want to stand up, leave, fly back. Back anywhere. Away. But I am glued to the chair. *'You insisted I come to Italy, and at your expense, to tell me the man I was engaged to left me for you. Why? What satisfaction does crushing your boot on a festering wound give you?'*

"*'I believe knowing the truth is healing. Truth brings clarity. You will hate me. Most people do. But you'll see, the hate will help.'* She is slurring her words. *'Martin the deceiver becomes Martin the victim of a conniving foreign woman.'*

"Fury gives me the strength to get up. *'I will be gone first thing in the morning.'*

"*'If you prefer.'*

"I start to walk away. Nora stops me with, *'This belongs to you.'*

"I turn. She is holding up the eighteenth-century watch fob I gave Martin as an engagement present. A gasp escapes me.

"*'No, Laetitia, he didn't give it to me. I took it from him when I said goodbye. He was too sick to notice.'* Nora is talking as if she has glue in her mouth. *'That's when I met you on the train. I had seen photographs of you among Martin's things. Our meeting was pure chance, if you believe in chance.'* She dangles the watch fob.

"I want it, but don't want to give her the satisfaction of taking it.

"*'Go on, it's yours.'* When I don't move, she tosses it at my feet. *'Buonanotte, Laetitia. I'm very tired. I will sleep here tonight. See you in the morn . . .'*

"She fell asleep midsentence. I picked up the watch fob and left her there," Miss Barron said. She leaned back, letting her head fall against the sofa.

Daniele had watched Miss Barron, fascinated by the control in her voice in contrast to the changing expressions on her face. Sadness, anger and now blankness. Had she just confessed? Nico had pushed himself forward in the armchair, his elbows on his knees. He could feel Nico's sudden tension. "Should I get her another drink or a glass of water?" Daniele asked.

Nico repeated the question in English.

"No." She lifted her head to look at Daniele. "Grazie."

Daniele smiled. *A lovely lady. Not a murderer.*

"I'm just tired. Baring my soul doesn't come easily. Over and out, Mr. Doyle."

"Thank you." Her story had moved him. She had told a painful story with incredible dignity, a story that he could now only hold against her. "The diazepam must have been in the Cognac bottle that was not found. You signed a statement in which you said you woke up when you heard the *Moonlight Sonata* being played."

"I did."

"I think something else woke you up."

"I have just signed my own arrest warrant, haven't I?"

"I'm afraid so, but which one? Obstruction of justice, murder or both?"

"Oh, I did want to smash her head in with a poker, I did. I could have, but someone took care of her for me."

"What did wake you?"

"Anger, I think. I was suddenly wide awake, ready to confront her, tell her how despicable she was. Martin could never have loved a woman like her. I put on a robe and went downstairs."

"What time was this?"

"The same time I told you. I didn't lie about that. I walked into the music room. It was dark. I had left the lights on when I'd walked out. I turned them on and saw Nora was no longer in the armchair. The glass and the bottle of Cognac were gone too. I was annoyed she'd slipped away to her bedroom. I turned around to leave the room and there she was on her back slumped across the piano bench, fast asleep I assumed. I went to the piano and standing over her I played the first movement. It doesn't take long. Just over five minutes. She didn't stir. I shook her to wake her up. Then I saw the cord. The shock sent me running upstairs to get my travel agenda for the right telephone number. I called the carabinieri station then went back into the music room and lifted her torso up and posed her, with her hand on the keys, as if she had just finished playing."

"Why did you do that?"

"She'd dreamed of being a concert pianist. I posed her like one in death. Out of spite or whether I felt suddenly sorry for her, I don't know. Does it matter?"

Nico sat back up. "It does to the law. Maresciallo Perillo will expect you at the station tomorrow morning at ten. He will have many more questions to ask you after you sign tonight's statement. The interview is over." He repeated that in Italian.

Daniele made his announcement and stopped recording.

"Miss Barron," Nico said, "I'm afraid I need to take your passport."

"I understand, although I'm far too tired to go anywhere but bed tonight. I always keep it with me when I travel abroad." She reached into her dark-blue clutch bag and handed Nico her British passport.

"You have a bottle of diazepam in your room. I will need to take that with me also."

"I would have thought you would be kind enough to allow me an escape, but it doesn't matter. I did not kill myself after Martin left me. I would not kill myself now." She took out a tasseled iron key from her bag and held it up. "Room 312. Medicine cabinet. Second shelf."

Nico pocketed it as he stood up. Daniele grabbed his phone and quickly got to his feet, eager to find out what he had recorded.

"Good night, Miss Barron," Nico said. "I will see you in the morning."

"You will," Miss Barron answered.

"I'll leave the room key at the front desk."

"Buonanotte, Signora," Daniele said with a slight bow of his head.

"Notte," she said, closing her eyes as if she could not bear to see them one more instant.

"What did she say?" Daniele asked Nico after he explained why they were going to Miss Barron's room. "She didn't confess, did she? If she did, she's lying. Or she regrets it terribly. Did you see her face? It spoke for her."

Nico retrieved the half-empty bottle, left the key at the front desk and walked to the parking lot. Daniele followed, saying, "No, I don't believe it. What did she tell you, Nico? How did she explain?"

Nico stopped. "Dani, it's late. Give me your phone. You'll read what she said tomorrow morning when you read what I've translated and correct it to proper written Italian. Buonanotte."

"Let me quickly text Stella."

Nico marveled at how fast Daniele's thumbs flew over the tiny keys. He could only type on the phone with his index finger. Daniele kept going.

"Are you writing an essay?"

"I'm just telling her why I love her so much."

Nico was anxious to get home. He had to call Perillo about the meeting in the morning and the translation was going to take forever. "Dani, enough. She already knows how you feel."

"I like to remind her why." He signed off and handed over the phone. "Ciao, see you in the morning. Bring Rocco. Vince and I miss him."

ONEWAG RAN AND STRETCHED against Nico's leg. "Hey, buddy." Nico reached down and scratched the top of the dog's head. Nelli came in from the balcony with a book in her hand. "Ciao, amore." She gave Nico a kiss. "How did it go?"

"Perillo will be pleased." He walked to the sideboard and plugged in Daniele's phone.

"She confessed?"

She confessed she had a surefire motive, Nico thought. *Whether that would get her arrested for murder was up to Perillo.* "She told me a long story, that's all I can say. I now have to translate it."

"Need my help?"

"Thanks, no. Daniele will polish it."

"Good. By the way, I wasn't just being curious."

"I know." He reached over and took her in his arms. "You were being helpful as always." He kissed her hair. "I better get to work. I told Perillo I'd have it ready for him at nine tomorrow morning."

"Then I'll take myself and my book to bed." She kissed him lightly. "I ate at Sotto Il Fico tonight. Your taglierini were outstanding."

"Glad to hear that."

"I was too." Nelli walked toward the bedroom. "Coming, Rocco?"

OneWag looked up at Nico, looked at Nelli, looked back at Nico.

"Your call, buddy."

With a look Nico interpreted as regret, the dog settled down on the hard floor and rested his head on his paws.

"Much appreciated, OneWag, but it's going to be a long night."

OneWag didn't budge.

FOURTEEN

Perillo looked up from Miss Barron's translated statement and rested his eyes on the woman. With her hands on her lap, she met his gaze with a serene face, the face of a woman who has accepted what was to come, Perillo decided. He had thought her guilty that morning at the villa but had changed his mind after meeting the victim's entitled and unpleasant family, letting his own prejudices get in the way. His first instinct had been right.

"Please impress on the signora that it is to her advantage to admit her guilt."

Nico translated.

"What advantage does it give me?" Miss Barron asked, speaking directly to Perillo. "I would go to jail anyway with no chance of an appeal. If I had killed her, I would have used the fireplace poker. One hard smash and she'd be done for. Strangling takes minutes, I think."

"You're not helping yourself, Miss Barron," Nico said, not wanting to translate what she said.

"Perhaps not, but I'm not sure I care."

"Did you kill Nora Salviati?"

"I wanted to."

Nico repeated the question.

Miss Barron's fingers clasped the watch fob. "She destroyed my life."

"I ask you again. Did you kill Nora Salviati?" He watched her debating how she should answer.

Miss Barron straightened her shoulders, released her fingers from the fob. "I did not."

Nico translated for Perillo.

"I don't believe her," Perillo declared. "In her statement she says anger woke her up. She went downstairs ready to confront the woman who had stolen her fiancé. Maybe the idea of killing her had not yet entered her head. She found Nora in a drugged sleep. Ah, how easy it is to eliminate this terrible woman. Maybe she saw the poker and was tempted to use it but realized the poker would splatter blood over her bathrobe.

"But strangulation is bloodless. Miss Barron went to Nora's bedroom, maybe the very place where Martin and Nora made love. Cut off the curtain tie with the scissors we found on the dresser, careful not to leave fingerprints, went back downstairs and strangled the woman who ruined her life." Perillo sat back in his armchair with a look of great satisfaction. "That's what happened."

It was very possible, Nico thought. "Do you want me to translate all of that?"

"Just this: Signorina Barron, I am detaining you because I believe you killed Nora Salviati by strangulation." Perillo nodded to Nico. Nico translated.

Perillo continued. "This detention lasts forty-eight hours, during which you will be interrogated by Prosecutor Della Langhe. If he determines there is enough evidence suggesting your guilt, you will be arrested and put on trial. An interpreter chosen by the prosecutor will assist you." After Nico had translated those words, Perillo added, "Brigadiere Dino will accompany you to your hotel to gather your belongings and then drive you to Florence." Perillo stood up. "I'll call Tarani from Vince's room. The case is really in his hands now."

Daniele made his announcement and stopped recording.

"It sounds terribly complicated," Miss Barron said after Nico translated. "Why can't you be my translator and why can't they just arrest me?"

"Italian law has its own intricacies. You've met Brigadiere Dino. He was with me when we searched your room. He will be your watchdog, I'm afraid."

"He seems harmless enough. Can I go now?"

"I think it better to wait for the maresciallo to come back."

Miss Barron examined Nico's face. "I'm looking for clues to what you think. I can't find any."

"What I think is not important."

"It is to me."

"Do I think you killed Nora? It does look likely. You have a very strong motive and easy opportunity."

"Do I hear a *but* in your voice?"

Nico hesitated. He didn't want to give her hope.

Her eyes entreated him. "Maybe a very small *but*?"

"Yes, there is," Nico admitted. *Maybe only because he really liked her.*

"Thank you. That makes me feel better."

They sat in silence, waiting. Daniele rewound the tape, put order to his already-neat desk. He was having a hard time accepting this nice, elegant English lady as a murderer. If she was, he could only blame Nora.

Ten or so minutes later, Perillo returned. "Done." He sat back down, his face brimming with relief. "She's due at the prosecutor's office at six o'clock this evening."

Miss Barron stood up and smoothed out the front of her dark-gray sheath. She faced Perillo. "Finito?"

Perillo raised his eyebrows, surprised by her Italian. "Sì. Finito."

She picked up her handbag with a satisfied smile and said to Nico, "Finito is what Leo always asks me after each course. I gathered it means, 'Are you done?' Goodbye, Mr. Doyle. Thank you for your help. I do hope I will have the chance to see you again."

Nico walked her out of the office. OneWag ambled out of Vince's room to wag once and sniff Miss Barron's shoes.

"You have a sweet dog, Mr. Doyle. I hope you deserve him."

"I try," Nico said. "You are a strong woman, Miss Barron."

"I try."

Dino, who had been waiting at the entrance of the station, stepped forward and offered his arm. Miss Barron took it and together they walked away.

Nico went back to Perillo's office, followed by OneWag. "Time for me to go."

"Thank you for all the help," Perillo said. OneWag scampered to the back of the room to see if Daniele had anything to offer. "Della Langhe will arrest her. I know you like her, but he'll have no choice. The evidence speaks for itself. Odd that she told you that story last night. Didn't she realize she was building her own cell?"

"She realized it at a certain point, but the need to unload was too strong, or Nora's revelation made her stop caring what happens to her anymore."

"I forgot to tell you when you first came in. They're releasing Nora's body this morning. Clara called to tell me the funeral will be at ten Thursday morning in the church of San Leolino. It's just above Panzano."

"I've been there. What about Marco?"

"Saturday in Lucca."

"I'll go to Nora's. Nelli will want to be there, and it gives me a chance to take a look at this lovely family you've been talking about. Ciao to both of you. I wish I could say I'm glad it's over, but I'm not."

"I feel the same way." Daniele was trying to grab the pencil OneWag had found on the floor and was now walking proudly around the room with in his mouth as if it were a trophy he'd just won.

"Well, I have to admit I'm relieved it's over," Perillo said, "but the devil knows how I would have rejoiced if I'd sent Fabio and/ or his wife to the prosecutor."

Nico snapped at his dog. "Drop it!" The morning's proceedings had put him in a bad mood.

OneWag looked back at Nico and sat down, pencil still in his mouth.

"Now, please." A gentle voice always worked best. "If you don't mind."

The dog padded closer to Daniele, waited until Daniele bent down and held out his hand, then gently dropped the scrunched and wet pencil into his palm.

"Thank you, Rocco."

OneWag ran to catch up with a departing Nico.

"HOW WAS BREAKFAST WITH Gogol?" Nico asked Nelli over the phone. He was at the Greve Coop picking up more onions and leeks for his pasta dish. Tilde had texted him to say she wanted him to make it again. She was taking care of the pasta. OneWag was waiting outside, chewing on a rawhide bone Nelli had bought him.

"He wanted to know why you and Rocco weren't with me. I explained you were working on a translation for the maresciallo."

He'd given up his morning run and his breakfast with Gogol to get the damn thing in decent shape.

"I'm driving him to the hospital this afternoon," Nelli said.

"I can do that."

"He doesn't want you to see him until he's back, the operation done. I think he's ashamed he needs the stent. He's a very proud man."

"I'm sorry it's all on you, Nelli."

"I'm happy to do it. I'm owed some time at work."

"Nora's funeral is on Thursday morning." He told her the time and place.

"Will you come with me?" she asked.

"Yes, I'd like to."

"I'm glad. I have to get back to work. Shall I come over tonight?"

"Of course, every night." Once Gogol was back and mended, he'd ask her to live with him. He wanted her to decide without distractions.

"I'll pick up OneWag and maybe I'll water the vegetable garden for you. Ciao."

"Thanks, Nelli."

"I said maybe."

"Thanks for being great whether you water the garden or not. I love you."

"You're going soft on me, Nico, but I think I like it. Love you back." She clicked off.

Nico held the phone to his ear for a moment, the silence still filled with Nelli's voice.

NICO WALKED INTO Sotto Il Fico loaded down with the Coop vegetables and Enrico's bread and prosciutto. Enzo took over the bread bags. "Another Nico dish?" he asked when he saw the Coop bag. He put the bags down on the nearest table.

"No, the same."

"Good. I'll write it in the menu. *Taglierini alla Nico.* My compliments. We ran out quickly."

"Leave my name out of it."

"Too late. That's how it was on the menu last night, that's the way it stays. Before you walk by my irascible mother on your way to the kitchen, be warned she's not happy with you."

"She didn't get the first taste?"

"She did since she put it together, but she wanted more and didn't get it. Tilde isn't as nice to her as you are."

"Not true. Elvira often has to remind me." Nico shouldered the Coop bag and walked to Elvira's corner. She was folding napkins, a pile already high on her lap.

"Buongiorno, Elvira." Nico kissed her cheeks.

She did not look up. "I pay you a salary, do I not?"

Guessing what was coming, Nico pulled a chair over and sat down facing her. "Yes, you do and I thank you for it." He felt like a schoolkid in front of the principal.

"And why do I pay you a salary?" She kept folding, her head down.

"To help Tilde in the kitchen. I know, I've taken a lot of time off. You have every right to be angry."

Her head snapped up. "I decide what rights I have to my emotions."

"Of course. Deduct the time I've taken off from my salary."

"That is too easy. You'll go off whenever you feel like it and leave us in the lurch. Last night, I helped prepare your dish. The two strands I tasted were good. For my work I deserved a full plate. In an hour it was gone. You weren't here to make more. I had to eat Tilde's usual fare."

"I will make you some now, if you'd like."

She looked down at her pile of napkins as if she didn't want Nico to see she was pleased. "It is my restaurant. I should be able to eat as much as I want of whatever we make."

"Absolutely." Nico stood up.

"Nico, I need you," Tilde called from the kitchen.

"I'm sorry, Elvira. Thursday morning I do have a funeral in San Leolino. After that I will be all yours."

Elvira clasped her hands together. "Let us thank heaven, then. The investigation is over and I can count on you to earn your salary again."

"Nico!" Tilde called out.

"Now go and make your dish."

"Right away."

"I wanted to get you away from her," Tilde said in a low voice as soon as Nico walked into the kitchen. "You found Nora's killer?"

"So it seems."

"You don't sound convinced."

He dropped the food bag on his side of the counter. "I'm just not happy about who it turned out to be."

"I'm sorry about that, but I'm glad it's over. You should have heard the fuss Elvira made about being deprived. I barely tasted it. We had a big crowd last night. Everybody seemed to want it. That's what happens when there's a new dish on the menu. Let's remember that next time you or I come up with something different." Tilde stopped tearing lettuce to give Nico a hug. "I've missed you!"

He hugged her back. "It's always great to be here."

Tilde went back to her salad. "Nelli was here last night. I saw her for all of five seconds. She looked very happy. So do you when you're not dealing with murder. Let's hope Nora's will be the last."

"Fingers crossed." He dug into the bag and took out Enrico's prosciutto slices.

Tilde watched him remove four slices.

"What are you doing? We're serving your dish tonight."

"Making the owner of Sotto Il Fico and the person who pays my salary happy."

"A noble attempt. Good luck."

WHEN NICO TURNED OFF his lights and got out of the car at ten-thirty that night, he felt as if a mask had been thrown over his face. The sky was a coal-dark dome. The front door light had burned out again. No lights in the windows. The air had turned chilly. He heard OneWag panting toward him, felt the dog's snout rub against his leg. "Hey, buddy." He bent down and gave OneWag a good back rub. "Where's Nelli?"

The dog trotted off into the darkness. Nico headed toward the vegetable garden in the back of the house. He didn't hear any water running. "Nelli?" He opened the gate and the crickets hushed for a few seconds. Nico bent down to touch the ground under a zucchini plant. Wet. Maybe she'd gone to bed. He closed the gate behind him. The crickets started again. A thought hit him. *No, she's not in bed. OneWag wouldn't be out.*

"Ciao, Nico."

His heart hiccupped. "Where are you?"

"Under your olive tree. I was fast asleep."

Nico walked ahead to the one olive tree that had escaped from Aldo's grove. When Nico had first rented the small farm, he'd instantly felt a kinship with the lone tree. Twisted and old, at least a hundred according to Aldo, it still produced. If the tree could do it on its own, maybe he could too. He enjoyed sitting under it to think, read, relax.

"What are you doing here?" All he could see was a long, dark lump. When he reached it, he turned on his cell phone light.

"Don't." Nelli covered her face with the blanket she was lying on. OneWag, now lying against her hip, closed his eyes.

"Sorry." He turned the light off. "For a minute there, I was worried."

Nelli patted the ground next to her. "I like to listen to the crickets. Their mating calls lull me to sleep."

"They keep me awake and I think it might rain."

"So let it." She patted the ground again. "Lie down beside me. If it rains you can use a little shrinking."

"Thanks." He lowered himself down and stretched out next to her. "Gogol?"

"Gogol's being operated on tomorrow morning. If all goes well, he'll be home no later than Saturday. And he is adamant about no one visiting him. Not you, not me. He will see us when 'the dreams of early morning are true.' Dante, of course, from *Hell*, I think."

"When he's his old self again?"

"His healthier self." Nelli turned on her side to face Nico. "Tell me about you."

"The case is closed for us. Miss Barron was arrested for the murder of Nora Salviati." Perillo had called him just before closing time. Della Langhe thought it would be an easy court win.

"That's wonderful." Nelli kissed him. "Back to normal life."

"Not for her."

"You care?"

"Yes, I do. I say this to you and no one else: Nora Salviati deserves what she got."

Nelli pulled Nico toward her. "Shh. Close your eyes and think of dreams coming true for Gogol, for you, for me, maybe even for Miss Barron."

"Hmm." Nico snuggled his face in the warm crook of Nelli's neck. It wasn't long before he fell asleep to the sound of crickets chirping for a mate.

FIFTEEN

On Wednesday, while Nico was plating more of Tilde's zucchini lasagne, Nelli called to give him the good news.

"He's in the recovery room, coming out of anesthesia now, muttering 'incomprehensible words,' according to the nurses. They let me take a peek at him."

Alba bumped her hip against Nico's. He moved aside to let her pick up the filled plates.

"The surgeon said the stent should allow him another ten years at least. I'm going to work now. For Nora's funeral tomorrow can you pick me up at eight-thirty?"

"I'm alone tonight?"

"I need to catch up on some of my own work. You've got Rocco. Ciao."

"Good news?" Tilde asked as she took another dish of lasagne out of the oven.

"Yes. Gogol's stent is in place and he's babbling Dante to the nurses."

"We'll drink to his good health on the terrace as soon as lunch is over."

"I'm all for it." They usually drank to lunch being over.

"Now that Alba's Cantuccini are so successful, are we going to lose her?" Nico asked.

"Never!" Alba said, her hands on her hips. "I need more lasagne."

Nico resumed plating.

"Tilde and Enzo gave me a job when I had nothing. For the cantuccini, I delegate. Ivana takes my place." Alba held up the six plates now balancing on her arms. "No one else can do this." With one graceful pivot, she exited the kitchen sideways.

"One day," Nico said.

"Don't even think about it."

THE FUNERAL MASS HAD started by the time Nico and Nelli got to the parish church of San Leolino. Nelli, pretty in a gray dress that matched her braid, had taken one look at the old dark suit Nico had on, a suit he had worn for his wedding to Rita, and insisted on going home with him. Out of the few clothes he owned, she selected a dark pair of slacks, a striped blue shirt and, for lack of anything better, a navy-blue cardigan. He wasn't bothered by her taking over one bit. It made him feel married to her.

When they walked into the plain Romanesque-style church, Nelli crossed herself and murmured, "So few people." Only the first three pews were filled.

The plain coffin, covered by a cape of multicolored roses, rested on a bier at the end of the center aisle. A wreath of peonies stood on a wooden easel to one side of the coffin. The wide ribbon declared: *FOREVER IN OUR HEARTS, THE ROSATI FAMILY*.

Nico heard his name whispered. He looked back. Perillo and Daniele, in uniform, stood erect next to the entrance.

"Why aren't you sitting?" Nico whispered as Nelli walked down the aisle.

"To show our respect," Perillo whispered back. "You just missed Adriana's speech." A woman was leaving the lectern in a knee-revealing white dress and trip-inducing heels. "She announced that her mother had always been difficult and now that her mother was dead, she hoped Nora was at peace. A tribute from the heart, eh?"

"She didn't lie. That's how she felt."

"At funerals lies are expected and forgiven."

"Later," Nico said and walked down the aisle to join Nelli, who had slipped into a pew a few rows behind the family.

A young man had taken Adriana's place behind the lectern. "I am honored that Adriana and Clara have asked me to pay tribute to their mother." Nico narrowed his eyes. The man looked familiar.

"My father had hoped to speak, but he found his grief too great to allow him to do so. I will speak for all my family. Nora was good to us. Welcomed us into her home . . ."

Nico tuned him out. "Who is he?"

"Stefano Rosati, the one from South Africa. I told you about him."

"Perillo liked him."

Stefano went on a few more minutes about the snacks Nora's housekeeper would send them while they played, how they were always forgiven when their tree-climbing ended up breaking branches. "Nora, I thank for your patience with us, for your generosity. I hope you have found in death the same beautiful home you had in life."

"That was sweet," Nelli said. "I think he meant it. Of the two Rosati boys, Nora told me Stefano was her favorite. He liked to sit in while I painted the girls and stare at Clara with lovelorn eyes. Adriana and Clara competed for Maso's affections."

"Odd name."

"It's a common nickname for Tommaso."

In the front row, a woman stood up and walked up the short stairs. She was wearing wide-leg black slacks, a black short-sleeved scoop-neck top and flat white sandals.

"That's Clara," Nelli said. "She always dressed her own way. I enjoyed that about her."

"Like you."

"That's right."

Clara turned around to face her audience. Nico instantly recognized the long messy hair, the pretty face. "I saw her at the Gravigna cemetery about a week ago."

"What was she doing there?"

Clara lowered the microphone. "In the movies, funerals are usually held in a downpour. My mother had enough rain in her life. For her the sun is shining today." The oblong window of the apse was filled with light. The gold altarpiece was bright with it. "I will always remember her in sunlight. I hope you will too. Thank you for coming. The burial is private. Our mother will rest in the Salviati vault of the Panzano cemetery."

"They didn't even give her a mass," Nelli said.

"We missed the service."

"We were only twenty minutes late."

Nico noticed Nelli's eyes fill with curiosity. "Did you talk to Clara at the cemetery? She's very attractive."

"Rocco caught her attention. She was moved because she thought Rocco was grieving on his owner's grave. I agree, she is attractive."

"I'm not the jealous type, Nico, but I am always curious. Clara must know someone buried there."

"She seemed to be in a happy mood."

Nelli and Nico stood up. Don Alfonso was coming down the aisle, head bent in prayer. Behind him Stefano and Fabio were guiding Nora's coffin by the handles of the bier. Nico studied Stefano's face as he passed, trying to match him to the man he'd seen at the cemetery.

Adriana and Clara followed the coffin, eyes straight ahead. The Rosatis came next. As Gianna passed Nico, she nodded to him. She was the only one who looked truly sad. He acknowledged her with a smile of regret.

The church emptied out. The door was wide-open and light poured in with the cool morning air. Daniele and Perillo had already left by the time Nelli and Nico slipped out of the row.

They walked to the car. "Are you off to work?" Nico asked.

"After you drive me home and I change. I'll see you tonight?"

"Yes, but let's not fall asleep on the grass again. I'm covered with mosquito bites."

"You're too sweet."

"They didn't bite you?"

"I'd sprayed myself. Ciao, bello."

AFTER DRIVING NELLI TO her house, Nico sat in the car and did a quick search on his phone. Satisfied with the result, he called Perillo. "I need you to put a tail on Clara Salviati."

"Why?"

"I think she could lead us to her mother's murderer."

"We already have Nora's murderer."

"I have a hunch that says we don't."

"And you think you know who she's going to lead us to."

"Yes," Nico said.

"May I ask who?"

Nico told him.

Perillo stayed silent for a moment, then said, "You are asking for a lot of manpower for just a hunch."

"Trail Clara for three days but start now. She's burying her mother as we speak. I'm sure they will all go to the villa afterward."

"She's been at the station more than once. She'd recognize all the carabinieri I have available."

"Ask Tarani to send a couple of men down, but it has to be done quickly."

"Tarani is going to have to pass this on to our esteemed prosecutor. Manpower involves money. I can't tell him you have an itch you want to scratch. I'll get a vaffa for sure."

"Tell him we're trying to avoid a possible miscarriage of justice, then. That our job is to find the truth without cost considerations. No, forget that." Nico realized he was so excited about his hunch, he'd stopped thinking coherently. "Remind him that we haven't found the jewelry yet. That was part of our job. No, your job, to be exact. I can go back to cooking and forget about it, if you like. It's up to you."

"Nico, you are my friend, and I will do my best to convince Tarani of the wisdom of your hunch, but if he says no, please do not blame me."

"I have no intention of blaming anyone but myself. Thank you."

"Let's just hope Signora Tarani hasn't gone into labor."

NICO DROVE UP TO the old town of Gravigna, left the car running in the main piazza and ran to get OneWag from Luciana. In a pinch she was the dog sitter. OneWag still couldn't be left alone at home or in the car. Whoever had locked him up in the past had caused deep wounds.

"I have peonies for Rita," Luciana said as OneWag wiggled his rear in happiness at seeing Nico.

"Thanks, keep them for me." Nico accepted her hug for a few embarrassing seconds. "I don't have time right now. I'm due in the kitchen."

"Tomorrow at the latest." Luciana had made it clear in unsubtle ways that she did not approve of his close relationship with Nelli. She had met Rita and liked her.

NELLI SHOWED UP AT Sotto Il Fico just as Nico was hanging up his apron. The diners had all left and the kitchen had been scrubbed down. "Nice surprise," Nico said.

"Ciao, cara." Tilde hugged Nelli and planted the standard kiss on her cheeks. "Always great to see you."

"I expected to meet you at home," Nico said.

"That's what I expected too, but Rocco showed up at the studio and insisted I follow him up here. He's outside waiting. What does he know that I don't?"

Nico laughed. Nelli's showing up unexpectedly filled him with joy. "OneWag could smell the steak we served tonight from the street. Since he doesn't get any until we go home, he was hurrying the process along."

Tilde picked up the plastic bag she had filled with steak bits and other food scraps. "I'd ask you to stay and have a glass of wine on the terrace with Enzo and me, but I suspect you're anxious to get home."

"We do have so little time together," Nico said.

"I know," Tilde said. "I've thought about that a lot recently."

Nico's cell phone rang. He looked down at the screen and felt a sudden adrenaline rush. "Excuse me, I have to get this." He walked out of the kitchen. "Yes or no, Perillo?"

"You're a lucky man, Nico. This morning Signora Tarani delivered twins, a boy and a girl. All three are thriving. Tarani is so happy his brain got disconnected. He's going to do as you asked without consulting with Della Langhe. He trusts your instincts and added that he prides himself in having all his investigations fully resolved. That includes finding the jewelry."

"Thank you, Perillo. Let's hope my hunch is right."

"I'm counting on it. The first man is on his way to the villa. The second will take over after twelve hours. You'll know the instant I hear anything. Ciao." The phone went dead.

"You're looking very satisfied," Nelli observed when Nico walked back into the kitchen.

"If I do, I'm jumping ahead of myself. It's time to go home. Good night, Tilde."

Tilde held out her hand. "Wait. Let me finish what I was going to say before you walked away. I've decided to change your hours. As of next week, you're going to have two nights and Sunday off. Enzo agrees and Elvira is only too happy to save the little money I will deduct from your salary."

Nico opened his mouth.

"Don't start sputtering protests, Nico. I've made up my mind. Finding happiness again does not come easily, and it can easily slip away. I love both of you. You need time together and I don't need a sous-chef that gets more compliments for his cooking than I do."

"You don't mean that," Nico said. "Everyone knows you're a far better cook."

Tilde winked at Nelli. "If you say so."

"How will you manage?" Nico asked. Having more free time to be with Nelli would be wonderful, but part of him felt rejected.

"I managed without you before, I'll manage again. I'm not saying this is forever. When the tourists start pouring in a couple of weeks from now, I'll probably need you back full-time. If you're willing, of course."

"Always eager. Always willing." Nico gave Tilde a hug. "Thank you."

Nelli put her hands on her hips. "Is anyone going to ask me how I feel about this?"

"The two of you will have to work that out."

Nelli hooked her arm in Nico's. "I suspect we will."

A bark rang out from outside.

Tilde handed the food bag to Nico. "You'd better go before Rocco wakes up the whole neighborhood."

Nico and Nelli thanked Tilde, kissed cheeks again. "Buonanotte."

"Sogni d'oro for both of you."

"WILL YOU HAVE GOLDEN dreams tonight?" Nico asked when Nelli and OneWag had joined him in bed. Once they got to Nico's place, they had not brought up Nico's upcoming free time. Nelli had talked about her visit to Gogol, and the mural she was getting ready to paint at the vineyard. Nico had listened while going over how best to word his invitation. The possible new lead in the murder case had momentarily receded to the background of his mind.

"Golden dreams because we can have more time together?"

"Well, yes."

Nelli turned to face Nico. OneWag had slipped in between them. "I found it a bit controlling on Tilde's part. She assumed we both want more time together."

"You don't?"

"Of course, I do. I love you, but I also have a life away from you. Sometimes I work in the studio until the early hours."

"I'm not going to take that away, but isn't it going to be nice to have dinner together every night instead of just breakfast?"

Nelli leaned her head over and kissed him hard. "If you cook it." She lifted OneWag, dropped him on her other side and snuggled closer to Nico. "Don't pay any attention to me. I'm happy we can be together more. I am. I've been living alone for over twenty-five years, and I'm a little set in my ways. For a minute there I felt threatened. As if your free time was going to impinge on my freedom."

Something that felt like a rock dropped in Nico's stomach. "That doesn't sound like a woman in love."

"I'm a modern woman in love. You have become the most important part of my life, but you're not all of it. I'm not all of it for you either, Nico. That's the way it should be. Obsessive, possessive love destroys itself."

Nico turned on his back and looked up at the ceiling beams. "I was going to ask you to come live with me." He didn't want to see her reaction.

"Now you won't?"

"You'll say no."

"I love going to bed with you at night, waking up together. I also love having a night and a morning all to myself. I prefer being with you but being with only me is still essential to me for now. We haven't spent a lot of everyday time together. Tilde understood that. That's why she gave you the time off. Let's explore this new time together, see how it works out. You may end up being bored."

"Never."

Nelli took Nico's face in her hands and turned him toward her. "I love you now, Nico, and I plan to love you forever. I hope you do too."

Nico took her in his arms and held her tight. "God, yes, I do and will."

"Then let's just enjoy that."

"I'll hold off asking until"—he dug his nose in her loose gray hair that smelled of sandalwood—"until I know you'll say yes."

"How will you know that?"

"I'll see it on your beautiful, smiling face."

WHEN NICO'S AND NELLI'S breaths finally slowed to a steady pace, OneWag gingerly climbed over Nelli's legs and burrowed himself between them. Peace now reigned.

SIXTEEN

The next morning, Friday, Nico went to the restaurant early with some ingredients he'd just bought from Enrico. Trying out a new spaghetti recipe would make him feel better. He was anxious to hear from Perillo, and last night's conversation with Nelli had left him worrying that he was rushing things, expecting too much from her.

Walking in he asked Enzo if he didn't mind picking up the bread. "I'm trying out something new."

"I'll be happy to. Something new from you is always welcome."

"Thanks."

"Nothing too expensive, I hope," Elvira said as he kissed her cheeks.

"For you only white truffles and caviar."

"I can't wait."

"You're early and brimming with energy," Tilde said as he strode into the kitchen with his grocery bag.

"Spaghetti alla Tilde coming up. If you like it, a modest thank-you for my reduced hours."

"I'll like anything you make and you know I'm not jealous. I just said that last night as a tease."

"I know." He spread out his ingredients on his usual

workplace. He washed the grape tomatoes and started cutting them in half.

Tilde looked at what he'd placed on his counter. "I see pitted Gaeta olives, anchovies in oil, brined capers and carrots. I'm salivating already."

"Basilico I'll get from the terrace and garlic from the basket. Slice the carrots paper-thin, cut up the rest, sauté everything in olive oil, add the basil and you've got Spaghetti alla Tilde. I'm making only three portions, you, Enzo and Elvira. After, you'll tell me how to tweak it." His cell phone rang. Nico dropped his knife and picked it up without looking, his stomach knotting. "Yes?"

"It's me," Nelli said. "Do you have a moment?"

"Sure." He slipped his phone between his shoulder and cheek and picked up his knife. The knot stayed.

"They're releasing Gogol early. I'm picking him up after work. He complained the hospital food is so bad 'the three-headed hound of Hades would not touch it.' If he's up to it, I thought I'd bring him over to Sotto Il Fico for an early dinner. I know he'll be happy to see you."

"Great idea." Nico started cutting the olives in half. "I'll make sure there's something good and healthy for him to eat."

"Thanks. Ciao." Nelli hung up.

"Who's coming for dinner?" Tilde asked.

"Nelli's bringing Gogol for Sotto Il Fico's good food."

"I'm glad to hear he's well again, but if you don't slow down, you're going to slit a finger with that knife. Relax, Nico. Your thank-you dish will be a great success."

That wasn't the success Nico was hoping for.

THE AFTERNOON BREAK CAME with no news from Perillo. Nico walked down to the main piazza. Luciana, dressed in her dark muumuu, was standing by the door of her flower shop and waved him over.

"I thought you'd forgotten," she said with an accusing tone. He was grateful. It meant she wasn't going to hug him.

"Here I am."

OneWag sniffed the hem of her dress in greeting. Luciana reached into her pocket and took out a cookie. The dog sat. She bent down a little. OneWag got on his hind legs and took the cookie from her fingers. "Somebody was going to pay me double the price I charge him for the flowers, but I said no." OneWag chewed the cookie. "They're for Rita, Nico's *wife*." She bore down on the last word.

"Thank you, Luciana. From now on, charge me more."

Luciana straightened up. "I just might the next time." She carefully made her way between the rows of potted plants and came back with three dark-red peonies.

Nico took them from her. "These are gorgeous. Thank you."

"Am I being too harsh with you?"

"No, you're just being loyal to Rita."

"Nelli is a good woman, and my thinking is old. And maybe I'm jealous." She started shaking with laughter and opened her arms. Nico had no choice but to walk into them. After a long thirty seconds Nico's phone rang. He gently extricated himself from Luciana's hug and picked up long enough to say, "I'll call you right back," before clicking off. "Sorry, Luciana, I have to run."

Knowing Luciana was good for only one cookie a visit, OneWag followed Nico to the cemetery.

"I just got a report," Perillo said when Nico called him back. "Adriana and her husband have left the villa. It looks like Clara is moving out. She put a full duffel bag in her car. I guess she's going back to her place in Lucca."

"No one else around?"

"No. That's all I've got."

"Thanks. Ciao." Nico walked into the cemetery, picked

up the pewter vase at Rita's grave, threw out the faded roses, changed the water and placed the new flowers just under Rita's enamel picture. OneWag, as always, lay down next to the grave. Each time Nico came, he would bring up a specific memory of her in his mind to bring her close. He tried now but failed.

Please forgive me, Rita. And wish me luck.

Nico still had half an hour before he needed to be back in the kitchen. He and OneWag walked all the way back up the Salita della Chiesa and parked themselves on a bench overlooking the golden valley, so called because it had once been covered in wheat. The gold had been replaced years ago by the green of vineyards. The old green was now covered in new-leaf green with tendrils reaching up to the sun, making the whole area seem like a blanket soft enough to jump into. OneWag sat next to him, exchanging wary looks with an orange-and-black cat lying on the hood of a parked car. Nico felt guilty for not being able to summon a Rita memory, but he was too tense. He hated having no authority and asking other people to work on a hunch that might turn out to be wishful thinking. If only he could proceed on his own. In the States a citizen's arrest was allowed. In Italy?

Nico took out his cell phone and searched. No, the rules were different here. He sat back to look at the view and scratched OneWag's head. One of his efforts had gone well, at least. His new dish had received five stars from Enzo and Tilde. Elvira had decreed that the dish would have been better with Castelvetrano instead of Gaeta olives and had given him three stars. Spaghetti alla Tilde would be added to the menu for tomorrow night's dinner with Gaeta olives and Tilde cooking it.

OneWag leapt off the bench.

From a side street a voice cried out, "Are you then Nico, are you the fountain that gives so freely of friendship?" OneWag ventured a wag and sniffed the old man's boots.

"Gogol!" Nico rushed to greet his old friend linking arms with Nelli. "You look wonderful. I've missed you."

Gogol allowed Nico to give him a quick hug. "You miss the crostini I provide."

"Which you always eat."

Gogol let go of Nelli, shuffled to the bench and sat down. "Your Beatrice has walked me far. Resting is good."

"Don't exaggerate," Nelli said, joining Gogol on the bench. "The doctor said you need to walk. A hundred meters is not far." OneWag jumped up between them. The cat on the car hood looked on bored.

"'The demon Charon led me to the eternal darkness of the other shore, but my friends took pity on me and brought me back to life and as I live, I will always voice my gratitude.' My gratitude will be even greater once my stomach has weight to it again."

Nelli looked at Nico. "I know we're early, but he didn't want to go home until he saw you."

Gogol lay his hand on OneWag's head. "And your one-headed dog." OneWag brushed his nose on Gogol's chin. "I will sit here with Rocco and your Beatrice until that time the perfume of your culinary efforts will reach our noses."

"It won't be long," Nico said. "What would you like? How about a vegetable soup followed by a sauteed chicken breast or veal scaloppine?"

"Feed that to the souls in Purgatory. Having been released from Hell I hunger for Heaven. Rigatoni with onions, arugula and sausage. A very big sausage."

Nelli raised two fingers with a sheepish smile.

"Amico, don't forget a sprinkling of hot peppers to remind me of where I've been, and a fistful of parmigiano to celebrate where I am now."

Nico started laughing. Gogol was back to his old self. "At your command."

Two hours later, after Gogol had finished his dinner on the terrace, Nelli took her happy friend back to his home. Sotto Il Fico was filling up, and Nico was busy in the kitchen. Perillo's phone call didn't come until Nico was driving home.

"Where is Clara now?"

"Her apartment in Lucca," Perillo said. "Three flights up with no elevator as my knee well remembers. The shutters are closed so there's no way of knowing if she's alone or not."

"If you're going to meet someone in a cemetery so as not to be seen together, you're not going to risk having him come to your apartment with the neighbors looking on."

"Her duffel bag is still in the car. That could mean this isn't her last stop. Or she's in no hurry to drag it up the stairs."

"I'm counting on her moving on, but not tonight. That's another hunch I have." He'd looked up flight schedules. Nothing left at night. "It would be a good idea for you and Dani to join Clara's tail before she gets up tomorrow and goes off to meet her lover. I'd do it, but as you know, in Italy I can only perform a citizen's arrest if I catch the person in the act of committing a crime. If I'm right, this crime was committed some time ago."

A long sigh reached Nico's ear. "I'll do it if you come with us. That's only fair."

Perillo was right. He should see it through. There was a good chance Elvira would fire him if he missed work—the chase could take only a few hours or go on for days—but maybe Tilde would hire him back. "I'll meet you at the station tomorrow morning at seven. I'll bring Jimmy's coffee and cornetti."

"That's the least you can do." Perillo clicked off.

SATURDAY MORNING, AFTER NICO, Perillo and Dani had their breakfasts, they took off for Lucca in Perillo's Panda. It took more than an hour to reach Clara's apartment. Luckily, she lived outside the old walls. In the historic center, parking would have been impossible.

"There he is," Perillo said, spotting a man sitting in an old green Renault. "He took over from a gray Citroën at six this morning."

Nico asked, "Don't they have names?"

"Mario, both of them. There was no activity during the night." Perillo swung the car into an empty spot a few cars behind the Renault.

"Where's her car?" Nico asked.

"Across the street from the Renault, a few cars up," Daniele said from the backseat. Nico's new development had brought him back from his Stella-loves-me bubble. He was now fully present. "The burgundy Ford."

"And now we wait," Perillo grumbled.

"And while we do that," Nico said, "who wants a custard-filled bomba?" He'd come well equipped in hopes of appeasing Perillo. "I've got two here and more coffee. I even brought a small bottle of grappa in case Clara decides to sleep late." The fourth-floor window shutters were still closed.

Perillo grabbed one of the round fluffy dough balls and bit into it, showering sugar over his jeans. "For all you know she may stay home for the next three days." He licked the custard off his lower lip.

Nico handed him a paper napkin. "Her duffel bag is still in her car, isn't it?"

"It's still in her car."

"Good." Nico handed the other bomba and a napkin to Daniele, who thanked him, and poured some coffee for himself.

Twenty minutes later, an excited Daniele whispered, "Look, she's awake." He caught a quick glimpse of Clara's dark hair as she opened the shutters of one window.

Twenty minutes passed. The other two windows of the apartment stayed shuttered. "The shutters' staying closed is a good sign," Daniele said, eager for the action to begin. "She's going out."

"It's only a sign she likes the dark," Perillo said. He'd been trying to nap but behind him Daniele kept moving. The plastic seat covers squeaked. "Dani, I know you're excited that we're on this great adventure, but I could swear I have mice back there."

Daniele froze. "I'm sorry, Maresciallo."

"Salvatore! How many times—"

"Here," Nico said, picking up the thermos. "Have some coffee, Perillo." He poured some into the tin cup and added a splash of grappa. "That should soften you up."

"Getting this over with will do a better job of that."

The sun rose higher. Perillo napped. Daniele sat still. Nico kept his eyes on the heavy wooden front door of the apartment building. At 11:21 the door opened, and Clara walked into the street wearing jeans, white sneakers and a white shirt under a dark-red blazer. The strap of a large handbag slipped down from one shoulder as she pulled a suitcase out of the door.

"She's off," Nico said, elbowing Perillo awake. "Turn the motor back on."

The seat in the back started squeaking again. Perillo shook himself awake and turned the key.

Clara walked past the green Renault. She checked her watch while waiting for two cars to drive by. She crossed the street to the burgundy Ford. As she opened the trunk, a large black car stopped in front of her building.

"Ah, he's picking her up," Nico said.

"That's a hired car," Daniele said, his younger eyes reading the license plate. "Only the driver's inside."

Clara pulled out the duffel bag, closed the trunk, stepped

out onto the street and waved at the black car. The sun flashed briefly on her raised hand.

Perillo shifted into first gear. The black car was moving forward. "This hunch of yours could be turning into a big hot balloon."

The black car stopped in front of Clara. The driver got out and opened the backseat door. Clara got in.

"Why isn't she driving her car?" Perillo asked as they watched the driver put her luggage in the trunk.

"Because where she's going, she won't need it," Nico said.

"Only the dead don't need a car."

Nico spotted Daniele crossing himself in the rearview mirror. "She's not going to die, Dani. I believe she's taking a trip."

"Ah." The seat squeaked under Daniele. "She's going to the Santa Maria Novella station."

"I'd say the airport."

The limousine drove off. Half a minute later, Renault Mario moved out of the parking spot and followed. Perillo waited another half minute and followed.

Fifty-four minutes and seventy-two kilometers later, the three cars entered the Florence airport. "Pisa is a lot closer," Perillo said. "Why here?"

Nico had looked into flights at both airports last night. "Pisa has fewer international flights."

"Paris. I bet she's going to Paris," Daniele said. "That's where I want to take Stella on our honeymoon."

"Dani, the optimist," Perillo muttered.

"We are going to get married!"

"I'm sure you are." Perillo kept his eyes locked on the black limousine four cars ahead of them. "I was thinking of Paris on a brigadiere's salary."

The limousine stopped in front of the crowded departure area. Renault Mario drove by the limo and found a lucky spot a few cars ahead. While Clara got out, the driver took her suitcase and duffel bag out of the trunk. Perillo double-parked two cars behind them.

"Call Renault Mario and tell him to follow her in," Nico said. A mixture of excitement and anxiety prickled his skin. His stomach muscles were tight. "She might meet Rosati at the airline counter. If she doesn't and Rosati doesn't show up, it'll be my bad luck, and Mario's to follow her to the gate."

"More mine than yours." Perillo picked up his phone and relayed Nico's instructions.

Nico let out a long breath. *Luck be with me tonight*, he thought. It was what his mother used to pray when his father went out drinking. "Keep your fingers crossed," he said out loud.

"That and a prayer from Dani." Perillo turned around to look at his brigadiere. "Put your heart into it."

"I always do, Ma . . . Salvatore," Dani said with a touch of resentment. "I've already prayed for all of us and Signorina Barron."

"What does she have to do with this?" Perillo asked.

Daniele glanced at Nico smiling in the rearview mirror.

Perillo caught the smile. "No, I don't believe it. You still think she's . . ." He stopped. The thought was too ridiculous to voice.

"It's a possibility," Nico said.

Perillo slapped his hand on the steering wheel. "Holy heaven, Nico! She has completely bewitched you."

"Ehi, look," Daniele interrupted. The maresciallo's disbelief made him uncomfortable. "Mario just followed Clara in. He's carrying a suitcase. That's clever. She won't notice him now."

The three men sat back and resumed waiting. Twenty minutes later, Perillo's phone rang. He handed it to Nico. "Your show."

Nico answered. "She's at the Air France check-in booth. The only person she's talked to so far is the booth attendant. Her flight is going to Paris, leaving in two and a half hours. Gate C6. She's heading to security now. I'm following."

"Thank you." Nico relayed the information. "We need to go in now."

As cars pulled out, Perillo slipped the Panda into the closest free spot. Before getting out of the car, he put a carabinieri special parking note on the dashboard.

Once inside the terminal they followed the signs to security. As they passed by the busy bar, Perillo slowed to give the displayed schiacciata sandwiches a wistful look. Nico gave his back a push. They stopped at the line for security and waited, letting travelers go in front of them. The next call came fifteen minutes later.

"She went through. I had to show my ID and explain why we were here. You'll just have to show your ID. I hope the American has his passport with him."

"I do," Nico said.

Renault Mario let out a short laugh. "All is well then. So far she's alone."

"Renault Mario is efficient," Nico said, clicking off. "Security knows we're coming, but once we've gone through, we stop and wait for the next call."

Nico was putting his shoes back on when Perillo's phone rang. "Yes?"

"Goal!"

"C6!" Nico called out and started running, forgetting his belt in the bin. Daniele ran after him with the belt. Perillo walked as quickly as his bad knee and dignity allowed.

Nico and Daniele stopped when they reached the C6 seating area. Clara and Rosati were sitting together in a row of seats facing the glass wall that looked out on the tarmac. An Air France plane was slowly moving into the gate.

Feelings of frustration and impatience Nico hadn't felt in a long time came over him. Rosati and Clara were his catch, but he could do nothing further except surprise Clara—if she would even recognize him without OneWag.

Perillo's heavy breathing reached them. Daniele turned around. "By the window." He pointed with his head.

Perillo took another deep breath and slowly said, "I can't tell it's him by his back. Are you sure it's Rosati?"

"Let's find out," Nico said and walked between a row of chairs and hand luggage. He swung in front of Clara's row and blocked her view of the tarmac. "Buongiorno, Signorina Clara. Remember me? We met at the Gravigna cemetery about ten days ago."

Clara looked up in surprise. The bag of potato chips she was eating fell to the floor.

Tommaso Rosati smiled as his arm slipped over Clara's back. His hand squeezed Clara's shoulders. His other hand lay relaxed on top of a black leather backpack on the seat next to him. "Clara was very taken by your dog."

Clara attempted a smile.

The family resemblance between the brothers was strong, Nico noted, but Tommaso had a leaner, more muscled body and was better looking. His picture on LinkedIn didn't do him justice.

"Where are you traveling to?" Tommaso seemed genuinely curious.

"Same place you are." Perillo stepped from behind the row of seats and joined Nico. "The Greve Carabinieri Station."

Nico watched as hot anger flashed across Tommaso's eyes. Clara let out a squeaky laugh just as a thickset man with a gun strapped to his hip stepped up behind the two of them.

"We're staying right here," Tommaso said. "We have a plane to catch."

The man behind Tommaso nodded to Perillo and Nico. "Not today."

"I need to get away from here," Clara said. "Mamma murdered, Marco killed by some crazy driver. It's too much. I need to get away."

Nico almost believed her.

Tommaso pulled Clara toward him. "You'll be fine." He looked up at Perillo, who hadn't budged. "Maresciallo, tell her she'll be fine. Let her get away for a while."

"And what are you doing here with Signorina Clara?" Perillo asked him.

Tommaso flashed a smile. "Clara and I are old friends. I ran into her a few days ago. She told me she was going to New York. I was flying back to San Francisco via New York. I suggested we travel together. I thought having company would cheer her up."

Renault Mario reached down and grabbed the backpack. Tommaso jumped up, reaching for the bag. "Ehi, that's mine!"

Renault Mario swung the bag behind him. "No need to get agitated. I'm not a thief." With his free hand, he pulled out his Nucleo Investigativo ID from his shirt pocket. "I'm only accompanying your bag to the carabinieri station."

"Your checked suitcases will join you a bit later," Perillo said. "Brigadiere Donato has gone to retrieve them from Air France. You are both under arrest on suspicion of carrying stolen jewelry out of the country."

Tommaso threw his head back and laughed. "That's a joke."

Perillo took out handcuffs from his pockets. "Please stand up and turn around, Signor Rosati."

Tommaso turned around, still laughing as Perillo handcuffed him. "This is ridiculous. What do I have to do with this?"

Clara turned around and offered her wrists without being asked.

THE JEWELRY WAS SCATTERED between a pile of socks and Jockey underpants. Perillo spread the pieces out on his desk. The only piece missing was the diamond bracelet Gianna Rosati had found buried under a laurel bush in her driveway and the ring found on Marco's body. They were sitting in the station's safe.

Perillo put his elbows on the desk. Tommaso and Clara, free of handcuffs now, sat facing him with blank faces. "Would either of you, or both, like to make a statement?" Perillo asked kindly. He was in a good mood. Nico's hunch had been right. All the jewelry was retrieved. The Melonis would no longer think of him as an idiot. "Brigadiere Donato has made the announcement. The tape is running."

Clara quickly glanced at Tommaso, then looked down at her feet. Tommaso seemed to be somewhere else, his eyes fixed on the window next to Daniele and his tape recorder. Renault Mario stood next to the closed door, his arms crossed over his chest. Nico was sitting off to the side, looking through the open carry-on bag at his feet, silently thanking Tarani for trusting him.

"You have nothing to say?" Perillo said after a minute or so.

Clara licked her lower lip, sat up straighter in the chair. "There is a very simple explanation, Maresciallo. If Adriana and I don't know what the jewelry is worth, we can't divide it fairly between us, so I decided to go to the diamond dealers in New York to get them appraised. You can understand that, can't you?"

Amsterdam is closer, Daniele thought.

"Besides, it's not stolen. I mean, half of it is rightfully mine."

"Not yet," Perillo said with a satisfied smile. "Half of it will be rightfully yours only when the probate court says it is."

Nico looked up from rummaging through the carry-on bag. "What was it doing in Signor Rosati's carry-on bag?" Nico asked.

Tommaso turned his head to look at Nico. "Why should I tell you?"

"Please answer Homicide Detective Doyle," Perillo said.

Tommaso turned his head back to face Perillo. "Clara told

me she was taking this valuable jewelry to get appraised. She seemed pretty nervous about it and I offered to put it in my carry-on. It was safer with me. I didn't know it was stolen."

"Well, it wasn't anymore," Clara added. "Mamma is dead. It's ours now. Mine and Adriana's. We're the only heirs." She stomped her foot. "This is an outrage. We didn't do anything wrong."

"We'll see." Nico walked over to Perillo's desk, pushed the jewelry to one side and placed the opal pinkie ring on the desk. "It was in Signor Rosati's shaving kit."

Clara stared, her mouth open. "That's Mamma's ring. She never took it off. When we viewed her body, it was gone, I thought someone working in the morgue had taken it. What—" The hand she pressed against her mouth stopped her from saying more.

Tommaso rested his shoulder against Clara's. She shivered and leaned away from him.

Tomasso caught his breath. "It was with the rest of the stuff."

"Didn't you slip it off Nora's finger because it used to belong to your mother?" Perillo asked him. "She may have told you she felt compelled to relinquish it to an insistent Nora."

"I haven't seen Nora since my last visit home. That was over two years ago."

Nico pulled his chair over and sat close to Clara. "I understand you didn't get along with your mother. She could be cruel. She told you she was going to sell her jewelry instead of giving it to you and your sister." He spoke in a soft voice. "She denied you the cash you needed to buy a better apartment. She offered the villa as collateral for a loan when she planned to sell it to a Swiss hotel company."

Clara had lowered her head.

"I can understand how her actions made you feel, Clara,

but why did Marco have to die? He loved you so much he was willing to steal for you. When he was killed, he was on his way to the villa to give you the ring your mother denied you."

She faced Nico now, pain etched on her face. "Why are you asking *me* that? I don't know why. There is no why. It just happened. Marco got run over by some crazy drunk who didn't care enough to stop."

"A convenient death, don't you think?"

"What do you mean?"

While Nico spoke, Perillo watched Tommaso's face stiffen and his eyes lower so they could not be read.

"Once the theft was done, what use was he?"

"What are you saying?"

Perillo took over. "Detective Doyle is saying that we believe your Marco was deliberately killed. Once you sneaked off to America with Tommaso and the jewels, he would be furious, don't you think? He might want to tell us how you hated your mother, how you had someone kill her as you had gotten him to steal for you. He might have pointed to Tommaso."

Tommaso raised his head. "You're talking nonsense."

"We would start looking into you. We already know your tech company is failing. You need a great deal of money. Selling Nora's jewelry is a start. Clara's inheriting a great deal of money would put you back in business. You also might have resented Marco. He'd bedded your woman. Clara cared for him. Eliminating him was a necessity for you."

Clara was now looking at Tommaso, her face churning between disbelief and doubt. "Maso?"

"Don't be stupid, Clara. Why would I be jealous of someone like Marco?"

Clara jumped out of her chair and started hitting and kicking Tommaso without uttering a sound. Tommaso stayed seated and let her hit him. Renault Mario moved to stop her.

Nico reached her first, wrapped his arms around Clara and pulled her away. When she went limp, he sat her down next to him.

Perillo glanced at Nico. Nico nodded.

Perillo got on his feet, pulled down his jacket, straightened his spine. "Both of you stand up, please."

They got on their feet.

"Tommaso Rosati, in addition to the charge of leaving the country with stolen goods, I charge you with the murder of Nora Salviati. I also charge you with the suspicion of murder of Marco Zanelli."

Tommaso jutted out his chin. "You'll have to prove that."

"We will," Perillo answered with a conviction he did not feel. He turned to Nora's daughter. "Clara Lamberti, I charge you with being an accomplice to the murder of your mother, Nora Salviati."

"You're crazy," she spit out.

Daniele announced the end of the interrogation.

"Get them out of here," Perillo said with a barely controlled voice.

Renault Mario stepped forward and handcuffed them. Perillo turned to look at Daniele. "Do you want to accompany them to Florence? Or I can send Vince or Dino."

Daniele's face broke into a wide smile, which he quickly tried to conceal. "I'd be happy to go, Maresciallo."

"Good. No need to come back tonight."

Daniele blushed with joy.

Nico zipped up Tommaso's bag. "There's nothing more of interest in here but have the forensics people go through his checked suitcase and hers. Who knows what else they're hiding."

Renault Mario picked up the two suitcases. Daniele grabbed the carry-on and together, they walked Clara and Tommaso out of the office.

As the Renault moved out of the station's parking lot with the two suspects seated in the back, Daniele called Stella. "I can spend the night with you."

All three of the other passengers heard Stella's happy laugh.

NELLI WROTE ADRIANA a note a few days later, expressing how sorry she was about Nora's death and Clara's arrest.

Adriana wrote back.

It was nice of you to write, Nelli, but then you've always been one of the nice ones. Mamma wasn't nice, but I miss her anyway. I will miss Clara even though we didn't like each other. I suppose you can dislike and love at the same time. We both loved Maso when we were small. I think part of me still does. He had a way of clutching my heart with his eyes. He only loved her. Clara stopped caring when we got older. She liked having fun with other men. That's why Maso went to live in San Francisco. A couple of years ago, I don't remember exactly when, Clara flew to San Francisco for a yoga convention. I guess that's when they started again. She took many "yoga" trips after that. I suspected Maso was the real reason for those trips and I wondered why she kept their relationship a secret. I thought maybe he was married. Who knows why anyone does anything. I often wonder why I married Fabio. I wouldn't steal Mamma's jewels to save his dental practice. But I'll help him with Mamma's money for Luca's sake. Sad. Sad about Mamma. Sad about Clara and Maso. Sad everything, except Luca. When he's older I hope you will find the time to paint his portrait again.

Until then,
Adriana

TWO DAYS LATER, Vince walked into Perillo's office with an open package and a grin on his face. "We checked. It's not a bomb. And there's no white powder."

Perillo looked up with a frown. "What the devil is it?" He'd been reading the newspaper article about Clara and Tommaso's arrest. Tarani got the credit for the arrest "with the added assistance of the Greve-in-Chianti carabinieri." He wasn't pleased.

Vince stopped grinning. "The package is addressed to Daniele."

"It is?" Daniele came forward and took the package from Vince. "Thank you."

Enjoy, Vince mouthed and hurried out.

Daniele took the package back to his desk and finished unwrapping it. "Oh, mamma!"

Perillo turned to look back at his brigadiere. "Your mother sent you a present?"

Daniele was blushing and laughing at the same time. "No. Capitano Tarani sent it. Look." He picked up the gift and the envelope, rushed to Perillo and set the gift down on his desk.

Perillo looked at the small black machine. "What is it?" *Something infernal for sure*, he thought.

"It's a Sony digital voice recorder." Daniele's voice was pitched high with excitement and relief. "We can retire the old tape recorder."

"But it's for you."

"No, it's for the office. There's an envelope addressed to you." Daniele gave him the envelope.

Perillo opened it and read:

A small thank-you for what you and your team accomplished. I am indebted to you, Nico and Brigadiere Donato for an excellent investigation. I am sorry I cannot

give you the public credit you deserve. Prosecutor Della
Langhe does know the truth.

Tarani signed it only with his first name—Carlo, a sign of
friendship, and he had included a picture of him smiling with
his newborn twins wrapped in his arms.

Perillo looked up at Daniele with a smile on his face. "A
good man."

Daniele nodded.

SEVENTEEN

The following Sunday, Tilde closed down Sotto Il Fico for a dinner to celebrate Nico's full-time return to the kitchen. A row of joined tables stretched out under the great fig tree. Elvira sat at one end of the table, Nico at the other end of one.

The guests were well into their antipasto course when Miss Barron, elegant in a pale-blue moiré silk dress, asked Nico, "I was right, wasn't I? Find the ring, find the killer."

On the other side of her, Perillo took his eyes off the antipasto plate. "Yes, Signorina Barron, but Nora's pinkie ring might not have been enough to convict. It's your word against his and with you under investigation—"

"But the prosecutor dismissed the charges against me."

Perillo clasped his hands to his chest. "I owe you many more apologies."

"No more needed. I'm here, celebrating with good food and wonderful company. It would be a great injustice to Adriana if they go free."

"They won't," Perillo said.

At the other end of the table, Elvira, dressed in her Sunday white and pearls, tapped a knife against her wineglass. "I find your mutterings down there frustrating. They won't what?"

Perillo forked the last grilled yellow pepper from the tagliere.

"Clara and Tommaso will be convicted." He slipped the pepper into his mouth.

Elvira shook her index finger. "You'll never have me believe Clara had anything to do with her mother's murder. No, no. You cannot kill the breast that fed you. It is against Nature."

Gogol dropped a prosciutto slice under the table for OneWag.

Enzo stood up and gathered the taglieri. "The next course is coming up and we're changing plates." Alba appeared with her swaying walk and ten empty bowls in her hands.

Ivana rose from the table. "Let me help."

"No, thank you. I get paid double time for this." Ivana sat back down. Next to her, Perillo was pouring Panzanello Riserva into the glasses he could reach. Alba went down the table picking up the dirty plates, replacing them with shallow terra-cotta bowls displaying the Chianti Classico rooster.

Tilde walked onto the terrace with a huge teaming bowl of the pasta. "Taglierini alla Nico. You want to eat this hot, so no more talking."

Stella stood up to lend a hand. So did Daniele. This time Ivana didn't move.

"Sit, both of you," Tilde commanded. "You're my guests."

"Our guests," Elvira corrected.

Tilde went along the table with Enzo serving. With all plates filled, they sat down on either side of Elvira. "Buon appetito!"

Alba picked up the pasta bowl and went back to the kitchen, where a full plate of Nico's pasta waited for her. In the oven, a pork roast was cooking very slowly.

For the next fifteen minutes, after variations of "This is delicious," "The best ever" and "Bravo, Nico," the only sounds came from forks hitting the bowls. OneWag, at Gogol's feet, waited for some buttery strands to come his way. When they didn't, he padded under the table between many legs and made his way to the shoes with the nice smell of talcum powder.

Elvira, who was a vacuum-cleaner-on-high eater, patiently waited for Perillo to clean his plate before asking, "That was a big—I would even venture—cocky statement you made earlier. What makes you so certain they will be convicted?"

Perillo raised his eyebrows and looked at Nico. "Tell her how cocky I am."

"With pleasure," Nico said. "In Tommaso's case, we found him in possession of a ring Nora always wore. We were worried it might not be enough to prove guilt, but then luck came our way."

"Luck is everything," Alba said as she came out to check if it was time to pick up the bowls. "It brought me to Italy, found me a job, a husband and now Ivana to help me with my cantuccini business."

Ivana checked Perillo's reaction.

"It's Ivana's luck and mine," he announced. He meant it. Ivana was happy and reenergized, and he would slim down, rediscovering his younger body.

Daniele leaned forward. "Tommaso had no luck."

"Dani's right," Nico said. "Nora was strangled with a curtain cord that had been cut from her bedroom curtains. Forensics found a jackknife in Tommaso's suitcase. The fibers of that curtain cord matched the fibers found on the joint of the jackknife. Tommaso Rosati will be convicted."

"What about Clara?" Elvira asked as Alba and Enzo started picking up bowls, replacing them with plates.

Daniele stuck out his head. "Maresciallo, may I?"

"Salvatore. We're with friends," Perillo reminded him. "It's all yours."

Daniele sat taller in his chair, drank some water and looked around the table with a serious expression on his face. "Clara confessed the next morning in front of the prosecutor." In a charged, loud voice, he repeated what he had read in the report Capitano Tarani had sent. "She was motivated to tell the truth because she was now convinced Tommaso had killed Marco to silence him. She admitted to asking Marco to steal the jewelry, admitted to letting Tommaso convince her to help him kill her mother for the inheritance money. She said she would never forgive herself for those two deaths."

"Thank you, Daniele," Elvira said, "although I haven't gone deaf yet."

"I'm sorry." Daniele swallowed and managed not to blush.

"I'm hungry," Elvira declared. "When is the roast appearing? It's my recipe for a change."

"It needs to rest for ten more minutes," Alba said from the other end of the table. She was waiting for OneWag to finish eating from the bowl Miss Barron had lowered for him. Tilde had gone back into the kitchen.

Stella noticed Daniele's crestfallen look. She stroked his arm. "Don't worry, Dani. I made a mushroom and baby artichoke casserole for you."

A bolt of love ran through Daniele's body. He hugged her. "Thank you."

Stella laughed with pleasure. "Taste it first, then thank me, but only if it makes you lick your whiskers."

"I'll have to grow some."

"There's more to the story," Nico said. "Now or after dessert?"

"Now," Elvira ordered. "I'll be asleep by dessert time."

Perillo leaned forward. "This part of the story is mine." He needed to stop thinking how perfect a cigarette would be right now.

Miss Barron lifted OneWag onto her lap, happy to hear more of the musical sound of the Italian language.

Perillo noticed her intent look and gave her a smile. "When Tommaso realized he wasn't going to walk free for a long time, he turned on his great love. He said she masterminded everything months ago when she learned he needed money to save his company. She duped Marco into thinking she loved him by getting engaged to him, then convinced him to steal the jewelry for her. She planned her mother's murder, gave Tommaso the keys to the villa and the bottle of Cognac she had filled with diazepam."

Nico quietly translated for Miss Barron.

"If he refused," Perillo continued, "Clara threatened to cut him out of her life. He'd been in love with her since they were children. The fear of losing her forever made him agree." Perillo sat back in his chair, arms spread out. "Somewhere between their two stories is the truth."

Gogol raised his index finger. "'Focus well on the truth.'"

"The truth is," Tilde announced as she walked onto the terrace carrying a large platter, "I invited you here to celebrate the good things in our lives."

"Finding justice is good," Stella said.

"All right, I'll concede that, but now"—Tilde lowered the platter next to Nico—"let's just eat, drink and enjoy each other's company. Serve yourselves and pass the platter around. Be careful. It's heavy."

"'O joy!'" Gogol declared. "'O ineffable gladness!'"

Tilde glanced at Gogol. "I'm glad to hear that, but you'll have to wait your turn. The only one who gets served is our vegetarian brigadiere."

Alba placed Stella's casserole dish in front of Daniele.

"You heard that?" Stella whispered. "Mamma said 'our.' You're in."

This time Daniele knew no amount of swallowing would stop him from turning red.

OneWag stuck his head out from under the table and nudged Tilde's foot.

Tilde looked down. "Oh, I forgot about Rocco." She took the small metal bowl she'd left on a nearby table and put it down in front of the dog. "He gets served too."

THEY FILLED THEIR PLATES with the pork loin with its melted butter and Dijon mustard sauce, the roasted potatoes and ate. OneWag, now sitting on the floor, was enjoying his rice and chicken dish. Nico raised his head to compliment Elvira. The others followed with their compliments, Miss Barron exclaiming, "Bellissimo." Elvira acknowledged them with a full-mouthed grunt.

More exchanging of plates, more wine and some conversation, followed by a salad of fennel, lettuce and arugula.

Nico patted his stomach. "I'll have to run to Siena and back to undo this meal."

"I might join you," Nelli said. "This has been the best meal I've ever had." A chorus of "Yes, indeed," "The very best," "Bellissimo" followed. Nico raised three fingers. "Michelin stars."

Tilde laughed with pleasure. Enzo brought out open bottles of prosecco followed by Alba with flutes. "Before we plunge into Nelli's lemon ricotta cake and Ivana's chocolate and almond Torta Caprese . . ." Tilde waited until all the flutes had been filled. "Alba, please sit down with us." Stella made room on her chair for Alba. "I want to propose a toast to the good things we have." Tilde raised her glass. "To newfound love and friendship. May we remember to hold on to them tightly."

Miss Barron turned to Nico. "May I add something?"

"Of course."

"To libertá."

"And to no more murders!" Perillo added.

Everyone raised their glass and shouted, "To everything!"

OneWag, his belly now full, burped his approval.

LIST OF CHARACTERS

in order of appearance

Nico Doyle—American ex-homicide detective now living in Gravigna

Nelli Corsi—Nico's artist girlfriend

OneWag—Nico's adopted dog, also known as Rocco

Salvatore Perillo—maresciallo of the carabinieri who needs Nico's help more than ever this time

Miss Laetitia Barron—the murder victim's English houseguest

Daniele Donato—blushing Venetian brigadiere and Perillo's favorite

Tilde Morelli—Rita's cousin and chef at Sotto Il Fico

Vince—always-hungry brigadiere at the Greve-in-Chianti Carabinieri Station

Dino—quiet brigadiere at the Greve-in-Chianti Carabinieri Station

Nora Salviati—the unloved murder victim

Adriana Meloni—Nora's snobby older daughter

Clara Lamberti—Nora's attractive yoga-teacher daughter

Dottor Gianconi—the medical examiner

Rita Doyle—Nico's deceased Italian wife

Enzo Morelli—Tilde's husband and Elvira's son

Elvira Morelli—the crotchety owner of Sotto Il Fico restaurant

Stella Morelli—museum guide in Florence and Daniele's dream woman

Gogol—Nico's Dante-quoting friend who needs an intervention

Sandro Ventini—Jimmy's husband and co-owner of Bar All'Angolo

Ivana Perillo—Perillo's newly independent wife

Marco Zanelli—Clara's fiancé

Enrico—owner of the town's salumeria and bakery

Fabio Meloni—Adriana's dentist husband

Riccardo Della Langhe—substitute prosecutor who has little regard for Perillo

Capitano Carlo Tarani—is therefore assigned the Salviati murder case

Jimmy Lando—cornetto baker and co-owner of Bar All'Angolo

Sergio—the butcher

Lapo Angelini—Villa Salviati's gardener

Beppe—always eager for news for his BeppeInfo blog

Luciana—hug-loving owner of the Gravigna florist shop

Laura Benati—manager of the Hotel Bella Vista

Alba—Albanian waitress at Sotto Il Fico and majority owner of Alba's Cantuccini Production Company

Sonia Rossi—Nora Salviati's loyal housekeeper

Gianna Rosati—Nora's grieving neighbor and bridge-playing friend

Federico Rosati—Gianna's husband who has known Nora since they were children

Avvocato Sbarra—Nora's lawyer who doesn't wait for a warrant

Cecco Angelini—the gardener's son who has health problems

Gustavo—a pensioner and leader of the Bench Boys

Ettore, Simone and Pippo—the other Bench Boys

Carletta—works for Alba's Cantuccini Company at Enrico's bakery

Stefano and Tommaso Rosati—Gianna and Federico's sons living abroad

Don Alfonso—the parish priest

Alberto Lamberti—Nora's rich philandering husband, now deceased

Marta Macchi—Nora's laundress

Celestina—Marta's protesting baby

Max Vitale—the laundress's much older husband

Claudio Nardi—restaurant owner in Gaiole and Nora's old beau

Leo—Hotel Bella Vista waiter

Aldo Ferri—owner of the Ferriello vineyard and Nico's landlord

Cinzia Ferri—Aldo's wife

Erica—a young woman who makes an ugly discovery

Maria and Pietro Zanelli—Marco's parents

TAGLIERINI ALLA NICO

Serves four

Ingredients:

- 8 thin slices of prosciutto
- 3 tbsp. olive oil
- 2 large onions, peeled and sliced thin (about 3 ½ cups)
- 2 medium-sized leeks, sliced thin and thoroughly washed and drained
- kosher salt
- 1 ½ cups chicken or vegetable broth

- 3 generous fistfuls of arugula
- 2 tbsp. unsalted butter
- 14 oz. fresh taglierini egg pasta (may be substituted with egg fettucine, preferably fresh)
- ¾ cup freshly grated Parmigiano-Reggiano

Instructions:

Start by cutting or tearing the prosciutto slices into small pieces. Lay them out on a microwavable dish and microwave on high for 1 ½ minutes. Set them aside.

In a 12-inch skillet add the olive oil over medium heat. Add the onions and leeks. Season with salt and pepper. Keep stirring occasionally, careful not to burn the onions and leeks. Once they have achieved a light golden color (20–25 minutes), put a pot of water to boil.

Add three or four tablespoons of kosher salt after the water boils. (The water should taste like seawater.)

When the onions and leeks have reached a deep brown color, add the broth, and stir. Once half of the broth has evaporated, add the hardened prosciutto pieces, the arugula, and the butter. Mix well.

Continue to cook until there are only two or three tablespoons of broth left in the skillet.

If pasta water is not yet boiling, turn off skillet heat and cover. Add the pasta to the boiling water. If it is fresh pasta it will cook in three to four minutes. If dry, follow directions on the package.

Turn heat back on under the skillet. Save a cup of pasta water, drain the pasta and add it to the skillet.

Add half of the parmigiano and mix well. If pasta looks too dry, add some pasta water and stir for a minute over the heat. Turn heat off and serve with the rest of the parmigiano on the side.

Buon appetito!

ACKNOWLEDGMENTS

With Covid loosening its grip, I was again able to go back to Panzano, the small Tuscan town in the hills of Chianti that I fell in love with seven years ago. The friendliness of everyone I met, the beauty of the surrounding vineyards, the excellent wines and the delicious food I could never have enough of gave me joy. I brought the town with me in my heart and my head back to New York and started writing.

I couldn't have started or continued the series without Lara Beccatini's friendship and Andrea Sommaruga's and Iole Como's welcome and wine expertise. I will be forever grateful to retired Maresciallo Giovanni Serra for his patience in answering my countless questions with a smile. In New York, I thank Dr. Barbara Lane for her sharp eyes.

For this new story I have been blessed with managing editor Rachel Kowal. I thank her for making this story so much better. I owe a big debt to Alexa Wejko, who does a beautiful job getting the word out.

My husband, Stuart, has been patient and understanding. I owe him much.

Last of all, I thank the people who animate this story, OneWag included, for letting me enter their lives. As Haruki Murakami said when asked where his characters come from, "I don't choose them; they choose me."